Undeniably You

USA TODAY & WALL STREET JOURNAL BESTSELLING AUTHOR

JEWEL E. ANN

UNDENIABLY YOU

MONTGOMERY SISTERS

JEWEL E. ANN

Cover Design: Sarah Hansen Okay Creations

Formatting: Jenn Beach

For my sister Kambra

Author's Note

Dear reader,

The thoughts and dialogue of these fictional characters do not necessarily represent my beliefs. They are representative of my perception of the world and the diverse opinions and language of humanity at the time of writing this story. Please understand that interpretation of words and beliefs change over time, as does my writing to reflect those changes and improve my craft. However, it's not realistic to continually edit a large and ever-growing backlist of titles. Thank you for understanding.

Prologue

June 22, 2013

THE WEDDING

A GAZILLION LAYERS of tulle engulf my five foot five, one hundred and fifteen pound body. I wonder how many grooms go MIA on their wedding night searching for their new bride in her Cinderella ball gown. My breasts and ribs protest as the weight of this strapless beast demands their full support for the next five or more hours. Long, dark ringlets pinned to one side cascade down my shoulder. Sweet floral aromas mingle in the air from my light pink rose bouquet and the lavender body spray still fresh on my skin.

A knock at the door startles me from my despondent appraisal of the reflection in the mirror.

"Come in," I call.

"Oh, Sam, you look amazing." My sister's hand rests against her chest as her gaping-mouth envy seeps into my conscience reprimanding it with a firm slap of guilt.

This is every girl's dream: the dress, the handsome

groom, the center of attention. There are those few unique females who are genetically missing the fairytale-dream gene. That's the rare and exclusive group to which I belong.

"Thanks, Avery," I murmur, meeting her watery blue gaze in the mirror.

"I wish Mom were here to see you." Her mouth sags in a frown.

Avery's words take me back thirteen years. It's not that those same words haven't drifted through my mind today, but Avery says it all the time. *"I wish Mom were watching this movie with us. I wish Mom could taste this amazing soup. I wish Mom could hear this song."*

I get it. I really do. Avery is two years younger than I am, but it feels like ten. Even today, she still reminds me of the broken eight-year-old lost without her mom—our mom. The fragile memories of feeling dependent on my mom are specks of sand fading from an hourglass in my mind. Taking the emotional leap from ten to fourteen in a matter of weeks to fill that "mother" gap does that.

Grabbing two fists full of tulle, I lift my dress and turn toward her.

"She *is* here. I'm looking at her now." Avery's long blonde Barbie locks and faded blue eyes hold such a ghostly resemblance to our mom it warms my heart and pulls my lips into a smile.

"Oh, Sydney!" As tears swell in her eyes, she comes at me with open arms and child-like fragility.

Crap! Avery only calls me by my given name when she wants to be coddled.

"Uh, uh, uh..." I hold my palms up blocking her approach "...white dress, white veil ... back away from the bride."

Avery comes to an abrupt stop. Her bereaved face melts into a soft smile as she dabs the corners of her eyes with the pads of her fingers.

"Sorry. You just always know how to say the right thing at the right time," she says while fiddling with her diamond tear-drop earrings.

Offering my hand, she looks at it for a moment before taking it. Squeezing, I look at those blue eyes, full lips, and blonde hair pinned up with a few stray spiral curls elegantly framing her face. I won't say it aloud, but I'm thinking it, too. *God, I miss you Mom.*

"You look beautiful, baby sister," I whisper.

Her exuberant full-teeth smile captures her eyes. "Thanks, I love my dress." Releasing my hand, she twirls around in her pale purple taffeta mermaid-style dress.

"You should, since you picked it out," I murmur with no response from her.

"Flower girl?" I ask with raised brows.

"Chasing the ring bearer behind the church ... or maybe it's the other way around," Avery dismisses with a shrug.

Shifting myself back toward the mirror, I take a deep breath and exhale a slow release.

"I'm going to check on your groom." Avery opens the door but pauses and turns with a reassuring smile. "He's the one, Sam. Handsome, kind ... and God, he loves you so much. It's fate."

The door clicks shut. *Fate.* The word echoes in the air. Is there such a thing as fate?

Chapter One

June 3rd, 2010

PALO ALTO

Sнɪт! It's everywhere and I've only been here for three hours. Thank God it's contained to the hardwood floors. I scramble to find a trash bag in the pantry as my phone chimes. Sliding it out from the back pocket of my short denim shorts, I swipe my finger across the screen.

"Hello?"

"Sydney?" An unfamiliar woman's voice sounds.

"Yes," I confirm with the phone pinched between my ear and shoulder as I peel open the trash bag.

"It's Kimberly from Dr. Abbott's office returning your phone call."

As I walk past the glass French doors to the patio, I'm met with two blue-grey eyes on the other side following my every move. Squinting and seething with contempt, I continue to the first steaming pile of shit.

"Oh, yes, thank you for calling me back. I'm house and *dog* sitting for my uncle and aunt, Trevor and Elizabeth Worthington. Their dog ... uh—"

"Swarley."

"Yes, Swarley has been shi—I mean pooping everywhere since they left early this morning."

"He might be nervous or apprehensive about them leaving. Dogs sense more than we realize. They're much smarter than we give them credit for being."

Yeah, this dog is real freaking smart!

"Anyway, Dr. Abbott has an opening at one o'clock if you'd like to bring Swarley in just to make sure it's nothing serious."

The ripe sewer stench wafting near my nose forces me to hold my breath as I rush to glove my hand in paper towels and wipe up the mess.

"One, thanks. See you then." The mordacious smell steals my voice.

———

House sitting is a great interim job, especially for someone with a bachelor's degree in art history. Pet sitting ... not so glamorous, but it comes with the territory. My dream of becoming a museum curator is going to be a long journey. It's virtually impossible to get an offer without a master's degree, and really, a PhD is preferred—especially among the larger, more prestigious museums. Feeling broke and drowning in debt since graduation, I've decided to work a few years before completing my schooling. However, if I continue to get into this sort of "shit," I may decide to sell my body instead of my time.

The first few jobs I took were in the Midwest, within driving distance from where I grew up in Rock Island, Illinois. After I banked some cash, I got my passport and applied for house sitting positions abroad. Over the past year I've traveled to Rio De Janeiro, Qatar, Ireland, Australia, and the UK. I visit every museum I can and dream of someday being the lucky person in charge of overseeing everything. It's a long shot at best, but a girl can hope.

When Avery took a job in L.A. as a massage therapist, I decided to look for something on the West Coast so we could see each other during the summer. As fate would have it, our dad's sister and her husband, who live in Palo Alto, decided to travel Europe in June. They were thrilled to hear that I was available to house-sit for them *and* watch their new dog. It's a five and a half hour drive from L.A., but at least Avery and I are in the same time zone.

"Get in, Swarley!" I hold open the back door to Elizabeth and Trevor's white Escalade.

Their two-year-old Weimaraner is infuriating, and we've known each other for less than twenty-four hours. It's going to be a long month.

I look at the time on my phone: 12:45 p.m.

"Ugh! You stubborn mutt, get in." I reach down and bear-hug his body, praying nothing squirts out of his backside as I thrust him into the backseat. After another five minutes of wrestling around trying to thread the seat belt through his harness loop, we're off to the vet.

I notice two other cars in the parking lot, so hopefully we won't have to wait long. The instant I unfasten Swarley, he bolts out of the backseat attempting to rip my arm off as the leash tourniquets around my wrist.

"Swarley! Dammit, stop!" He drags me through the grass

7

along the side of the building. I think he's chasing a squirrel, or a bird. Hell, he could be chasing his tail for all I know. I'm too busy trying to avoid all the steamy land mines. What happened to dog shit pick up etiquette?

Swarley stops to lift his leg to a tree, giving me a reprieve. Digging the embedded leash out of my skin, I choke up on it about an inch from strangling his neck.

"Let's go!" I yank his leash.

Approaching the door, my face wrinkles. I'm not sure if I'm smelling something new or if the pungent odor from earlier this morning is still lingering in my nose. Grabbing the door handle to steady myself, I lift my right foot to inspect the bottom of my shoe. *Clean.* I lift the left.

"Shit!"

Literally, all over the bottom of my sandal. Swarley pulls on the leash, going spastic, so I wriggle my sandal off and take him inside.

"Swarley!" The woman behind the desk cheers as she jumps up and greets us, well ... him.

"You must be Sydney. I'm Kimberly, we talked on the phone."

"Yes, hi." I smile.

"Come on back. Dr. Abbott is just finishing up. He shouldn't be too long." Kimberly escorts us to an exam room. "Have a seat. I'll get Swarley weighed and bring him back in."

She leads him away while I sit in a small armchair by the window overlooking the dump yard. Glancing down at my feet, I realize how ridiculous I look with only one sandal. Will I look better without shoes? No shoes says I'm one of those weird dirty people who never wears shoes. One shoe says I either lost my other shoe or stepped in dog crap. Either explanation is feasible. After all, I've lost count of how many times I've driven down the street and seen just one shoe in the middle of the road. It's solid evidence that there is an entire population of people running around with only one shoe. I assume these are bikers or motorcyclists losing their shoes. It's too implausible that I brought Swarley to the vet on a Harley or Schwinn, so I think I'll stick with Option B: shit happens.

"Here we go," Kimberly announces while guiding Swarley back into the room.

Following her through the door is Dr. Hottie Vet. A thick head of dark hair brushes past his brows just above rich, light brown eyes that crinkle at the corners matching his bright friendly smile. Perfect-fitting black pants hang from his tall, lean frame. The light gray button-down shirt under his white lab coat exposes a teasing of dark chest hair where the top buttons are left casually open. Swarley gives a kind greeting to his crotch while the vet offers his hand to me.

"Good afternoon, I'm Dr. Abbott ... or ... Dane." His long fingers are warm and his grip is nervously firm.

"Sydney, and I think you already know—" I try to hide my grin, gesturing to Swarley who continues to give a rude sniffing to Dr. Abbott's crotch.

"Swarley. Yes, I've been seeing him since he was just a pup."

Swarley's magnetic attraction to a certain crotch is distracting. Although he's not my dog, and I'm sure Dr. Abbott is used to it, I feel the need to explain his behavior.

"He must think you have a big piece of meat in there."

The words come out of my mouth, and my brain—that

9

apparently has a two-second delay—catches up as I turn crimson. Dr. Abbott is discernibly embarrassed by my comment because the shade of his face mirrors mine while he averts his eyes to the chart he's holding. Kimberly coughs and turns her back to us. It's obvious she's trying to stifle her reaction as well.

"Oh my God! I didn't mean ... or what I meant—" Swarley has diarrhea of the ass and I have diarrhea of the mouth. Could this day get any worse?

"Sydney, it's fine," he recovers with quick composure. "How long has Swarley been having—" He pauses and I notice he's looking at my feet.

Yes, this day just got worse. I wiggle my toes then cover my barefoot with the one that has a sandal.

Dr. Abbott smirks and his eyes meet mine. He exudes a subtle shyness that I'm guessing is masked by his white-coat authority and the *Dr.* before his name.

"When did Swarley start having diarrhea?" he asks with a genuine smile.

"This morning. I arrived late last night, but I didn't meet Swarley until early this morning when Elizabeth and Trevor left. They didn't mention him having any issues, so I assume it's just been today."

"Did you bring in a stool sample?" he questions, jotting some notes on the chart.

"Um, no. Sorry."

"It's fine. I'm going to do a quick exam, but it's most likely just a case of nerves and anxiety. To my knowledge he's usually on a strict feeding schedule so I'm doubtful it's anything that he's eaten."

I nod and observe as Dr. Abbott guides Swarley onto a

hydraulic lift table. Kimberly puts him in a headlock-type hold while the good doctor does his exam.

"Everything looks fine. Make sure he has water and keep him off food until morning. Maybe by then he'll be settled. If it persists or gets worse, give the office a call. In fact, I could stop by on my jog in the morning and see how he's doing."

Kimberly raises an eyebrow in his direction. He's tapping his pen on the chart.

"Oh, that's not ... necessary. I mean, I'll just call if there's an issue. No need to go out of your way."

"It's not really. Actually, I jog by there every morning. I only live a few blocks away."

He runs his fingers through his hair and looks down at his feet shifting his weight from one to the other. *Holy crap!* He's flirting with me and Kimberly is *so* onto him.

"If you have time, but really, don't go out of your way." I smile as I stand.

He glances at my feet again. I bend my knee and hide my barefoot behind my other leg as I shrug my shoulders.

"Stepped in shi—poop outside."

"Oh, where'd you leave it?"

"Outside."

"Kimberly will finish up the paperwork and bill the Worthington's account. I'll get your shoe cleaned off."

"What? No!"

He holds up his hand and shakes his head. "I insist. It's the least I can do. I think you have your hands pretty full with this guy." He scratches Swarley behind his ears. "I'll be back in a few minutes."

He leaves and I look at Kimberly as she fills out some paperwork. "Is Dr. Abbott this nice to everyone?"

She grins but doesn't look up. "Nice? Yes. But if you're asking if he routinely cleans shit off shoes? No."

Kimberly tucks her chin-length auburn hair behind her ear. She looks about forty, but I'm not the best judge of age.

"If your next question is whether or not Dr. Abbott is married, the answer is no."

Now I'm officially uncomfortable and just as anxious as this spastic dog to get out of here.

"That's interesting, but I wasn't going to ask. I don't live around here and I'm leaving in a month. Trust me, I'm not looking for—" My thoughts trail off. *Looking for what? Romance? A date? Sex?*

"Suit yourself. But he'd be quite the catch."

The nervous tension is building. This trip is about Swarley, not finding a fix for my nonexistent social life. I twirl my long, dark brown hair around my finger as Dr. Abbott returns with my sandal.

"Good as new." He hands it to me.

"Thanks, uh ... it really wasn't necessary, but thanks, Dr. Abbott." I bend down and slip it on. Standing up, I notice Mr. Quite the Catch is looking at me, but not at my eyes.

I clear my throat and his gaze finds mine again.

"Oh, um, my pleasure, and call me Dane. Until tomorrow." He nods and steps aside.

Swarley wastes no time dragging me back to the waiting room. Before I push open the door, I glance back and wave.

"Thanks again, bye."

We pull out of the parking lot, my mind reeling. *"Until tomorrow."* Who says that?

———

Glancing at the clock in the kitchen, I realize it's been over five hours since Swarley has had the squirts. He's resting on his plush I-am-the-most-spoiled-dog-in-the-world bed in front of the coffee table in the living room. Elizabeth and Trevor don't have any children and it shows in their immaculately kept house. It's spacious, but not overwhelming like a few that I've stayed in. The main floor has an open foyer with a formal dining room on one side and an office on the other. All the floors are hardwood or tile, with large traditional wool rugs in each room.

The dark earth-tone walls are nothing like what I remember in our house when I was younger. Theirs lacks the artistic crayon and marker masterpieces etched on the lower half. The crisp white, wide trim and arched doorways are absent of dents and scratches from collisions with toys with wheels and metal parts.

At the back of the house is a kitchen and great room combination that overlooks my favorite part of the whole house—a mammoth deck and a large rectangular swimming pool. This is not an average deck. There is a hot tub on one side and a pergola-covered outdoor bar area with a large stainless-steel grill and stone-covered pizza oven on the other.

Avery is going to freak when she comes to visit. This is our first time at Elizabeth and Trevor's new house here in Palo Alto. It's also my first time housesitting for family. I can already see us lounging by the pool, sipping margaritas, and listening to music flowing from the outdoor speakers.

It's nearly four o'clock. I open the refrigerator door to get some iced tea and the doorbell chimes. Making my way to the entry, I see through the daylight windows a guy with short, golden blonde hair standing with his hands shoved in his khaki cargo shorts pockets. He's wearing a red Stanford T-shirt that looks like it's a size too small, but the way it hugs his defined arms and chest, I find it difficult to wish it were the correct size.

I'm not expecting anyone today, but I have a vague memory of something about a pool guy coming on Wednesday. I thought it was next week, but I could be wrong.

Opening the door, the most spectacular blue eyes framed in long lashes suck the air right out of my lungs.

"Hi," I whisper, unable to find my full voice.

"Hi." He drags the word out into two long, silky syllables. Eyes of iridescent blue oceans with the intensity of a brilliantly cut sapphire and a few specks of soft summer forget-me-nots travel the full length of my body.

My skin tingles and I'm hyperaware of how short my faded denim shorts really are, and I can't remember what color my bra is under my fitted white tank, but I don't think it's white. I feel naked under his gaze as he grazes his perfect white teeth over his bottom lip eliciting an immediate flushing of my skin and a little lightheadedness. I'm a voodoo doll and with one look he's working his sexual black magic on me.

Taking a slow exaggerated swallow, I close my eyes and shake my head.

"You must be ... uh ... Aaron?" I cross my arms over my chest because his sultry look has my nipples at attention.

Head cocked to the side, his bold gaze takes an encore trip down and back up the entire length of my body.

"The pool guy, Aaron, right?" His calculated silence drives me crazy.

He gives me a slow nod. "The pool guy."

"I'll have to look at the schedule, but I'm pretty sure

you're not supposed to be here until next Wednesday." I fiddle with my hair and internally scold myself for my breathy voice and school-girl gaga gaze.

He shrugs and flashes me an innocent boyish grin. "I guess I should come back next week then, *or* I could just check out the pool now."

Mirroring his casual attitude, I shrug my shoulders. "That's fine. If it's not too soon. You're the expert."

Stepping back, I gesture for him to come in. His whole face is one big grin.

"Don't you need anything from your truck?"

He walks past me and I look out front to the paved stone circle drive. Parked at the end of the walk is a black Toyota 4Runner.

"Don't you drive a company vehicle?"

Without turning back, he walks toward the kitchen to the deck like he owns the place. "The supplies are probably out back and the pool guy van broke down," his voice echoes.

Shutting the door, I pause a moment and shake my head. *"Probably out back? Pool guy van?"*

Out the back window I see his flip-flops on the deck. As he walks toward the pool house, he shrugs off his shirt in one smooth motion.

Oh. Sweet. Hell.

What is it with the guys here in Palo Alto? They don't grow them like this where I'm from. Pulling my phone from my back pocket, I call Avery but press *End* right away.

"No, better yet," I whisper to myself with a sly smile pulling at my lips.

When Aaron comes out with the long-handled pool skimmer, I take a picture of him and send it to Avery.

2 words: Pool Guy – 3 words: Life is Good

A short two seconds pass before my phone vibrates with a text.

NFW!

I laugh then text back.

Way!

My phone rings Beyonce's "Single Ladies," which is fitting for my party-loving sister.

"Jealous?" I answer.

"Sam! Oh my God. Pool guys do not look like that in real life. Is this a joke?" Her enthusiastic shriek pierces my ears.

Aaron walks with slow calculated moves around the pool running the skimmer through the water. Ironically, when I was out earlier the water looked clear, pristine, and free of bugs and leaves.

"I don't think so, but it might be. He's not really doing anything. Shouldn't he be checking the chemicals or changing a filter or something like that?"

Avery snorts. "How should I know? I live in an apartment building with a pool guy that looks like Shamu. I go out of my way *not* to watch what he's doing. Tell him you think there's a slimy film on the bottom of the pool."

"What? Why?"

"Duh ... so he has to get in and check it out."

As Aaron rounds the corner of the pool, he looks up and smiles at me. I make a quick retreat away from the window.

"Uh, I don't think he brought his swim trunks."

16

"And?" Avery questions in her *duh* tone.

"*And* he's not going to jump into the pool fully clothed."

"Or—"

"*Or* naked."

"Ugh, my next client is here. You'll have to fill me in later. And by the way, I marked off my schedule for a few days starting next Friday so I can drive up and stay with you."

"Great! You're going to love this place. Talk to you later."

I pour a glass of iced tea and start to walk toward the deck. Then I turn around and pour another glass. "Hospitality is a good thing," I tell myself, needing only to convince the rational part of my brain.

"Tea?" I offer, walking over to the pool.

Aaron sets the skimmer net along the side of the pool.

"Thank you." The smirk on his face is suspicious and makes me feel like I'm missing some inside joke. He takes the glass from me and I move past him to get a closer look at the pool because I can't look at him without his shirt and not break into a sweat.

"What are you skimming?"

"Nothing really. I'm stirring the water," he says matter-of-factly.

This guy is not for real. What does he mean by "stirring the water?" He's up to something. It's obvious why Aunt Elizabeth hired him. She must properly clean the pool after he leaves so Trevor doesn't get suspicious and fire his ass ... a very *fine* ass I will confess.

"And *why* is it you need to *stir* the water?" I turn toward him and my eyes dart straight to his broad muscular chest and well-defined abs all kissed by the sun. Jeez, he's too perfect and I'm ... something. Distracted? Mentally lethargic? Crazy? Horny? BINGO!

"So there's an even consistency of chemicals when I test the water."

My mouth is agape and I cannot stop looking at him. He bends down to physically capture my attention. *Shit!* I show no shame staring at his bare chest.

"Hello?" he says, forcing my eyes back to his.

Shaking the inappropriate thoughts from my head, I take a quick sip of my drink to mask my embarrassment.

"Do I need to put my shirt back on?"

I choke on my tea. "No—" I can't stop coughing. "I mean —" Clearing my throat, I notice his cocky smile. "Put your shirt on or leave it off. Why would I care?"

God, Sydney, could you be a bigger disaster today? The flap of the dog door distracts me. Swarley leaps down the deck stairs. Aaron hunches down like a lineman in anticipation of his overzealous greeting. The problem is, as Swarley races closer I realize he's not aiming for Aaron. He's aiming for—

"Oh shit!" I'm catapulted backwards into the pool.

My body makes its descent to the bottom while I open my eyes to see the blurry magnification of Mr. Sex on Legs pool guy standing at the edge looking down at me. I'm considering seeing how long I can hold my breath. Maybe he'll decide to leave and I can surface from the depths of my own personal Hell without an audience.

Yes! That's it. I can do this.

I still hold many records from my high school swimming career. Holding my breath until he leaves should be easy. Unless he decides to be heroic and jumps in to save me. Not a bad scenario either. Then at least we'll both be drenched in our clothes.

Like a leaky raft, I release my breath one bubble at a time and take a seat at the bottom of the pool. *Ha!* He's emptying his pockets. Looks like I won't be the only drowned rat. Wait. *What the hell? No he's not. Oh dear God, yes he is.* Sex on legs dives into the pool, sans shorts *and* underwear! The two haunting notes from *Jaws* sound in my head while I scramble to the surface in the opposite direction, desperate to get away from him.

The sweet relief of air filling my lungs is squashed by the anxiety of being chased by a naked stranger.

"Oh my God! What are you doing?" A frantic yell breaks out with the remaining breath in my lungs while I swim toward the ladder, barely escaping him. I leap out of the pool with superhuman speed. Wrapping my arms around myself, I scramble to the pool house, my heart racing and my whole body shaking as I fumble for a towel.

"The water feels great today." His voice sounds behind me.

I whip around and gasp, wide eyed. A wet, naked, sinful-as-a-hot-fudge-sundae body greets me a few feet away. Hands fisted, his arms are casually crossed at his wrists covering part of his junk in the front. The perfect cover to *Sports Illustrated* stands before me, and all I want to do is smack him across the face to wipe the stupid smirk off it. Then, of course, I want to jump him and rub every sensitive part of my body against his, because right now I'm so pissed and so turned on, I need to dive into the pool again before I self-combust.

"Finish up and get out," I mumble as I toss him a towel

and stomp toward the house. On my way, I pass Swarley beached out in a lounge chair by the pool.

"Evil demon dog!" I scowl at him.

———

HOPEFUL THAT HE'S GONE, I pull my long, wet hair into a ponytail as I tiptoe downstairs in a dry pair of shorts and a green T-shirt from Ireland that says *Dublin your pleasure.* Unfortunately, the shirt does not impart the luck of the Irish. He's still here, perched on a barstool in the kitchen.

Watching my approach, he stands.

"Hey, I think we got off on the wrong foot," he says with a megawatt smile.

"Are you done?" I ask, leaning against the cabinets with my hand resting on my hip.

"Done?"

"With the pool?" I say in exasperation.

He rolls his eyes. "Sure, I'm done."

"What's that supposed to mean?"

His face scrunches like he's ready to tell me something as my phone vibrates in my back pocket.

"Hello?"

"Hi, Sydney. It's Elizabeth. We just got off the plane and I wanted to make sure you were getting acclimated to the house okay or if you're having any issues with Swarley."

"Um, Swarley had some ... uh ... tummy issues this morning so I took him to Dr. Abbott. He thinks it's just nerves or something, and Swarley's been fine since." I think it's too early to tell her Swarley might be chained to a stake in the yard by the time they get home.

"Oh dear, I'm sorry you had to deal with that, but thank you. Any other issues so far?"

"Not really. Aaron came to service the pool today," I say with my eyes squinted at him.

He's biting at his lips, averting eye contact and rubbing the back of his neck. This behavior is polar opposite to the guy who showed up at the door an hour ago.

"Aaron? Really? He wasn't supposed to be there until next week. I thought he was still recovering from his gastric bypass surgery. Anyway, I guess that's one less distraction you'll have next week. You've got our cell numbers. Don't hesitate to call if you have any questions."

"*Aaron*" shifts his wide-eyed gaze to mine while I listen to Elizabeth and ease my way through the kitchen. Without taking my eyes off him, I reach behind me in slow motion and grasp the handle of a large butcher knife in a hardwood block.

"Thanks, Elizabeth, enjoy your trip."

Holding my phone in one hand and the knife in my other so he can clearly see them, I continue to move farther away.

"Listen, I don't know who the fuck you are, but I suggest you get out of here before I call the police or ... cut you!"

His eyes flash between mine and the knife, yet his look is one of amusement with his lips curling at the corners.

"Cut me?" he says with a raise of his brow.

Waving the knife around with reckless abandon, I growl. "Yes, cut you, stab you, castrate you."

Squinted blue eyes twinkling with mischief stare at me. "Castrate me?"

"Yes, chop off your penis!" I slice the knife through the air in an X.

"Castration would be removing my testicl—"

"Get out!" I lunge in his direction.

Jumping back, he holds his hands up. "Okay, okay, jeez take it easy. I'm going."

Keeping a safe distance, I follow him to the door. It shuts and with swift fingers I lock the deadbolt. I freeze mid turn at the sound of a knock on the daylight window. Cupping the sides of his face, he's peering inside. His smile is sexy but, under the circumstances, a little creepy.

"Wanna go to the beach tomorrow?"

Scowling, I stab the knife through the air in his direction. Shaking his head, he walks to his 4Runner. I wait until he's gone then retreat to the kitchen.

Chapter Two

June 4th, 2010

SWARLEY WAKES me way too early. His eating schedule is suited for early risers. That, which I am not.

"Go away, dog!" I groan as he attempts to lick my eyelids open.

It's six-thirty and the sun is peeking through the shades. I'm missing the motorized blackout shades I've experienced during some of my housesitting adventures. The sheer window coverings here suggest Elizabeth and Trevor rise with the sun.

"Alright already, let's get you fed." It's hard to be too upset with Swarley, for this anyway. He hasn't eaten in twenty-four hours per Dr. Abbot's orders, which reminds me, he might be making a house call this morning. Swarley is supposed to get a walk or jog an hour after he eats so I change into my running shorts and a racerback running top.

Pulling my hair into a ponytail, I look at the hazel eyes staring back at me in the mirror. My wandering mind sees a different reflection—the most striking blue irises I've ever seen. His smile, the messy, golden blonde hair, and that body ... oh my. Rippling muscles. Strong Jaw. Full lips.

Shaking my head, I try to banish the absurdity of it all from my mind. Today is a new day and I have to believe it's going to be less ... *shitty*.

I scroll through my e-mail and texts while sipping coconut water on the deck. Of course there's one from Avery.

> Hey, Sam, sorry I didn't call you back last night. I went out with some friends and ended up drinking too much and waking up ... well I'm sure you can guess :) Call me later, I think you have a story to finish ;D

"Okay, dog, it's seven-thirty. Let's do this so we can get back and plant our asses by the pool for the rest of the day."

Not only was I on the swim team in high school, I also played soccer. In college I participated in intramural soccer, volleyball, and flag football. Running, however, has never been my choice activity. Pounding the pavement for miles and miles doesn't "clear my mind." I'm sure orthopedic surgeons love runners—joint replacement by age fifty. I'll pass, thank you very much.

On the front porch I get Swarley into his harness.

"We jog for two miles then walk home. If you need more exercise than that, I'll strap your hyperactive ass to the treadmill downstairs for the rest of the afternoon. Capiche?"

"You could just tie his leash to the bumper and drive around town."

Eyes wide, I whip around. Dr. Abbot is standing behind

me and Swarley makes an immediate dash for the crotch greet.

"Crap! You scared me. I ... I was just—"

"Joking? I hope." He smiles. His navy jogging shirt is wet and clinging to his lean runner's figure, and his shorts are too short for his long legs. Then again, mine are probably too short for running in public at all. His dark mop of hair is stuck to his forehead and dripping sweat down his flushed face.

His irresistible innocent charm brings a smile to my face. "Yes, at least today I'm joking."

"Rough day yesterday?" He chuckles.

"There were definitely a few unexpected events, starting with the trip to your office." I offer a tight-lipped smirk with my hands crossed over my chest.

He squats down and gives Swarley a playful rub behind the ears. "You look good today, big guy." Swarley goes crazy licking him. His whole body wags in excitement.

"We haven't had any more messes since yesterday morning and he inhaled his breakfast an hour ago."

"So two miles huh?" he asks.

"Yes, that's my limit today." I nod.

"Well, that's about all I have left before I need to get ready for work. Want some company?"

"Dr. Abbott, I don't want to slow you down."

"It's Dane and I've already jogged eight miles. I think a slowdown would be just fine." He shifts from side to side, stretching his inner thighs.

Tightening my ponytail, I consider his offer. With twenty-nine more days to go and a completely unpredictable mutt, it might not be a bad idea to make nice with the cute vet who lives in the neighborhood.

"Come on, it's just a jog." He rests his hands on his hips and cocks his head.

I nod. "Fine, but I'm serious. The legs on this five foot five inch body have to work twice as hard to keep up with your six-foot-five frame."

"Six-foot-three and I'll go slow."

We head north at the end of the drive, and Dane starts playing twenty questions.

"So how do you know Trevor and Elizabeth?"

"Elizabeth is my dad's sister."

"Where are you from?"

"Illinois."

He laughs. "Midwest girl, huh?"

"Yeah, yeah, Midwest girl." I try to keep my grin contained, but I can't.

"Did you go to college?"

"Yes."

"Don't elaborate." His voice is deep with sarcasm and not at all labored from his already eight mile run.

I'm not usually a talker when I jog, not enough oxygen.

"University of Iowa. Art History. Mom died. Dad's a minister. Younger sister. Your turn."

Dane laughs. "It's like jogging with a robot. Swarley has more enthusiasm than you right now."

I stop as Swarley pulls me off to the side to drop a load.

"Poop looks good." Dane grins.

I bag the poop and we continue.

"Veterinary Medicine, UCD. Parents in Los Angeles. Younger brother in Seattle. Older sister in San José."

He gives me a sideways glance, but I don't say anything in response nor does he add anything else as we jog in silence.

"This is me." He points off to the right at a two-story red brick house.

Bending over, hands resting on my knees, I catch my breath while Swarley lifts his leg to anything and everything.

"Can I get you some water before you head back?"

"Thanks, but I'm good. Come on, Swarley."

"I enjoyed our jog ... uh ... maybe we can do it again sometime?" Dane shifts his weight from one foot to the other. It must be a nervous habit, or maybe he needs to use the bathroom.

"Sure. Swarley would love that. Well, you know where to find us."

"Bye, Sydney."

"Later."

———

As soon as we turn the corner into Elizabeth and Trevor's long drive, I stop. A familiar black Toyota 4Runner is parked by the front walk. *Crap!*

"Okay, dog, when I say attack you'd better obey."

I tread up the drive and as I come around the corner of his 4Runner I'm taken back by the sight on the porch. Pseudo pool guy is sitting on the steps holding a huge bouquet of wild flowers and beside him is a drink holder with cups and a white sack.

"Attack," I whisper, releasing the leash.

Swarley runs up the steps and starts licking pool guy's face.

Stupid dog.

The I-couldn't-wait-to-see-you-again smile that graces his

27

face melts my resolve and those blue irises ... My God, they render me speechless.

"I thought we should call a truce before you have access to any cutlery." He licks those full red lips and my tongue mirrors his.

Catching myself, I bite them together with a tight smile. "Mmm ... wise." I step closer.

Swarley finds a patch of shade near the front door and collapses.

Standing, he holds out the flowers. "Truce?"

This guy is off-the-charts irresistible wearing black and gray striped board shorts and a black muscle shirt with aviator sunglasses hanging from the front. Everything about him screams dangerously sexy. Today, however, I'm deaf.

I bring the vibrant flowers to my nose, walking past him. "What do I call you?"

Turning my head, I raise a questioning brow and his grin doubles. "Lautner Sullivan."

I keep walking and open the door without looking back again. Swarley jumps up and heads into the kitchen.

"Aren't you going to invite me in?"

Pausing in the middle of the doorway, I contemplate the sanity of inviting a total stranger into a house that doesn't belong to me. Okay, I did it yesterday, but completely under false pretenses.

Twisting my lips to the side, I shrug my shoulders. "Depends. What's in the bag?"

"Cherry-almond galettes."

I grab the bag and look inside. It's a done deal. He's officially invited in, and if one of those four cups is a chai tea latte, I will drop to my knees and give him the best damn blow job he's ever had.

"After you." I grin and pivot to let him in.

"Thank you—?"

"Sydney." Our eyes meet.

"Just as I suspected. Beautiful name for a beautiful woman."

Oh jeez, this is not good ... not good at all.

In the kitchen Lautner takes a seat at the counter while I grab plates from the cabinet.

"Hope I brought something you like. I have plain decaf, Frappe, green tea, or chai tea latte."

Chai tea latte? Oh dear God!

One of the plates slips out of my hand and crashes against the counter. By some miracle, it's not broken.

"Shit!"

"Sorry, you're probably an orange juice girl. Huh?"

Sydney! Get a grip ... figuratively and literally.

My whole body warms and I know my face is flushed. I can't look at him without thinking about giving him head. I'm quite certain I will never drink another chai tea latte without thinking about giving Lautner a blow job. *Shit!* I hope he's not a mind reader.

"Is something wrong?"

"No." I clear my throat with a quick recovery, setting the galettes on the plates without making eye contact.

"Are you sure? You seem ... flustered."

"Fine, I'm ... just ... fine. Chai tea latte, please." I regain some composure and look at him as I take a bite of the galette. It's so good!

Seemingly satisfied with my persuasion, he slides my tea over to me and starts eating.

"So I take it you're dog sitting for the owners?"

Swallowing, I nod. "Housesitting. The *pleasure* of taking care of the dog is just a bonus."

"Not a dog person?" he asks with a knowing smirk.

"No, I'm a dog person. I'm just not sure if I'm a Swarley person."

"Maybe he's an acquired taste, like me."

I choke on my tea because I can't believe he just said that. I'm trying desperately not to picture him naked, which is hard to do because I've actually seen him naked. Why did he have to say that? *Is* he reading my dirty mind?

"Are you okay?"

I nod, covering my mouth and stifling my cough. Who the hell is this guy and why does he affect me so?

Remember, Sydney ... guys are serpent-like distractions, fairytales don't exist, and you're allergic to pixie dust.

"I'm ... fine. Swarley, in a world where dogs are considered family members, is my cousin. The homeowners, Elizabeth and Trevor, are my aunt and uncle. It worked out that I wanted to be on the West Coast, closer to my sister, around the same time they needed a house and dog sitter while they travel through Europe this month."

Lautner sips his drink and nods. "Well, lucky me."

"Yeah about that ... let's acknowledge the elephant in the room. Who are you and why were you here yesterday?" I ask, taking a seat at the counter, making sure to leave an empty chair between us. I don't trust him yet, but worse than that ... I don't trust myself in his close proximity.

He finishes chewing while a sly smirk pulls at the corners of his mouth. "Funny thing actually, my friend moved into a house at 1109 SW Vine. I didn't write down the address, I was going by memory and as you know this house is—"

"1109 NW Vine," I finish. "So you were just at the wrong address?"

"Crazy, huh?"

"No. Crazy is impersonating the pool guy just so you can stalk an unsuspecting young woman staying alone in someone else's house."

He twists his lips to the side and scratches his chin. "Hmm, when you spin it like that it makes me sound like some sort of predator."

"How exactly would you explain yesterday's events?" I raise a brow at him and sip my tea.

Teasing his tongue over the corner of his mouth, he rolls his eyes to the ceiling for a moment. Bright blue irises meet mine and his face softens.

"Boy meets girl. Boy physically feels like he's gasping for air because the girl before him is just stunning, absolutely ... breathtaking. An unfamiliar feeling seizes boy—fear. Fear that he's taken a wrong turn for all the right reasons. Fear that the moment could slip away and for the rest of his life he'd live with the excruciating agony born from the soul-snatching 'what if?'"

Lips parted, my eyes blink rapidly.

Speechless.

What if?

Silence hangs in the air like a heavy cloud waiting to burst. I'm staring at him, but his head is bowed looking at his plate while he pushes a few crumbs around with his finger. His eyes risk a peek up at me and I see something in his somber expression that I haven't seen yet—vulnerability.

I wrinkle my face and squint my eyes. "Worst pickup line ever."

Holy Shit! Best pickup line EVER!

I'm lost in blue irises, but he doesn't hold my gaze. He looks back down at his plate and shrugs with just a mere hint of a smile.

"Can't blame a boy for trying."

"True. But your sappy,"—*actually, boombox-over-your-head-banner-in-the-sky-no-other-guy-will-ever-compare*—"explanation doesn't explain why you nearly let me drown before you jumped in the pool after me ... completely naked."

This time it's his squinted eyes that snap back to mine. His head juts forward and his jaw drops.

"Drowning? Yeah, right." He laughs. "Because people who are drowning sit cross-legged at the bottom of a pool with their hands folded in their lap."

"Whatever." I wave my hand in a dismissive gesture. "Still doesn't explain jumping in the pool naked."

"You were playing around, so I thought I would too. Don't act all Goody Two-shoes. You were eye-fucking me from the moment you opened the door, and when I took my shirt off it was like nothing above my neck even existed."

"*Eye-fucking* you? Don't flatter yourself." I stand and take our plates to the sink.

I was totally eye-fucking him, but come on ... how ungentlemanly of him to call me on it.

"I guess we'll just have to agree to disagree. However, I will concede that I may have over shot it a bit by jumping in the pool naked." He holds up his thumb and index finger about an inch apart.

A very unladylike snort escapes me. "Jeez, what makes you think that?"

Biting his thumbnail, he smiles. "I'd have to say the butcher knife. Did you really think I was a threat?"

Leaning against the counter, I smile. "No. You were playing around, so I thought I would too."

"Touché, Sydney." The shimmery reflection in his eyes and the unrestrained smile possessing his lips consumes me.

He stands and moves with slow caution toward me. Every muscle in my body contracts. I'm frozen, numb, and completely raptured by blue irises. We're so close I can feel the warmth of his breath on my face. I jump at the touch of his thumb on my chin.

"Crumb," he whispers, brushing it off.

My brain is screaming, *say something!*

"Let's go."

"What? Where?" I shake my head to clear the fuzziness his close proximity has created in my jumbled head.

He steps back and I draw in a quick breath to keep from withering to the floor. The way my body involuntarily responds to his is magnetic and alarmingly dangerous.

Retreating another few paces, he leans against the opposite counter. "The beach."

"I can't go to the beach with you," I retort without hesitation.

"Why not?"

Why can't I go to the beach with Lautner? I don't know, but my instincts tell me it has something to do with self-preservation. That, and it's the correct response to a person I've known for two seconds. Who in their right mind would do something so reckless as to say "what the hell" and jump into a stranger's vehicle because he said "what if?"

Me. That's who.

Barely able to contain my nervous excitement, I twirl my long hair around my finger and grin that you-might-be-Ted-Bundy-but-fuck-it-I'm-going-with-you-anyway grin.

"I'll grab my suit."

———

"THIS IS INSANE." Skipping down the porch stairs, I sling my bag over my shoulder. Lautner leans against the front of his 4Runner with one leg casually crossed over the other. A pang of disappointment threatens my beaming grin as I notice his sunglasses hiding those hypnotic blue irises. I make a quick recovery when his lips part into the most infectious smile.

"I'd hardly call a day at the beach insane." He opens the passenger door and takes my bag, grazing his fingers over my bare shoulder. My breath hitches at his electric touch and my lips pull to a tight grin to hide my nervousness.

"Thank you," I whisper, relinquishing my bag. He tosses it in the back then shuts my door. The man I threatened with a knife less than twenty-four hours ago is taking me to the beach. He's hijacked my ability to reason. I'm going on impulse and it's exhilarating, liberating, and *insane*. What if he's luring me away from safety to rape me, cut me up into tiny pieces, and throw my body in the ocean? Maybe I've watched too much *Dexter*.

The slam of the driver's door sends a shiver of doubt through my body. My heart races in my chest, stomach knotted, lungs gasping for air. His hand rests on mine which is white-knuckled into the charcoal leather armrest.

"Everything okay?"

My gaze fixes on his hand. The searing sensation of his touch frazzles my focus. Is he running a fever? Why does he feel so hot? Maybe I'm sick. I feel chilled and slightly disoriented.

I drag my eyes to his face. He slides his glasses up on his head.

"Sydney?"

Blue irises. They're so indescribable. It's more of a feeling. My chills evaporate and blood surges through my body heating the surface until it glistens. No words can escape, just the faint whisper of a satisfied sigh as my posture relaxes. It's as if all the wonder and nostalgia of the most surreal places on Earth have been captured then released from his gaze. It's crazy, I know it, but there are blue eyes and then there are *blue* eyes. It's like God decided to give one man infinitely beautiful irises, a passageway to forever, a glimpse of Heaven, and I'm looking at him. It's the only explanation because it's not possible—or fair for that matter —to have eyes so mesmerizing.

"Fine ..." It's all I've got. One word.

Flipping his sunglasses back over his eyes, he removes his hand from mine and starts the engine.

Fucking Medusa eyes! Get a grip, Syd.

"You look a little nervous, that's all." He puts the 4Runner in gear.

"Nervous? Why would I be nervous? It's not as if I'm going to the beach with a complete stranger who could rape me, chop up my body, and feed me to the sharks."

A deep staccato chuckle reverberates from his chest. "Sydney, I'm not going to *rape* you."

And ...?

An eerie silence hangs between us as I give him a sideways glance. Focused on the road, his slightly crooked smile is filled with mischief.

"And ...?" I tilt my head in his direction waiting for a more reassuring response.

"And what?"

"And I'm supposed to take comfort in knowing that my virginity will be preserved when I'm butchered and fed to the sharks?"

Lautner's head whips in my direction. "You're a virgin?" he emphasizes the last word with a high-pitched tone.

"No, of course not. It's just a saying."

He shakes his head. "Being 'nervous as a long-tailed cat in a room full of rocking chairs' is just a saying. 'My virginity will be preserved' is not a saying. It's a declaration, an announcement, a disclosure ... a big reveal. But it is *not* a saying."

I shrug a single shoulder and look out my window. "Yeah, well maybe not where you're from."

"Sydney, it's okay if you're a vir—"

"I'm not a virgin! Jeez! What do I have to do to make you believe me?"

"Well—" His new smirk is laced with devilish intentions as his tongue eases out to wet his full lips before he bites the edge of his bottom one.

"Not happening," I affirm.

"Okay," he mumbles.

"I'm serious. I am not sleeping with you."

"I said, okay." He laughs, inching his head back and forth.

"No, you didn't just say 'okay,' you said 'okay,'" I mock, "but what you meant was 'whatever, baby, you know you'll never be able to resist my hypnotizing sex appeal.'"

Laughter erupts from deep within his belly, as if he's just heard the most amusing joke of all time. "God, Sydney, you're a real spitfire."

A warm breeze twists and pulls my hair as we pick up

speed out of town. Taking the hair tie off my wrist, I pull back my wild locks and secure them in a ponytail.

"We can roll up the windows," Lautner offers.

"No way. Since we're not taking a convertible to the beach, windows down is a must. By the way, what beach are we going to?"

"Not sure yet. Just thought we'd head west to Highway One then see what waves call to us between there and Santa Cruz."

The morphing view of green peaks and valleys peppered with colorful remnants of spring blossoms along the winding road is spectacular. I've seen the ocean countless times, but I still buzz with giddy anticipation as we venture toward the surging coastline of California.

"So, Sydney, do you have a last name or are you a celebrity that goes by one name?" Lautner's silky voice infiltrates the windy buzz in my ears.

"Montgomery." I grin, looking out my window.

"Well, Sydney Montgomery, are you from California?" His formal interviewer's voice is amusing.

"Illinois. I've been housesitting all over the world for the past year since I graduated. I've been able to see the most amazing places, but as I said earlier, I wanted to be closer to my sister this summer. She's a massage therapist in L.A. so Trevor and Elizabeth's vacation was perfectly timed.

"Hmm ... from which college did you get your degree in housesitting?"

I meet his sideways glance and goofy smirk with an eye roll. "University of Iowa. I have a bachelor's degree in art history, but my dream job requires a bit more school and a lot more money so I'm taking a couple of years off to save up."

Keeping his eyes on the road, he nods. "Yeah, it's crazy

how much money it takes to get a good job, or your dream job..." he glances over at me with raised eyebrows "... which is?"

It's impossible to hide my enthusiasm and my broad grin shows it.

"A museum curator."

"Ah, so you're the artsy type?"

"Not necessarily artsy, I mean, I like to draw and I love photography, but art history is my passion. I could spend all day researching and never tire of it. My college instructors said I have a knack for organization and an eye for the unique. Which is ironic because I'm a mess at home. Anyway, somewhere along the way I set my mind on becoming a curator and I've never looked back." Slipping off my flip-flops, I prop my feet up on the dash.

Lautner is quiet, like he's processing what I've just told him.

"So what's your story? How is it that a grown man has nothing better to do on a Thursday than go to the beach with a stranger?"

"Good question, and you're right ... you are a little strange."

"Shut up!" I pinch the taut skin on his arm with my nails. I can only pretend to be offended when he has such a gregarious grin on his face.

"I'm on a break, at least for the next week and a half."

"Break, huh ... are we talking jail break or—"

With a quick grab, he squeezes my knee. The shrill sound that escapes me threatens to shatter the windshield. He releases my leg, but the heat from his touch still lingers on my skin.

"For your information I'm getting ready to start my residency in pediatric medicine."

I could not be more shocked if the car grew wings and flew us to the moon.

Lautner has a playful grin, not arrogant, just confident.

"You're a doctor?" I can't hide my wide-eyed stare.

"Yes." He gives me another sideways glance and rolls his eyes. "Don't look so surprised."

Redirecting my gaze to the road, I sigh. "Hmm, that's—"

"Amazing? Awesome? Fascinating? Wonderful? Marvelous?"

Pursing my lips, I shake my head. "No ... I was going to say *unexpected*."

"Oh, well I'd hate to be predictable. However, I am a little disappointed by your reaction. After all, aren't you trained to see a diamond in the rough?"

I guffaw. "Oh my! You're calling yourself a diamond in the rough?"

He shrugs. "Sure, why not? I have to at least be considered a good catch."

A good catch? Is it possible to meet two "good catches" in less than twenty-four hours?

I cross my arms over my chest and watch the hilly terrain pass by. "You might be. Not that I would care. I'm not looking to *catch* anything or anyone."

"You could be in trouble then. We're all unsuspecting fish in the sea being lured by temptation."

I snort. "If you're calling yourself bait, then I'll concede you are distracting, trouble, bad news ... but tempting? No. I'll willingly swim into the net when I'm ready, but that won't be anytime soon. Not to sound *shellfish,* but I don't have time for the fisherman right now."

He roars into a boisterous laughter. "Shellfish? God, Sydney, you're too much."

A warm feeling of content washes over me. Lautner isn't laughing at me. He gets my quirky sense of humor, which puts him in a small but elite group of people. Authenticity is often an illusion, yet in this moment, being myself has never felt so real.

"No worries, Sydney, I'm not looking for distractions either. I have three years of fifty-plus hour work weeks ahead of me with lots of on-call time. Someone like you would not be a good thing."

"Ouch!" I feign offense, pressing my hand flat to my chest.

He shakes his head. "You know what I mean. Women can be evil little temptresses, and I think that's exactly what you are underneath that flawless, innocent, Midwestern girl persona."

It's my turn to laugh. "Whatever."

I can't get a mental grip on him. He's emotionally intense one minute, saying things you'd only hear in the movies, then he's cocky and aloof the next.

"Okay. What would you be doing today had we not met yesterday?"

He shrugs. "That's easy, surfing."

"So you didn't plan this day special for me?"

"Don't flatter yourself. As I said, I have a lot going on in my life. No time for romantic grand gestures."

Oh, he's smooth. I suck in a breath and bite my upper lip to keep my reaction neutral. He's definitely proving to be a worthy adversary.

"Then what do you call the galettes and tea this morning?" I raise a single brow.

Keeping his eyes on the road, he grins. "Breakfast."

"And the flowers?"

"A momentary lapse of sanity." He glances at me with a smirk. "But I'm okay with it. The line between insanity and genius is often blurred."

"Yeah, that's kind of what I thought when I agreed to come with you today."

Holding the top of the steering wheel with his left hand, he moves his right arm behind my seat with his hand on the back of my head rest. "That it was genius?"

I try not to look back at his herculean arm. "Or insane," I mumble, tensing from his close proximity.

The rest of the drive is peaceful. Neither one of us say much, but it's not an awkward silence. A mix of music blares from the speakers, and I find myself wanting to sing along, but I'm not confident with my voice or Lautner's reaction. That might be too *real*. The coastal drive down Highway One is filled with a breathtaking panoramic view of the Pacific. White crested waves crashing onto smooth sandy beaches. Herons and Terns scavenging in the shallow waters. Fishing and sailboats in the distance mixed with the occasional wave runner or parasailer. Could anyone ever get tired of this view?

Lautner exits and pulls off onto a flat dirt area at the bottom of a grassy knoll.

"What beach is this?"

He unfastens his seat belt and opens his door. "This is our beach for the day."

I hear him open the back latch so I slip on my flip-flops and hop out. There are no other cars around and I can't see past the hill to the beach, but I assume it too is vacant.

When I come around to the back, he hands me my bag then grabs a cooler with two Whole Foods sacks on top.

"Are we allowed to be here?" I grab one of the sacks off the cooler.

Lautner turns a complete three hundred and sixty degrees. "Looks like the coast is clear."

"Ha, ha. I don't have anyone to bail me out of jail if we get arrested." I shuffle my feet along the dirt behind him as he lugs the cooler toward the hill.

"We're not going to get arrested. Just keep your bikini on ... or not," he calls over his shoulder.

"If I recall correctly, that's your MO not mine."

I ready myself to climb the hill until I see him head down a narrow path that winds around to the beach. He plops the cooler in the sand.

"I'll get the boards. Help yourself to a drink in the cooler."

From the looks of the worn dirt path, more than just our feet have trod through the brush here to play in the sun and sand. I slip off my shoes, pull off my tank, then shimmy out of my jean shorts. There wasn't enough time to give much thought to my choice of bikini. It's a simple black halter with a tie in the front and low rise bottoms. Nothing flashy, then again, who am I trying to impress? *Yeah, right!*

The sand falls back away from the water to the winding lines of the grassy knoll making this area of the shoreline feel secluded, like a private beach. Reaching into my canvas bag, I pull out my camera bag. I rarely go anywhere without it. It's the first real investment I made after saving up money lifeguarding the summers of my junior and senior years in high school. My dad suggested an eight hundred dollar used Canon on Ebay after my first summer, but I waited until the next year and dropped close to three grand on a Nikon. Best decision ever.

"Ah, the lover of photography."

I turn as Lautner sets the surfboards down. He's already taken his shirt off, and I'm once again challenged to keep my lips closed and panting to a minimum.

"Yes," I reply, messing with the dials to look like I'm doing anything but staring at him.

He removes his sunglasses and tosses them on his shirt that's been wadded up and left in the sand. Just when I think his eyes can't get any more stunning, they do. Maybe it's the lighting, or maybe it's just the way he looks at me, but I'm so lost in his eyes.

"I'll do you if you do me?" In his hand is a bottle of sunblock.

Great. I nearly melted when he touched my hand earlier. We might as well see if my body can completely vaporize.

"Okay." I snap a few pictures of him. In case I end up dead, at least my camera will have evidence on it.

"Let me put my camera back in its bag." My hands are shaking; this is not good.

"Here." He hands me the bottle.

"Reef Safe biodegradable Sunscreen."

"Gotta protect the marine life. My dad is a marine biologist, it's all I know." He smiles then turns his back to me.

I'm glad he can't see me because my hands are still shaking as I squeeze the bottle. Way more comes out than I expect. I hand him the bottle then start applying it to his back. My mouth is cotton and I feel sweat beading on my brow and between my cleavage, but it's not from the sun. His back is a bumpy terrain of firm muscles. With slow movements, I knead each one.

"You have strong hands."

The sound of his voice paralyzes me. Jeez, I haven't been applying sunblock, I've been massaging him ... feeling him up.

"Uh—um—I—I got too much sunblock and I'm just trying to rub it in."

He raises his arms and laces his fingers together on top of his head. I whimper—yes, actually whimper—as his body shifts and his muscles flex. My hands itch for my camera. He's a masterpiece and I'm dying to capture him from every angle.

"Just rub it around to the front," he suggests, thankfully without acknowledging my needy noises.

My hands, still heavily slathered in sunblock, work their way around to his chest and oh-so-firm abs. In this moment I become hyperaware of how little I'm wearing. It wasn't a big deal when we were at a safe distance, but now I feel naked to his heated gaze just inches from my body. I chance a glance up, imagining him with a cocky smirk. Instead, I'm met with firm eyes and moist parted lips.

Shit! Not good.

"There." I look away.

"Turn around," he demands.

The spurting sound of him squeezing the lotion tingles my skin. I'm nervous, awaiting his touch.

My breath catches with the moment of impact. His large hands glide over my back in slow, circular strokes. The feel of his fingertips grazing just underneath the edge of my bikini bottoms has me turning around in a quick reflexive motion.

"That's good ... thanks. Uh, I actually don't burn that easily, so no need to over apply."

He rubs the excess from his hands over his arms while I rush to finish applying it to the rest of my body.

"Have you surfed before?" he asks.

"Yes, but I'm not that good." An understatement. I suck. The last time I tried surfing I ended up with five stitches on my head when my board completely rejected me two seconds after I popped up.

"Let's do this." He hands me a board.

"Uh ... maybe I should watch you for a while. I mean, shouldn't we spot each other or something?"

"Yes, we should. I'm going to spot you first." He grins, still holding my board.

"Oh, well ... o—kay." I take the board and drudge my way through the sand. The poor guy is clueless. Every fantasy he's ever had about sexy girls in bikinis catching the big wave is about to be shattered and ruined forever. He will never be able to un-see what's about to happen.

I paddle out on my stomach, attempting to duck under the breaking waves. No good. I capsize and get slammed back into the sand under the relentless succession of waves. Refusing to look back at Lautner, I start my second attempt. This time I make it past the breaking waves and straddle the board with my butt situated just behind the center point. The perfect wave catches my eye. I turn the nose of my board toward the beach and begin paddling.

Brilliant!

My stomach flips as I feel myself rising with the wave. "You're mine, bitch." *Paddle, paddle, paddle ...* Guess it wasn't my wave after all. I'll catch the next one. Here she comes ... Okay, not mine either. This goes on for eternity. Finally, roughly fifteen attempts, five capsizes, and seven wipeouts later, I catch one. Dropping into the trough, I remind myself to be patient and wait until I'm in the flat water at the front of the wave. "Oh yeah!" I pop up and look toward the beach to gloat. Wrong move! Nosedive.

Don't panic. Close your mouth. Go with the flow.

I'm crawling—yes, crawling—in the sand with my head down. My hair is matted to my face, and I have so much sand in my bikini bottoms it feels, and I imagine looks, like I've shit my pants. Balancing on my knees and one hand, I attempt to wipe my hair out of my eyes with my other hand. Two large feet in the sand with foamy waves cresting over them come into view. I sit back kneeling before him with rhythmic waves flowing over my legs. After smearing the rest of my wet tangled hair back away from my face, I look up at Lautner. He's no longer wearing his sunglasses and his hands rest casually on his hips.

"That was ..." The smile on his face is tense, like he's in pain. He's nodding his head but then he changes direction and it's now a back and forth movement. "Wow, you must be ... *exhausted* ... and this *isn't* your first time?"

I shake my head with a wrinkled-nose smile, squinting from the bright sunlight. He fetches my board then offers his hand. Taking it, I clamber to my feet. He's trying to hide his grin, but failing miserably. Releasing his hand, I start to walk forward.

"Sydney, do you ... maybe want a *private* moment in the water?"

Crap!

He's looking at my backside. Specifically the sand turd clump weighing down the back of my bikini bottoms. There is no use trying to hide it. He's already seen it. So why am I backing into the water like a dump truck instead of turning around first? Simple. I'm trying to preserve the one small shred of dignity I have remaining.

I'm safely neck deep in the cool Pacific so I fiddle with my bottoms to wash out the sand turd. Lautner acts the part of the perfect gentleman by keeping his back to me as he rummages through the cooler. I tug and pull at my top to straighten it out and free the sand from it as well. Leaning my head back in the water, I try to rinse out my hair, but some of it is tangled in the ties of my top.

Seeing that Lautner is still occupied with setting out food and drinks, I make quick moves to untie the front and neck straps of my suit and untangle my hair. My hairband is knotted in part of my hair so I pull it out. I hold my top in my teeth while I work to tie my hair back into a bun so I can get my top back on without my hair in the way.

"Water or iced tea?" he yells, thankfully still not looking at me.

"Wa—ah—shit!" There it goes. The last shred of my dignity just caught a wave and it's riding my top all the way to the beach with its tongue out and hands fisted above its head, thumbs and the pinkies pointed out.

Dammit, Sydney! Tea, you love tea.

Tea is easy and natural to say with clenched teeth. For example, if a person were to ... oh, I don't know, hold onto their bikini top in their mouth while saying "tea," no problem. "Water" ... not so natural.

What. Are. The. Chances?

"Coming Sydney? I have turkey or salmon sandwiches. Maybe you're a vegetarian. Are you?"

No, Lautner. I'm not a vegetarian. I'm stuck in the ocean without my top!

My arms are crossed over my chest with my hands

cupping my breasts. Can I run and capture my top then retreat back into the water before Lautner looks in my direction? Maybe. It's a fifty-fifty chance—okay, more like forty-sixty. I was never that great at capture the flag, but the odds should be in my favor since Lautner is not yet privy to the fact that there is even a game going on.

I inch my way toward the beach with stealth-like movements. *That's it, big guy, you just keep focusing on making me a kick-ass sandwich while I retrieve my runaway top. There's nothing to see here. Nope—*

"SHARK!" I scream while sprinting to the beach. My hands are fisted as I frantically pump my arms for momentum to propel my body out of the water. Lautner jogs toward me, and I leap onto him throwing my arms around his neck.

"Oh my God! Sha—shark. Did you see it? It's pointy ... fin thingy is sticking out of the water." My heart is racing as I struggle to catch my breath.

I'm still holding onto him like the shark is going to grow legs and chase me up the beach. He wraps his arms around me and hugs me to himself as he lifts me off the ground and turns us so I'm facing the water when I look over his shoulder.

"That fin?" he asks.

I squint my eyes, although I have twenty-twenty vision. Near the shore is a ... *cardboard box*. Most of it is saturated and below the water but one corner, a triangular-shaped corner, is still dry and bobbing on the surface of the water. It's drifting closer to my—

My top!

Quick assessment: a box disguised as a shark is floating in the water; my bikini top is sunbathing without me several yards away; and my naked breasts are pressed against Lautner's bare chest.

"I seem to recall suggesting you keep your top on? *Not that I'm complaining.*"

I'm now fully aware of how his bare chest is pressed against mine. I'm praying, begging, offering Swarley as a sacrifice that my nipples don't deceive me or his ... guy thingy doesn't ... *oh, God, too late.*

"What are you doing?" My voice is a desperate whine.

"Sorry, it's not like I have a whole lot of control over—" He starts to release me.

"No!" I tighten my grip around his neck, which also brings me closer to his *problem.* "I'm not wearing a top."

I have a gift for stating the obvious when I'm nervous, and as far as situations go, this one has me *very* nervous.

"Uh ... yeah, I know. About that, why exactly did you take off your top before you ran from the *cardboard box?*"

"I didn't take off my top when I saw the ... *shark.* I'd already taken if off to get the sand out and tie my hair back, and then I chose water when I should have chosen tea and—"

"Sydney?" He brings me out of my nervous rant.

"Mm hmm?"

"You can let go now. I've already seen your boo—breasts."

"Well, once is enough so ..."

"I'd have to disagree with you on—"

"Lautner! Just close your eyes, let go of me, and count to one hundred."

He chuckles and releases me. Suddenly, I'm hanging from him with my tippy-toes grazing the sand. "One ... two ... three ..."

His eyes are closed so I make a mad dash for my top.

"... Thirty-three ... thirty-four ..."

I don't work well under pressure. My hands fumble with the ties.

"... Sixty-six ... sixty-seven ..."

"Done!"

He peeks one eye open at a time. I stand tall with my shoulders back, chin up, and hands planted on my hips. What am I so proud of?

Lautner has a close-lipped grin. He nods his head toward our stuff. "Let's eat."

There's a large plaid blanket on the sand with a bag of potato chips, green grapes, carrots, and two paper plates with artisan bread sandwiches.

"Turkey or salmon?"

"Salmon, thanks."

With the food in the middle, we sit on the blanket facing the water.

"It's a great day," I murmur through my mouth full of sandwich. I'm not sure why I said it, other than the awkward need for small talk.

He looks over at me with a single raised brow. "I'm glad you still think so."

We both gaze out at the water and continue to eat. Through the corner of my eye, I can tell Lautner's body is shaking and I hear a funny noise as if he's choking. Setting my plate down, I lean over and see his hand is fisted at his mouth and he has twisted his torso away from me. I had CPR training but it's been awhile. If I recall correctly, he's too large for back blows so I'm going to need to get my arms around him for abdominal thrusts, unless he passes out.

"Hey, are you okay?" I ask, concern evident in my shaky voice.

He nods his head as I lean even closer to see around to his face.

"Oh my God! Are you laughing at me?"

He no longer can hold it in. Uncontrolled laughter escapes as he tries to keep from choking on the food in his mouth.

"You shit!" I shove him so he falls over on his side.

"I'm sorry ... it's—" He's laughing too much to finish. "I've never seen ..." He coughs to clear his throat and uses the back of his hand to wipe tears from his eyes. Holy Crap! He's laughing so hard, *at me*, that he's crying.

"What's so damn funny?" I ask with my own goofy grin. "Is this about my surfing or the shark? Or are you laughing about my clothing mishap?"

His face is beet red and wrinkled in contortion from trying to contain his hysteria. It's a textbook ugly laugh.

"Oh God ... it's all of it." His breath is labored as his body tries to regain some control. "I mean, it's not just that you had trouble catching a wave, or standing up, or even just straddling your board for that matter..." a few more errant chuckles escape "...it's that you were so determined. God ... it was painful to watch." He continues to take a few deep breaths while I grab my camera and start shooting one shot after another of him.

"Hey, what are you doing?" He tries to cover his face with his arm.

"Well, I heard there were hyenas around these parts, but this is the closest I've gotten to one so I thought I'd get some shots."

"Okay, okay, okay. I'm sorry." He peeks under his arm that's covering his face.

I snap one more shot and set my camera down. As much as I want to keep an angry scowl on my face, I can't.

"Your turn. Now get going." I make a shooing motion with my hand. "My turn to spot you. Although, after your incredibly rude display, I can't guarantee I'll save you if you start to drown. So make sure you leave the keys with me so I can get home in time to feed Swarley."

Lautner stands and swipes my camera from me.

"Hey!" I yell.

He snaps several shots of me then hands it back. "Watch and learn." He smirks as he grabs his board.

———

WE'RE DRIVING BACK to Palo Alto after Lautner's Olympic performance on his surfboard. I must have taken over a hundred pictures of him. He was crazy-good, and I told him as much ... minus the "good" part.

I'm tired. The long day in the sun has zapped my energy. Well, that and being waterlogged.

"You wanna grab some dinner? Pizza or something?" Lautner doesn't sound tired at all.

"Thanks, but not tonight. I have to get Swarley fed and I'm not that hungry."

He smiles, but it's faint.

"Raincheck?" I offer.

Now he perks up. "Definitely. Tomorrow?"

I match his smile. "Okay."

"Great! I'll bring pizza and beer. You provide the entertainment."

"Entertainment?" I question with a sideways glance.

"Yes, entertainment. Did I stutter?" He grabs my leg again, eliciting another squeal.

Shoving his hand away, I shake my head. "There's a pool, hot tub, satellite TV, and a Ping-Pong table in the lower level. The entertainment provides itself."

"Good point. Shall I bring my swim trunks?"

"Only if you plan on getting in the pool or hot tub." I shrug, looking out the window.

"Oh, I plan on getting in both. I'm just confirming whether or not I need my swim trunks."

Turning, I punch him in the arm, which is the equivalent of a bug hitting the windshield. "Shut up! From now on, we *both* keep our clothes or suits on. Got it?"

"Hey, I'll follow the rules if you do." He chuckles as we pull into the drive.

He turns off the ignition and retrieves my bag from the back while I slip on my flip-flops and get out. Instead of handing me my bag, he shrugs it over his right shoulder and surprises me by clasping his left hand to my right, leading me up the porch steps. We stop at the door. Releasing my hand, he faces me and hands me my bag.

"So tomorrow ... five o'clock?"

I nod. My eyes move from blue irises to his full lips and back to his eyes. Why do I feel like I'm sixteen and on my first date? Is he going to kiss me? Do I want him to kiss me? What the hell is wrong with me? My pulse quickens. He steps as close as he can to me without actually touching me. Taking a deep swallow, I lick my lips that are dry from my heavy panting.

"Can I kiss you?" he whispers.

What?

I've never been asked that before. Most guys just do it.

Speak, Sydney!

"Um ... I'm leaving in a month."

Nice ... newsflash, he already knows that!

"Then I'd better not linger, huh?"

He rests his finger under my chin and tilts it up as his lips descend to mine. They're warm and the kiss is gentle and slow. I close my eyes and find myself leaning into it, trying to deepen it. Lautner ends the kiss leaving me wanting more. My knees are weak so I lean back against the door to keep myself upright.

"Goodnight, Sydney." He turns and walks down the porch steps.

I run the tip of my tongue over my lips. "Night." I sigh.

Chapter Three

June 5th, 2010

Day three in Palo Alto and I've had a handsome veterinarian flirt with me; a hot stranger jump in my pool naked; I surfed, which I swore I'd never do again; and I rubbed my breasts against said hot stranger's bare chest. Then there were those blue irises and ... the kiss.

"Yes, Swarley! I'm up. Jeez, must you lick my entire head?" It's 7:00 a.m., so much for sleeping in. "Don't think I didn't see you licking your ass last night. Now my head is covered in your ass germs. Where are your manners?" I mumble, putting on my jogging shorts and T-shirt. He plops down with his head resting on his front paws that are crossed. I'm getting the "puppy dog" eyes.

"I'm not buying the act. Let's go."

I get Swarley his breakfast and there's a knock at the door.

Approaching the front door, I see Dr. Abbott balancing

on one leg while pulling back his other leg to stretch his quads.

"Dr. Abbott ... I mean, Dane."

He wipes the perspiration from his forehead with his arm. "Hey, good morning. Hope I'm not waking you."

The nervousness in his shaky voice is obvious. As I predicted, his confidence is much higher when he's wearing his white lab coat.

"I wish, but unfortunately that's Swarley's job. You want to come in?" I gesture with my outstretched arm.

"No ... or, well yes ... or what I mean is I can't. I have to get ready for work. I just thought I'd see if you were ... or if you wanted ... well that is if you're not too busy, to um have dinner tonight ... with me? 'Cause, I mean, I'm sure you want dinner, and I like to eat dinner too ... so maybe we could eat together. If you want ... or not, I mean ... whatever."

Paging Dr. Abbott. There is an impostor in your body and he has diarrhea of the mouth. Please don your white lab coat and come restrain him, STAT!

Swarley finishes with his breakfast and greets Dane with his usual eagerness and signature crotch sniff.

"Hey, Swarley." He bends down and lets Swarley lick him all over.

Swarley can't get enough of Dane's face. He must taste like a salt lick after all that running. I don't confess Swarley's anal cleaning habits to Dr. Abbott. I'm sure in his profession he's exposed to more ass germs than a fly in a barnyard.

"I appreciate the offer, but I have plans tonight. Maybe another time?"

Dane stands as Swarley bolts out the door to chase an unsuspecting squirrel.

"Yeah, sure um ... absolutely. How about brunch tomorrow?"

The awkwardly shy doctor is persistent. I think just being in the proximity of an animal gives him a boost of confidence.

"Brunch? Okay, why not?" I'm navigating a slippery slope for only day three, but he is the vet and I can't alienate my greatest ally in Operation Thirty Days of Swarley.

"Great. I'll pick you up around eleven?" His face beams.

"Sounds good." I return a polite smile that doesn't show my teeth.

"Good, great ... um, I'll see you then ... tomorrow. At eleven."

Swarley gives up on the squirrel and races past us into the house. "Eleven." I close the door as he turns to jog away.

———

Sunshine, pool, lounge chair, good book, and exhausted dog—it's going to be a good day.

I took Swarley on an extra-long walk this morning. Then we played frisbee in the yard. Now he's passed out in the lounge chair next to me. Mission accomplished.

I reach for my phone and call Avery.

"Hey, Sam. What happened to my phone call yesterday? Were you too busy doing the nasty with the pool guy?"

"Avery, last I knew you had my number too. I was home all evening. Why didn't you call me?"

"Hmm, let me think ... where was I last night?"

"Let me guess. Over-served and passed out in some stranger's bed?"

Avery sang in our church choir throughout high school.

She and her friends wore purity rings and vowed to save their virginity until their wedding night. Ryan Michelson, also in the church choir, took Avery's virginity her sophomore year after the homecoming dance. Avery prayed for forgiveness and a spiritual revirginization. Since then, she has treated the purity ring like a vampire daylight ring. As long as she's wearing the ring, she won't burn in Hell for her sexual indiscretions.

"I won't even justify such a hurtful accusation with an answer."

She doesn't have to. We both know that's code for "WTF happened to me last night?"

"Anyway, enough about me. What happened with the pool guy?"

"Well, you were right. Pool guys don't look like that. Long story short ... he showed up here by mistake, wrong address. Apparently he thought he 'took a wrong turn for all the right reasons' and so he played along with my assumption that he was the pool guy."

"He said that? Oh my God, how romantic." Avery's sappy voice is a shrill.

"Now, that's exactly why you end up in the worst relationships, Ave. You think it's romantic if a guy licks tequila out of your navel."

"Yeah, well I might not think that if a guy ever said something like that to me. So I take it you called his bluff and kicked his ass to the curb?"

I think for a moment. Do I fill in all the blanks? The skinny dipping. The castration threat. The flowers and pastries. I opt for the sugarcoated highlights.

"I let him know that I was ... a little upset. Then he

brought me flowers and breakfast yesterday as an apology. We ended up at the beach surfing all afternoon."

"Stop right there! You *surfed* again?"

"Yes, I surfed again. It went ... fine." *Sugarcoated highlights.*

"Are you going to see him again?"

"As a matter of fact, we're having pizza and beer tonight."

"Does he know about your inability to commit?" she questions in a mocking tone.

"Pot. Kettle. Black. Don't even go there with me, Miss I-Don't-Know-Where-I-Woke-Up-This-Morning. Yes, he knows I'm leaving in a month and I'm not looking for a relationship. In fact, he's not either. He's getting ready to start his residency in pediatrics."

"No. Fucking. Way!"

"Way ... so don't get all up in my face about some guy who will drift out of my life as quickly as he drifted in."

"If you say so. I guess that means you won't mind if I test your pool guy out when I come to visit."

Do I mind if she tries to sleep with Lautner when she comes to visit next week? *Over my dead body, slutty little sister!*

"Whatever. It's not like he's my boyfriend," I say in a casual voice while I twirl my hair around my finger.

"Great! I can't wait. See you next week."

"Bye, Ave."

———

AVERY IS RIGHT, although I will never say those words out loud. My stern focus on nothing but achieving my goals is usually a turnoff to most guys. They'd be fine with a one-night stand, but that's Avery, not me. So I end up being the unattainable "tease." And by "tease" I mean men thinking that if a girl is attractive but not promiscuous, she is a *tease*. I rarely show interest in guys; I notice them, but I don't actively look for them. My current situation is different. Truthfully, I wasn't *looking* for anyone. Swarley got sick, so Dr. Abbott's office was an unexpected but necessary trip my first day, and Lautner ... well, he too was unexpected, but a nice surprise. I can do casual. Fear of commitment is usually what kills a relationship. Good thing neither one of us is looking for commitment.

Looking in the full-length mirror, I give myself a nod of approval. I've chosen a pastel striped bandeau bikini top with a string tie bottom. Over it I'm wearing a hot pink, above the knee spaghetti strap sundress, and my toenails are painted a matching pink. My long brown hair is ironed straight with a wisp of bangs off to the side.

"What do you think, Swarley?" He's sprawled out at the end of the bed keeping a watchful eye on me.

"I agree. I look appropriately hot. Not too slutty, not too prudish."

It's a few minutes before five o'clock and I turn on the surround sound system. A playlist from my iPhone flows through both the indoor and outdoor speakers. Kings of Leon's "Use Somebody" starts when there is a knock at the door. I'm nervous. It's ridiculous since we spent most of the day together yesterday, but it ended with a kiss and that's where my body is still frozen.

"Hey." I greet Lautner with a nervous smile.

He's wearing red board shorts and a gray Stanford shirt. My brilliant assumption is that he attended college at Stanford. He's holding a pizza box in one hand and a six-pack of bottled beer in the other. At the moment, his blue irises drink me in and my skin blushes from the heat of his gaze.

"Hey, yourself. You look ... amazing."

"Thanks, um ... come in." I take the pizza box and head to the kitchen. "Smells good. I'm hungry."

"I forgot to ask what kind of pizza you like so I played it safe and ordered veggie, no onion."

Hmm, is he assuming I don't like onion or that we don't need onion breath for ... whatever reason?

"Perfect. Let's eat out on the deck."

I set the pizza on the table as Swarley greets Lautner, thankfully not with the eagerness that he does Dr. Abbott. It might just be me, but the tension is thick. I've been hanging since Lautner kissed me last night, and I want him to hurry up and do it again so I can relax and not spend the evening wondering when or even if it's going to happen again.

God, it better happen again!

While I set a slice of pizza on each of our plates, he opens two bottles of beer. His bare leg brushes past mine under the table as he scoots his chair in. I give a quick glance down to make sure my dress conceals my hardened nipples. I'm a mess. Can't we just squeeze in a quick inning first, where he makes it to second base and my body gets a reprieve from being on such high alert.

"What did you and Swarley do today?"

I take a pull of my beer, hoping it will calm my nerves. "Not much. After I wore his butt out with a long walk and Frisbee, we lounged by the pool most of the day."

"Rough job," he replies with a smirk.

"I know, right? Someday when I'm up to my ears in school work again, I will reminisce about my carefree housesitting days."

"You're quite driven. Is that an inherited trait?" He takes a bite of pizza, keeping his eyes fixed to mine.

"My mom was going to school to become an architect when she met my dad. They married six months later and I was supposedly a honeymoon baby. Then after I was born, she gave up on school ... She gave up on her dream. My dad told her she should finish her schooling when I reached preschool age. But that got delayed because of my sister. One thing led to another and money was tight with just my dad's income, so my mom continued to postpone her schooling. Then she was diagnosed with cancer and ..." The words are too raw. I'm not ready to have Lautner see me cry.

"You're worried you'll get sidetracked from your dreams." It's not a question.

I nod and take another much needed swig of my beer.

"I understand. I've put a lot of blood and sweat into my schooling ... my future, and I don't want to get sidetracked either." He holds up his beer bottle. "To not getting side-tracked."

I smile and tap my bottle to his. "To not getting side-tracked." It might be the alcohol or our mutual understanding, but I feel more relaxed.

"Did your mom—"

I nod and swallow hard, but the lump is still there so I drink more beer and wait for the numbness.

"So your dad's a reef-safe-sunblock-wearing marine biologist. What about your mom?"

He picks at the label on his beer. "My mom is a special education teacher ... she's also a breast cancer survivor."

Soft blue irises shine at me. He doesn't say it, but I can hear the unspoken words. We share a bond. Both of our moms had cancer. But his mom is a *survivor* and mine is not.

"She's the reason I'm a doctor. Originally, I was going to specialize in oncology, but when I did my oncology rotation all I could see was my mother hanging on for her life." He takes a long pull of his beer. "But then I did a pediatric rotation and working with the kids just clicked. I knew it was my calling."

I nod, wondering if I have a *calling*? Is being a museum curator my calling? It all sounds too "fate-like" to me, and I don't believe in fate.

"Siblings?" I ask, keeping the focus on him.

"No. My mother had trouble conceiving, so I was, in their words, 'a miracle.' When I was two, she was diagnosed with stage three breast cancer. Now she's the 'miracle.'" He leans back and interlaces his hands behind his head. "Do you want to talk about this anymore?"

My eyes fall to his chest and arms, admiring the flex in his large, defined muscles.

"Nope. Hot tub or pool?" I speak the words without thought, or maybe my subconscious thoughts are all about getting Lautner to remove his shirt.

"Hot tub. We should let our food digest before we swim."

"Good call."

Standing, I brush a few crumbs off myself and walk to the hot tub, shrugging my dress off on the way. I take the tie from my wrist and pull my hair up into a messy bun. Pausing with my hands still above my head, I turn and Lautner is standing behind me. His bare chest greets me. I wet my lips and force my gaze to his, but his eyes are exploring every part of my body except my eyes.

"Beer?" He holds up a new bottle.

"Thanks." I take it and turn. Easing myself down to sit

on the edge, I dangle my feet in the steamy water for a moment before scooting all the way in. "God, this feels good."

The hot tub accommodates at least eight. Much to my liking, Lautner takes a seat next to me but turns so we're at a comfortable angle for conversation.

"Okay, you know I like surfing. What about you?"

Our feet and legs occasionally touch, and I find myself back to my original nervous state.

"Surfing, not so much." I roll my eyes. "You're older than I am so you must have more to share than surfing and medical school."

He runs his toe under my foot and I jump, eliciting a chuckle from him.

"I'm not that much older. What are you ... twenty-three? Twenty-four?"

Rubbing the top of my beer bottle over my lips, I smile. "Twenty-three. How old are you?"

"Older."

I nudge him with a playful kick to his leg. "Duh! Let me see ... four years of undergrad plus four years of med school..." my eyes roll while I do the mental math "...twenty-six?"

"Good guess ... twenty-seven."

"Mmm, so you recently had a birthday or you failed a grade."

He pinches his bottom lip between his teeth with a slow nod. "Yeah ... something like that."

I tilt my head to the side, squinting one eye.

"Your turn. Tell me more."

"What?" My voice shrieks. "You still haven't—"

"Ladies first." He smirks.

"Fine! About me, hmm ... soccer and swimming, at least that's what I did in high school. I played intramural volleyball, flag football, and soccer in college. I'm kind of a tomboy. Kudos to you yesterday for finding the one sport I suck at." I roll my eyes and take another pull of my beer.

Laughter vibrates from his chest and his blue irises sparkle with delight. "My bad, we'll have to rectify that unfortunate situation with an activity of your choosing next time."

Next time? I like the sound of that.

He sets his beer down and then surprises me by taking mine and setting it behind us next to his. He scoots closer, resting his arm behind me on the edge of the hot tub. My heart surges against my chest. He's not rushed. Every move he makes is patient, calculated, and agonizingly slow. His eyes focus on my lips and I swallow in breathless anticipation as he leans in toward me.

"Sydney, you look nothing like a tomboy." His voice is a deep whisper.

I watch his left hand move to cup my jaw. Our faces are so close. His thumb brushes over my bottom lip. My mouth relaxes and I let the tip of my tongue taste his thumb. I'm dying! He's hovering so close, yet the mere inches that separate our lips feel like an ocean. Is he waiting for me? Is he having second thoughts? Is he—

Thank you, God! His mouth is on mine. It's slow like last night, but with an undercurrent of intensity. My tongue brushes his top lip and I expect his to reciprocate, to deepen our kiss, but he pulls back. I've never felt like the aggressor. I'm usually the one putting on the brakes, but Lautner is *baiting* me, stringing me along. He's giving me just enough to drive me crazy. By now, Avery would have her top off and be straddling him. Her tongue wouldn't ask for permission with a shy brush. She would lunge forward and demand attention.

"Sydney, you're so damn sexy."

Show me!

"You're not so bad either." My voice is barely audible.

He scoots back a bit. "It's getting hot in here." To my disappointment he climbs out and takes a long pull of his beer.

Hiking my arms up behind me, I lift myself up to sit on the edge leaving my feet in the water. Lautner walks down the deck stairs and takes two long strides before diving into the pool. I'm befuddled. That wasn't my first time making out in a hot tub, but it was definitely the shortest. I'm not sure it really even qualified as making out. Now he's walked away and jumped in the pool. I have no idea what to think or what my next move should be. Do I get in the pool too? Do I wait here?

The lounge chairs on the east side are still catching some sun as it hasn't moved below the trees yet. I get out, grab my beer, and lie back in one of the chairs with the warm setting sun against my face. Lautner is swimming laps. The back stroke looks good on him, showing off his taut abs. Swarley, as predicted, finds me and claims the chair next to mine.

"Are you getting in?" Lautner calls. His arms are folded along the edge of the pool with his chin resting on them.

"Are you thinking a race?" I ask, squinting at him while trying to shield my eyes from the sun with my hand.

"I was thinking a dip in the pool, but if you're feeling a little competitive ... we could race. I won't even use my legs, just my arms."

I jump up and stomp over to the edge of the pool with

my arms crossed in defense. "I'll have you know I was a state swim champion three years in a row. You're not only going to need your legs. You're going to need divine intervention to beat me."

"You're on." He grabs my leg and yanks me in the pool.

I surface and wrinkle my face into an evil grimace. "That's going to cost you, buddy." I swim to the edge where he's already waiting with a cocky smile.

"Name your stroke."

His eyes widen. "The *breast* stroke of course, but we'll save that for later."

I adjust my top. "Whatever, so far you're all talk and little action. Crawl stroke, down and back five times, go!"

His mouth is agape. My brazen accusations have rendered him speechless as I tuck my chin and push off the wall. He's on my tail in no time. I keep a half-body length distance between us, but I'm just warming up. On the last flip turn he starts to gain on me. I kick into high gear. Images of him laughing at me yesterday fuel me to the finish. He comes in a *distant* second. I'm breathless and so is he as we rest our arms on the edge.

"Jeez, Sydney! I underestimated you."

My you-bet-your-ass-you-did grin says it all. I'm very competitive. That's why I took such punishment in the water yesterday. I'd rather look pathetic but determined than to bow out gracefully.

"Because I'm a girl?" The defensive tomboy in me emerges.

Lautner chuckles. "No, because you looked ... awkward in the water yesterday."

I swipe my hand along the surface, splashing him in the face. "Shut up!"

Lunging at me, he grabs my waist and pulls me into him pinning me against the side of the pool. I gasp. His bare skin is flush with mine, but not like yesterday. That was embarrassing and awkward. This is heated and sensual.

"So all talk and little *action*."

I nod once, looking into his blue irises as my tongue traces my bottom lip.

"You want *less* talk and ... *more* action?" he whispers a breath away from my lips.

"Yes," I exhale.

His mouth descends on mine, but it's not slow. It's urgent and demanding. He's not asking, he's taking. I release a soft moan as his tongue plunges into my mouth exploring with erotic strokes against mine. My arms wrap around his neck while he slides his hands from my waist to the back of my legs, lifting and guiding them around his body as I drift closer to him. I suck in a deep breath when his mouth breaks from mine. My fingers dig into his shoulders and his lips brush along my jaw to my ear. Another moan escapes while his tongue grazes below my ear and his right hand slips under the back of my bikini bottoms. His thumb hooks on the outside as his fingers squeeze my bare skin, pulling me closer yet.

"Oh God." I feel his lips against my neck pull up into a smile. He grazes his teeth along my skin then gives me a quick nip, making me jump and giggle because it tickles. Our eyes meet.

"Is this what you had in mind?" he asks, slipping his hand out of the back of my bikini bottoms. "Or did you have something else in mind?" With his eyes fixed to my lips, his hands move up my back to the hook of my top.

I pause in thought, but I'm not Avery. Releasing my legs

from his waist I smile. "You've more than exceeded my expectations. We should get out."

He grins and releases his hands from my straps.

I climb up the ladder and grab two towels from the pool house. When I turn around, Lautner is standing in the same spot he was two days earlier. Only this time he's not fully exposed. I hand him a towel. He dries his face and hair then pulls the towel to his chest.

"Stop picturing me naked." He's not even looking at me, but his lips are twisted into a cocky grin.

I stand idle with my towel hugged to my front. My eyes snap to his that are now focused on me. "I—I'm not picturing you naked." Wrapping my towel around my chest, I brush past him.

"It's okay if you are. I sure as hell am picturing you without your top on."

I ignore his comment and continue toward the deck. "Beer, we need more beer."

———

AFTER WE BOTH finish our third and last beer and our suits are dry, we decide to go downstairs. There's a Ping-Pong table, wet bar, and brown sectional in front of a large LED TV. I have my dress back on over my bikini and Lautner has his Stanford shirt back on, much to my disappointment.

"Is Ping-Pong in your repertoire of mastered skills, Sydney?" He picks up a paddle and taps it against his hand.

I grab the other paddle and ball. "Why? Is losing more than once tonight going to damage your ego?"

"God, you're almost as cocky as me." He grins. "How about a little wager?"

I flip my hip out to the side and tap my opposing foot on the ground while I dribble the ball on my paddle. "I'm listening."

"If I win, I stay the night." The megawatt smile appears.

"Lautner, I told you before. I'm not sleeping with you."

"Who said anything about sleeping?" His voice is deep and sexy.

I jerk the paddle and the ball bounces off the ceiling. My hand, hell, my whole body is shaking. I clear my throat. "And if I win?"

He shrugs. "Name your prize."

Pinching my bottom lip with my fingers, I tug at it. My eyes jump to his and my lips curl up into their own beaming smile.

"If I win, you pick up Swarley's shit in the yard ... tonight, with a flashlight."

Lautner chuckles and shakes his head. "Interesting choice but whatever, deal. You can have first serve."

"Best of five or seven?" I ask.

"Five if I take the lead. Seven if you take the lead."

"Seven it is," I confirm with a wink.

I easily take the first three games. Lautner takes the next three but in close matches. Then something happens on the seventh game. Lautner wins ten points ... In. A. Row.

"Oh my gosh! You played me," I yell, heaving my paddle at him. He deflects it to the ground.

"What? No, I just got lucky, or maybe you were getting tired." He feigns innocence as he struts toward me.

I shove him away. "Bullshit! I wasn't *tired*."

"Okay, I may have played you a little." He scratches his chin and scrunches his nose.

I fold my arms over my chest, sulk over to the sectional,

and plop down. Flipping on the TV, Tom Cruise is scaling the side of a tall building in *Mission Impossible.*

Lautner kneels down in front of me. I keep my eyes focused on Tom.

"I'm sorry. Do you want me to pick up shit and go home?"

"Yes," I snap with squinted eyes and pouty lips.

He slides his hands along my bare legs and leans up so his face is in the crook of my neck. I tense from his hot breath on my skin and his hands squeezing my legs with gentle pressure. His thumbs trace circles on my inner thighs, and his hot, wet tongue sears my skin from my shoulder to my ear.

"Are you *sure* you want me to leave."

"Maybe," I whisper. Yet, my body says otherwise as I tilt my head to give him better access. My nails claw at the couch as I fight to keep from touching him.

With his right hand, he slides the strap of my sundress off my shoulder, following its path with open-mouth kisses. My pulse throbs in my neck, my breasts, and between my legs. Every breath I take becomes increasingly shallow and ragged. An uncontrollable tremble vibrates through my nerves. He ghosts his lips lower to the swell of my breast. The heat of his breath lingers over my skin, driving me insane with need. I arch my back until his lips touch me. His left hand tightens around my leg, and his thumb caresses my inner thigh less than in inch from where I'm dying to be touched. He traces his tongue along the swell of my breast where my bikini top meets my flesh.

"Lautner." I'm breathless and losing control. Taking his hand that's still holding my dress strap, I move it to my breast. He pulls back and meets my heated gaze.

"Touch me," I whisper.

His eyes stay fixed on mine while his thumb slips under my top. The pad of it brushes over my erect nipple. I expect him to put his mouth where his hand is, but he doesn't. He's watching me, my reaction to his touch. He cups my breast and lifts it out of my top, still holding my gaze. Blue irises glaze with lust as he kneads it between his palm and strong fingers, repeatedly circling the pad of his thumb over my nipple.

Fucking blue irises. They're as seductive as his touch. My eyelids are heavy. He's so damn intoxicating. I bring my other hand to the back of his head and pull him to my lips. My soft moan invites his tongue to meet mine.

There is a rhythmic vibration. I try to ignore it but I can't. It takes us a few seconds to realize it's not us and it's not an earthquake. Lautner's hand on my breast stills. Our kiss breaks and we both look to the side. Swarley is humping the cushion next to us. We turn back toward each other and start to kiss again, but I get an untimely case of the giggles. Lautner, like a true gentleman, pulls my top back up over my breast.

We're both laughing now. He shakes his head and sits next to me on the couch. Maybe Swarley's done or just quits because he has an audience, but he hops down and heads upstairs.

"I should go pick up some shit and head home," Lautner says as he covers a yawn with his fist.

"Don't pick up the shit. It's dark out and technically you won so let's call it even. Okay?"

He stands and holds out his hand. "Okay."

We walk upstairs to the front door. "Thanks for the pizza and beer."

"Anytime." He steps closer to me and brushes a few

errant strands of hair away from my face. Leaning down, he places a soft kiss on my lips. I close my eyes while he rubs his nose against mine.

"I'm leaving in less than a month." I breathe out, reminding myself as much as him that whatever this is, it's temporary.

"I'm letting you go in less than a month. Even when you beg me not to because you are an evil little temptress."

Fisting his shirt to hold him close, I kiss him. I've never tasted anything so addictive. Breathless, I pull back.

"I think it will be the other way around, buddy. Don't forget, I come from the art world. I don't have to possess something to enjoy it."

He opens the door. "Fair enough. I'll let you *enjoy* me until *I* let *you* go."

"My sister is coming into town next Friday and staying for a week. So either you make yourself scarce while she's here or find a friend to keep her entertained part of the time."

He purses his lips to the side and squints his eyes. "What does your sister look like?"

"Me with blonde hair."

"Consider it done. I'll see you in the morning." He bends to kiss me again, but I turn to dodge him.

"Um ... about tomorrow. I sort of have plans, but I should be back by two."

Lautner cocks his head to the side. "What sort of plans?"

My face wrinkles. "Brunch with Dr. Abbott."

"Dr. Abbott?"

I nod. "Swarley's vet. He asked me out."

"And you said yes?"

I shrug. "Well, he's good with Swarley and I've already

needed his help once so—"

"So what? He's a vet, that's his job. I'm sure your aunt and uncle will pay the vet bills. You don't have to barter."

I step back and plant my hands on my hips. "It's just a meal and he's a really nice guy. I like making friends when I travel. It makes me feel less like a drifter."

Lautner cups my face and gives me a sound kiss on the lips and steps out the door. "Dr. Abbott?"

"Yeah, why?"

"I'll Google him when I get home."

"Because ...?"

"So I can size up my competition."

Shaking my head, I shove him toward the porch stairs. "Get out of here, *pool guy.*"

"Two o'clock," he hollers back as he swaggers to his 4Runner.

I shut the door and lean back against it. "Oh boy."

Chapter Four

June 6th, 2010

Dr. Abbott picks me up precisely at 11:00 a.m. That's when he knocks on the door anyway. However, I saw his metallic silver Lexus SUV parked outside at 10:45 when I glanced out the upstairs window while brushing my teeth.

"Good morning, Sydney."

"Dr. Abbott."

"Please, we're going to brunch. Call me Dane."

He leads the way down the porch stairs. Dane is a handsome guy. His faded jeans hang nicely from his tall, fit frame, not like some guys who are missing an ass altogether. The navy blue short-sleeve button-down shirt he's wearing casually untucked hides the definition of his upper torso, but I know he has some because I've seen him in his running attire. He opens the door for me, and I'm reminded he has such an adorable, shy school boy smile and straight white teeth.

"Thank you." I slide into the comfy leather seat and fasten my seat belt while he gets in. "Is your car new?"

"No, it's five years old." He starts the ignition.

His vehicle smells brand new and everything from the leather seats and floor mats to the dash and chrome accents looks immaculate. It hits me that I may be dealing with Dr. OCD. I'm now nervously aware of myself. Did I check the bottoms of my sandals before getting in? My floral skirt doesn't reach my knees. Is the lotion from my legs rubbing off on his seats?

"I hope you don't have Celiacs," Dane announces without further explanation.

Do you like pancakes? Is there anything you don't eat? Do you have any food allergies? But, *I hope you don't have Celiacs?* Dane is one odd duck, but I find his quirkiness humorous. I prefer it to stuffy and pretentious.

I can't help but laugh. "No, I don't have Celiacs. Why? Are we going to IHOP?"

With a quick sideways glance he smiles. "No ... but uh ... we could. I mean if you—"

"Dane? Wherever you take me is fine."

His perfect posture relaxes a fraction. "I'm taking you to a café just off campus. The food is incredible."

We arrive fifteen minutes later and the parking lot is full, so we park along the street a few blocks down.

Dane rushes out to open my door.

"Thank you." I sling my purse over my shoulder and straighten my pale yellow sleeveless blouse.

As we walk toward the café, Dane fidgets with his keys. He shoves them down into his pocket then wrings his hands together. Surprising me, he reaches down and takes my hand in his without looking at me. His nervousness is palpable. I repress a smile because he makes me feel like we're in junior high, and it's so damn cute. My conscience questions the intimate gesture, but it's too innocent to worry about right now.

There's a crowd waiting out front. Some people are standing in small groups, others are sitting on benches scattered around the flowerbeds that line the walkway to the entrance.

"Don't worry, I have reservations," Dane assures me.

We worm our way through the crowd.

"Sydney?"

I twist my head to the right and then to the left. Dane's grip on my hand tightens as the crowd gets more congested near the door.

"Sydney?"

Dane hears my name too, because he stops and looks as well. I take another backwards glance and spy Lautner standing next to an older couple. I retreat a few steps with Dane in tow.

"Hi, uh ... what are you doing here?" I ask with a nervous smile.

Lautner's gaze is fixed on my hand clasped in Dane's.

"Lautner?"

His eyes meet mine. "I'm having brunch with my parents." He gestures to the couple next to him. "Mom, Dad, this is Sydney Montgomery. We met unexpectedly the other day. She's housesitting in Palo Alto this month. Sydney these are my parents, James and Rebecca."

A warm inviting smile creeps up my face. I'm not sure why I'm so pleased to meet Lautner's parents, but I am. "Nice to meet you. This is Dr. Abbott, my ... *friend*. He's

Swarley's vet. Swarley is the dog I'm watching as well." *This isn't awkward at all!*

Dane releases my hand and shakes their hands.

Lautner gives Dane a one-word greeting as he shakes his hand. "Lautner."

Dane smiles but his eyes are tense. He looks confused.

James and Rebecca smile and offer friendly greetings to both of us. I'm mesmerized by his parents. Lautner shares his dad's build, but his dad is nearly bald and what little hair he has is gray. His dad's eyes are brown, so it's possible his hair was originally dark as well. Rebecca is very petite. Her pixy cut golden blonde hair matches Lautner's color and her eyes are blue, but not quite as brilliant and mesmerizing as his.

"Well, we'd better get inside before they give away our table." Dane grabs my hand and gives it a gentle tug.

"Lovely to have met you. Enjoy your brunch." I hold my hand up in a friendly gesture.

"You too," both James and Rebecca reply in unison.

Taking a few steps toward the door, I glance back at Lautner. His face is unreadable. I smile, but his mouth is set in a firm line.

The place is packed. We're seated at a small table near the window overlooking the street. The waitress hands us menus and asks us if we'd like to start with something to drink. Dane orders orange juice and a decaf. I get an unsweetened iced tea with lemon.

"How did you and Lautner meet?" Dane's tone is even and casual as he looks over his menu.

Thinking for a moment, I decide to go with the *sugar-coated* version. "He showed up at Elizabeth and Trevor's by mistake. We shared some casual conversation before he left, then one thing led to another and we ended up going surfing the next day."

Dane raises his eyes to mine over his menu. "Really? Do you know who he is?"

"Uh ... what do you mean? I know he just finished medical school and he's getting ready to start his residency."

Dane nods, looking at his menu. "Do you follow football?"

"I followed it a little in college but not obsessively. Why?"

His eyes peek at me over the top of the menu again. "Lautner Sullivan played wide receiver for Stanford."

I shrug. "Hmm, makes sense. He looks like a wide receiver." My outward reaction is controlled, but inwardly I'm reeling. Why wouldn't Lautner mention that? I shared all my high school and college activities with him.

Dane sets his menu down and starts fiddling with his napkin. "Interesting."

"What is?" I furrow my brow. Dane is acting weird, even for Dane.

"It's just odd Lautner didn't mention his college football years."

"Maybe. It's not like he's playing in the NFL."

Dane's eyes widen. "He could have. He was a candidate for the Heisman Trophy his sophomore year and was predicted to be a first-round draft pick."

Hello!

"What? Seriously?" I'm starting to understand Dane's surprise to my lack of knowledge about a guy who, around here, was or still may be considered a celebrity. "So he didn't get drafted?"

"He chose not to enter. Rumor has it he was spooked by

a knee injury his senior year. The doctors cleared him to play after rehab, but when interviewed he said he wanted to pursue a career in medicine instead. It was quite a news story at the time. You just don't turn down an opportunity to get drafted in the NFL."

"Are you ready to order?" the waitress interrupts as she sets our drinks on the table.

"Yes." Dane nods at me to go first.

"I'll have the Italian veggie omelet with Nutella wheat toast."

Dane points to his menu. "I'll have the sausage breakfast burrito with a side of fruit and a blueberry scone."

"Okay, I'll get your order placed right away." The waitress smiles as she takes our menus.

Dane adds cream and sugar to his coffee. "If you don't have plans later, you and Swarley could meet us at the dog park."

"Us?"

"Salt and Pepper, my black and white Jack Russell Terriers."

"I'm sure Swarley would love it, but I do have plans later." I squeeze lemon into my tea.

After Lautner's conservative response to meeting Dane, I'm not sure if I do still have plans later.

"No problem, maybe some other time."

"Sure." I smile.

Brunch is great. I see why there is such a huge crowd waiting outside. Our conversation is polite and easy. Dane is very attentive and I find his company relaxing. The Lautner revelations make it hard for me to stay fully focused on Dane, but I don't think he notices.

He pays the bill and we decide not to linger since

there are so many people waiting for a table. Just as we're exiting, I see Lautner and his parents seated at the opposite end of the café. He and his dad are talking but his mom sees us leaving. She smiles and gives a polite wave. I return her gesture as Lautner glances in our direction. His lips pull into a small, forced smile then his eyes drop to his plate.

The ride back is quiet, as if we've run out of things to talk about. I keep hoping Dane will turn on the radio to ease the awkward silence, but he doesn't. When he stops in the drive, I'm relieved that he stays in his seat.

"Thank you for brunch. It was really good."

"I'm glad you liked it. Um ... should we exchange numbers or something, in case you decide you want to meet up at the dog park sometime?"

I bite the corner of my bottom lip. "Mmm, okay. Swarley would like that. Actually, I have your number from the visit to your office."

He nods and I see the disappointment on his face as his eyes drop and his smile fades. I'm sure he'd like for *me* to like it too and had a certain pool guy not shown up at my door I would have been more enthused about hanging with Dane.

"Hey, my sister is coming to visit next weekend. We'll probably end up having a pool party. Maybe you could come by." Once again my mouth works quicker than my brain. Why does Dane make me feel so sorry for him? And why do I keep falling for his pouty looks?

"That sounds great. So ... I'll wait for your call?"

I nod as I open the door.

"Bye, Sydney."

I close the door and wave.

Stupid, stupid, stu ... pid, Sydney!

———

I'M NOT HOLDING out hope that Lautner will be coming by today. My contingency plan is a no-brainer—pool. By 2:00 p.m., it's eighty degrees under a sunny but hazy smog-filled sky. Swarley and I have taken our customary spots in the lounge chairs by the pool. Flo Rider serenades me through the speakers, and I have a blended strawberry margarita next to me with condensation dripping down the sides. Life. Is. Good!

Swarley startles me with his quick leap from the chair. He races toward the deck. Lautner is coming down the steps. He bends down and gives Swarley a few firm pats on his side. Content with Lautner's acknowledgement, he trots back over to his chair next to mine.

I flip my sunglasses up on my head and raise the back of my lounge chair.

"Hey." My voice is reserved as I try to gauge his mood.

"Hey." He straddles my chair facing me. I pull my knees to my chest.

"I didn't know if you'd come." I take a sip of my drink.

"Why wouldn't I?" He wraps his hand around mine and pulls the glass to his mouth. "Mmm, good." He licks his top lip.

I set the glass down. "You seemed quiet, maybe even jealous this morning."

"Why would I be jealous?" He traces his finger from my knee to my ankle leaving a wake of goose bumps tingling my skin. "You're not mine."

I can't hold in my laugh. "Jesus, Lautner, It's 2010. I'm pretty sure women are no longer considered possessions."

His full lips pull up to a smile as I melt into blue irises. What is my obsession with his eyes?

"You have the most amazing eyes."

He looks down, like I've embarrassed him. I duck my head to follow his gaze. He lets me catch it again.

"You do. I'm serious, they're ... stunning. This can't be the first time you've heard it."

I readjust myself, now kneeling on the chair so I'm at eye level with him. He's letting me free-fall into the blue abyss. I rest my palm on his cheek and brush my thumb over the gradual curve of his thick brows. He wraps his fingers around my forearm and presses his lips to the inside of my wrist. Lautner is a large, strong man; yet his strength is magnified most by his soft, soothing gaze and the restraint in his gentle touch.

"If you must know, I get more compliments from women about some of my other body parts." There are a thousand notes of sexual innuendo in his voice. He's an irresistible flirt.

Time to change the subject.

I tug at the leg of his cargo shorts. "You didn't come dressed for the pool."

"Didn't stop me before." He wiggles his eyebrows.

I cross my arms over my chest and squint my eyes. "Not today, big guy."

"Oh, so you do know what part of my body gets the most compliments."

"Ugh! You're incorrigible." I huff, shoving his solid chest.

He chuckles and reaches in his front pocket. Pulling out his wallet, phone, and keys he sets them under the lounge chair. This scene is too familiar. The realization of what he's doing hits me.

"No! Don't you dare," I warn.

The playful smile on his face grows as he shrugs off his shirt. Then he stands and unfastens his shorts.

My hands fly to my face, covering my eyes. "Stop stripping in front of me!"

"Once again, not something a girl has ever said to me before."

I have to confess. Two of my fingers are spread just far enough to see him. His shorts fall to the ground and he's left wearing black boxer briefs. He leans down and hooks his arm around my waist and snags me from my chair.

"Stop!"

We're midair. *Splash!*

I scramble to the surface and move to the shallow end. Lautner has me in his arms before I can get away. "Let go!" I plead with my eyes closed tight.

"Sydney, open your eyes." He's laughing ... again ... at me.

I open them but look anywhere but at him.

"Why won't you look at me? I'm not naked and anyway you've already seen—"

"I didn't look—"

"Oh, you looked—"

"No, I didn't and now you're only wearing your underwear and I can see your ... or the outline of your ..."

"Penis? Cock? Dick? Wood? Schlong? Womb broom? Clam hammer? Yogurt slinger?"

"Stop!" I meet his eyes.

He's loving this. His eyes dance and his grin is confident and yes ... *cocky*. Any attempt to escape his hold will be futile. I know what I have to do. It's a little risky, but I have no other choice. With unwavering determination and a firm tenacious grip, I grab his *package,* an admittedly *large* package.

His eyes bulge open and he sucks in such a quick breath he comes close to swallowing his tongue.

"Okay, *big* guy. You've made your point. Now let your *clam hammer* know he's swimming in restricted waters."

Lautner's hold on me vanishes. I climb out of the pool before his body and mind become coherent again.

With an exaggerated swing to my hips, I mosey over to my chair without looking back. My whole body teems with exhilaration because I've never done anything like that before. I feel confident, strong, sassy, giddy, and oddly ... turned on.

Swarley has gone in the house and left my towel covered in dog hair. *Thanks for that.* I shake it out and flip my head down to dry my hair.

"Oh God!" I jerk up and whip around. Why did I turn around? I don't know. I caught an upside down glimpse of what was behind me; I didn't have to turn around. But here I am, staring at naked Lautner and his ... man thingy is ... Oh. My. God! I'm not sure what's most bizarre about this situation: Lautner being so casual and comfortable with exposing himself to me, or that I cannot peel my eyes off of ... *it.*

He's wringing out his underwear as leisurely as if it were a shammy he used to dry off his car.

"Wh—what—" My mouth is dry, utterly parched.

"Oh, this. Well, Syd, you can't wear that string bikini mere inches from me while grabbing my junk and not expect me to have a raging hard-on." He drapes his underwear over the back of the chair and slips back into his shorts. My eyes, which will never be the same again, climb up his body to his face.

"So what should we do now?" he asks, fastening his pants.

All words have escaped me. I take my margarita and gulp down every last drop.

"Shit!" I grimace and rub my temples. *Brain freeze!*

Unsuspecting hands cradle my face and hot lips meld to mine. The warmth of his tongue heats my mouth and my brain freeze evaporates. He pulls back and rubs his nose against mine. "Better?"

Lautner is flat out crazy and unpredictable. He's too much to handle, yet I can't get enough.

"What was that? Brain freeze CPR?"

"Worked, didn't it?" He winks and grabs his shirt slipping it on. "What do you think about remote control airplanes?"

I wrap my towel around my waist. "You'll need to elaborate."

He slips his keys, phone, and wallet back in his pocket. "My friend Caden is taking his little brother to fly remote control airplanes not too far from here. He invited us to join them."

He's done it again, flipping the switch from cocky to sweet. The truth is, Lautner is all sweet. Even his cocky side is more playful than anything else.

"In that case, I think I should go change. Want me to throw those in the dryer?" I nod to his wet boxer briefs.

"Nope, I'm good." He grins.

"Of course you are," I mumble as I turn and walk to the house.

"What's that?"

"Nothing."

———

I CHOOSE black capris and a lilac racerback tank top. Predicting windows down, I pull my hair back into a high ponytail then dig through my shoe bag, that I still haven't unpacked, and find my Keen sandals.

Lautner is waiting on the front porch in an Adirondack chair. I shut and lock the front door. He stands and gives me a slow perusal and an appreciative smile.

"So damn sexy." He shakes his head.

I sense a warm blush surfacing on my cheeks and neck. He reaches for my hand and leads me to his 4Runner. Opening my door, he looks to the sky. "Hope we don't get rained on. Clouds are moving in."

He gets in and buckles up.

"Should I grab an umbrella?" I ask.

"I've got one. We're good."

On the way to the flying field, Lautner rests his right arm behind me. This time it's on my neck and he caresses the tips of his fingers over my skin. The windows are open and Jeffrey Gaines is singing my favorite Peter Gabriel song, "In Your Eyes." I close mine and drift off with the lyrics that have me lost in blue irises. *The light the heat ... I am complete.*

There are about a dozen cars in the lot when we pull in. I see only two kids in the field and one is a girl so I think it's going to be easy to find Caden and his brother. As we approach, the boy who looks about ten passes off the remote to the guy standing next to him then he rushes toward us.

"Sully," he yells.

"Hey, Brayden." Lautner opens his arms and Brayden embraces him.

Sully?

Lautner didn't mention it, but I notice Brayden has Down Syndrome. He has the characteristic flat facial profile, upward slanted eyes, and protruding tongue. His speech is slightly impaired but not enough to cause any communication problems.

The guy with the remote walks our way with the plane in his other hand.

"Sully, my man." He and Lautner perform an unusual series of handshakes. "And this must be Sexy Sydney."

I raise a brow with a sideways glance at Lautner, whose jaw is clenched, lips set in a less than appreciative smile at his friend.

"I never called her Sexy Sydney." Lautner shakes his head.

"True. But he did say you're the sexiest thing he's ever laid eyes on. I coined the term *Sexy Sydney*, and look at you, rightfully so. I'm Caden by the way." He holds out his hand and I return a firm shake.

Sexiest thing he's ever laid eyes on? Crap! I'm in trouble.

"Nice to meet you. You're the first of *Sully's* friends that I've met." I look to Lautner again.

"Sully's my nickname." He shrugs.

"Yeah, because his favorite movie is Monsters, Inc.," Brayden adds enthusiastically.

I cock my head to the side with wide eyes. "Is that so?"

Lautner playfully messes Brayden's hair. "If Brayden says it's so, then it's so. Brayden, this is my friend Sydney."

"Sexy Sydney," Brayden says it as if it's my full name.

I roll my eyes, giving Caden a playful squint. "Nice to meet you, Brayden."

"Bray, the sky's not looking too promising. If you want to

show off your aviator skills for Sully and Sydney, then we better get going."

Brayden is quite good with controlling his plane. Lautner and I sit in the grass and watch while Caden supervises the path of the plane.

"His fine motor skills are amazing. He's doing better than some of these adults out here," I comment.

"Their mom is an occupational therapist, so he's more advanced than most other Down Syndrome children his age. Brayden is a great kid. He's the water boy for his school's football team, and he has dreams of being a wide receiver someday."

"Why wouldn't he? Rumor has it he's friends with a college legend."

Lautner picks at the grass between us. "Someone's been doing her homework or *research*."

"Not this time. But Dr. Abbott sure knows your stats."

"Yeah, well I'm sure he also gave you the speech about what a 'disappointment' I was to football fans when I chose med school over the NFL."

"Why did you?"

"I thought I'd quit while I was ahead, and by my senior year my heart just wasn't in it. I was behind in school..." he looks over at me "...because premed requires a lot of difficult classes, not because I flunked anything." He nudges into my side.

I nudge him back, remembering my comment about his age.

"The money and fame aren't worth the risk of early arthritis in my joints or possible brain damage. Don't get me wrong, I love the game, but that's all it is for me ... just a game."

My eyes scan his bare legs and I notice a faded scar along his right knee. I reach over and trace it with my finger. He tenses, his eyes following my finger.

"And this?"

"Torn ACL." He doesn't elaborate.

"Is that why you stopped playing?"

His eyes remain on my finger still tracing his scar. "It's on the list."

I bend down and press my lips to it. He sucks in a quick breath. Sitting up, I'm met with firm eyes and a tense brow. I take his hand and run his finger along my scalp just above my forehead. I let go of his hand, and he continues to feel the raised area of skin under the pad of his finger.

"Soccer injury?" he asks.

I shake my head and grin. "First time surfing."

The sparkle returns to his eyes as he smiles and leans down to kiss my head.

"Brayden is done, so we're taking off," Caden says as they approach us. "Besides it's looking like the clouds could open up at any moment."

The sky is getting darker. We both stand. Lautner gives Brayden another hug. "Great job today, buddy. Later, man." He puts his hand on Caden's shoulder and gives it a firm squeeze. "Remember, next weekend party at Sydney's."

I eye Lautner because we hadn't actually had a discussion about a *party*, even though I did invite Dane to this supposed party when my sister comes next week.

"Looking forward to it. Nice to meet you, *Sexy Sydney*." He grins and they walk away.

I turn and cross my arms over my chest. "So, *Sully,* why do I get this feeling that you and your buddy have spent a fair amount of time talking inappropriately about me?"

Lautner mocks me by crossing his arms over his chest. "Now why would you think that?"

A rumble of thunder distracts us from our standoff and with barely a moment's notice we're pounded by rain.

"Oh, shit!" I squeal.

Lautner grabs my hand and we make a mad dash for the vehicle. He's shoving his hands into his pockets but coming up with nothing. I'm drenched. At this point I don't know what the hurry is.

"My pockets are too damn wet. I can't get my hands down in them to get the keys!" he yells. "Maybe you should try. You have smaller hands."

"What?" I squint my eyes against the rain, looking up at him. He can't be serious. They're flipping cargo shorts for goodness sakes. They've got like ... twenty pockets on them. Why wouldn't he put the keys in one of the outer pockets on the legs instead of his hip pocket.

"Ugh! This is ridiculous," I reply.

He holds his hands up in surrender. I shake my head and stick my hand down in one pocket.

It's empty.

Then I stick it down his other pocket, but I can't feel his keys.

"Maybe you should move it around a little more."

What?

I hear the double beep of the doors unlocking. Looking up, I see the keys dangling from his finger and he has the biggest shit-eating grin on his face.

"Why you son of a—"

He puts his finger to my mouth. "Now, now ... that's my mom you're talking about."

I swing open the door and slide in, slamming it behind

me. If he didn't already have the keys I'd lock his ass out. I'm soaking wet and water is dripping and pooling all over his leather seats.

Too damn bad!

He gets in and shakes the water from his head like a dog. I think it would take an act of God to wipe that smile off his face. "That was fun!"

I scowl at him and turn away.

"Buckle up," he says.

I don't budge.

"Sydney, come on. We're not leaving until you fasten your seat belt."

There's no way in hell I'm acknowledging him right now. He leans across and tries to grab my seat belt. I ram my shoulder into him.

"What the hell?"

My response is a firm glare. Our faces are a breath away and the crackle of lightening surges untapped emotions that are charged and out of control. My angry eyes fall to his lips a split second before I claw my hands in his hair and pull him to me. I'm not asking. I'm taking. My demanding tongue reaches for his.

Heart pounding. Breath quickening.

My clenched fingers tingle with need, and my flesh burns for his touch. He grabs my waist with both hands and drags me onto his lap so my knees are bent straddling his. His eager lips continue to attack mine as his left hand fumbles the side of the seat. It inches back until it won't go any farther. I move my hands to the hem of his shirt and claw at it. Tugging and pulling it until he leans forward allowing me to peel the heavy wet cotton off him. We break our kiss long enough to pull his shirt over his head. It slaps against the back seat as I toss it aside. My lips feel bruised and numb, but I don't want him to stop. This craving is insatiable.

After a few moments, I sit back and we pause, completely breathless. My hands are aching to touch him, so I ghost my fingers down the bumps and curves of his firm, defined chest and abs.

"Lautner ..." I whisper. "God, you're so ..." I'm not sure what the words are.

His hands are on my hips and he inches them up just enough that his fingers are skimming my abs. It's a searing touch. I cross my arms and curl my fingers around the hem of my shirt, pulling it over my head. He adjusts his hips and the slight shift has his large erection straining against his shorts pressed between my legs. A slick warm sensation floods my core.

Lautner's gaze fixes on my breasts. His hands skim up my sides and his thumbs trace the skin under my bra. The rise and fall of my chest escalates with building anticipation. His patience is agonizing. I watch his eyes as I unlatch my bra in the front. His eyes meet mine for a quick moment as his lips part and his tongue slides out to wet them. His gaze returns to my chest as I pull the pink satin and lace away from them.

"Sydney ... they're ... fucking perfect." His raw voice makes my nipples pebble as my skin craves his touch.

I'm waiting, eager for his next move. His hands are static, just hovering below my breasts. I feel him twitch between my legs. At last, both of his hands move up to my breasts.

"Ah ... oh, Lautner," I moan and close my eyes, arching my back. My breasts feel full and heavy in his large hands as he begins to knead them in his firm, sensual grip. A soft whimper escapes me when his thumbs graze my nipples. I sit up on my knees a little more and thread my fingers through his hair, pulling his head closer. He flicks his tongue over my nipple and my whole body jerks.

"Lautner! Oh my God!"

He flicks his tongue over my other nipple then sucks it into his mouth. My clenched fingers yank his hair harder. He releases a guttural growl. I sit down and devour his mouth. His hands continue to give my breasts the sweet torture I've been dying to feel. My core is engorged and on the verge of an orgasm. It's almost painful. I start to grind against him and he grabs my hips, digging his fingers into my flesh.

"Christ, Sydney, what are you doing?" he groans into my mouth.

His firm grip stops my motions.

I don't want to stop. I can't stop. My fingers fumble with his pants. He grabs my hands.

"Sydney, stop. This is going too far."

I brush my lips along his jaw and run my tongue down his neck. He tastes so good and my hunger for him is ravenous.

"Please ... don't stop." I beg. I can't believe I'm begging.

He brings my hands up and sets them on his shoulders. Then he unfastens my pants.

"Are you on birth control?" he asks.

His tongue swipes over my nipple again.

"Sometimes," I breathe out.

He stills and pulls his head back. "*Sometimes?*"

I graze my nails along his shoulders. "Most of the time ... except when I forget. Don't you have a condom?" I can't hide the agitation and neediness in my voice.

"Jesus, Sydney! No, I don't have a condom."

"Why not?" I sit back. My body is buzzing, heart pounding, and I'm breathless.

He rolls his eyes and sighs in exasperation. "Because I don't make it a habit of having random sex in my car."

Random sex?

My chest is bared to him, but it's no longer sensual and erotic. I'm now nervous and aware of my exposed chest, and the shift in conversation is embarrassing. I pull my bra over my breasts and hook it.

Were we on the verge of having random sex? If so, does that bother me? I've known this guy for four days. Is it too soon? In the scope of what can only be a thirty day relationship, day four is like two months if we had a year. Most people have sex by the time they've been dating for two months. I mean, surely a guy buys a pack of condoms by the second month, right?

I grab my shirt and put it on. It's wet and cold, but that's probably what my libido needs right now.

"You're right. We need to slow down." Lacking any sort of grace, I maneuver myself to the passenger seat.

Lautner reaches back and snatches his shirt. As I put on my seat belt he rests his hand on my leg and squeezes it.

"Are we good?"

No, we're not good.

I feel like a total hussy for throwing myself at him. He must think I travel around and sleep with *random* guys. God, I can't believe I stooped so low as to beg him to have sex with me. I was pleading. Could I be anymore pathetic?

With a quick sideways glance, I smile and give him a single nod. The ride home is uncomfortable. We didn't say much on the way either, but the air wasn't thick with uncertainty and insecurity. The rain has let up by the time we pull into the drive. I leap out of the vehicle before he gets it in park.

"Sydney?" he calls chasing after me.

I'm shivering in my cold, wet clothes, and my fingers won't cooperate as I fumble to get the key in the lock.

"Sydney?" Lautner clutches my arm and turns me around. "What's wrong? I thought we were good?"

I jerk out of his grip. "I lied. We are *not* good! I feel like a complete idiot. I'm embarrassed ... and ... angry ... and ..." I whip back around and unlock the door then slip in the house and slam it behind me, locking it with quick fingers.

He pounds on the door. "Come on, Sydney. I'm sorry. What do you want me to do? I'll go get some condoms."

The nerve—

I lean to my left and shoot him my most menacing death glare through the window. "Go. Away!" I march upstairs without looking back.

Chapter Five

June 7th, 2010

GREETINGS, monthly friend. I stand by my belief that I had every right to be upset with Lautner yesterday. However, I will concede that my reaction may have been a little ... extreme. The tinge of blood on my panties this morning may be a plausible explanation. It's 5:30 a.m.—too early—but I can't sleep. The dull pain between my legs has me awake so I might as well take Swarley for a walk before his breakfast. Exercise seems to help my situation. I also would like to avoid a certain vet who conveniently jogs by the house between 6:30 and 7:00 every morning. In fact, given my current state, mixed with yesterday's embarrassing fiasco, I declare the next four days men-free.

We walk. We eat. We go back to sleep. Monday is shaping up to be a better day already. I post a note on the door to keep the pesky vet and the striptease away.

Beware!
Red Angry Bitch Inside
Evacuate the premises immediately!
Come back on Friday.

By 10:00 a.m., the doorbell rings. I peek around the corner and see Lautner walking away. I creep toward the door as he pulls out of the drive. Opening it, I spy on the ground a bouquet of colorful flowers, a pastry bag, a hot drink cup, and a bottle of Advil. I carry the goods to the kitchen and put the flowers in water next to the first bouquet that has started to wilt. There's a card taped to the pastry bag.

SORRY

I inhale the cherry-almond galette and sit on the porch sipping my chai tea latte with a mischievous grin on my face and dirty thoughts in my head.

Going through my duties, I pick up poop, mow the lawn, and set out the trash and recycling bins before retiring by the pool for a late afternoon nap with Swarley.

———

June 8th, 2010

BETTER SLEEP. I've discovered Swarley will let me sleep in longer if I let him in bed with me. A fair trade.

It's 7:30 a.m. and I choose to feed Swarley first and walk him in an hour. Once again, my strategy is to avoid Dane on his morning jog. While Swarley's food is digesting, I call Avery.

"Jeez, Sam, do you know what time it is?" Her voice is groggy.

"Yes, it's 8:oo a.m. on a Tuesday. Don't you have a job?"

She laughs. "You're one to talk. Miss I-Get-Paid-To-Lie-By-The-Pool. Anyway, my first client isn't until eleven. You're not calling to tell me not to come, are you?"

"No, of course not. I'm looking forward to seeing you. There's an overload of testosterone around here. I need you to help even things out."

"Oh, really? Well, if there's one thing I like it's a healthy dose of testosterone. You haven't staked your claim on pseudo pool boy have you? I've been using his picture as a visual when I find myself under someone who is ... not so visually appealing."

"Nice, Ave. Why would you even sleep with someone you weren't physically attracted to?"

"Boredom." She giggles.

I roll my eyes. "You need a hobby."

"Maybe sex is my hobby."

"Great, write that on the Christmas card you send Dad."

"Oh, Sam, don't be such a prude. Maybe if you took advantage of that hot eye candy in the photo, then you wouldn't be so judgmental."

I've tried!

"Yeah, yeah, whatever. When will you be here on Friday?"

"I'm leaving in the morning, so I should be there between two and three."

"Okay, drive safe. I love you."

"Love you too, Sam. Bye."

I take Swarley for his walk then we play Frisbee. I sit on the couch checking my computer for e-mail, specifically job opportunities. The doorbell rings. Once again, I see Lautner walking away. When he's officially gone, I open the door—flowers, bakery bag, and a hot beverage.

I sit on a kitchen barstool and open the envelope taped to the bag. There are two museum tickets, one to de Young and the other to Legion of Honor, both in San Francisco. There's also a note.

PLEASE

Please what? It doesn't matter. Right now I'm too busy digging into another cherry-almond galette and sipping a chai tea latte. Damn, it's good and so are the dirty thoughts I've attached to it.

"Sorry, Swarley, you're on your own for a while today. I'm going to San Francisco," I announce with a broad smile.

———

June 9th, 2010

I ENJOYED both of the museums yesterday. Just being surrounded by what I love reminded me of my goals and my unwavering commitment to them. I'd happily take a curator position at either one. The upside to working in California would be the proximity to Avery. A weak voice in my head whispers Lautner's name too, but I'm not ready to think about a relationship. I will not give up on my dreams. A part of me feels like pursuing my career with steadfast focus is a tribute to my mom who lost her chance. I have to believe she would be proud of me and equally disappointed if I gave up my future for a man.

Swarley is crowding me, which should be hard to do in a king-sized bed. The clock reads 7:45 a.m. We're gaining on it. By this time next week, I could be sleeping in until 9:00 a.m. Elizabeth and Trevor might not appreciate Swarley's new schedule, or his new sleeping arrangements, but I'll deal with that later.

"Let's get you fed, you big beast."

While Swarley eats I step out onto the mammoth deck. It's cloudy again today. I hope we can get his walk in before it rains, otherwise I'm going to be stuck in the house all day with a dog who has more energy than I can handle.

We manage to get back from our walk just as a few drops start to fall. We're walking up the drive and I see something by the front door. I can't make out what it is yet, but I grin with giddy enthusiasm because I already know. A bouquet of flowers, a bakery sack, and a hot drink cup.

Today the note reads:

FORGIVE

Then there is a piece of paper titled *Rainy Day Entertainment* with a long list of website links. I bring my laptop to the kitchen and type in the links while I eat my cherry-almond galette and drink my chai tea latte ... and of course, think dirty thoughts.

"Oh, jeez!" I say aloud, shaking my head. The links are to YouTube how-to surfing videos. There must be fifty links listed. Lautner makes me smile even without his presence. The thought is equally endearing and terrifying.

By the end of the day, I've watched them all. It did rain

most of the day, but tomorrow it's supposed to be sunny and warm. I'll get to meet the real pool guy as well. He was scheduled to come today, but the rain changed those plans. Elizabeth's description of him leads me to believe there will be no gawking or sneaking photos to send to Avery. Just as well, I have my hands pretty full as is.

———

June 10th, 2010

8:07 A.M. "YES! Good boy, Swarley." I rub his tummy. "See, sleeping in rocks." I'm feeling energized this morning. My sister is coming tomorrow, and awesome weather is predicted for the day.

Swarley eats, then a little after 9:00 we go for a jog. Yes, a jog. I need an outlet for my new found energy, and Swarley has an unlimited supply so we make the morning count. As predicted, but nonetheless a phenomenally sweet gesture, there are flowers at the front door with a bakery bag, hot drink cup, and ... oh ... my ... God ... condoms.

The note on the bag reads:

ME
SORRY PLEASE FORGIVE ME

There's another note taped to the box of condoms.

Not being presumptuous or pushy, just prepared.

The condoms on the counter make it extra hard, no pun intended, to keep my head out of the gutter as I drink my chai tea latte and eat my cherry-almond galette. I decide to take the *Red Angry Bitch* sign down before Aaron, the pool guy, shows up. After four days of Lautner special deliveries, the bitch is gone, the anger has dissolved, and the only red left is the flush that comes over my skin when I drink my chai tea latte and think of gratitude blow jobs.

Aaron is right on time. He's also a large man with a severe case of plumber's crack. I make myself a sandwich in the kitchen while he gets the supplies from the pool house.

Oh, no, please don't. No, no, no! Ugh!

He bends over, showing way too much crack for my "taste." I look at my sandwich with disgust. My appetite is gone, maybe for the rest of the day.

"Swarley!" I call as I set the plate on the floor.

Another broken rule Elizabeth and Trevor would not be too happy about. *No table food.* Technically, the sandwich never made it to the table.

Twenty minutes later Aaron comes to the back door and slides it open. "Sydney, would it be too much to ask for some ice water?"

I set down my book and get a glass down. "No problem. Is it getting pretty hot outside?" I hand him the glass.

My bikini is easily visible through my sheer, white cover-up. He drags his eyes over my body with blatant shamelessness. I wonder if he sees my skin crawling. *Yuck!*

"Yeah, it's real *hot*," he says in a creepy voice as sweat races down his large torso.

His gaze keeps moving to the kitchen island behind me then back to me with a suggestive grin. I glance back.

Oh, fuck!

There are two things on the island. My laptop and the box of *condoms*.

My eyes bug out as I suck in a breath. "Okay, well I have to run an errand. Let yourself out when you're done."

He nods. "Maybe I'll catch you later."

Dear God, I hope not!

I force a tight smile as he goes back to the pool. Snatching the condoms, I sprint upstairs to change into shorts and a T-shirt. I was going to wait until later to run to the grocery store, but now is definitely the best time to go.

My mental list consists of all the essentials: snacks, beverages, alcohol, and an assortment of things to throw on the grill. I make a second run through the store to make sure I didn't forget anything ... and to make sure I give Aaron plenty of time to finish up and get the hell out of there.

Chapter Six

June 11th, 2010

TGIF ... well, for people with real jobs anyway. I wake up early, even before Swarley. Call it karma, but I drag his butt out of bed, feed him, walk him, and smile as he's once again crashed on the lounge chair by the pool. And it's only 9:00 a.m. I take a shower and shave all the hair on or near my lower extremities. Why? My subconscious sneaks around behind my conscious thoughts and prepares for the "what if."

I forego drying my hair since I'll be jumping in the pool anyway. When the doorbell rings my heart slam dunks into my chest and my stomach does a front aerial flip with a half twist. I open the front door with an embarrassingly large grin. At my feet on the porch is a bouquet of flowers, a bakery sack, and a hot beverage. No vehicle in the drive, no Lautner. My smile fades and a pang of disappointment seizes my heart. I pick everything up and turn to go inside.

"Good morning, beautiful."

I turn around. *Blue irises.*

"It is now." My enthusiasm recovers in a blink. Narrowing my eyes, I tilt my head to the side. "Were you hiding?"

He grins and nods once, moving up the porch one slow step at a time, holding a tall cup of coffee.

"Why?" I purse my lips to hide my excitement.

"I wanted to see your face when you opened the door, so I could gauge my chances of getting invited in today." He moves to the threshold.

I bring the flowers to my nose and inhale the sweet smell of fresh lavender. "And?"

He pulls a pink daisy from the bouquet and tucks it behind my ear then runs his finger down my neck. "I think my chances are pretty good."

"Where's your vehicle"

"Parked on the street."

I turn and walk toward the kitchen. When I look back Lautner is still standing at the door. Motioning toward the kitchen with my head, I smile. He takes an exaggerated cautious first step inside. I shake my head and keep walking. The kitchen counter near the windows is filled with glasses and vases of flowers.

"Someone must think you're pretty special."

"Just some guy I met last week. All these flowers are obnoxiously over the top." I add the new bouquet to water. "Then there's all the pastries and sweet creamy tea. I think I've gained five pounds."

I still, sensing his nearness behind me. He pulls my hair back over my shoulder and brushes his lips along my neck.

"Sydney," he whispers and I close my eyes. "I'm sorry

about the other day. You are special and being with you would never be *random*."

Sirens should be screeching in my head. *Danger! Hot guy is trying to derail your future!*

I turn. I'm not thinking about the next twenty-one days, or a future driven by a stolen past. Lautner, standing before me, owns my every thought. Resting my palms on his chest with splayed fingers, I breathe in his unique scent. It's become familiar; it's just *him*, sometimes mixed with sun, ocean and sand, or earthy grass and rain. I curl my fingers into his shirt and pull him closer. Our eyes meet.

Letting my analytical brain steal this moment would be like flying to Paris and not seeing the Eiffel Tower. I have to experience this moment, it's not a choice ... it's instinct.

Pushing up onto my toes, I stretch my neck and brush my lips against his. He grins so I bite his bottom lip, dragging it through my teeth.

"Don't tease me today." I tug harder on his shirt.

Strong hands wrap around my waist and lift me to the counter. He pulls his shirt off. My hands grip the edge of the counter at my sides.

Blue irises.

Deft fingers work the small buttons down the front of my pale yellow sundress.

Blue irises ... they're all I see.

Nerves are soothed. Fear vanishes.

In this moment there is nowhere I'd rather be and no one I'd rather be with.

When the last button is pulled through, Lautner spreads open the front of my dress. I'm wearing a simple white lace bra and matching thong. He sucks in a slow, deep breath. My flesh warms under his lustful gaze. I love watching him look at me. No man has ever looked at me this way, and it's gut-wrenching to know that our timing is all wrong because I'm certain no other man will make me feel the way I do right now ... with just ... one ... look.

"Sydney, you're breathtaking." Patient hands cradle my face. Sliding them back and weaving his fingers through my hair with a soft pull, he brings our lips together.

I move my hands to his biceps. They flex under my touch as he pulls me closer, deepening our kiss. My legs wrap around his waist, and I slide my hands around his neck. My skin prickles with tingly excitement under his touch. The pull of his strong arms lifting my body from the counter elicits a soft moan from me. He releases my lips and turns, carrying me away from the kitchen to the stairs.

With effortless strength, he carries me to the bedroom. Our eyes feel connected like our bodies, and we stare at each other in silence. Near the foot of the bed, he eases me to my feet. I shiver in breathless anticipation. He feathers his hands down my neck to my shoulders then slides my open dress back until it falls to the floor. Every move he makes is slow and measured. It's seductive and sensual. I'm a cool drink in the sun melting in surrender to his touch. The familiar full-ness returns to my breasts as he unhooks my bra letting it drift to join the pooled sundress at my feet. My nipples firm under the veil of my dark hair covering my breasts.

Lautner kneels before me, ghosting his hands down both sides of my torso. He leans in, touching his lips to my stomach. My breath catches as his tongue dips into my navel. Fingers curling under the waist of my thong, my knees feel weak as he pulls the lacy material down my legs. I take a deep swallow when blue irises gaze up at me. They're tender and patient. My whole body is vibrating. I wonder if he notices the soft shivers of nervous arousal that flow through me in small waves. He stands. I'm held hostage in his invisible hold. Sculpted abs merge to a point where his shorts hang low.

The pull of a button. The inching descent of a zipper.

As his shorts and briefs slide down his firm legs, I hold my breath. I've seen him before, but with the anticipation of his naked body against mine, it's like seeing him for the first time.

He's ... stunning. Taut, bronzed skin covering every inch of his strong muscular form. Large defined quads and calves. Ripped chest and abs. Brawny arms angled from broad shoulders. The low line along his waist, where tanned flesh fades to a paler shade, awakens me, an erotic reminder that I'm looking at part of Lautner that is not seen by everyone else.

It's not about belonging to someone. I belong to no one. It's surrendering to a physical need that outweighs all reason. The rapturous flood of sensation that comes from being taken, controlled by another for pleasure. I want Lautner to take me, control me, drown my senses in a sea of physical euphoria.

Lost in a slow blink. The distance between us vanishes. His hands tangle in my hair. Our tongues claim each other. I wrap my arms around his back and slide my hands to his glutes, curling my fingers into firm muscles that flex as his pelvis tilts forward. His erection presses into my stomach, and my sensitive nipples brush against the soft hairs on his chest. My head falls back and I close my eyes as his lips and tongue caress the thin flesh of my neck.

"God ..." I moan in breathless pleasure, "Lautner ..."

"Sydney ..." he whispers below my ear.

He drags the duvet off the bed and lowers us to the cool sheets. On our sides, our legs entwine. The warm friction of his hard body moving against mine is intensely erotic ... surreal. He inches his head down my neck to my chest and captures my breast in his mouth.

"Ahh ..." I cry, arching my back and rocking my pelvis so my sex brushes against his leg that's scissored between both of mine.

He rolls us so I'm on my back and hovers over me on his hands and knees. His mouth is back on my breasts and the sensual assault is sending a crescendo of fireworks straight to my core. I fist his hair and pull his mouth to mine. His tongue makes deep, slow thrusts into my mouth. I keep one hand fisted in his hair and slide my other down his chest. He moans into my mouth as I wrap my hand around him and squeeze his hard length with upward strokes.

"Syd—Sydney ... oh God ... stop!" He sits back on his knees between my legs. Eyes fixed to mine, lips parted, quick ragged breaths flow from him. "Condom?"

Wetting my lips, I grin. There's an unrestrained satisfaction that comes from making him want me. I look to my right and his gaze follows to the nightstand where I've set the box. He leans forward and grabs it. I'm mesmerized by him rolling the condom onto his huge erection. My teeth nervously work the corner of my bottom lip. I think it's too big. Is that possible? Surely not. After all, women push babies out of the same opening. I look at Lautner and his heated expression now has a hint of a smile. I'm sure he notices my wide eyes staring at his ... *sizable contribution* to my pleasure.

Placing his hands on my bent knees, he slides them up

my thighs. Eyes connected to mine, he pushes his finger between my slick folds and swipes it up over my clitoris.

"Ung!" I yell, jerking my hips off the bed. It's official, my sex is throbbing.

Lautner smirks and slides two fingers into me. I buck into his hand and moan again. My eyelids are lead and I fight to hold back my orgasm, overwhelmed with the most arousing sensations.

He removes his fingers and my eyes flutter open. His head ducks to my hips. Slow, wet kisses heat my flesh as he works his mouth up my body. Stopping at my breast, he covers my nipple with his mouth and tugs at it with teasing teeth. Continuing past my neck, he pauses. He hovers over my lips, and I feel him bring his sheathed erection to my entrance. I suck in a quick breath and hold it in anticipation. Simultaneously, his mouth consumes mine and he eases into me. I release a moan into his mouth. I'm being stretched farther than I've ever been before. The fullness is intense. A balance between pleasure and pain.

Lautner stills and looks at me. My chest pulses with rapid, shallow pants.

"Are you okay?" he asks. Every muscle in his body contracts, as if he's fighting a primal urge by taking it slow with me.

I nod.

He pulls back a little then thrusts into me.

"Gaaahhh!" I cry. It's pleasure, it's pain ... it's mind blow-ing, and I don't want him to stop. He hesitates again as I yell, but I hurry and pull his head to mine, attacking his mouth while I move my hips toward his. That's all it takes. He's setting an intense pace. I dig my nails into his backside.

"Sydney ..." My name oozes from his mouth like slow, sweet honey.

Sex with Lautner is beyond anything I ever imagined possible. I can't think. My mind is fuzzy. I feel dizzy. I'm drunk on him. His pace quickens as his hand slides between us to touch me.

"Lautner!" I cry, out of control with my eyes rolling back in my head while the most unimaginable orgasm rips through my body in relentless waves.

"Oh God ... Sydney!" Lautner stills deep inside me then circles his hips once as his lips find mine. The room is filled with soft moans of gratitude as we hum into each other's mouths. My legs snake around his, silently begging him to not move. My hands frame his face, holding his mouth to mine. Sex was the main course, but this is dessert. The urgency has subsided and we're lost, savoring the moment of this languid, eternal kiss. Every craving I have for the rest of my life will be compared to this moment.

He eases out and falls onto his back beside me. A breathy laugh escapes him. "That was ..."

"Sam?" I hear an echo from downstairs.

"Shit!" I gasp leaping from the bed.

I grab Lautner's shorts and throw them at him. "Get dressed. You have to get out of here."

"Who's Sam?" He's still lying on the bed.

"I'm Sam. Now, get up. Hurry!"

My moves are quick and erratic as I fumble with my bra and thong. I can't button my dress with shaky hands, so I toss it aside and grab a pair of shorts and a T-shirt from the dirty pile of clothes in my open suitcase on the floor.

"You said your name is Sydney?" he questions as he

walks into the en-suite bathroom, presumably to dispose of the condom.

"It's my nickname," I mumble, zipping my shorts.

"Sam? Are you here?"

"Is that your sister?" he asks, walking out of the bathroom, thankfully with his shorts on.

"Yes. Where's your shirt?"

"It's downstairs in—"

"I'll get it to you later." I push him toward the window.

"What are you doing?" His voice is laced with confusion and his brows are furrowed.

"You have to go out the window. Don't worry, there's a metal lattice you can climb down." I open the window.

"You don't want your sister to know about us?"

"No. She's planning on sleeping with you." I hold back the curtains.

"What are you talking about?"

"She asked if I was planning on it and when I said no, she asked if she could."

"Jesus, Sydney! You're trying to pimp me out to your sister?"

"No! Well ... yes, but it's not what you think. I'll explain later, now go."

He shakes his head, moving his leg out the window. "What about my shoes?"

"You can get them in a little while. Climb down and wait about fifteen minutes then ring the doorbell."

He huffs out an exasperated breath and he climbs down.

"Oh ... and, Lautner?"

He stops and glances up.

"Best sex I've ever had." I grin and shut the window.

He's still shaking his head, but it's not enough to keep a smile from creeping up his face.

———

"Avery!" I yell, coming down the stairs. She's hunched down letting Swarley lick her like a lollipop. *Ass germs!* Some guard dog he is. However, I owe him an extra walk or a special treat from the dog bakery for being my decoy and buying me extra time to get Lautner out of the house.

"Sam!" She stands and we embrace. "I left extra early this morning, and you know I'm not a morning person, but I wanted to surprise you."

I release her and flash an exaggerated gummy smile with my eyes wide. "Mission accomplished."

She purses her lips and tilts her head. "What were you doing?"

"Uh ... nothing. Why?" She messes with my hair, brushing a few stray strands away from my face.

"You're hair is all disheveled and you look flushed."

"I've been hanging out by the pool for the past week. It's just a tan, and I didn't dry my hair after I showered this morning."

"Mmm, it's not a tan, but whatever. If you're watching porn on your computer that's your business not mine. Your secret's safe with me."

"Avery, I don't look at porn on—"

"No need to explain." She waves her hand in the air while walking into the kitchen and looking out the patio doors. She whistles. "Now that's a backyard—pool, hot tub, and badass outdoor kitchen. This is officially party central for the next few days."

While she's distracted, I snatch Lautner's shirt off the floor and shove it in the kitchen drawer just as she turns.

"What's with all the flowers?"

"I like having fresh flowers around." I shrug while twirling my hair.

"Since when?" She crosses her arms over her chest.

"Since ... I've been housesitting. It ... um ... brightens my mood when I'm lonely."

I'm in such a hole right now I'll never be able to dig my way out.

"Why two cups?" she motions to the island.

"I haven't thrown away the one from yesterday."

Avery picks one up, the one that's Lautner's. She opens the lid and sniffs. "Coffee. You hate coffee."

"I know. Stupid barista gave me the wrong one, but I didn't notice until I'd already left."

She sets down the cup and raises an eye at me. "It's half empty."

"Spilled. Yeah, in the car." I stutter like the worst liar ever.

The doorbell chimes. *Thank God!*

"Ave, that's probably FedEx. Will you take Swarley out back?"

"Sure, I need to check out the pool anyway. Come on, Swarley," she calls as she opens the back door.

I grab the T-shirt out of the drawer and run to the front door picking up Lautner's shoes before I open the door.

"Hey!" I exclaim as if I didn't know exactly who was at the door. Stepping out onto the porch, I hand him his stuff and shut the door behind me.

"Hey," he returns with a slight nod while poking his tongue into his cheek. "Aren't you going to introduce me to your sister?" He slips on his shoes and pulls his shirt over his head. "After all, we should get acquainted before we ..." He suggestively moves his eye brows up and down.

Before I can respond, the door opens behind me.

"Well, well, well ... who do we have here?" Avery's high-pitched, ditzy blonde voice sounds. She's not at all ditzy. Avery is quite smart, but somewhere along the way she figured out the clueless damsel in distress gets the most attention from the opposite sex.

I turn with a fake, tight smile. "Avery, this is Lautner. Lautner this is my sister—"

"Avery, and it's a true *pleasure* to meet you." She bumps me aside and offers her hand.

"Avery, the pleasure's all mine. Sydney told me you were pretty, but that's an understatement. You're just ... wow!"

She giggles. "Oh, stop."

WTF!

"Sam, let's not be rude. We should invite Lautner in for a drink or a dip in the pool."

She turns, still holding his hand, and pulls him into the house. He flashes me a this-should-be-fun grin and shrugs his shoulders. I scowl.

"Sam, you should make margaritas. Sam makes killer margaritas," Avery gushes as she scoots her barstool closer to Lautner's. "Sam was a bartender her last two years of college."

"Avery!" I growl between clenched teeth.

"Chill out, Sam. I didn't say you used to get drunk and dance on tables ... oops, guess I did now." She turns to Lautner, resting her hand on his leg. "After Sam's high school sweetheart snatched her virginity and made himself scarce her first week of college, Sam decided to try out the role of preacher's daughter, you know, wild and crazy? She sucked at it; that's my role."

I dump ice into the blender, slam the lid on, and flip the switch. Anything to drown out my annoying sister. I'm tempted to add an extra shot of tequila in my glass to take the edge off, but I decide it's best to keep my senses with my sister seducing Lautner right in front of me.

"Thanks, sis." Avery takes a sip and licks her lips like she's auditioning for a triple X movie. "Mmm, we should take these by the pool. I'm going to go put my bikini on."

"Avery, Lautner doesn't have his suit," I interject.

"Who needs a suit?" Lautner pipes up, looking at me with a stupid smirk. His hypnotic blue irises are dancing with excitement. Avery's Wikipedia report of me seems to please him.

The scowl that was on my face when he came in is still in place. I think it's here to stay for the next few torturous days.

"I like the way you think," Avery calls from the stairs.

Leaning against the counter, I sip my drink and shoot daggers at Lautner. "Having fun?" I chide.

He stands and saunters over to me, taking my glass and setting it aside. Resting his hands on the counter to either side of me, he skims the tip of his nose along my neck and inhales. "Mmm, you smell like hot, sweaty sex and ... me."

"What are you doing?" I whisper as my pulse starts to quicken.

"Just killing time until your sister comes down in her *bikini*," he whispers back.

"Don't be a jerk and lead her on."

"Sam? Do you have a hair tie I can borrow?" Avery calls from upstairs.

Lautner takes a step back. "Who said I'm leading her on?"

I squint my eyes and shrug past him. "Ugh, whatever!"

———

AVERY IS the only person I know who shows up at a pool wearing a bikini and stilettos.

"Gee, Ave, I think you forgot your sash and tiara." I roll my eyes as she comes outside.

"You like them? They're new." She pivots her feet to show off her shoes, completely ignoring my intentional jab.

Lautner's shirt is off—thankfully only his shirt—and he's relaxing in a lounge chair on his stomach. I'm still in my dirty, wrinkled shorts and T-shirt, apparently smelling like sex, sitting on the edge of the pool dangling my feet in the water. There's a cold shoulder situation going on, but I'm not sure if I'm on the giving or receiving end. Lautner and I haven't spoken to each other since we came outside a few minutes ago.

I think I'm pissed at him, but I'm not sure why since I basically gifted him to my sister before she ever showed up. Maybe he's pissed too and this game he's playing is to make a point. What point? Not sure about that either.

"Need some suntan lotion on your back?" Avery offers Lautner.

He lifts his head and smiles. "Sure."

She lathers up her hands and massages it into his back. "Did Sam tell you I'm a massage therapist?"

"No. But I can tell. That feels so good," he moans.

"I'm going to put my suit on," I announce. "Not that anyone cares!" I mumble to myself.

———

THE DUVET IS STILL on the floor, so I straighten the sheets and make the bed. I pick up the box of condoms and turn in circles trying to figure out what to do with them. "Where to hide the stupid condoms?"

I started talking to myself when I began housesitting a year ago. It might not be the healthiest mental behavior, but sometimes it helps stave off loneliness. "Might as well put them in Avery's room so she has them when Lautner screws her tonight." I speak in a fake catty voice.

"I'm not going to *screw* your sister tonight."

I jump and turn toward the door. Lautner is leaning against the frame with his arms crossed over his bare chest.

"Shit! You scared me." I rest my hand over my heart.

"Who are you talking to?" he asks as he enters the room, shutting the door behind him. "Sam? Your alter ego?"

I shove the box of condoms under the pillow. "Where's Avery?"

"Sunning herself. I told her I needed to use the restroom. I thought we should talk."

I sigh as I sit on the edge of the bed and stare at my fingernails. This isn't supposed to be so complicated.

"I don't know how to navigate this. If I tell Avery that we've had sex, then she'll make me rationalize it. I'll be forced into labeling *us*. Either we're just messing around, which in her eyes still makes you fair game, or we're in some committed relationship which is not an option for me at this point in my life."

Lautner sits beside me and holds my hand, interlacing our fingers. "Twenty-one days?"

I nod and look at him.

"I'll take it, whatever I can get. We don't have to call it anything. It just ... is. So, tell your sister. Don't tell your sister. It's up to you. I won't *lead her on* and I won't *screw* her. Okay?"

I smile and look over at him without quite making eye contact because I'm embarrassed that I made such a brass assumption. "Okay."

He stands and pulls me up to him. I love the feel of being held against his bare chest. Maybe too much. I already feel my pulse quickening so I step back.

"Uh ... you should get back down stairs. I need to change and Avery will be wondering where you are." I slide past him and rummage through my stuff for my bikini.

"So are you going to tell her? I just need to know how to act."

Finding my bikini, I stand. "I'll handle it when I come downstairs."

He moves to the door and pauses. "Sydney, for the record, best sex I've ever had too."

He's gone and I'm flying high. It's ridiculous to think that I could possibly be the best sex Lautner has ever had. I was a jittery wreck. However, I'm still bubbling over with giddiness that he even thought to say it.

———

AVERY's in the kitchen refilling their margarita glasses and Lautner is sitting next to Swarley by the pool.

"Hey, Sam, cute bikini. We're draining the rest of the margaritas. Do you want to throw something on the grill for lunch?"

I'm fidgeting with my hair and chewing on the inside of

my cheek. I have to tell Avery about me and Lautner. She's going to analyze the hell out of the situation, but not because she cares about my sex life. She wants to prove that my attempt to control my future is absurd.

After our mom died, I became focused on the future and achieving my goals before something unforeseen happens ... like cancer. Avery focused on living in the moment. It's crazy how something so tragic affects people differently.

"Earth to Sam? Lunch?"

"Yeah, something on the grill sounds good."

"Great. Will you get the door for me?" she asks, holding the margarita glasses.

"Ave ... uh ... about me and Lautner ..."

She furrows her brow. "Yes?"

The words are all jumbled in my head.

"What is it, Sam?"

I take a gigantic breath. Here goes nothing.

"I had the best sex of my life this morning; that's why my face was flushed and my hair was a mess and there were two cups on the counter and one was coffee, which you're right I don't drink, and I didn't spill it in the car. It was just a cover-up, and I didn't buy the flowers. They've been delivered to the front door daily for the past five days while I was having my period and refused to see men." My stomach is contracted, lungs deflated, and I'm gasping for air, but at least I got it all out—at auctioneer speed.

Avery's saucer eyes are appropriately complemented by her jaw on the floor. "Wow ... I mean ...wow! I don't know what to say, other than who's the guy?"

As oxygen infiltrates my brain again, it occurs to me that in my hurried spiel I never said Lautner's name.

"Oh, it's Lautner."

"*Lautner,* Lautner?" she clarifies.

"Of course Lautner, Lautner. How many Lautners do you think I know?" I stand firm with my arms crossed.

"Sam, you don't have to do this. It's not a competition." Her eyes are rolling around while she shakes her head as if it's the most preposterous thing she's ever heard.

"Do what?" I demand.

"You're jealous that I'm here now, and I'm the one getting all the attention. So naturally you want me to back off so that Lautner pays more attention to you."

"What? Are you crazy? I'm not making this up."

"Prove it then." She glares at me.

"Fine, lets go ask him if I'm lying." I step toward the door but she grabs the handle to stop me.

"No way. You two probably have some agreement or made some deal. He's a nice guy. I'm sure he'd do that for you. So how will I know if he's telling the truth?"

Now it's my turn to roll my eyes. "Then how do you expect me to prove it to you?"

Her face scrunches as she looks to the ceiling. "I got it! Take off your top then go out there and give him a long, sensual *open-mouth* kiss." She grins with mischief.

"No way! That's ridiculous and completely stupid."

"Suit yourself, but don't get all doe-eyed with jealously when he's all over me later." She opens the door and reaches for the drinks again.

"Why do I have to take my top off?"

"A kiss is nothing more than an intimate wink, but a bare bosom says 'remember me?'"

"Stupidest thing I have ever heard, but fine!" I untie my top and toss it on the counter.

Avery stares at me, expressionless, as if she's not sure whether I'm bluffing or not.

I'm not.

I march out the door and when I reach the stairs Lautner looks up. His wide eyes say it all: shock. I get closer and his jaw moves as if he's trying to speak but nothing comes out. He's reclined in the lounge chair and I crawl up between his legs.

"Syd—"

My *open* mouth is on his with my tongue tracing the seam of his lips, asking for permission to enter. He obliges after a moment of hesitation. I know Avery's watching. This is only to prove a point, and I'm enjoying it more than I should be. We've gone beyond public display of affection. The point was confirmed before now, but he tastes so damn good I have to force myself to stop. I release his lips and the aliens-just-landed-on-Earth look is priceless, but not nearly as much as Avery's when I walk past her to retrieve my top.

"Satisfied?" I glare.

"Oh my God!" Her mouth drops as she gasps following me back into the kitchen. "You had sex with him?"

Securing my top, I smirk. "Told you."

"Sam, why didn't you tell me earlier?" she asks in a hushed voice while shutting the door and taking a quick look back at Lautner.

"I knew you'd make it into more than it is."

"Which is?" She raises her brows.

"I'm immersing myself in the local *culture*. You know ... taking in the *scenery*, going on a few *excursions*."

We both surrender to our impending grins and chime into a fit of giggles.

"You mean the *culture* is immersing itself in *you*." Avery snorts.

I start to reply just as Lautner opens the door.

His eyes scan between us. I turn away and clear my throat, digging deep for some composure.

"I'm ... uh ... going to go ..." Avery stammers, pointing outside, still grinning but not making eye contact with Lautner.

He walks toward me and I turn, backing up until the wall stops me. With the look of a predator, he captures me and I'm trapped with nowhere to go. I bite my lips together in a half-ass attempt to conceal my smile. My performance outside was for Avery, but I sense Lautner is ready to critique it. He's a breath away. I want to press my lips to his chest and trace every muscle with my tongue, but I don't. Instead, I bat my eyes and wait for him to make his next move.

He feathers his finger along the swell of my breast while his eyes consume me, drinking me in, one sensual pull at a time. "Interesting way of telling your sister, but I like how you *handled* it."

"Yeah, well ... you know, a picture's worth a thousand words."

He cups my breast over my bikini top and circles his thumb over my nipple which hardens instantly. "That it is, Sydney, that it is."

The words twenty-one days flash through my mind.

Ah, screw it!

I put my hands on his chest and lean into him, kissing his pecs and gliding my fingertips over his abs like a car easing over speed bumps. His fingers tangle in my hair and a soft growl vibrates from his chest.

"Sydney, God, I want to rip those flimsy pieces of material off your body and take you against the wall, but I think your sister has seen enough today. And I've been getting mixed signals on the dress code. I don't have my swim trunks, which I assumed would be a requirement with Avery here, but then you came out without—"

I giggle and push his chest. "Go get your suit. I'll make some lunch."

After I get done fantasizing about you nailing me to the wall!

He grabs my wrists and guides my arms around his neck then palms my ass lifting me to my tippy-toes. I melt with a soft moan of satisfaction as he kisses me. The languid stroke of his tongue against mine is sensual and consuming. He makes me teeter on the verge of losing control, yet he exhibits such bridled restraint.

"See you in a while." He squeezes my ass while his nose brushes mine.

Thank God there's a wall to my back, otherwise Avery would have to mop me up off the floor.

———

THE MOMENT LAUTNER LEAVES, Avery grills me on everything from the size of his penis to what I imagine our kids would look like. She's trying to crack my resolve and convince me that being hell-bent on my future is going to lead to regret. I feel just the opposite, but it's a point that's been rehashed too many times, and I'm no longer in the mood to have the same argument.

We decide to have our official pool party tomorrow. Reluctantly, after my unbelievable morning with Lautner, I still make the call I promised to make. Dane is overjoyed about coming tomorrow. That makes just one of us ... okay, two, counting Swarley.

"So let me get this straight. You have Lautner, who is just off-the-charts hot, and, in your words, a 'handsome vet' both pining for you?" Avery cuts up vegetables while I cube the salmon and season it for the kabobs.

"I don't know if I'd say they're *pining* for me." I laugh.

"I guess I'll be the judge of that tomorrow. Speaking of ... will there be anyone else coming?"

"Hmm, maybe. I think Lautner's friend Caden is coming."

"Oh, is he hot?" Her whole body perks up.

"He's hot enough. Short dark hair, maybe six feet, dark eyes, and a nice body ... You've done worse." I can't hide the smirk on my face.

"What's he do?" she asks, completely ignoring my last comment.

"I don't know. Does it matter?"

Avery shrugs. "Not really. Only if he's ugly. Then he has to be rich and successful to make him more appealing."

"Jeez, you're something else. Did it ever occur to you that you don't have to sleep with him. Maybe you could just be here to visit me and make friends ... platonic friends."

"Okay, I could give it a try. But you have to agree to not screw Lautner while I'm here."

"What? That's just stupid!" I burst out, even shocking myself with my reaction. Is the idea of not having sex with Lautner for a few days really so unimaginable? *After this morning, yes!*

"See, you don't want to go without sex, so why should I?"

Frustrated, I jab the bamboo skewer missing my palm by

millimeters. "It's not about going without sex like I'm some addict. It's about me and Lautner, but for you it's about you and sex … with anyone."

"Low blow, Sam," she replies as I hear the front door open.

I raise my eyebrows at her. "Maybe, but true. Am I right?" I whisper as Lautner nears the kitchen.

Avery rolls her eyes. "Whatever."

"Ladies," Lautner chimes as he walks into the kitchen.

Just his presence raises my body temperature a few degrees. "Hey, you wanna fire up the grill? We're just about done with the kabobs."

I glance back at him and he has on his board shorts and a gray T-shirt that, once again, looks too small for his arms. Screw the kabobs, I'll take a second helping of Lautner and be completely satisfied.

He winks at me. "You got it."

Over lunch we fall into casual conversation, mainly about Avery and how much she loves L.A. Lautner questions us about our dad and the whole "preacher's daughter" stereotype. The rest of the afternoon is spent in or around the pool. Lautner and I can't keep our hands off each other, but we try to be discreet so Avery doesn't feel uncomfortable. To my surprise and disappointment, Lautner informs me he has plans this evening with some friends from school. He extends an invitation to both me and Avery, but when I find out we would be the only girls, I decline … much to Avery's disappointment. She is not happy, but I assure her we'll have a girls' night out instead and she's once again back on board.

Chapter Seven

June 12th, 2010

Iᴛ's 2:00 a.m. and I'm startled from my sleep. Avery and I were out barhopping until after midnight. She passed out in the cab on the way back. Thankfully, the cab driver helped me get her to the door. I was on my own from there, so she's currently on the couch because there was no way I was going to get her up to the bedroom.

I rub my eyes and listen again for the sound that woke me. I whip around to my right. There's a tapping noise. I peek behind the curtain. Lautner's at my window.

"What are you doing?" I whisper, opening the window. My head is heavy, still carrying a slight buzz from my evening out.

He clambers inside and shuts the window. I sit on the edge of the bed as he stands in front of me kicking off his shoes. His greedy eyes rake over my body. I grab the sheet and hold it to my chest with a sudden awareness of my breasts being so easily visible through my thin white tank.

"I had to see you." His voice is raspy and seductive.

I watch with wide eyes as he pulls off his top and removes his shorts. *Good lord!* His briefs are tented, not like a one person pop-up, more like an eight person tent that you can stand in the middle of. And his eyes ... *fucking medusa eyes* ... are doing naughty things to me. I squeeze my legs together and squirm in nervous anticipation.

He drops to his knees in front of me and smirks while he tugs at the sheet I hug to my chest—a chest that's rising and falling in rapid succession from my sky rocketing pulse.

"What's this? Hiding something?"

I wet my dry lips as he yanks the sheet away. His gaze focuses on my exposed legs and translucent top. "You're sexy as fuck, Sydney."

I think I detect alcohol on his breath, but it could be mine. Alcohol and Lautner is a heady mixture, so I can't think straight right now.

His hands slide up my bare legs, and his fingers curl into my panties peeling them off.

"Lie back."

I swallow and ease back, keeping my knees pinned together.

"Relax, Syd," he whispers. Grabbing my feet, he rubs his thumbs along my insteps with firm pressure. It feels so good. My muscles soften with his touch. He rests my feet on his shoulders and I suck in a deep breath. The lights are off but the moonlight filters in through the sheer shades. I'm fully exposed to him, and it's unnerving and erotic at the same time. His once smooth face has a rough stubble to it as he sucks and licks his way up my thigh. God, I love and hate how he leisurely works me up. I don't want it to end, but I need more than he's giving me. My core is wet and slick for his touch. He's so close I can feel his warm breath. I tense as his nose brushes over me and he inhales. I'm quivering with each ragged breath. He cups his hands under my knees and spreads my legs wider. The cool air on my exposed sex is replaced with his tongue.

"Aahh!" I moan, clawing at the sheets.

He pulls back and presses his lips to my inner thigh. I feel his smile against my skin. He knows what he does to me, so he does it again. This time my hips jerk from the bed, chasing his touch as his pulls away.

"Lautner." A whimper escapes me as my hands reach for his head. Clenching his hair, I pull him to me. He doesn't stop this time and lost in the chaos of physical ecstasy is a trace of embarrassment that I come so quickly.

He hums and moves up my body, taking my top with him. I lift my arms and fade into his gaze as he slides my tank top off. His large hand palms my ass, lifting and scooting my body farther onto the bed. Cupping my breast, he teases his tongue over my nipple. I work my foot up to his waist and hook my toe into his briefs and push down. Balancing on his knees and one arm, he pushes down the other side.

"Kiss me," I whisper.

Our mouths mesh. Tongues exploring. Hands caressing. I feel so small with his large, strong body hovering over mine. I'm aroused by the thought, but I also feel protected and safe like the world could crumble around us and I would survive in the safety of his arms.

"Sydney ..." he whispers my name like a prayer as his mouth moves over my flesh.

"Don't make me wait." Drowning in desperation, I reach for him.

Not caring that his expert tongue just gave me an amazing orgasm, I greedily want more.

His mouth pulls from my skin and his chin drops to his chest as I stroke him. The only sound I hear is his heavy breath as his hips move with slow deliberate thrusts into my touch.

Without warning, he rolls over taking me with him. I sit up straddling his pelvis. He grasps my hips and slides me back and forth over his length. My heavy eyes close with the stimulation that's bringing me closer to the edge again.

Lautner digs his teeth into his lower lip, watching me. "Put a condom on," he says in a husky voice.

I'm tempted to look around the room, thinking surely he's not talking to me. The good news is there's nobody else in the room with us. The bad news is he's talking to me. I suck in my lips and bite them together for a moment.

"Um ... okay." I crawl off him and sit on the edge of the bed. Taking a condom from the box, I tear it open. It's wet, lubricated I guess. My hands are shaking.

It's a freaking condom, Syd, just roll it on him!

I slide it back in the foil packet and set it on the nightstand. Lautner is ghosting his fingers over my back.

"Got it?" he asks.

"Uh ... yeah, just a sec." I pull out the instructions but the moonlight is not enough to read them. Reaching for my phone, I set it between my legs and illuminate the screen to see the instructions.

"Is that your phone?"

"Yes ... uh ... thought I got a message. Just a sec."

1. *Carefully tear open the package, don't use scissors, teeth* ... blah, blah, blah.

Good.

2. *Making sure the roll-ring is on the outside, place condom on the head of the penis.*

Okay.

3. *Make sure to leave space at the tip for the semen.*

Good idea.

4. *Gently squeeze tip to prevent air from being trapped inside.*

This isn't sounding as easy as it seems.

"Syd, what are you ..." Lautner rolls toward me and I try to hurry and get the instructions back in the box. "What the —Are you reading the instructions?" he asks incredulously.

"Yes ... I mean, no." I snatch the condom and crawl back on the bed. He lies back with his arms clasped behind his head. I sense his smirk but I don't want to ruin the moment so I keep my eyes focused on what I'm doing. After I successfully roll it on, I can't help but smile at my handiwork. It's the artist in me.

"Not bad." He chuckles and I'm snapped out of my reverie.

"Are you laughing at me again?" I start to move off him and he grabs my arms and hugs me to his chest, our faces nearly touching.

"You're adorable," he murmurs.

I roll my eyes. "Puppies are adorable. I'm a disaster. How did I go from being 'sexy as fuck' to 'adorable?'"

His lips capture mine while his hands slide to my head holding me close. Our bodies shift again. I'm on my back and he's kissing me with renewed passion. With a gentle hold, he hikes my leg up and sinks down, filling me one agonizingly slow inch at a time. The deep appreciative sigh I hear from him blends with my own soft moans. He moves in me and I feel like I'm being transported to another dimension. It's a feeling I've only felt with Lautner—his body reading mine, giving me what I need without asking. I don't want him to ever stop.

When he finds his release, I move in desperation to find mine that is so close but just out of reach. His head falls to my shoulder and my nails dig into his butt as his movements slow.

"I got ya," he mumbles with his lips brushing over my skin, nipping and sucking. A little pressure from his fingers circling my clitoris and I'm gone.

"Yes, oh, yes!" I pant.

———

LIGHT FLASHES as my eyes squint open. I'm oblivious to the time and confused as to why I haven't been awakened by Swarley. What I do know is that I feel warm and cozy and there's a soothing rhythm in my ear. I'm sprawled out on Lautner's chest and I've never felt so at peace. Ever so slowly, I tilt my head up to see his face. I'm met with blue irises.

He smiles. "Good morning."

I grin. "Good morning. How long have you been awake?"

"Awhile."

"Why didn't you wake me?"

"Because I like the feel of your sexy, little, naked body draped across mine." He brushes my hair away from my eyes. "And then there is your long dark hair fanned out in all directions. You look like a goddess."

"Hmm, well, I like the feel of this too."

The tips of his fingers strum along my back. "So *Sam* is your nickname? Why?"

"Dr. Seuss, *Green Eggs and Ham*. It's my favorite book ... Sam I am."

Lautner tickles my sides making me squirm and wriggle. "Liar!"

I giggle. "Okay, okay, it's my initials, Sydney Ann Montgomery. Avery started calling me Sam when she was old enough to figure out that my initials are Sam. My friends heard her calling me it, so after a while they started calling me Sam too."

"But you like Sydney better?" he asks.

I feather my fingers over the thin hair on his chest. "Yes, it was my mom's middle name."

"Mmm. Sam and Sully," he chuckles.

"Who first started calling you Sully?"

"My college football coach. One of the defensive linemen had the last name of Sullivan too, so Coach and everyone else started calling me Sully. Even the press used my nickname when interviewing me."

"I'm not going to call you Sully. I like Lautner."

He squeezes me to him. "I like Sydney too." He sighs. "So a preacher's daughter, rebel bartender that was shit on by her high school sweetheart, huh?"

"Yep, stupid me. He was older and I thought he was Jesus."

"Huh?"

"Walked on water."

Lautner laughs. "Ahh ..."

"Anyway, as you know, thanks to blabber mouth, I gave him everything and he left me. The lesson was mine to learn."

"Which was?"

"Don't fall in love."

"Ouch, a little extreme don't you think?"

"Maybe someday it will be, but not for now. Sex is sex and love is love. You don't need one to have the other."

"So I'm sex?"

I kiss his chest. "No, you're ecstasy, which is in a class all its own. But I still can't love you."

"That's fine. Just sex the hell out of me and drive off into the sunset at the end of the month."

"Oh, I plan to." I giggle.

"But there is an issue that I think we should address."

I look up at him again. "What's that?"

"Your lack of *prophylactic* knowledge."

"Oh my gosh! I can't believe you're bringing that up." I roll off his body and smack him in the head with my pillow then wrap the sheet around myself.

He's cackling so much I think I just heard him snort. The bemused smile on his face is devilish. I expect to see horns emerge from his head.

"Enough, you dumb shit! Just because you're too lazy to put on your own damn condom doesn't mean you have to make fun of me. We're not talking about putting your shirt on backwards. Incorrect application could result in an eighteen year gift that I'm not asking for."

He hugs my pillow to his chest with that same shit-eating grin.

"Besides, it's just like a man to dismiss the importance of reading instructions to something. I'd like to see you insert a tampon or a diaphragm in me."

"Christ, Sydney, I'm a doctor. I could probably insert your tampon or diaphragm better than you."

I laugh and shake my head. "Boy, I've met my match. Any other guy would declare defeat at the tampon and diaphragm comment, but not you."

He tosses the pillow aside and grabs me, pinning me under his massive frame. "Bow down to a challenge? No way in Hell. I've never met anyone as stubborn..." a kiss to my nose "...feisty..." a kiss to one cheek "...competitive..." a kiss to my other cheek "...and a total fucking turn on as you." A kiss on my lips that deepens.

Twisting to the side with his mouth still pressed to mine, I glance at the clock. It's 9:30 a.m.

"Holy crap!" I shove his chest. "Swarley must be starving. I can't believe he's not crying at the door." Apparently I had more to drink last night than I thought. I usually don't shut the door. After getting Avery to the couch I went on auto pilot to get myself into bed.

Jumping out of bed, I throw on the first clothes I can find. Lautner enjoys the show with his hands-behind-my-head-I'm-so-damn-sexy pose. The sheet is draped low on his waist but not completely covering his large erection. Either he's aroused by our kiss or he gets off on embarrassing me. I hope it's the former.

"I'm going to feed the mutt. I'll meet you in the kitchen." I open the door.

"Can I take the stairs this time?" he chides.

I roll my eyes without a response.

———

AVERY IS facedown on the floor in front of the couch—snoring. Incredible. Is it even physically possible to snore on your stomach? Swarley is on the couch—also snoring. Note to self: Avery plus Swarley equals sleeping in.

"Rise and shine!" I yell, yanking on the cords to the blinds.

Swarley's a dalmatian in a fire drill leaping from the couch. Eyes wide. Ears back. Tail wagging.

"What ... the ... fuck?" Avery moans, rolling onto her back while covering her eyes with her arm.

"I'm going to feed Swarley and you're going to get up and take a shower. Then you're going to take Swarley for a walk."

"Me? That's your job," Avery whines.

"Yeah, well I paid for the food and booze *you'll* be enjoying this weekend so you owe me."

She staggers to her feet, still squinting her eyes. "What are *you* going to do?"

"Lautner is taking me to breakfast."

"He is?" a husky voice behind me questions.

Turning, my eyes are greeted with my sexy jock dressed and looking mouthwateringly delicious with messy hair and sexy lips that have expertly tasted every inch of my body. I stretch up on my toes and pull his head to mine. I start to hum into his mouth, and he willingly takes everything I offer.

"Ahem, hello? I'm standing right here," Avery interrupts.

Reluctantly, I peel my lips from Lautner's. "Yes, you're taking me to breakfast. I think it's time you reveal your secret little bakery."

"Then it won't be a secret." He tucks my hair behind my ear in an affectionate gesture.

I whisper in his ear, "Guess when we're going to have sex again?"

"When?" His eyes perk up.

"It's a secret." I smile.

"I'll go shower and be back in thirty."

———

"Hello, fat ass and flabby arms. This place is ridiculous." I'm staring at four large glass cases filled with every baked good imaginable: pies, cakes, cookies, turnovers, sticky buns, scones, muffins, Dutch letters, fritters, galettes, and the list goes on.

"What are you going to get?" Lautner asks as the lady behind the counter smiles at us.

"Cherry-almond galette and a medium chai tea latte."

"Make that two," Lautner adds.

I find a booth while he pays.

"What are there, like over a hundred different choices? And you choose the same thing I've been bringing you all week." He sets our drinks on the table and the lady brings our galettes behind him.

"Thank you." I smile at the lady.

Wrapping my hands around my cup and blowing at the rising steam, I shrug. "Why knock a good thing? Why did you get tea today?"

He takes a sip of his. "Thought I'd see what all the fuss was about. Every time you drink it you get this seductively satisfied look."

My eyes widen. "I do?"

"Yes, it's like coffee shop porn. You even purr."

"Shut up! I do not."

I think I do ... but it's not what I'm tasting, it's what I'm envisioning.

He chuckles. "You do. It's adorable and hot all at the same time."

Wasting no time, I dive into my heavenly galette. "So tell me about Caden."

He wipes his mouth. "We played football together and he was my roommate in college. He's a software engineer."

"No girlfriend?" I question, knowing Avery will be on the prowl this afternoon.

"Actually, he was engaged for about six months and his fiancée broke it off a couple of months ago. She wanted to move back to Oklahoma were she was originally from, but Caden refused to leave Brayden."

"Hmm, that sucks. Is he over her?"

"I suppose. We're guys, we don't analyze our feelings with a bottle of wine and a box of tissues."

"Yeah, whatever tough guy. You just shower women with gifts during their menstrual cycle."

"Women? No." He taps his foot against mine. "You? Yes."

"What a waste. You could be wooing your future wife, but instead you're investing, admittedly grand romantic gestures, in a relationship that has an expiration date."

He shrugs and sips his drink. "Maybe that's why I'm doing it. Maybe you're my guinea pig. You know, see what works and what doesn't. Then when the right girl comes along I'll have perfected the 'wooing' and be effortlessly irresistible, all thanks to you."

Jesus! Look in the mirror, fucking Medusa eyes. You already are effortlessly irresistible.

My gaze falters and the smile I'm trying to force wavers. I'm leaving Palo Alto in twenty days. So why am I experiencing a jabbing pang of jealousy from Lautner talking about "the right girl?"

"I see, well, anyway, the reason I asked about Caden is because Avery is going to pounce on his ass this afternoon. She's ... how shall I say it? *Flirtatious* and she likes to have a good time, but a committed relationship is not really her forte right now so—"

"So ... you want me to forewarn Caden that she's not marriage material."

"God no! That's not what I mean, well, not exactly. I'm sure she'll be marriage material someday. She just has another silo or two of wild oats to sow."

Lautner chuckles. "Thanks for the warning, but in case you've forgotten, I've had first-hand experience with your sister. Besides, Caden's not looking for a replacement bride. I think he's going to be a little commitment shy for a while."

I nod.

"Is this the real reason for breakfast?" he questions.

"Partly." I work my lip between my teeth with nervous apprehension. "And I also need to tell you that I ... uh ... invited Dane to the pool party." My face wrinkles waiting for his response.

He rubs his chin and purses his lips. "The vet, huh? I'm not really into that kind of threesome, I prefer two girls and one—"

"Shut up!" I kick his shin.

"Ouch! What?" He laughs. "As I recall, you two were holding hands and looking quite cozy at brunch."

I finish my drink. "I knew you were jealous that morning."

His head jerks back. "Jealous? You've got to be kidding. I don't get jealous."

I stand and brush a few stray crumbs off my top. "So when I introduced you it was just a figment of my imagination that you pulled back your shoulders and puffed up your chest like a damn rooster before you shook his hand?"

"I have no idea what you're talk—"

"Yeah, yeah ... let's go. I have a pool party to prepare for."

———

It's NEARLY eighty degrees with a cloudless sky. Lautner and Caden man the grill, Avery mixes dip and cleans veggies while I'm making margaritas—blended and on the rocks. Then, there is Claire. She is Lautner's "friend" from med-school who he decided to invite to even the numbers. He also mentioned that there would be a single guy, Dane, who she might like to meet. My favorite flirtatious and totally awkward vet has yet to arrive, but I'm not holding out hope for Lautner's decoy.

Petite, long wavy blonde-haired Claire, who has not offered to help do anything, is sitting by the pool, in the shade, with a brimmed hat so wide that anyone within a six-foot radius of her will be guarded from the sun. What my sexy pool guy has yet to notice is Claire's aversion to Swarley. I don't think it's *Swarley*, I think it's dogs in general. Much to my surprise he has been on his best behavior today. But when Claire arrived, he sniffed her hand and I assume his nose must have touched it because she immediately went to the sink and did a good three minute surgical scrub. Then there's been the shooing and scatting. *"Scat dog ... shoo, ya big mutt!"* Now, I'll admit, I wasn't the biggest Swarley fan when I first arrived, but my reaction was provoked, hers is instinctual.

"Sam, get the door!" Avery yells over the shrill of the blender. I flip the switch and answer the door.

"Hey, Dane, glad you could make it."

He's the picture of cool and casual with his T-shirt, board shorts, sunglasses, and carton of bottled beer in each hand. "Thought I'd contribute." He gestures to the beer.

"Great, I'll put them in the fridge. Come on in."

As he follows me to the kitchen, my curiosity is wide eyed and anxiously waiting to see how this is all going to play out. When Caden arrived an hour earlier, Avery was on him like Swarley to Dane's crotch. Caden appeared equally as interested in Avery. However, Dane's arrival could alter the chemistry of the afternoon. Avery is anything if not unpredictable. She could see Dane and decide to keep her options open. My sister's dating motto is "equal opportunity."

Everyone's out back as I lead Dane through the kitchen, dropping his beer contribution off on the way to the patio.

"Hey, everybody, this is Dane Abbot. Dane, this is my sister, Avery."

She offers her hand to him while standing close to Caden. "Hi, Dane, nice to meet you." Avery is friendly, but not ditzy and giggly. *Hmm, interesting.*

"This is Caden," Avery introduces him as though she and Caden are already a couple.

He must be on a few second delay because Swarley is just now barreling toward Dane. I smirk and inwardly roll my eyes. *Crotch, you remember nose. Nose, you definitely remember crotch.* Dane must buy his toiletries at one of those specialty stores that offers bacon scented soap.

"And you've met Lautner," I continue.

Lautner nods, but not a standoffish or jealous nod. No way, because *he* doesn't get jealous!

"Yeah, I thought I recognized you last week at the café. I'm a huge Stanford fan and I loved watching you play, man."

Dane's fan confession has Lautner relaxing a bit. "Thanks. It's crazy people still recognize me."

"Don't be so modest, Sully. You could be playing for the 49ers ... you would have been a first round draft pick, dude!" Caden has no qualms with singing Lautner's praises.

"Yeah, whatever." Lautner takes a pull of his beer.

The sun-fearing beauty makes her way up the stairs. If she turns her head too fast her Saturn-ringed hat could decapitate Dane. What's interesting, and has been since she arrived, is she seems to only have eyes for Lautner.

"Ahem ..." I clear my throat.

Claire turns and spares Dane's life by mere inches.

"Dane, this is Claire. She graduated with Lautner."

Dane is still rubbing Swarley's head with one hand but offers his other to Claire. "Pleasure to meet you."

Claire offers a weak, fingertips-only shake. Since Dane's hand has been on the toxic germ infested dog, I'm certain Claire will feel compelled to go inside and scrub another three layers of skin off.

"Hi, I'm Dr. Brown." Clare replies.

It's probably just me, but I'm fighting the urge to bust out laughing. Dr. *Brown?* I didn't ask what her specialty is but if it's gastroenterology, I may just wet my pants.

Dane smiles. "Well, in that case, I'm Dr. Abbott."

Ouch! Nice zinger.

I'm seeing Dane through a new light, and he doesn't just act funny. He genuinely has a great sense of humor.

"Drinks?" Avery jumps in to save the train wreck that's happening in front of us.

I head into the kitchen to get drinks for everyone and Lautner follows me. Grabbing my waist, he pulls me into him. I snake my hands up the back of his shirt to trace the defined muscles I've come to know so intimately.

"Have I told you how damn sexy you look today?" his voice is low and raw.

I'm wearing the infamous black bikini from our surfing outing and a pink sheer wrap skirt. Grinning, I shake my head. He wastes no time showing me. I release an appreciative moan as his lips consume mine and our tongues leisurely slide together. My pulse accelerates. His fingers dip below my bikini bottoms, curling into my ass.

"Drinks," I remind him, breathless.

He bites his lip and looks out the window discreetly adjusting himself. "God! You've got me hard already."

Turning my attention to filling up the margarita glasses, I shake my head. "You did that all on your own, buddy. Don't blame me."

He grabs a few bottles of beer from the refrigerator. "Dane was kind of a jerk to Claire."

"What?" I whip around to look at him. "Did you just show up from some alternate universe? Because had you been here about five minutes ago you would have witnessed what everyone else did. *Dr. Brown* being completely stuck-up and pretentious to a seriously nice guy."

"Oh, so now Dane's 'a seriously nice guy?' What does that make me? A schmuck?"

"Enough, Mr. I-Don't-Get-Jealous, you're missing my point."

"Which is?"

I throw my hands in the air and growl in frustration. "You invited some girl who is clearly here for you, not Dane.

In your words, she's been 'eye fucking' you for the past hour. *And* she's obviously not a dog person. Hello? Why would you try to set your dog-hating friend up with a veterinarian?"

"That's not fair. Swarley can be a little overbearing—"

"Bullshit! Swarley's been on his best behavior today and you know it." I grit my teeth while poking his chest with my finger.

"Is ... everything okay in here?" Avery asks opening the door. "Thought you two were bringing drinks."

"We are," I snap with residual rage that's not meant for Avery.

I set the drinks on a tray and brush past Lautner without meeting his eyes.

Avery passes out the drinks while Dane and Caden get everything off the grill. Lautner follows with the bottles of beer, but I ignore him. Everyone finds a seat around the table. I'm conveniently nestled between Lautner and Dane, but Claire chooses to take the other seat next to Lautner instead of sitting by Dane. In keeping with the boy-girl pattern Caden sits between Claire and Avery, who is next to Dane.

Avery and Caden successfully engage Dr. Brown in conversation—conversation about her of course. Come to find out, her specialty is anesthesiology. Guess Dr. *Brown* won't be the *butt* of my jokes after all. Lautner joins in, sharing his upcoming residency schedule, which starts in two days. Dane decides to start his own conversation with me. We talk about Swarley, his dogs, and even his new jogging route.

Lautner manages to ignore me the entire meal, not that I am vying for his attention. Dane leans back in his chair and sips a beer in one hand while his other casually rests on the back of my chair.

"I have season tickets to the Giants. Are you a baseball fan?" Dane asks.

We officially have Lautner's attention now. He turns and zooms in on Dane's hand resting on my chair.

"Yeah, Syd, are you a baseball fan?" Lautner's hand rests high on my leg giving it a gentle squeeze. His eyes widen and his mouth sets in a challenging smirk.

Dane's eyes fall to Lautner's possessive hand, and he removes his arm from the back of my chair.

"Sure. I like baseball." I scowl at Lautner and turn back to Dane. "But Avery does too. She'd be pretty jealous if you took me to a game."

"Damn right!" Eavesdropping Avery pipes up.

"Oh ... well maybe you two could take my tickets and see a game this week."

"Woot woot! Thanks, Dane." Avery bounces in her chair, clapping her hands.

I shake my head. "Yes, thanks. That's really nice of you."

Dane takes another swig of his beer and nods. I'm sure he didn't see his propositioning me for a date turning into a ticket donation for a girls' day out.

"Yeah, real nice of you, Dr. Dane," Lautner adds with a satisfied smile.

I push his hand away and glare at him. Standing, I grab the empty plates and take them to the kitchen. To my utter surprise, Dr. Brown follows me with the rest of the dishes.

"Thanks." I smile and take them from her.

"So ... Lautner tells me you're only in town until the end of the month."

"Correct." I arrange the plates in the dishwasher.

"So it would be accurate to assume whatever is going on between the two of you is ... temporary?"

Obviously her attempt at domestic labor was just a front to be alone with me.

"Why do you ask?"

She glances outside then steps closer to me. "Lautner's my *friend* and we've both worked really hard to get to where we are. He has a very demanding three years ahead of him and I just would hate to see him get *distracted*."

Shutting the dishwasher door, I lean back against the counter and cross my arms over my chest.

"Distracted or taken."

"Excuse me?" Her voice raises a few notches while her posture stiffens.

There's a knock at the French door. Avery is holding up her empty glass. I nod and grab the margarita pitcher.

"Don't sweat it, *Doctor*. I'll be out of your way in a couple weeks." I leave her in the kitchen and head out back.

"What's up with Claire?" Avery asks as I refill her glass.

"She's worried I'm invading her territory."

"Oh, cat fight?"

"Hardly, Ave, she's not worth the energy." I grab my drink and claim my lounge chair next to Swarley.

All three guys are in the pool. They've stretched the net across and are playing water volleyball. Of course Dr. Stud is on his own. It'd probably take both Caden and Dane to beat him.

"Come on girls. Get your asses in here," Caden yells.

Avery has a nice buzz going so she jumps in without hesitation. "Come on, Sam," she hollers.

"I'm good. Besides, if Claire doesn't play then it will be uneven."

"I'm in." I hear Claire call as she moseys to her lounge chair on the opposite side of the pool. "I just need some sunblock on my back. Would you mind, Lautner?"

He glances at me but I divert my eyes. I refuse to give him the satisfaction of acknowledging that I heard what she just asked. Instead, I grab the beer beside my chair and start chugging it. I'm not sure whose it is, maybe Dane's, but I don't care.

"Sydney Ann Montgomery, get your ass in the pool," Avery calls again.

I remove my skirt and adjust my top. The surge of alcohol from the margaritas and the beer rewards me with my own little buzz. I pull my hair back into a ponytail and cannonball into the pool. When I surface, Dane grins and Caden and Avery chuckle in unison.

"Sam is such a fish." Avery shakes her head.

"Guys against girls?" Caden asks.

"That won't be fair," Lautner calls. He's rubbing sun lotion on Claire's back. I remember when he rubbed it on mine at the beach, but the thought only pisses me off now. I'm pissed that he's doing it, and I'm pissed that I'm pissed.

"Lautner's right. The last thing this party needs is three bruised male egos. Which is exactly what we'll have after we girls kick your arrogant male asses." I'm basically meaning me and Avery because I'm not sure if Ms. SPF 100 can even tread water.

"You're on!" Caden says, swimming to the other side of the net. Dane shrugs his shoulders and follows Caden.

"Let's do this, bitches!" I yell, feeling a little more than tipsy.

"Ah, I love drunk Sam. She's so much fun when she gets her sailor talk on," drunk Avery squeals.

I'm not drunk—yet—but if Lautner doesn't get his fucking hands off albino girl, I'll be sucking down straight tequila.

Okay, I might be a little drunk.

———

A WHIPPING, spanking, and merciless humiliation sums up this game. As predicted, Claire has been no help. She even claps for Lautner every time he scores against us. Dane, my only true ally, has to leave because he received a call about a poodle that got into a bag of chocolate. Claire has stayed another hour since Lautner so kindly applied another coat of sunblock after we all got out of the pool. She let me know that she rents the apartment above Lautner's. So while he walks her to the door, I imagine her reminding him of his curfew and to avoid any distractions that would prevent him from getting good sleep.

"Where's Lautner?" Avery asks, looking very comfortable sitting on Caden's lap.

I take a long pull of beer. "He's say—ing goodbye to Doc—tor Bitch ... I mean Brown." I giggle. Warm all over from way too much alcohol, I'm finding it hard to think before I speak.

"Claire is just a friend," Caden speaks up in Lautner's defense no doubt.

"Friend." I slur the word like I'm testing it. My eyes are closed and I'm absorbing the end of the afternoon sun. "Yes, they seemed very *friendly* together."

"Who seemed very friendly together?" Lautner's voice muffles through my fuzzy head.

"No one," Caden offers a quick response.

"Sydney's drunk. She doesn't know what she's talking about."

"I ... am *not* drunk. Y—you...uu are drunk, Ave."

"I haven't had any alcohol for the past two hours, Big Sis ... it's all you. Unfortunately, you're on your own. Caden is taking me out tonight." She moves her mouth to my ear. "Don't wait up," she whispers.

Hell, I can barely keep my eyes open now. I don't think she has to worry about me waiting up for her.

Chapter Eight

June 13th, 2010

"**Ouch**!" My head is killing me and so is the stupid light filtering in from those damn sheer curtains. I'm sprawled out on my stomach. Brushing my hair away from my face, I squint at the clock. *6:05 a.m.* I try to move but my legs feel like lead.

"Swarley." I cough through my cotton mouth, realizing he's beached out on my legs. He jumps off the bed and goes through his morning yoga stretches. As much as I don't want to, I have to get up. Oddly enough, I feel dehydrated and yet my bladder is ready to burst. I grimace while sitting up and swinging my legs off the edge of the bed. *What the ...* I'm naked. In spite of my stiff protesting neck, I whip my head around. Lautner is sleeping on his back with his hands resting on his bare chest and one leg flopped on the outside of the covers.

We must have had sex last night, but I can't remember. God, that could not have been good. Or maybe it was good.

It's possible I'm quite the minx in my drunken state. He looks peaceful, maybe even ... *satisfied*. I grin until I ease to my feet with a suppressed moan. My fingers circle my temples with firm pressure to alleviate the throbbing in my head and to keep it from exploding.

After relieving myself and washing my hands, I duck my head down to the faucet and slurp in gulp after gulp of cool water. The soothing sensation feels like Heaven and hopefully so will the two Advil before too long. My mouth still tastes like ass. *Yuck!* Grabbing my toothbrush, I squirt a mammoth glob of toothpaste on the worn bristles and scrub the hell out of my mouth.

Swarley has claimed my spot in bed.

"Move," I whisper. He tucks his snout under my pillow and sighs. "Now, Swarley, move it!" I nudge him and he returns a low growl without looking at me. "Stupid mutt!"

There are three other beds and two sofas, but I want to be next to Lautner when he wakes up. After what was probably some pretty adventurous sex last night, I have no doubt that he'll want to wake up next to his *sexy Sydney*. It's a king-sized bed and while my massive pile of hot, sexy muscles takes up his half, Swarley is balled up near the edge leaving me a nice pocket to slide into between the two of them. I shimmy my nakedness under the covers, resisting the urge to knock Swarley's K-9 ass onto the ground. Sucking my bottom lip in between my teeth, I lift the covers with stealth control to sneak a peek at Lautner—*all* of him. To my surprise he's wearing a pair of jogging shorts, although nicely tented.

Suddenly, I feel a little underdressed. I ease onto my elbows to scoot out but not before Lautner's long lashes flutter open revealing the blue irises that always paralyze my body and suck my thoughts dry. Sliding back under the covers to hide my breasts, I relinquish a shy smile.

"Good morning," his husky voice vibrates.

I roll to face him, bending my elbow and propping my head up on my hand while clutching the sheet to my chest. "Good morning."

Clenching his fists, he stretches his arms out over his head and yawns. My lips part and my tongue traces my lower lip as I watch his muscles flex and ripple with each movement.

"That was quite a night, huh?" He grins.

I knew it! My legs press together as I try to remember what happened last night. His grin says it all. I was an uninhibited sex goddess. Now the only downside is I have something pretty spectacular to live up to but I can't remember what. I trace his abs with my fingertips.

"Yes, it was," I purr seductively.

He raises a single eyebrow and turns on his side mirroring me. "Let's just say I hope for both of our sakes it doesn't happen again anytime soon."

What!

I pull my hand away from him as if he just burned me. "What part didn't you like?"

His eyes double. "Uh ... basically all of it."

I'm shocked, just speechless.

He grins a little. "Well, except for the striptease. That was *entertaining*."

I want to throw the covers over my head and disintegrate into the depths of humiliation hell. "I was that bad?" My voice is weak and my words are slow and incredulous.

"Bad's an understatement. I was relieved when you finally passed out. Honestly, I felt so sorry for you. Had you been in your right mind I'm sure you would have been embarrassed."

He reaches over and brushes a few strands of hair away from my face. "I don't want you to worry about it. After the striptease things got a little messy, but then you passed out and I got you out of your clothes and did what I needed to do."

I can't believe he is saying this. Admittedly, I've had some bad sex in my life, but I would never chastise someone by being so degrading. And what kind of sick bastard has their way with an unconscious person?

"I think you should leave," I say with monotone controlled emotion.

"What? Why?" Lautner's head jerks back.

"Why? You really have to ask me that?" I sit up bringing the sheet with me. Swarley must feel the tension because he jumps down and exits the room.

"Maybe you've been around too many cadavers or some weird shit like that, but where I come from having sex with an unconscious person would be considered rape."

My heart is working a marathon in my chest and my blood is racing hot in my veins, but the sick bastard lying next to me has the audacity to laugh.

"Oh God, Sydney." He laughs, buckling at the waist the way he did when we were at the beach.

I scoot over to the warm spot where Swarley had been, tugging more covers and increasing the distance between us. I'm appalled that he thinks this is so funny.

"Oh jeez, Syd, we didn't have sex. After your little strip-tease attempt you vomited on yourself and then passed out. I had to get you out of the rest of your clothes and give you a bath. Then after I got you in bed I had to go clean up the rest of your mess and take a shower myself."

Dear God, I feel like a complete idiot. I've known Lautner for all of eleven days now and he's seen me at my worst on more than one account.

I shake my head. "Why would you do that? I mean, seriously, what are you still doing here? Most guys would run for the hills. You've known me two seconds and you're cleaning up my vomit and tucking me into bed?" I wiggle the sheet gesturing to my body. "Albeit naked." I raise my brow at him and he smirks.

With a swift, unexpected motion he grabs my waist and pulls me down flat on my back, losing the sheet along the way. He hovers over me, resting his forearms on either side of my shoulders.

"I'm not *most guys,* Sydney, and you ..." He sighs while shaking his head but doesn't continue.

"I'm sorry," I whisper.

He rubs his nose against mine. "For what?"

"Everything ... drinking too much, vomiting everywhere, leaving you with a mess to clean up, then accusing you of ..."

He grins and dips down to trail kisses along my neck. "Raping your unconscious body?" he murmurs over my skin.

I lace my fingers through his hair and close my eyes as his touch sears my skin. "Yeah, that."

His mouth finds mine. Our tongues lazily slide together with soft strokes. His torso sinks just enough that my nipples bud under the tease of his skin. I moan and skim my hands over his shoulders and down his back, curling my fingers into his firm flesh. He shifts his body so he's cradled between my legs. I bend my knees and relax my legs to accommodate him. The kiss deepens. He plunges his tongue deep in my mouth while simultaneously rolling his hips allowing his rock hard erection to press right where I need it. I whimper and buck my hips, silently cursing his damn jogging shorts.

"Take off your shorts." I break our kiss.

He skims his hands over my hips, along my ribs, and across my breasts. Working my nipples between his fingers, he trails his tongue along my jaw to my ear where he grazes his teeth over my ear lobe.

"No time for sex. I've got to get going," he whispers in my ear.

"What?" My voice is a pathetic, desperate whine. I dig my nails into his back, threatening to draw blood.

His body vibrates with his chuckle. Grabbing my arms, he pries my nails from his back and pins them above my head. I wiggle my hips, enticing him to stay, but he rocks his pelvis firmly to mine, halting my movements. His blue irises sparkle and his cocky grin taunts me.

"I'd love nothing more than to consume every inch of your sexy body until you're screaming for mercy ... but I have to go."

Holy shit! Screaming for mercy?

I'm completely frazzled and my chest works overtime to bring in some much needed oxygen. My core is melting from his steel rod wedged into the apex of my thighs.

"Wh—where are you going?" He keeps my naked body pinned to the bed underneath his deliciously rock solid frame. He's assaulted my mouth with his expert tongue, thrust his hips into my warm slick sex, and stimulated my nipples into firm erect peaks ... but he has to go? The hell!

His mouth drops to mine and he bites my lower lip pulling it between his teeth with a slow drag. "No pouting. I'll make it up to you later."

I barely blink and he's out of bed pulling his shirt on. Looking down at my naked body, I grab the covers and drag them over me, but he yanks them away and shakes his head in warning.

"I have nineteen days to look at your mind-blowingly sexy body. You can cover it up in July." He grins and saunters into the bathroom.

"Humph!" I crawl out of bed and follow him.

He looks in the vanity mirror messing with his hair, which is a joke because he makes messy sexy. I press my bare chest to his back, snaking my hands around him and sliding them up under his shirt.

"Can't I change your mind?"

He laughs and turns letting his eyes caress my naked body like a soft brush flowing over canvas. I'm comfortable in my skin but not usually to the point of letting someone leisurely stare at my nude figure. But Lautner makes me feel beautiful. It's not lust, it's more. I recognize it. It's the way I look at a piece of art and see something nobody else does.

He pulls me into him and skims his large hands down my back and over the soft curve of my ass. "Unquestionably, you could change my mind. That's exactly why I have to get out of here." He lifts my hair off my breasts and pushes it back over my shoulders. "Mmm ... mmm ... mmm," he hums shaking his head, "you and your long, dark, sexy goddess hair cascading over your flawless skin. God, I've gotta get out of here." He leans down and brushes his lips over mine. "I'll see you later, my seductive goddess." He walks out leaving me boneless and dizzy.

I shake off his captivating spell, grab my robe, and chase after him. He's by the front door putting on his shoes and talking to Swarley as I reach the top of the stairs.

"You never said where you're going ... and how will I contact you?"

He looks up and gives me a fetching smile. "I have a tee time with my dad in thirty minutes. It's his birthday."

Opening the door, he winks. "I'm in your phone, beautiful. Later."

———

WALKING Swarley and listening to Avery share *every* detail of her night with Caden has kept my mind off of Dr. Sexy and his distracting presence in my life. I'm off kilter. As crazy and demented as it sounds, I needed Lautner to be the twisted guy who unscrupulously took advantage of me in my altered state last night. I'm twenty-three and working for my future—my dreams. I want marriage and children, but not for another decade or so. The worst thing that could happen to me would be finding the right guy at the wrong time. I like Lautner ... a lot, maybe too much. This is worrisome.

"What's your deal, Sam?" Avery asks, pushing down her sunglasses so she can glare at me over the frames.

I flop over onto my stomach and untie my top to even out my tan for the afternoon. "I'm not following."

"I just spent the past hour gushing about Caden and the dance club he took me to and the insanely expensive restaurant, and the mind-altering sex we had, yet you haven't given me the big sister speech. What gives?"

Squinting at her, I shrug. "Maybe I've given up on you. Hell, you've slept with half of L.A., it was only a matter of time before you ventured into new territory." I laugh because I know what's coming.

"Bitch!" She tries to act offended but she knows it's futile with me.

"You're leaving in a few days and Caden knows it. So if you're both fine with ... *recreational sex*, then who am I to judge?"

She laughs. "Yeah, especially after last night's little show."

I push up onto my forearms. "What exactly are you referring to? You weren't here last night."

"Lautner called Caden because he needed to ask me about feeding Swarley. I asked how you were doing and he said you were passed out, but not before you scolded him for rubbing his hands all over Dr. *Skank*."

"What?" I jump to a full sitting position, tying my top back on. "I did not!"

"Well, I wasn't here to witness it myself, but I believe him because you were in a drunken, jealous fit before we left. Why do you think you were so drunk?"

"Oh God!" My head falls into my hands.

"You've got it bad, Sis. Lautner could be a deal breaker."

Snapping my head back up I shake it. "No way. He's fun and good in bed." *He's a sex savant!* "But not a deal breaker. A catastrophic natural disaster or a car accident leaving me in a vegetative state is a deal breaker. No *guy* will ever be a deal breaker."

"Mmm hmm," she hums.

I squint my eyes and huff, stomping toward the house.

———

It's 6:00 p.m. and Avery has taken off with Caden again. I'm surprised I haven't heard from Lautner yet, and I'm internally scolding myself for even caring. After messing with my computer and flipping through the channels, I grab my phone and see if he's really under my contacts. Yep, he is. *Lautner Sullivan*. I have his phone number, address, and email. He obviously messed with my phone after bathing me and putting me to bed—*naked*. I wonder what else snoop dog did?

I set my phone on the counter and stare at it. "Just call him, it's no big deal. No, wait for him to call if it's really no big deal. Or just commit yourself to the nearest mental institute because you're talking to yourself so damn much. Arg!" I yell and run my fingers through my hair. This is crazy. Even when my jerk of a boyfriend plucked my cherry and ran with it I didn't fret about it as much as I am over this stupid phone call.

"Screw it!" I call him and as it rings I feel insanely nervous. His mouth has explored every inch of my naked body. So why am I literally shaking with the phone held to my ear?

"Hello?" His voice is groggy.

"Hey, uh, did I wake you?" My finger is working a nervous twist in my hair.

"Yeah, but I need to be getting up." He clears his throat bringing strength to his voice.

"Jeez, sorry, uh, long day?"

He chuckles. "Long night with some drunk girl and an early morning of golf with my dad followed by lunch at the clubhouse."

"Yeah, about last night ... it's been brought to my attention that I may have been a little out of line with somethings I *did* and *said* so—"

"Really? Such as ..."

I can't believe he's going to make me say it. He's so frustrating. One minute he's cleaning puke off the drunk girl, showing his kind side, and the next he's trying to humiliate me. Granted, I do a pretty good job of setting myself up for it.

"*Such as* drinking too much to begin with, then maybe giving the impression that I was ... jealous of Claire, or Dr. Brown."

"You mean Dr. Skank?"

Shit!

"Yes—I mean—no, not Dr. Skank. I don't remember calling her that, but if I did then I'm sorry. I didn't mean it." *I may have meant it.*

"Don't sweat it, Syd. I think you're adorable when you get all jealous."

"I was not jealous!" I yell in a high-pitched voice.

"Uh ... your striptease was entitled 'Where Lautner's hands will never be again if he doesn't keep them off Dr. Skank.'"

Kill me now and never let another drop of alcohol pass my lips.

"So how was golf?"

Lautner laughs. "I take it we're done talking about last night?"

"It's pointless because it's your word against mine, unless Swarley goes all Bush Beans Duke on me."

"God, you're something else. So what did you call about?"

"Oh ... just to ..."

"I'm just flipping ya shit. I know why you called."

He does? I'm not entirely sure *I* know why I called so how can he know?

"You do?"

"I left you in a hot mess this morning and you need to be serviced." His voice drips of confidence or most likely arrogance.

"What? No, that's not ... um ..."

"Sorry, babe. I didn't realize just how tightly wound you would be by now. Damn, you can't even form a coherent thought. Get naked, I'll see you in ten."

"Lau—"

He hung up on me!

———

"Hey." I answer the door with a goofy grin.

Lautner's blues scan my body. "I must be early." He crosses his arms over his chest.

I turn and walk toward the kitchen hearing the door close behind me. "What do you mea—"

I'm swooped up into his arms and the air from my lungs releases with a squeal as he takes the stairs two at a time.

"Lautner!" I cry.

He tosses me on the bed and shrugs off his shirt. "Naked ... did my phone cut out?"

I shake my head, drinking in the full expanse of his ripped chest and abs. "You came over here for sex?" I ask in a breathy voice.

He drops his shorts and his arousal springs free. My eyes widen and I gasp. *Sweet Jesus!* He came over here commando. I'm paralyzed but not for long. He grabs my ankles and tugs me to the foot of the bed pulling me up and making haste with my top.

"I came here for you. But let's be honest, you've been thinking about this all day."

He has me naked and his frantic movements halt. Liquid blue irises flow over me. He stands before me, every muscle perfectly chiseled, every inch of him solid except for his face. His expression is soft, parted lips and heavy eyes like he's drunk on me. With a deep swallow, I break the silence.

"So how's the zero percent body fat thing working for you?"

My comment pulls at the corners of his lips, and his eyes dance with playful delight. He kneels on the floor and takes my foot, rubbing deliciously firm strokes with his thumb along my instep. "How's the sexy-goddess-every-other-girl-in-school-must-have-hated-you thing working out for you?"

I lean back and moan in appreciation as his magic hands work all the muscles in my feet making slow strokes up my legs.

"I told you, I was a tomboy in school. Nothing about me was sexy, unless you're turned on by bruised knees, scabby elbows, and chlorine-damaged hair."

His lips brush along my knee. "*Everything* about you is sexy."

My insides clench and heat. I feel my skin flush. "Kiss me."

I love the way I feel his smile against my skin before I ever see it.

"Patience, Sydney." He flips me over and my flesh tingles under his soft, caressing lips and hands.

"What are you doing?" I whisper.

"Memorizing you." He breathes over my back, easing my hair away from my shoulders.

"Why?"

"Because you're going to leave me and this is going to feel like a dream. I want to..." he kisses my neck "...remember..." he kisses the side of my breast "...every..." he kisses the subtle curve of my hip "...detail."

"Lautner?" I breathe out with a shaky voice.

"Hmm?" His mouth vibrates against the small of my back while his fingers dance along my arms.

"Don't." My voice breaks.

He stills and I roll to my back, pulling his face to mine, rubbing my palms against his scruffy face. I blink back unwelcome emotions and shake my head. "Please ... don't."

Blue irises explore my lips, my hair, my cheeks, and finally meet my gaze. He nods and gives me a reassuring smile, but it doesn't reach his eyes. Without a word, he reaches for a condom and rolls it on. The silence around us screams but the lump in my throat is too big for words to escape. His lips attack mine in a renewed urgency. I feel desperation as his tongue dives into my mouth making firm deep strokes against mine, hands eagerly claiming my breasts bringing my nipples to firm peaks.

He's gone from the controlled animal stalking his prey to the attacker taking everything with relentless desire. We're all over the bed, twisting and tangling sheets. My body fights to match his every move of driving intensity. He growls as I grab and tug his hair, and the guttural noise he releases makes me pull it even harder.

"Lautner ..." I moan as he pins my arms above my head and laves slow stokes with his tongue over my nipple. "Ahh!" I yell when he sucks it into his mouth, grazing his teeth over my sensitive flesh.

His hand skims down my stomach and my legs part inviting his touch. But his hand holds firm to my abs, fingers splayed across my quivering skin. My arms are still bound together in the strong grip of his other hand and I'm withering beneath him. He's consuming me at his own agonizing pace with complete control over me.

The ongoing tugging and teasing of my nipples is too much. My nerves are firing under his touch and the sparks of intensity are all building in one spot ... the spot his hand is less than an inch from touching.

"Lautner!" I cry. My arms wriggle in his grasp as my pelvis rocks off the bed searching for touch—any touch.

"Sydney, you're driving me fucking crazy," he mumbles into my neck.

I'm driving him crazy? Not ... even ...

He releases my arms and I waste no time clawing his back trying to pull his body closer to mine. It's in vain. I'm no match for his strength. This will be on his terms. I just hope it's before I lose all dignity and start begging and pleading.

He pulls my leg up over his shoulder and my breath hitches as my muscles stretch. I'm not a contortionist and his bold assumption that he can pretzel my body into crazy sexual positions takes me by surprise. I don't have time to focus on my flexibility because my mind explodes when he slips two fingers into my slick channel.

"Oh God." I throw my head back and moan.

I want to look into his lust-filled eyes, but I can barely keep mine open as he works his fingers inside of me. Removing them, he pauses and I drag my eyes open again. I feel him at my entrance and the anticipation is hypnotic— the way he watches me and silently demands my full attention as he sinks into me. I bite my bottom lip to the point of pain as I try to relax my muscles to accommodate all of him.

"God, this is perfection, Syd." He groans as he stills, buried inside me.

Running my tongue over the teeth marks on my lip, I nod several quick times. This is perfection.

I find my breath and pull his head down to mine. Our tongues mirror our hips while we suck and moan into each other. He pulls out and then inches back in with a drawn out breath. I let myself be consumed by the moment and not rush to the finish, even though every other part of my body is frantically wanting to surge forward. He releases my leg and my muscles sigh. The rocking force of his hips is an erotic ebb and flow, and despite my efforts to pace myself, I find my legs locking around his waist and my fingers tormenting his hair. I feel his muscles going rigid against my body and his cock thickening inside me. His control is slipping, and with each thrust I nearly tip over the edge.

"Let it go, Sydney," he growls, fighting for control, but he loses it and stills buried deep in me, releasing a string of expletives as if chastising himself for not holding back a little bit longer.

He circles and grinds into me and that's all it takes ... I'm gone too.

"Oh God, Lautner!" I cry and bury my face in his neck, sucking and biting at his firm skin while waves of indescribable euphoria ripple through my body.

He collapses on me which does nothing to restore oxygen to my drained lungs, but I'm too sated to care about something as trivial as air.

I'm not sure what the count is for calories burned but it's high. We're both covered in sweat and I'm famished.

"That was ..." The two hundred pound pile of dead weight on me breathes into my neck.

"Sextacular." I giggle.

His body shakes on a laugh and I feel his head nodding. A rush of wind infiltrates my chest as he lifts himself from my body. I can barely move my legs. I think they're permanently molded in the shape of his pelvis. He saunters his sexy ass of flexing muscles into the bathroom. The stupid grin on my face feels permanent. Lautner comes back out of the bathroom minus a condom.

"I'm starving, but I don't think I have the energy to walk downstairs to scavenge for food," I say, lying unabashedly naked and limp on the chaos of bedsheets.

"Hmm, well that could be a problem." He sits on the side of the bed with his back to me.

I can't resist running my hand over his defined muscles. "Problem?"

He turns with a devilish grin and a foil condom packet in his hand that he tosses on the pillow. "Yep ... problem. I'm not done with you yet." Strong arms pull me onto his lap.

We're face to face and my eyes are wide with excitement. "You're not?"

"Not even close."

———

THE HUNGER PAINS ARE GONE. I've feasted on Lautner for nearly two hours. Now I'm standing by the front door in a long T-shirt and messy, matted sex hair. Goodbyes suck! But I have to get used to it.

"Do you have your scrubs ironed for your first day, Dr. Sullivan?"

He smoothes his thumb over my bottom lip and smiles. "Something like that."

"So ... I'll see you again before I leave, right?" I'm trying not to sound nervous or desperate, but casual is failing me.

"I'll have a few hours to spare at some point. Where are you going next?"

"Paris." There is lackluster in my voice which should not be there. I've been waiting to see France and the Louvre since I took my first art class in high school. Damn Lautner for dulling my enthusiasm.

He tilts my chin up. "I'm happy for you. You're getting to see more of the world in a year than most people do in their lifetime. I'm sure your mom would be proud."

I bite my quivering lip and nod.

"I'll call you." He presses his lips to mine.

"Bye." I suck in a deep breath and let it out, fighting to keep my composure.

I can't peel myself away from the door. Even after his taillights fade into the night, I continue to stare into the darkness.

Chapter Nine

June 14th, 2010

I<small>F THERE EVER WAS A BITTERSWEET</small> night, it was last night. I took a gazillion pictures of Lautner and some of us both. They were of us in bed naked, but the photos are PG and tastefully beautiful. Half of them were close ups of his face. I think I managed to photograph nearly every muscle of his body. They would sell nicely as stock photos, which I've done before, but I won't sell these. These are for my eyes only.

I'm in blue iris Heaven flipping through them on my computer while Swarley beaches out on the floor by the window where the sun beams its rays on the pooped pooch. Our three mile jog was just what we both needed. My muscles felt a bit sore this morning and my girly parts felt gloriously overused. They're going to get some much needed rest whether I like it or not. Lautner's residency is demanding and time ... is not on our side.

"Hey, Sam!" Avery calls from the front door.

"In here, Ave," I yell from the kitchen table.

She dances in like a graceful swan, all dreamy eyed and giddy grinned. "Sydney—"

I raise a suspicious brow. Avery doesn't call me Sydney. Something's up.

"I'm in love."

WTF?

"You'd better be talking about some handbag or pair of shoes and not—"

"Caden." She sighs and closes her eyes.

"It's Monday, Avery. You haven't known him forty-eight hours. You're delusional." I dismiss her lunacy and continue flipping through my photos.

Her eyes snap open and then she squints them in a grimacing scowl. "I'm not delusional."

She walks behind me, looking over my shoulder. "Holy fuck! Is that—"

"Nothing." I slam my MacBook shut.

"Oh ... my ... God. Those photos are of Lautner." She grunts. "You're the delusional one, Sam."

I grab some grapes from the refrigerator and pop one in my mouth. "I'm not in love," I mumble.

"That's why you're delusional. You've found *the one* and you're too blind and stubborn to see it."

"Shut up, Ave. He starts his residency today and I'm leaving in a couple weeks. I'm not even sure if I'll get to see him again."

"Jeez, Sam. Yes, he's starting his residency, not enlisting in the military. You'll see him again. Besides, you're missing my point."

"Which is ..." I say in exasperation.

"That you're in love with Lautner."

I go to interrupt but she shakes her head and holds out her finger. "Uh, uh ... let me finish. Sam, you can't blame fate and you can't control it. You could have found a job in L.A. closer to me, but then Aunt Elizabeth called and this job fell into your lap. Fate. Then Lautner just happens to show up here by *mistake*. Fate. And he's perfect for you. He's educated, athletic, fun, and hot as hell ... and he adores you. It's fate, Sam. You can't plan your whole damn life. We're just not meant to have that kind of control over the universe."

I'm mentally counting down the hours until Avery gets in her car and goes back to L.A. "You really expect me to listen to someone who has never had a relationship last longer than one week and who just walked through the door ten minutes ago declaring her love for some guy she met two days ago? Come on, Ave. Seriously?" I walk off and head upstairs for a shower.

"You're going to leave California with a broken heart in two weeks and you know it!"

———

June 15th, 2010

LAUTNER MESSAGED me late last night. He said his first day went well, just long. I didn't mention my sister's crazy declaration of love for his best friend, which led to us sitting by the pool in silence most of the afternoon until she left to meet Caden for dinner. I also failed to mention that Swarley and I met Dane and his Jack Russell Terriers, Salt and Pepper, at the dog park for a playdate. He gave me the baseball tickets for tomorrow's game.

It will be me and Avery's last hurrah before she goes

back to L.A. In spite of her recent pestering about my feelings toward Lautner, deep down I know I'm going to miss her. Caden took the day off to spend it with Avery. I guess that should mean something, but after what Lautner told me about Caden's past, I don't put too much weight in the gesture.

Dinner is pasta and salad for one on the deck with the tiki torches lit, John Legend flowing through the speakers, and a great bottle of local Pinot Grigio. I hate that as much as I've been alone over the past year, I've never felt lonely ... until Lautner. By the time I'm halfway through the bottle of wine, I hate that I miss him now. With the last drop of the bottle and a warm buzz enveloping my body, I hate that Avery's right. I'm going to leave Palo Alto with a broken heart. I hate bad timing. I hate the idea of fate. I hate feeling so lost. But mostly, I hate my heart for betraying my brain.

———

June 16th, 2010

Number one sign that I'm losing it ... I wake up and find myself spooning Swarley. Elizabeth and Trevor are not going to be happy about me humanizing their dog.

"Let's go, Swarley. Jog then breakfast."

When I open the front door, I initially feel elated then a pang of disappointment hits me just as fast. There is a beautiful bouquet of flowers, a hot drink cup, and a pastry bag ... but no Lautner. There's a note with the flowers.

Early morning, you might have to reheat the

tea. Didn't want to wake you ... scratch that ... DID want to wake you, but I would never have made it to the hospital on time. What if I said I'm missing you more than I should? ~Lautner

"Ouch, Swarley," I say, holding my hand protectively over my heart. "What's a girl to do?"

We run extra hard and then I indulge in my galette and lukewarm chai tea latte that still tastes great. I send my favorite pool guy a text.

> Yummy, thank you xx! What if I said I wish you would have given me the chance to make you late for work? ~Sydney

I'm surprised at his quick response. But it makes me smile.

> Mmm ... What if?

———

AVERY and I make a day of it in San Francisco: shopping, lunch, and a great Giants' game. The tension between us has eased. I'm still not openly admitting that I may have complicated feelings for Lautner, not to Avery and certainly not to him.

"So are you seeing Caden tonight?" I ask on the drive back to Palo Alto.

"Mmm hmm. I'm spending the night at his place then I'll come by in the morning to say goodbye before I head back to L.A."

"I hesitate to even breech the subject again, but has he said that he loves you?"

She shrugs while weaving through traffic like a maniac. "Kinda."

"Kinda? How do you kinda tell someone you love them?"

Her small grin is overshadowed by the tense wrinkle of her nose. "Well, he said it once during ..."

I roll my eyes. "Sex? Right?"

She nods. "Yes, but he wouldn't have said it if he didn't mean it, right?"

My laughter cannot be contained. "Oh, Ave ... if it was in the heat of the moment, it might not mean anything. Did he say it early on or did he yell it out during his orgasm?"

"Don't laugh at me!" She's trying to be serious, but I see her lips quivering to resist her impending grin. "It was in the middle. He said, 'I fucking love you, Avery.'"

"Ave, I've heard you nearly orgasm eating a chocolate truffle, and if I recall, you also declared your love for it."

"Why are you spoiling my moment?" She pouts.

"I'm not trying to spoil anything. If he says it again, fully clothed, before you leave tomorrow, then I think you might have something to hang your hopes on. But if he doesn't ..."

"So you don't think I should quit my job and move to San Francisco yet?"

We both laugh and I'm glad she sees the insanity of it all.

"Okay, your turn. Where do you and Lautner stand?"

"Ave—"

"Don't Ave me. Sam, I'm not stupid. He's more than just sex."

I look out the window and watch the surroundings morph into familiarity. We're almost home. "I like him ... a lot. The timing is just wrong for both of us. It will be hard to leave Palo Alto in two weeks, but ... that's just life."

————

June 17th, 2010

DANE CONVENIENTLY HAPPENS to catch Swarley and me on our jog. I knew it was possible given our early rise time, but I'm no longer trying to avoid him. I'm actually happy to see him.

"Hey, Dane. Thanks again for the tickets. We had a great time."

"And they won," he adds, wiping his brow with his arm and slowing down to match my pace.

I grin. "Yes, they did."

"I watched the game on TV, but you and Avery didn't make it on the Jumbotron."

"Which is surprising since Avery was dressed in her sexy Giant attire and giving Lou Seal some competition for attention."

"I bet she was," he laughs.

We jog for a bit in silence until we approach Dane's house.

"Do you have time to come in for something to drink?" he asks.

I twirl my ponytail and twist my lips to the side. I'm leaving soon and nothing's going to change that so I decide to just enjoy myself and not analyze every stupid little decision.

"Sure, but I can't stay long. Swarley is going to be demanding breakfast soon."

"That's fine. I have to jump in the shower and get to

work in an hour so I'll be kicking you out in about fifteen minutes anyway." He winks.

"How hospitable of you."

We let Swarley out back to get reacquainted with Salt and Pepper.

"Your house is amazing. It looks pretty old from the outside but you've obviously done a lot of work inside."

"It's was built in the sixties. I bought it from the original owners when they moved into assisted living. Water, coconut water, orange juice—"

"Water is fine, thanks."

He hands me a water and leads me out to the deck with the dogs. "Anyway, I basically gutted the interior one room at a time. The previous owners had only updated on a need-to basis."

"*I* meaning you actually did it or you hired out the work?"

Dane gulps down the rest of his orange juice. "I did everything except the electric and plumbing."

My eyes widen. "You have some serious skills."

"Internet." He smiles. "There's a how-to video for anything you could ever want to do. My dad taught me a lot when I was younger too."

Swarley runs up to me and sits on my foot.

"Hmm, someone's hungry." I baby talk to Swarley.

"Where do you go after Palo Alto?" Dane asks.

"Paris. I've wanted to go there more than any other place in the world, and it's finally going to happen."

"And Lautner?" his voice is cautious.

I twist the lid back on my empty water bottle and watch his dogs chase each other. "Lautner started his residency on Monday. He has three tough years ahead of him."

"And you?"

I meet his gaze and smile with a resigned shrug. "I'm going to housesit for another year then I'm going to start grad school and finish what I set out to achieve."

"No distractions?"

"No distractions." I hand him my empty bottle and put Swarley's leash back on. "Thanks for the water and thanks again for the tickets. I know you really intended to take me to that game."

He nods. "True, but it worked out for the best."

"Bye, Dane."

"See ya around, Sydney."

Swarley is scarfing down his breakfast when Avery arrives.

"Good morning." I hug her.

"That it is." She's holding back. I can tell by the look on her face.

"Out with it." I shake my head and pour a bowl of cereal.

"He wants to see me again." She smiles and flutters her eyelashes.

"Anymore declarations of love?" I mumble with a mouthful.

"No ... but he's going to drive down to L.A. on Saturday and spend the weekend with me."

"Well, that's good. You do know he was—"

"Yes, I know he was engaged. I'm not asking for a proposal. He's just the first guy that's made me not want to be with other guys."

I gasp and slap my hand against my chest. "Avery in a monogamous relationship. Quick, grab my jacket, Hell must be freezing over."

"Oh, stop it!" She punches my shoulder. "I really like him."

We're both somber and it's silent for a few minutes. I love my sister and want nothing more than to see her happy. But I'm also protective of her, and lately her own worst enemy has been herself. Caden changes everything. For the first time in years, Avery is in a vulnerable situation. I'm trying to be happy for her, but the mother in me, the one that's been dominant since Mom died, is scared for her.

We both stand and embrace. "Safe travels, Ave. I love you."

"Love you too. If I don't get back up here by the end of the month you'd better call me before leaving the country."

"I will."

She slings her bags over her shoulder. "Tell Lautner bye for me."

I nod and smile.

When she shuts the door, I let a few tears fall down my cheeks. I don't know what's happening, but every day I feel a little more alone.

MY NEW BEST FRIEND, Swarley, and I hang out by the pool the rest of the afternoon. I haven't heard from Lautner in over twenty-four hours. I have no idea what he's doing or what his schedule is, so I refrain from calling or texting him. Instead, I stare at my phone for hours like a pathetic clinger waiting for him to call. I've played every version of "In Your Eyes" that's ever been made, and I've set it as my ring tone for him. I'm having severe blue iris withdrawal. I can't imagine what it's going to feel like when there is a physical ocean separating us. I have to believe immersing myself in all that is magnificent about Paris will dull the inevitable heartache that I'll be taking with me when I leave.

It's 10:00 p.m. and I decide to drag my ass upstairs and fall into the sea of covers that smells like Lautner. I really need to wash the sheets. We both were a sweaty mess, but I can't let go of the musky soap smell that I associate with the sexiest guy I will ever know.

I hear "In Your Eyes" and I spit toothpaste out of my mouth and sprint to the bed. My heart is leaping from my chest and I take a deep breath before answering.

"Hey!"

I don't hear anything.

"Hello?" I say slower.

"God, your voice is like the sun rising after days of darkness. I miss you so fucking much."

The heartache officially ... just ... started.

"Mmm." I'm swallowing my entire heart that's stuck in my throat constricting my air.

"Syd?"

"Hmm?"

"Is everything okay?"

I nod and blink back the impending flood as if he can see me. It's too much. I can't talk and hold back the tears, so I let them go and find my voice. "Fine, everything's fine," I respond with a nervous laugh, brushing away my tears. This is ridiculous. What's my problem? "How's life as a resident?"

He sighs. "Insane. I keep telling myself that my busy schedule will keep my mind off the sexy goddess that has consumed my every thought."

"Well, good thing I'll be leaving soon. You can forget

about me and concentrate on being the brilliant doctor I know you are."

"Sydney ..." he whispers my name like a prayer.

Don't, please don't! My mind screams as the eerie silence weighs heavily between us.

I clear my throat. "So, think you can squeeze me in for a cup of coffee or something in the next two weeks?"

"I'm off Sunday. I have some research to do, but I wouldn't miss seeing you for anything."

"Okay." I sniffle and suck in my top lip tasting the saltiness from my tears.

"Sydney, are you sure you're okay?"

"Yes. Why do you keep asking me that?" I turn to grab a tissue on the night stand and there he is ... blue irises and a megawatt grin on the other side of the window. I shake my head and wipe my eyes. "I hate you," I whisper over the phone before pressing *End* and opening the window.

I grab his phone from his ear and toss it on the floor. "You shit!" I grin.

He climbs in and shuts the window. His I-caught-you smirk has to go.

"You don't hate me."

"I do ... so much." My arms fly around his neck and our lips collide. He hugs me and lifts me off the floor. The old T-shirt I'm wearing slides up my backside as my feet dangle in the air. His hand palms my bare ass exposed from my thong. I moan into his mouth. He tastes divine and my greedy tongue can't stop exploring every inch of him. I'm faintly aware that he's set me down on the ground, but Lautner has me flying so high I'm certain I'll never find my feet again.

He steps back and pulls off his top. My palms automatically flatten on his firm chest. I feel his finger under my chin tilting my head up to meet his hypnotic gaze. His thumbs brush across my cheeks.

"These tears weren't for me, were they?"

I wrap my hands around his that are cradling my face. "Never." I want to look away, but I can't.

Without a single word, he draws me into a place I've never been. I grasp the hem of my shirt and pull it over my head, now standing before him in only my lacy thong. He keeps his eyes fixed to mine and I wait. I know he's going to look at me ... all of me. He does, and I heat under his gaze. I love the way he looks at me. It's an aphrodisiac. I pray time will steal the images of him from my mind, but I don't ever want to forget how those blue irises make me feel like I was made for his eyes only.

In slow motion, I unfasten his pants and his eyes shift to my hands. Lips parted and chest rising with a deep inhale, he waits with eternal patience. I squat down taking his pants and briefs with me. He steps out of them and I rest my hands on his firm quadriceps. I kiss his shins and his knees, lingering over his scar and feeling his muscles flex under my lips. My hands skim up to his hips while my lips follow with a trail of tender kisses. I look up at blue irises while tracing the pads of my fingers over his washboard abs. My lips oh-so-lightly graze the entire length of his smooth, firm erection. His limp hands at his sides ball into fists and his stomach muscles steel under my touch while his eye lids fall heavy over fading irises. I tease the tip of my tongue over the head of his length. He hisses as his eyes fly open. I smirk while he shakes his head. Large, strong hands thread through my long, dark locks. I continue my journey, leading with my hands and following with my lips over his abs, chest, arms, and neck. Ending with his perfect ... sexy ...

mouth. Still smirking, I trace my tongue along his bottom lip.

"I'm not going to let you go," he whispers.

I feel the joy in my face fade and my head drops. Pressing my mouth to the center of his chest, I close my eyes and drown in the rhythm of his pulse against my lips. My tears bleed down my cheeks and I'm helpless against their need to escape.

"Look at me, Sydney."

I'm ripped open with a vulnerability that leaves me completely wrecked, and I am weak. In this moment he does the one thing I swore no man would ever do ... he owns me.

Blue irises ...

"I love you," he whispers.

Shattered.

It doesn't matter that my eyes are flooding and my nose is a sniffly mess. I've never felt so beautiful and ... loved.

"Then you'll let me go," I choke out with a strangled sob.

I can physically feel the anguish in his face, but he rescues me anyway with just one ... single ... nod.

Hungry lips meet like they've been starving for a lifetime. It feels like every second of my life has inexplicably led me to this single moment, and I'm giving everything I've ever had to give in this one kiss. I may leave completely empty in two weeks, but it's worth it ... he's worth it.

Our entwined bodies melt to the bed and time stops. It doesn't matter that we've known each other only two weeks ... I've known his touch forever in the warm sun, his breath in the wind, his eyes in the sea.

"Sydney ..." I love my name wrapped in his voice. It feels like he's branding this bond between us into the depths of eternity.

He caresses my neck with gentle lips and my breasts with patient hands. The yearning inside me to feel one with him is overwhelming, but I refuse to rush anything. Lautner is making love to me and *nobody* has ever made love to me. In this moment, I'm certain no one will ever make love to me again.

"Beautiful ..." seductive lips whisper over my navel.

I'm mesmerized; everything about him is breathtaking. While I ease my fingers through his thick blonde hair, I'm rewarded with blue irises.

"If I were to go blind tomorrow, the last thing in the whole world I would want to see is your eyes," I whisper with a weak raw voice.

He rests his chin on my stomach and smiles. "You want to know what you see in my eyes that's so amazing?"

"What?" I whisper, brushing my thumb over his thick brow.

"Your reflection."

There are no words. I nudge him with my knee, and he willingly rolls to his back. I straddle him and he grabs my hips. Exposing my breasts, I brush my long hair back over my shoulders. He wets his lips and smiles in appreciation.

"I've been taking my pills." I stroke him from the base of his cock with a firm grip. "I want to feel you inside me ... just you."

I expect hesitation in his analytical doctor mind, but if there is any, his body hasn't received the signal. He lifts my hips and I clasp his firm arms to steady myself as he lowers me onto him, sliding in one breath-hitching inch at a time. My heavy lids close over my eyes while my head falls back with a soft moan vibrating in my throat. I'm filled completely with him, and it feels exquisite having his warm flesh rubbing against mine. It's so much more intimate.

"Sydney ... you feel so damn good."

"Mmm," I hum, still absorbing the fullness. I swallow hard and peel my eyes open to find his blazing at me ... and then we start moving together. It's an easy, savoring, languid rhythm. I'm not thinking about an orgasm. I'm enraptured in the moment and I don't want it to ever end.

I lean forward. "Kiss me."

His hands feather across my back taking my hair with them, then he brings my head to his. We're completely connected, our tongues syncing to the motion of our hips and our hearts keeping beat to the beautiful symphony of love we're making.

Time starts to tick again as our movements become more urgent and erratic. The fullness in my breasts and lower abdomen match the engorged feeling between my thighs. I feel Lautner thicken inside me and his breaths are quick and shallow. As much as I want to control it ... make it last, I can't. His hand moves from my breast to my clitoris. He pulses his middle finger against my tight bundle of nerves and rocks his hips up to me in several short, firm thrusts. Hot fluid fills me and he breathes my name at the same moment I call his and fall apart around him. Circling my hips, I take everything he has and give all I have left.

Exhausted and sweaty, I lie limp on his chest with my face pressed to his neck. The soothing touch of his fingers strumming gentle strokes along my back lulls me to sleep.

Chapter Ten

June 18th, 2010

4:00 a.m.

NESTLED ON LAUTNER'S CHEST, I don't think I moved all night. His confession still haunts me. The most amazing man I have ever met loves *me*. It hurts so damn bad. All I want to do is love him back. Screw grad school. To hell with stupid dreams. Nothing will ever compare to how I feel right now. That's how I know it's too good to be true. I'm blinded by love. If I don't find perspective, I'll end up crashing to the ground when this illusion evaporates.

I ease off him and grab my laptop. Intending to distance myself from Lautner, I click on iPhoto to delete the pictures I took of him. Blue irises stare back at me as my finger hovers over *delete*. Turning my head, I look at Lautner. Long lashes resting on his cheeks. Full lips slightly parted. One hand resting on his chest, rising and falling with slow, even breaths. I can't do it. It feels like goodbye. I'm not ready to say goodbye. I will never be ready to say goodbye. But I'll do it anyway, just not now.

I click on another album I've been working on for the past month.

"What's that?" Lautner's groggy voice startles me. He sits up and leans against the headboard next to me.

"Hey, I didn't mean to wake you."

Leaning into me, he nuzzles my neck. "You didn't. I have to get going soon. I need a shower and a change of clothes before I head back to the hospital."

I tilt my head to the side resting it on his.

"Where did you get those pictures?" he asks.

"I took them."

"Are you serious?"

I laugh. "Yeah, I'm serious. Why?"

He shrugs. "Just ... they're incredible. Why'd you take them?"

"A couple I housesat for have a granddaughter with leukemia. They made calendars for donation gifts. It's actually benefiting twelve children with leukemia, one for each month. Anyone who donates gets a calendar. A local printer gifted all the printing services and I took the photos free of charge."

Lautner doesn't speak. He's just staring at the screen. The photos are of children with leukemia. They are black and white images, but the props—toys, hats, dress up clothes —are all in color. Most of the children have lost their hair to chemo and they have a thinner frail look to them. But the smiles on their faces and the sparkle captured in their eyes is pure joy. I remember every one of them. Their names, their stories, and their courage is etched in my head and held in my heart. The children felt like celebrities, dressing up and posing for the photo shoot. They felt extra special in that moment. And for one day, they felt normal.

"Sydney, you're so talented. I mean ... these are *really* good."

I nudge him playfully. "Says the soon-to-be pediatrician who obviously has a soft spot for kids."

"Yes, I love kids, but I'm talking about the photos. The lighting, the angles, the added color, the candidness of each one is so ... *raw* and essence-capturing. Your work is ... wow!"

"Yeah, yeah, I'm the next Annie Leibovitz. Whatever. It's just a hobby." I look at him and he's shaking his head and pursing his lips in annoyance. "Okay, I'm sorry. Thank you. I really do appreciate the compliment. It means a lot coming from someone with so many talents of his own."

A sheepish grin slides up his face. "I want a calendar. I'll pin it up in the staff lounge as a reminder of why we're there."

I nod and smile. "Okay." Closing my laptop, I set it on the nightstand. I crawl onto his lap straddling him with my arms wrapped around his neck. "Don't go," I say, sticking out my lower lip.

He leans in and bites it, slowly dragging it through his teeth. "I'll stay if you stay."

I wiggle my hips suggestively. "Mmm, okay. I don't have anywhere to be."

His fingers curl into the skin on my hips to still me. A seriousness washes over his face.

"No, I mean I'll stay if you *stay*."

I nod once in understanding, letting my eyes fall from his gaze. "Then you'd better get going." I climb off him and scoot down turning my back to him and pulling the covers up. The balance in the mattress shifts as he stands.

"I want you to stay." His voice is soft behind me as he dresses.

"I know," I whisper.

He walks around the bed and hunches down so his face is inches from mine. "I love you."

"I know." I close my eyes, suck in a slow breath, and let it out in a huff.

"I'm not expecting you to say it back. I just need you to know so I don't spend the rest of my life wondering *what if.*"

Another nod. "I know."

I refuse to open my eyes. He'll have me. One look and I'll be his. Hell, I already am his. I just haven't said the words and I won't ... I can't.

Warm lips brush across my forehead. "You know, huh?" His voice is weak and defeated. "Okay then, I'll call you later."

One last nod is all I give him. My heart surges into my sternum like a warning signal, but it's not my brain so I have to ignore it. Emotions are unreliable, dangerous, and misleading. Fate is for fools who believe in fairytales. I didn't buy into the whole princess dream when I was a little girl, and I'm sure as hell not going to jump into the golden carriage now only to find myself sitting on a pumpkin surrounded by mice when the ball is over.

―――

June 19th, 2010

"Hey, Ave. What's up?" I answer my phone while walking Swarley.

"I'm making breakfast for Caden. He's still in bed. We've

had the best weekend." Her voice is soft, just above a whisper.

"Wow! Have you ever made breakfast for a guy before?"

"Do you really have to ask?"

I laugh. "I suppose not. So things are getting serious?"

"I think so. He's so different from any guy I've ever known. He's smart and sweet and he's so *attentive* in bed. If you know what I mean." She giggles.

Scrunching my nose, I respond. "Yeah, I know but I don't really want to."

"I like him, Sam." The seriousness in her voice brings out the protective big sister in me.

"I'm happy for you, just … be careful. He's been burned and that could make him emotionally unavailable for a while. You have to consider the possibility that he's a nice guy who is good in bed, but it doesn't necessarily mean anything more than that. Okay?"

"Duly noted, Sam. I have to go. Call you later."

"Bye, Ave."

I sigh and look down at my walking partner. "Oh, Swarley. Avery is getting in over her head. I think I may be too. Any advice?"

Swarley stops and drops a load in the grassy easement.

"Nice. Is this your response? What are you trying to tell me. Shit or get off the pot? Or just that I'm full of shit?"

———

I FEED SWARLEY, shower, and wait on the front porch with my beach bag. This is our last full day together. I'm anxious for it to begin, but once it does, I'll never want it to end. Lautner called me Friday after he got home. We made small talk. He sounded tired and I wasn't sure of what to say, so we didn't talk long. Yesterday he texted me during his lunch break to let me know what time he would pick me up today. I want to say that I didn't wait up for him to call me last night ... but I did. However, he never called.

I woke with a heavy heart this morning, so I decided to just say "fuck it." It would be insane to not enjoy every day of a vacation just because it's inevitably going to end. Lautner and I are going to end. The timing is all wrong and I will not be fooled by the illusion of fate. But I am going to enjoy every second I have left with him. I've surpassed the you-might-get-hurt line by the span of an ocean. I'll deal with the consequences later.

As the familiar black 4-Runner turns into the drive, I jump to my feet and grab my bag. There's no time for cool and casual. I fly down the stairs and sprint to him just as he gets out. I'm airborne leaping into his strong arms, wrapping my legs and arms around him.

"Whoa! Someone's a little excited to see me." He laughs, hugging me tight to him.

I pull back to find *my* blue irises. My face hurts from grinning so big. "Shut up and kiss me."

Lautner doesn't hesitate. Everything about him over-whelms my senses: his minty mouth, his intoxicating, musky scent, his strong body that envelopes every inch of mine, his sexy growl, and those fucking Medusa eyes.

My legs squeeze him with everything they have while my hands splay across his cheeks reveling in the smoothness of his freshly shaven face. Our kiss ends breathlessly.

"I love it when you're bossy." He rubs his nose against me.

"You do, huh? In that case, take me to the beach ... a very *private* beach." I wiggle my eyebrows suggestively.

He sets me down and smacks my butt. "Get in, we have a quick stop to make before you go streaking across the beach."

Walking around to my side, I stick out my tongue. "Not funny."

———

WE PULL up to a community center where there is a large bus painted white and red with a heart on the side and the words: *Give Blood for Life.*

"Did you have breakfast?" he asks.

"Yeah—"

"Are you hydrated?" he continues.

"Uh ... yeah. I drank a bottle of water on my walk with Swarley, and I had a can of coconut water when I got back. Why? What are we doing?" I attempt to keep my voice strong and steady in spite of the nervous apprehension that floods my system.

"Donating blood. My mom and a group of her friends organized a blood drive in honor of their friend who was recently hospitalized after a severe car accident."

"Oh ... okay."

"Have you given blood before?" Lautner asks while he unfastens his seat belt.

"Once, my senior year of high school when we hosted a community blood drive."

"Great, so you know what to expect." He gets out and comes around to my side.

Yeah, I know what to expect: blurred vision, muffled

hearing, dizziness, and the pungent smell of ammonia bringing me out of the darkness.

He opens my door and my knees are already weak.

"Let's go talk to my mom."

We walk over to where a group of ladies are standing around tables filled with water, juices, and cookies.

"There's my boy," Rebecca calls, opening her arms.

Lautner embraces his mom with affection. "Hey, Mom." He releases her and grabs my hand again, interlacing our fingers. "You remember Sydney."

"Of course. So nice to see you again. I really appreciate you both coming by to donate today."

"It's for a great cause. However, I'm sorry to hear about your friend."

"Thank you, dear. She's been in a coma for two weeks now, but we're very hopeful she'll come out soon."

I nod and smile politely.

"Come on, baby, let's get our paperwork filled out." Lautner pulls me toward another table with clipboards and forms to fill out. I look for a reaction from his mom after he uses his term of endearment—*baby*—but it doesn't seem to phase her at all. I like Rebecca. She seems genuine and kind. It shouldn't matter since I'm not planning on returning to Palo Alto, but I want her to like me. I don't want her to remember me as the girl that broke her boy's heart. Is it possible I could break Lautner's heart?

We fill out our forms and Lautner takes the first opening.

"Sydney Montgomery." A young short-haired brunette calls my name.

My mouth feels dry and my clenched teeth begin to chatter. "Me." I force a smile while walking to the bus.

Lautner's smile beams the moment I walk onto the

bloodmobile. "Right here." He pats the seat next to him with his free hand.

I try not to stare at the needle in his arm or the blood draining into the tubing. It's not that I normally get queasy or light-headed from someone else's blood, but the anxiety over what I'm certain is about to happen has me feeling all sorts of unwelcome sensations.

"So I see on your form you've donated before but you fainted afterward?"

I look at Lautner while she puts the tourniquet around my arm. His brows furrow a bit.

"Low blood sugar?" he questions.

I shrug with a sheepish smile. "Maybe."

It has nothing to do with my blood sugar, but I choose to stick with that explanation anyway.

"Well you had a good breakfast and we'll get you some juice right away so you'll be fine."

"Yeah ... I'll be *fine*." I repeat with a tight-lipped smile, nodding my head repeatedly.

A quick alcohol swab, a small stick, release the tourniquet, and viola, the clear tubing turns red. This is the easy part. I have good veins and the stick doesn't bother me. It's standing up when I'm done that seems to be the problem. I've donated blood only once, but I faint every time blood is taken. It doesn't matter if it's less than an ounce or a full pint ... I'm out for the count.

"We won't be surfing today. No strenuous activity after donating blood."

I look at him. "Surfing is a strenuous activity?"

He purses his lips to the side and smirks. "Well, it is for one of us."

"Once again, not funny." I roll my eyes.

Lautner waits inside with me until I'm done. He hands me a cup of juice before I even try to stand. "Drink this and just give yourself a moment before standing. Okay?"

I nod and do as I'm told.

"Did you know every two seconds someone needs donated blood? And for every donation up to three lives can be saved?" Lautner hunches down between my legs with his hands on my hips.

I love his passion for helping people. It goes beyond the obvious, his degree in medicine. There's no doubt in my mind that had he followed his career in football he would have been one of those players who used his money and celebrity status to do great things off the field too. The first day he took me to the beach I saw him picking up trash along the shoreline while I was making a fool of myself in the water. He has an innate desire to do good.

"You're a good man, Lautner—what's your middle name?"

"Asher." He leans down and kisses my bandage. "It means happy and blessed."

"Well, you're a good man, Lautner Asher Sullivan."

"That means a lot coming from you." He winks.

"Pfft ... I may be a preacher's daughter, but I'm not exactly a missionary out to save the world."

"No, you just gave up your childhood to help raise your sister. Now you're working to put yourself through school and volunteering your professional photography skills to help families of children with leukemia. *And* you just donated blood."

"Thanks, Saint Lautner." I grab his face and kiss him soundly on his lips. "Now, let's get this over with."

He stands and holds out his hand. "You're fine."

Okay—

I stand and Lautner gives me the see-I-told-you-so look. Then, with little warning, my hearing goes, my head is dizzy, and the lights fade. I'm out.

————

"Now I just feel like crap," Lautner says, setting out our lunch on the blanket at what I'm officially calling "our beach." "I'm still amazed that you fainted. Are you sure you ate breakfast?"

I lie on my back and flip my sunglasses down over my eyes. "It's no big deal. And yes, I ate breakfast. I can't believe you're still here. Seriously, I'm a disaster. I'm noncommittal. I'm a fainter. I'm a terrible drunk. And I advertised my menstrual cycle to you after knowing you for only five days. *Five days!* You should have been yelling 'crazy bitch' and running for the hills."

He hands me my sandwich and shakes his head. "I wouldn't trade a single second of your 'crazy' for a lifetime of sanity."

I take a bite of my sandwich and watch the waves crash into the shore. Lautner says the most incredible things with the casualness of ordering a coffee.

"What if you never find crazy again?" I glance over at him.

"What if a complete stranger never jumps into your pool naked?" He takes a bite of his sandwich.

I giggle. "What if you never get another drunken striptease?"

Now he laughs. "What if you never eat another cherry-almond galette?"

I can't help but smile, looking to the infinity of the ocean. *What if I never see the world in blue irises?*

"Yeah ... what if ..." I whisper.

We eat the rest of our lunch to the soothing white noise of the breaking waves. There are so many unspoken words between us. Sharing them will not change anything, it will only cause more pain. I believe the emotions between us are magnified because they are so new. Time will fade old memories and new ones will replace them. I never imagined not feeling the pain of my mom's death weighing heavy on my heart, but it doesn't anymore. There is and always will be an emptiness inside me that will never be filled, but it doesn't hurt. There's a layer of scar tissue that has numbed the pain. Lautner is leaving his own mark on my heart. It too will become a painless reminder of a special person who passed through my life.

He pulls me between his legs and I rest my back against his chest. "Had you not gotten injured would you still be playing?" I ask, focusing on his scar.

"I don't know ... maybe."

"Do you ever regret not continuing to play? I mean, a lot of players get injured but continue playing."

He folds his arms around me and kisses the top of my head. "Sometimes when I go to games or watch it on TV I miss it, but I can't say I regret it. A lot of people thought I was scared to play even after my injury healed, but the truth is I was more scared to not play. It was the one thing I was really good at and I loved playing. It was all I knew."

"How'd you know you were making the right decision?"

"I didn't ... I still don't. It's hard to let go of what you love and it's even harder to move on. But not looking back is the greatest challenge." He kisses my head, again. The strongest arms I have ever known embrace me—all of me. He speaks to me with touch and holds me in the space between words.

If this isn't love, then it doesn't exist.

We walk a ways up the beach holding hands and sharing the happier moments of our childhoods. No surprise, a lot of Lautner's childhood revolved around sports. He played just about every sport but also taught himself how to play the guitar. Just when I thought Lautner couldn't possibly get any hotter, he had to add sexy hunk with a guitar to my already scorching hot visual of him that I carry around in my head.

"I expect a private performance before I leave."

He slides his arm around my shoulders and pulls me into his side. "I'll have to check my concert schedule."

I pinch his hard glutes. "Okay, tell me more. Were you the perfect boy scout—polite, charming, kind?"

He's quiet so I'm not sure he heard me. Glancing sideways, I notice him gritting his teeth, lips pressed tight.

He clears his throat. "Not all the time. Looking back, I'd have to say there were a few things I did or participated in that might not look good on a résumé."

My favorite eyes are avoiding me, making him look the guilty part. "Such as?"

"In the eighth grade my friends and I started a club." He pauses.

"What kind of club?"

The chuckle that escapes him suggests it wasn't a chess club.

"A jock club. The treehouse in my backyard was our clubhouse. Although, we were really too big by that age to be squeezing into that thing. It's a miracle it didn't crash to the ground under our weight. Anyway, we discussed important *sports* matters."

"Oh, I get it. That was the age you and your buddies thought you needed to start wearing protective gear—jocks and cups. But you didn't have the courage to ask your parents to buy them, so you got together everyday after school and whittled little penis cups out of driftwood and finger-knitted jockstraps out of scrap yarn you stole from your mom's sewing room—" I squeal as he grabs me and tosses me over his shoulder potato-sack style.

"*Little penis cups?*" He growls, smacking my barely-covered ass.

"Stop! Let me down!"

Inch by agonizing inch, he lets my body slide down the front of his, stopping when our eyes meet. I'm waiting for his lips to torment mine or a snarky comment back, but he's just shaking his head with a tight grin.

I'm dropped to my feet.

"As I was saying..." he interlaces our fingers and pulls me back in the direction of our stuff "...our Jock Club discussed girls. Specifically those who planned on trying out for freshman cheerleading. We picked our favorite candidates based on looks, popularity, and bounceability."

"Bounceability? As in how high they could jump?"

He smiles and it's a big one, but I can't define it.

"As in boob size."

Never mind. I just defined it. It's an I-was-a-horny-perverted-teenager-and-I'm-still-kind-of-proud-of-it smile.

"We called our rating system The Bounce Factor. A *five* causing black eyes and a *one* not even requiring a training bra."

So much for Saint Lautner.

I don't want to laugh—degrading women, making young

girls self conscious, and all that—but I can't hold it in. It's too damn funny.

"You're laughing?" he says in a slow voice filled with incredulity.

"I know … I know, I should be offended." I shake my head and catch my breath. "Maybe if I hadn't been such a tomboy at that age I would be more offended. If there's such a thing as the opposite of a cheerleader, then that was me."

Lautner tugs at my ponytail. "Do tell, it's my turn to get the dirt on you."

"*Dirt* is right. During my short-haired tomboy phase, I had an obsession with digging through the dirt behind our house. I'm pretty sure *Fear Factor* stole my idea a year later. A few kids in the neighborhood, mostly boys, and I played our own version. I've eaten one of about every species of bug there is in Northern Illinois, along with a few rabbit turds and a frog's eye."

His scrunched face is hilarious.

I nod, pointing a finger at my mouth. "Oh yeah, buddy. That's right. You've kissed this mouth—turds, frog eyes, and insects."

"Nasty … there's no other word." He closes his eyes and does a quick skin-crawling shiver.

We've reached our beach area again.

"We should get back. I have some research to do and your favorite dog is going to want dinner." Lautner pulls me into his chest. The water foams around our feet.

"A quick dip first?" I suck my bottom lip between my teeth and make a pathetic attempt at puppy dog eyes.

"It's a little cooler today. You're going to be cold when we get out."

I shrug and pull him toward the water.

"Eek!" I squeal as the cool tide flows over my shoulders. Lautner pulls me into him and we share a deep kiss.

"Turds, frog eyes, and insects," I mumble against his lips.

"Shut up."

He grabs my ass and I wrap my legs around him. The feel of his arousal beneath his trunks has me wanting more. With adept thumbs, he eases the cups of my top over my breasts, his palms rubbing over my nipples. This is by far the sexiest thing I have ever done. My fear is that Lautner's analytical brain is going to kick in and steal the moment. I squeeze him tight, working myself against his cock in hopes of preventing the invasion of any rational thinking on his part or mine. He walks us closer to the beach, and I feel a pang of disappointment as he sets me down in water up to my knees. I start to cover my breasts back up.

"Uh, uh, uh ..." He shakes his head and I want to scream with elation as I watch him inch his swim trunks down just past his hips. Falling to his knees in the shallow water, he sits back on his heels and tugs me onto his lap. There's no one around, but the fact that someone could appear over the grassy knoll has me feeling naughty. The moment is sexy and exhilarating.

His mouth covers one breast and his hand kneads the other. Clutching his hair, I tug him closer, moving one hand down to his erection and stroking it until he moans against my breast. My breath catches as he bites my nipple. Reaching between us, he pulls my bottoms to the side. I dig my feet in the sand and push up just enough to maneuver his firm cock between my legs, sinking onto him.

"Oh God." As he fills me, I'm transported to a whole new level of paradise.

His hands grip my hips and his mouth takes mine as I

begin to move up and down on him. For a slight moment my mind wanders to sharks that are probably making their way closer to shore with dusk approaching.

"Ahh!" I yell as Lautner thrusts up into me. Visions of sharks vanish in an instant as I start to feel the slow building of my orgasm. We're both working up to a fast pace as water sloshes against my back.

"Harder!" I cry, throwing my head back, feeling so close.

"Christ, Sydney!" He growls with one final surge into me and we both climax at the same time.

Our hips make a few slow deep circles riding out every last sensation. I feel the ocean in me and all around me. His head collapses against my chest, and I rest my cheek on the top of his head.

"That was ..." I breathe out in labored exhaustion.

"Fucking amazing," Lautner finishes.

"So much for avoiding strenuous exercise." I laugh and he does too.

I FALL asleep on the way home to the soothing strokes of Lautner's fingertips along my forearm.

"I'll be right back, baby," he whispers. I hear his door close and my eyes fight to open. I don't recognize where we are, but it looks like the parking lot of an apartment building. Lautner goes in the bottom door, but I lose him from there. He returns carrying a duffle bag in one hand and a messenger bag slung over his shoulder.

"What are you doing?" I ask as he opens the driver's door.

"Staying with you until you leave. I packed enough for a

few nights anyway." He buckles up and backs out. "I'm still not going to be able to see you that much with my long hours, but even just crawling in bed with your sleeping body is more than I've had this past week."

I'm thrilled, completely elated.

"Unless you don't want me to stay?" he questions as we pull out of the parking lot.

I shrug. "Whatever. You're not the worst thing to wake up to. I suppose you can stay ... if you want."

"You suck at nonchalance, baby. But that's okay. I'll play it your way. Oh please, Sydney. Let me stay with you and put my mouth where you like it best until you're screaming my name, making Swarley howl, and the neighbors alert the authorities."

I punch him in the arm. "Jeez, I can't believe I fell for the whole, blood donating-child loving-marine life preservation-ist-flower sending act. I thought you were a good guy. But now I think you're just like every other arrogant guy." I cross my arms over my chest.

"I am a good guy ... with a bad boy side too. You know you love it."

I really do, but I'll be damned if I ever openly admit it. There's nothing sexier than a guy who thinks he has something to prove.

Chapter Eleven

June 25th, 2010

PURE BLISS. There's just no other way to describe the past week. Lautner has been working long hours, but he always ends up next to me in bed. I know he's silently counting down the days, as am I. We no longer speak of *the end*, but the air around us keeps getting thicker making it harder to breathe as each day passes. It doesn't matter what insane hour Lautner arrives. We take each other in a frenzied passion. Words are not needed. The inevitable is felt in bruising kisses, desperate hands, insatiable stamina, pleading moans, and the way our bodies stay entwined for hours.

Seven days. I've thought about staying—a lot. It's really all I've been thinking about. But at twenty-three I still can't choose a handbag without making a dozen trips to the mall. Why the hell would it make sense for me to think I've found the love of my life in less than a month?

That's easy. He sucks me in, bleeds my sanity, arrests my

heart, and bares my soul. And that's just with his eyes. *Fucking Medusa eyes.*

There's a knock at the door and Swarley goes crazy. His boredom with me is apparent, and he can't help the exuberance he feels at the prospect of someone—anyone—more interesting than me walking through the front door. Lautner has been spoiling him with treats from the dog bakery. I can't complain. When Swarley's preoccupied with a delectable goodie, he gives us more privacy. It doesn't bother Lautner at all, but Swarley sits by the bed and cries when we're having sex. He's made me lose two impending orgasms in the past week. Both of which Lautner heroically chased after and captured for me after kicking Swarley out of the bedroom. I want to believe Lautner's ability to make me come in under ten seconds is due to his extensive studies in human anatomy and not years of sexual experience.

Dream on, Syd! He was a freakin' Heisman Trophy candidate.

"Oh my God! What are you doing here?" I squeal in shock embracing Avery.

She attempts to hug me back with her huge purse hanging from one shoulder and an overnight tote slung over the other. "Surprise!"

"Why didn't you call?" I ask, stepping back so she can come in.

"Kinda would have ruined the surprise. Don't you think? Yeah, yeah, I see you Swarley." She drops her bags and bends down to pet the pestering pooch.

"How sweet, you came to say goodbye again before I leave next week." My voice is nauseously sweet and I'm working overtime batting my lashes.

Avery squints at me then rolls her eyes. "Sure, that too."

"Caden's got you all tied up, huh?"

She smirks. "Figuratively and literally."

"TMI ... thanks for the visual." I grunt and walk to the kitchen. "Does he know you're here, or are you going to just show up at *his* door too?"

"Bingo. I found a job in San Francisco, Sam. I haven't taken it yet, but I think after this weekend I just might."

"What happened to 'I will die in L.A.?'"

"What can I say? I've grown up." She pulls her shoulders back like better posture will drive home her point.

"You're twenty-one. Six months ago you were carrying around a fake ID, but now you've *grown up*?"

"So how's Dr. Sexy?"

"Nice diversion, Ave. Dr. Sullivan is fine."

I hand her a glass of iced tea. "Fine or *fine*?"

The shit-eating grin I'm trying to hide wins over. "*Fine* ... very, very F. I. N. E."

"I bet he's a fucking machine in bed. Am I right?"

"Avery! Watch your mouth. I thought you were here to see Caden?"

She laughs. "I am. But Jesus, Sam. Lautner is an Adonis and those eyes ..."

"Fucking Medusa eyes," I finish with a blank stare into my glass.

Avery giggles. "Nice description."

"Mmm ... so when are you going to surprise Caden?"

"Soon. He only works until noon on Fridays. But I wanted to see you first."

"Oh really?" I question in disbelief.

"*Really.*" She stands and saunters into the foyer, grabs her bag, and heads upstairs. "And I need to freshen up and change into something sexier after my long drive."

Of course she does.

———

It's a picturesque Friday so I pack up my new four-legged friend for a drive to take some photos. Redwoods from every possible angle. I stick to the flora because Swarley is not a photographer's best asset when trying to capture wildlife. I love playing with the light and different filters. It's easy to get lost in the lens when I'm surrounded by such marvels of nature.

I take a picture with my phone of me hugging a tree and send it to Lautner. He's a little treehuggerish so I think he'll get it.

> **Thinking of you!**

After loading up Swarley and my camera bag "In Your Eyes" chimes. "Hey, you didn't have to call me."

"I'm grabbing a quick lunch. I like the picture and the naughty innuendo." Lautner's voice is low and sexy.

"Naughty innuendo? What are you talking about? It meant treehugger."

He chuckles. "Yeah, I suppose it could mean that too, but I like my interpretation better."

"Which is?" I fasten my seat belt and start the car.

"You miss my *big wood.*"

"Oh my God! And they let you work with children? You're such a pervert."

"So you don't miss my big wood?"

"Wha—where are you? Are people hearing you? I'm embarrassed for you!" I sigh.

"Relax, I'm tucked back in the corner of the cafeteria by myself. I have about five minutes so let's continue. What are you wearing?"

"What do you mean what am I—jeez, I am not having phone sex with you while you're at work and I'm in the car with Swarley."

"Suit yourself, but just remember, you started it, Syd."

"Ugh! I'm hanging up now, bye."

"Sydney?"

"Yeah?"

There's a pause of silence. "I'm going to miss you."

Kill me now.

"I'll see you later," I whisper and press *End.*

It's late afternoon, I have my photo fix for the day, and Swarley is ready for a nap. Pulling into the drive, I'm surprised to see Avery's white Honda Pilot. I proceed with caution into the house, hoping I don't come across a naked porn film by the pool starring her and Caden. I'm relieved when I see Ave in a lounge chair by the pool—clothed. Something is off. She's not in her suit and she's drinking beer which she only drinks when she's pissed because it won't cause her to vomit quite so quick.

"Hey, Ave." The words ease out of my mouth as I walk down the deck stairs. Her large black sunglasses cover most of her face, but they don't hide the tears on her cheeks or her runny nose that occasionally sniffles.

"I'm so stupid," she sobs.

I sit at the foot of the chair and squeeze her hand. "What happened?"

"Fucking Caden happened, or more like Caden fucking." She swipes the tears on her cheeks and sniffles again.

"I don't understand."

"I—I showed up and—he—he was screwing some oth—other girl!" Her body shakes with each word and I'm hurting so bad for her.

The default mother in me stands at full attention and I'm ready to go to war for my baby sister. Kick ass now, take names later.

"What did he say?"

"He said he thought we were just having some fun. God! I can't believe I fell for the nice guy act. At least with most guys I know they're just a one night stand. They don't call and text and stay the whole fucking weekend at my place! They don't tell me about their family and introduce me to the little brother with Down syndrome. They don't tell me that they miss me and that they wished I lived closer."

I don't know what to say. I'm livid and ready to drive over to Caden's and rip his balls off and pulverize them with a pair of four inch stiletto heels.

"I'll deal with this." A surge of angry heat burns my skin.

"No, Sam. He's obviously not worth it." Avery removes her glasses and my heart clenches at the sight of her red swollen eyes.

I've never seen Avery this broken over a guy—ever. She took a chance and had her heart trampled. I know she's missing our mom right now. Dad wouldn't know what to say and most likely would give her some condescending sermon that would only make her feel worse. Not Mom. No matter what she'd think of Avery's cavalier lifestyle, she would comfort her baby. Mom was always unconditional with her love.

"Then what can I do for you, Ave?" I scoot closer and pull her into my arms.

"Just remind me that guys are only good for sex. I'm

never making that mistake again. In fact ..." She releases me and sits back while wiping her eyes and sucking in a deep breath. "Nice guys are officially off my list. I'm sticking to the bad boys. With them, what you see is what you get."

"Ave, not all guys are like Caden. You just need to slow things down in the future. Don't get caught up in the whirl-wind of romance and fairytales that don't exist."

"Except for you. Lautner would never do this to you."

My gut tells me that she's right, but it doesn't matter. I'm not getting ready to rearrange my life to be with him. I'm getting ready to say goodbye.

"Maybe ... but it's irrelevant. In another week I'm going to be leaving for Paris, my dream destination, and you're going to be back in L.A. leaving Caden and all his shit behind."

"The Montgomery girls are going to be sassy, sexy, and single again," she declares with a confident, resolute nod.

I laugh in spite of the pain that I won't let Avery see. "Watch out world!"

I TREAT Avery to dinner out and let her drown her residual sorrows in her favorite Riesling. Between the wine and her long day of complete mental exhaustion, she crashes in the guest room as soon as we get home. Swarley keeps me company on the bed as I sort through all the photos I took earlier today. He jumps from the bed startling me, and I look up to see my sexy doctor in a sky blue T-shirt and faded jeans standing in the doorway. Lautner gives Swarley his daily treat, which he immediately trots off with downstairs.

"Hey," I say with a slight grin. My emotions have been dampened by today's events.

He sits beside me on the bed and presses his lips to mine. I want to talk to him about Caden and Avery, but I need this first. His tongue slides between my lips and mine greets his with fervor. I frame his face with my palms and hmm a soft appreciative moan. Lavishing my jaw and neck with open-mouthed kisses, he closes my laptop and slides it off my lap.

"Lautner, wait ... We need to talk."

His hands slide up my bare legs. Muscles tense under the touch of his thumbs circling near the apex of my inner thighs.

"I am. Don't you hear what I'm trying to say?" he mumbles against my neck.

Lautner owns me ... or at least my body. Thoughts dissolve. Sensations surrender. The rest of the world ceases to exist.

"I do ... and dear God, I love the way you say it, but—"

He pauses, leaving his thumbs a breath away from the meltdown button to my brain.

Blue irises shine and it takes me a moment to catch my breath.

"Have you talked to Caden today?"

Lautner sits back and the loss of his touch is my answer.

"He feels like shit."

I claw my hands into the mattress to scoot up straighter then cross my arms over my chest. His eyes fall to my arms as he chews the corner of his lower lip.

"Well, poor Caden. Maybe I should send him some flowers tomorrow to cheer him up. Remind me to do that after I send my sister and her crushed heart back to L.A. in the morning." My intention is not to take out my anger on

Lautner, but I can't keep the sarcasm from dripping off my words.

"Syd, he had no idea she was coming to visit this weekend."

"That's not the fucking point!" I yell with little restraint.

"Jesus, Sydney!" He holds his palms up in surrender.

I let out a long breath. "I'm sorry. I'm just so pissed off right now. Avery hasn't looked this broken since our mom died."

He grimaces. "I'm not trying to sound insensitive, but this *is* Avery we're talking about."

"What's that supposed to mean?"

"I'm just saying she's kind of a ..." He stops short and watches me.

I know he's trying to gauge me like a trapped animal.

"She's kind of what?" I raise my eyebrows.

He runs his hands through his hair and sighs with a slight shake of his head. "Nothing. Listen I'm sorr—"

"No! Say it!"

"Jeez, Syd!" He groans in exasperation. "Your sister was all over me two seconds after we were introduced. Then you insisted I take you to breakfast so you could warn me that she was going to 'pounce' on Caden. You said she was 'flirtatious' and still 'sowing wild oats.' So now Caden's somehow the bad guy for not throwing a ring on her finger and promising forever?"

"She's a human being, Lautner! Nobody deserves to walk in and see the person they love screwing someone else."

"*Love?* Are you serious? Did she tell him that she loves him? Did he profess his love to her? Did they agree to be in a committed relationship?"

"That's not the point." I look away from him.

He stands and puts his hands on his hips. "Then, please, enlighten me. What *is* the point?"

"He drove down to L.A. to spend the weekend with her. He shared personal information with her. He introduced her to Brayden. He was putting on quite the 'nice guy' act."

"Caden is a nice guy! It's not an act. The poor guy was dumped by his fiancée and maybe he's sowing a few of his own wild oats before he risks getting his fucking heart ripped from his chest again. He wasn't trying to rub it in her nose. She should have called."

I pull my knees to my chest, needing an extra shield. We're three feet apart but he's standing over me like a tower, and his stance is just as defensive as mine. The voice of reason whispers something in the back of my mind, but I can't hear it over my ruffled ego screaming in my ears.

"She was offered a job in San Francisco. A job that she was going to accept to be closer to Caden. Avery wasn't spying on him or trying to catch him in the act. She was trying to surprise him. Like 'Surprise! Remember me? The girl you've been screwing the past couple weeks. The girl who is willing to give up her dream of living in L.A. to be closer to you.'"

Lautner shrugs and shakes his head. "I'm sorry, Syd. I know you want me to be mad at him. But I can't. I get it. Avery's your sister, but Caden is the closest thing I have to a brother. Besides this isn't about *us*."

"You're right. This isn't about us. There is no *us* because I'm leaving next week. Maybe you should go screw some random girl tonight and plead innocence because you didn't throw a ring on *my* finger and promise *me* forever."

"You're being ridiculous," he mumbles while scrubbing his hands over his face.

"You're being condescending," I retort.

"Ugh! I'm not being condescending. Do you even know what that means?"

"Yes! I know what it means and you just did it again!" I yell.

Standing, I brush past him to open the bedroom door. It's taking everything I have to hold down my dinner. The knot in my stomach, the lump in my throat, the barbed wire around my heart ... it's all too much. He doesn't move and neither do I.

"Just leave." I sigh in exhaustion.

"I'm not leaving and I'm not going to screw some random girl." He shrugs off his shirt then removes his jeans before slipping into bed.

He's so damn stubborn and frustrating. I stomp over to the bed and grab my computer. Before I can escape he grabs my arms, pulling me inches from his face. I swallow and divert my eyes.

"Look at me, Sydney."

I shake my head.

"I love you."

"Just STOP!" I yell.

He releases my arms with a look of defeat. I go to Avery's room, shutting and locking the door behind me.

———

June 26th, 2010

THANK YOU, Swarley. The one morning I need you to sleep in and not cry outside the door is the one morning you compose the longest freaking "feed me" solo ever.

Avery is facedown but still breathing. She had enough alcohol in her body to sleep through the fight I had with Lautner *and* my sobs that eventually wore me out and lulled me into the most restless sleep ever. I'm emotionally drained and physically exhausted. It's not going to be a good day.

I tiptoe down the hall and peek into my room. Lautner is gone. I wonder if he stayed or left last night. Swarley is glued to me, tail wagging and smiling. Yes, he's actually smiling. At least one of us is going to have a good day.

Entering the kitchen, I'm greeted by a very large bouquet of flowers, two hot drink cups, and my favorite bakery sack. I get the pathetic pooch his breakfast and read the card with the flowers.

I love you. I love you. I love you. I love you … only you … always you … forever you.

I hate him more everyday. He has nothing to lose and everything to gain by saying those three words. I, on the other hand, have nothing to gain and everything to lose.

When my dad woke me up to tell me that hospice called and said my mom died, I didn't want to believe it. And I didn't, not until I saw her body in the open casket. Sometimes I think if I hadn't seen her there, a part of me would have forever believed she wasn't really gone.

As much as I don't want to live my life with such childish mentality, I can't help it. I still believe in the creative power of words. So if I don't say the three words I desperately want to say to Lautner, then maybe they won't be true. For some reason holding them back feels like keeping just enough of myself that he can't completely consume me, break me, and take away my dreams. However, I think he knows he can. Everyday he makes another crack in my resolve.

"Dear God. More flowers?" Avery's raspy voice startles me.

She looks like hell and that's not an easy task for her.

"Coffee?" I ask, taking off the lids to the cups and claiming my tea first.

"Yes, definitely coffee," she replies taking the cup and sitting on the barstool. "Mmm, good, but not so hot anymore."

I sip my lukewarm latte. "I think he was probably at the bakery when they opened the doors. I know he has to be at the hospital pretty early."

"Why'd you come into my room?" she asks.

I furrow my brow in confusion. "How'd you know I came in last night? Did you wake up in the middle of the night?"

"Nope. Your computer is on the nightstand. So spill. What happened?"

Grabbing a galette out of the bag, I tear off chunks to feed my nervous frustration. "I confronted him about Caden."

Avery sets her coffee down and rests her folded arms on the counter. "And?"

"*And* he acted like it wasn't Caden's fault. I got my back up, he got his up, and we argued until he tried to change the topic to *us*, which I then proceeded to tell him there is no *us*."

She gives me a tight, pained smile. "Thanks for sticking up for me, Sam. But now I feel like I've split the two of you up."

"Ridiculous," I mumble with half the galette shoved into my mouth. I finish chewing and take a drink.

"I'm leaving in less than a week. We both knew our..." I air quote "...*relationship* had nowhere to go. It was over before it ever started. And I didn't just stick up for you because you're my sister. I did it because Caden was being a complete ass. He took advantage of your lack of communication. He used it as an excuse to sleep around. Sometimes feelings are implied without ever having to say the words—"

I have just rendered myself speechless with my own damn words.

"You amaze me, Sam. No matter how low I sink, how many one night stands I have, you always see the good in me and never hold my indiscretions against me."

I shrug. "Nobody is doomed. Not even my skanky sister from L.A."

"There she is. Welcome back." Avery laughs as she grabs the card from Lautner off the table. Holding it up I can see the WTF look on her face.

"Don't ask," I deadpan.

"Oh snap!" She looks up after reading it.

I bust out laughing. "*Oh snap?* I look around. "Did Dad just walk in or something?"

Avery giggles. "You're right. Fuck me sideways. This is some seriously deep shit!"

I roll my eyes. "You could use a good preachin', that's for sure"

"Sydney ..." She draws out my name and furrows her brow.

Tears sting my eyes and all the humor is sucked out of the room. "Sydney" coming from Avery means it's time to be serious, but I don't want to be serious.

I grab the card from her hand. "It's nothing. He just feels bad about fighting last night so he's overcompensating. I'm sure he was tired and not even thinking about what he was writing."

"*I love you .... only you ... always you ... forever you.* Once again you amaze me. I walk in on my dream guy screwing some other girl and you get *this?*" She gestures to the flowers, drinks, pastry bag, and note. "You won the goddamn lottery of eligible guys and you're ripping up the winning ticket! It doesn't make sense."

My jaw is clenched. I know damn well that Lautner isn't *a* catch, he's *the* catch. But it doesn't change the circumstances. It's like finding your favorite five-hundred dollar shoes are half-off but you don't have ten dollars in the bank. It's the perfect opportunity at the wrong time. It is what it is.

"Mom—"

"Don't!" she interrupts. "Don't you dare give me some spiel about making Mom proud or living the life she never had. I hate it when you make it sound like her life was a disappointment. It makes me feel like she regretted having us. Is that what you think we were to her? Mistakes?"

"No! That's not my point!" My muscles steel in defense. "I hate when you try to make me feel guilty for being ambitious."

"Fine! Be ambitious. Spend the rest of your life going to school and finding the perfect job. Wait until you're forty to get married and start a family, but do it for you. Don't do it for Mom. Don't do it because you think that's what she would have wanted you to do. Don't do it because you think she missed out on following her own dreams."

I rest my hands flat on the counter and take a slow breath. "I'm flying to Paris next week, for me. I'm going to grad school for me. These are my dreams. Mom's dead. It's too late to make her proud." The words taste like acid in my mouth.

"I hope so. Because you're officially risking everything."

"Go big or go home," I reply with a hint of snide in my voice.

"Yeah, well, yesterday I went big and today I'm going home in worse shape than when I left. Worth it? Hell no." Avery throws her arms in the air.

I laugh because this conversation is diving into philosophical depths that neither one of us are adept to deal with. "So ... is that supposed to relate to Lautner or my future. It's a risk either way. But I don't think my dream job is going to disappoint me. I think your point proves that *guys* are unpredictable and not worth the risk."

Avery stands and stretches with a big yawn. "Guys aren't worth the risk, but love is." She walks toward the stairs.

"I never said I love Lautner."

"You never said you didn't."

―――――

AVERY TAKES a walk with me and Swarley then leaves after lunch. We both apologize for our emotional outbursts and chalk it up to men messing with our heads. Lautner has frayed my nerves. I feel on edge and ready to attack if the wind brushes my skin. It's insane, but I envy Avery's circumstances. I'm sure seeing Caden with another girl was crushing, but making the decision to leave him was easy. Walking away from Lautner, no matter how hard I try to make him out to be a bad guy, is not going to be easy.

I head out to the pool and my phone rings the moment I sit down.

"Hey, Elizabeth," I answer.

"Hi, Sydney. How are things going?"

"Good." I stop short of mentioning Swarley is off his normal diet and sleeping schedule. Nor do I mention that he sleeps in their bed, a bed I've been having hot sex in for the past three weeks and the sheets smell like Lautner, me, and sex.

"Oh, that's great. Say ... we're going to be coming home early."

"Really? How early?"

"Tomorrow. Trevor got food poisoning and has been miserable for the past three days. He's feeling better now, but he's exhausted and wants to go home."

"Oh jeez, that sucks. There's nothing like being sick a million miles from home. Been there, done that."

"Yeah, he's kind of a germaphobe so hugging the hotel toilet and lying on the bathroom floor about killed him."

I laugh thinking of Trevor's OCD. Even his look says OCD with his head shaved for optimal cleanliness and his clothes perfectly pressed, tucked in tight, and buttoned to the top. Elizabeth can downplay it and call him a germaphobe, but I've seen him in true form. The thought paralyzes me with anxiety. I have less than twenty-four hours to make this place fit for their return. *Not good!*

"So when will you arrive? And do you need me to pick you up from the airport?"

"Not until 9:15 p.m., and no, we've arranged transportation home."

"Okay then, I'll just see you tomorrow night."

"Bye, Sydney."

"Bye."

The adrenaline kicks in and my day in the sun has officially been canceled.

"You're on your own, Swarley. I've got some major cleaning to do."

My mental pen starts making a list of everything that needs to be done: laundry, bathrooms, dusting, sweeping, mow the lawn, clean the dog hair out of the back of Trevor's Escalade, and replenish some of the food and alcohol I consumed. Just as I make it to the laundry room with the sexed-up sheets, I receive a text.

> You're welcome for breakfast. I'm sure I
> just missed your "thank you" text :)
> Because there's no way you could possibly
> still be upset about last night. Right?

Am I still upset about last night? I don't know. I can't think about that right now. There's too much to do. I'll deal with Lautner later.

> Thank you.

I stare at the message and contemplate elaborating, but I don't know what I should say so I just send the two words.

Chapter Twelve

June 27th, 2010

TWELVE HOURS ... ticktock. I'm up and Swarley's had his walk and breakfast. My uniform for the day is old denim short shorts, a black tank top, and yellow rubber gloves. Laundry is done—their linens and my clothes. Elizabeth and Trevor have a cleaning lady who comes every two weeks, but I told them I would take care of the cleaning while they were gone. Now, I'm wishing I wouldn't have made that offer.

It's a big ass house, or at least it seems big when it's time to clean everything. It took me two hours to dust everything yesterday. Let me rephrase. It took me two hours to dust to Trevor's perfectionistic expectations. The wide, wood trim work is beautiful but a nightmare to dust. I might have to skip lunch and bathroom breaks, but I think I can have everything whipped into shape by the time they get home tonight.

The doorbell chimes while I'm on my knees scrubbing the toilet in the upstairs hall bathroom. With an exasperated huff, I climb to my feet and go downstairs. The last person I need to see is standing in front of the daylight window melting my panties with his huge grin. I peel the glove off my right hand and open the door.

"Hey, beautiful."

I roll my eyes. "Now you're just being stupid. Look at me." I hold out my arms so he can get a good look at my old clothes, makeup-less face, and hair pulled into a messy ponytail high on the back of my head.

"I graduated top of my class in medical school. I assure you I'm not stupid." His tongue lazily grazes his bottom lip while his fucking Medusa eyes rake over my entire body. He steps forward and I take a step back.

"Don't you have to be at the hospital today?"

He shakes his head just once. The lust in his eyes is predatory.

"Well, I'm busy so I'll call you later." I back up another step.

"Sydney ..." He grabs my gloved hand and pulls off the glove, dropping it to the floor.

"I don't have time—"

I'm in his arms tasting mint, smelling his aftershave, feeling large hands palm my ass lifting me off the ground.

I turn away from his kiss. Lips attack my neck.

"They—they're coming back—tonight. I have to clean." Unconvincing words come out with each labored breath.

Thunk.

My back hits the wall as my legs search for leverage around his hard body. His hands skim under my shirt until they find my breasts.

"God, Sydney. Where's your bra?" he moans against my neck along the sensitive skin behind my ear. He rocks his hips up and my breath hitches when the erection beneath his shorts rubs against the apex of my thighs.

"They're all clean—I—didn't want to—dirty them." I grab his hair and yank on it until his face is level with mine again.

A breath away, we just stare at each other. My full breasts are supported by his hands, thumbs brushing over my nipples. I force a deep swallow and wet my lips. Heavy eyes drowning from his touch.

He feathers his full lips over mine with calculated restraint. "I'm sorry about last night, baby." A soft kiss. "I wasn't trying to be insensitive." Another kiss to the corner of my mouth. "God, I love you so much." The gentle slide of his tongue along my top lip relaxes my jaw allowing him access to my mouth, and he doesn't hesitate.

Our bodies flow in sync: his pelvis moving up again and again; mine matching his, vying for a little more friction each time. He's sucking and licking my tongue, claiming all of my mouth. I resent every thread of clothing that's separating our naked bodies. His right hand moves from my breast to grip the top of my leg. He eases his thumb up my inner thigh sliding it under my shorts and dipping it under my very wet panties.

"Jesus, Sydney ... you're drenched," he moans into my mouth.

"Hmm ..." is all I can manage.

He slides his thumb in and out of my wet channel then circles it over my clitoris.

"Ahh ..." My head falls back against the wall with a *thump*.

A knock at the door stops us both. We're frozen in place, our desperate breaths the only sound slicing through the silence. We're hidden from the visual path of the daylight windows by mere inches.

"Expecting someone?" Lautner whispers with one hand still on my breast and the other planted firmly on my leg, thumb still pressed to my core.

My eyes bug out as I shake my head. Then I remember the call I made yesterday and blow out a frustrated sigh.

"Shit!" I whisper.

Lautner raises one curious brow.

"It's Dane."

I'm quickly dropped to my feet. I adjust my top and shorts while Lautner draws in a controlled breath.

"Dane?"

I walk toward the door. "Yes, Dane."

Opening the door, I pray my face is not painted as red with embarrassment as it feels.

"Hey, Dane!" I smile. "Thanks for doing this for me."

Swarley comes running for his Dane fix. He squats down to greet him, accepting his enthusiastic licking.

"Hello, Dane." Lautner's arms snake under mine as he pulls me back against him.

"Lautner." Dane looks up and smiles.

Both of their greetings are a few notes shy of friendly.

"What brings you by?" Lautner asks.

Dane stands but before he can answer, I speak up. "I called Dane last night to see if he'd be so kind as to take Swarley for a few hours so I can vacuum and mop the floors."

I grab Swarley's leash by the door and hand it to Dane.

"Well that's very kind of you." Lautner offers a tight-lipped grin.

"Yes, *it is.*" I wriggle out of Lautner's possessive grip, making sure to look back and give him a warning sneer.

"You must be part of the cleaning crew?" Dane directs at Lautner.

"Yes," I say with a big grin. "Lautner came by to mow the lawn and clean out the Escalade. Then he's going to skim the pool and check the chemicals."

Lautner purses his lips and squints his eyes at me with a slow nod. "Yeah ..." He draws out the word. "That's exactly why I'm here." He crosses one arm over his chest resting the elbow of his other arm on it. He makes a fist and brushes his thumb—*that thumb*—over his lips letting just the tip of his tongue out to graze it.

NOW, I'm red—bright red.

"So, I should be done in a couple of hours." I offer a nervous smile to Dane and pat Swarley on the side a few times.

"Sounds great! Don't work too hard." He turns and leads Swarley down the stairs.

I shut the door and Lautner is on me in a heartbeat, pinning me firmly against it with his body. His hands pressed to the door on either side of my head.

"Now ... where were we?" He breathes into my neck.

I shove his chest and duck under his arm. "No way! I—scratch that—*we* have to clean up. Elizabeth and Trevor will be home by ten." I grab my gloves from the floor. "The lawn-mower is in the garage. Do you need me to show you how to put gas in it and start it? Oh, and don't forget to pick up the dog shit first."

He swats me on the ass eliciting a *yelp* then shrugs off his shirt. My hungry eyes take in the firm chiseled terrain of his drool-worthy torso. His shirt hitting my face snaps me out of my daze.

"If you need me or this..." he gestures to his half-naked body and smirks "...we'll be outside."

Smart-ass!

———

Floors mopped and vacuumed. Bathrooms scrubbed. Kitchen restocked and cleaned. Then there is my heartbreakingly handsome hunk pretending to be the pool boy again. *Swoon!* The yard is perfectly manicured; Lautner may have a little OCD too. The Escalade is also detailed to perfection and free of Swarley hair.

"Stirring the water, *pool boy?*" I lower my voice to a soft seductive tone.

Lautner grins and winks. "Step back, ma'am. I'd hate for you to fall in. There's no lifeguard on duty, which means I'd have to rescue you .... naked, of course."

I walk up behind him and slide my hands around to his chest. "Mmm ... I've never wanted to be a damsel in distress so bad in my life." I kiss his back while scratching my nails along his rigid abs.

"Don't start something you can't finish," he warns while working the skimmer along the top of the water.

"Who said I can't finish?" My right hand starts to slide under the waistband of his shorts.

He grabs it and pulls it away. "One 'almost' today is enough. It's nearly five o'clock and I'm sure your favorite vet will be showing up with your favorite pooch any minute. If you insist on starting something now, I will not ... I repeat, *I will not* stop no matter who's watching us."

He releases my hand and I slip both of them into his front pockets. "Why, Dr. Sullivan, how brash of you."

"Last warning, Syd."

I pull my teasing hands out and smack him on the ass the same way he did to me earlier. "You're no fun." I saunter back to the house.

"Oh, I'm plenty fun ... just wait," he yells toward the house.

As if on cue, the front door opens and Swarley runs to me.

"Hey, Swarley. Did you have fun with Salt and Pepper?" I take off his leash and he runs out the dog door to see Lautner.

"Thanks, Dane. I really appreciate your help. We got a lot done. Hopefully Swarley won't mess up the floors too much in the next couple of hours."

Dane laughs. "I wouldn't worry about it. Swarley is their dog after all. Unless you lock him out of the house or kennel him, you're not going to be able to keep everything spotless."

"True," I concede.

"Well ..." Dane rocks back and forth on his feet.

"Yeah, well ... in case I don't get a chance to see you before I leave, it's been fun." I step toward him and give him a hug.

"Hey, if you're out west again visiting give me a call and we'll do lunch or something."

I nod as he opens the door.

"Enjoy Paris."

"I will, thanks!"

The door closes and I turn. Lautner is leaning against the wall by the kitchen with his hands shoved into the front pockets of his shorts.

"Stay with me."

I can't read his face or the tone of his voice. "Stay" is a little vague and I don't know how far to read into it.

"Stay?"

"Until you have to go." His eyes fall to the floor. He is so big and strong, yet in this moment, I see a sad vulnerability that tugs at my emotions, my heart, my resolve.

"That's only five days."

He nods. "I'll take all I can get."

"I'm sure Elizabeth and Trevor are expecting me to stay here until I leave. What am I supposed to tell them? 'Hey, I met this guy who swept me off my feet with flowers, pastries, and sweet tea. We've been having mind-blowing sex in your bed and oh, by the way, I'm going to stay with him instead of you until I leave for Paris.'"

He smirks. "Yeah, pretty much. Except the part about the pastries and sweet tea ... that's kind of personal. Don't you think?"

I'm struggling to keep a straight face. Elizabeth and Trevor blindsided me with their early return, now Lautner is doing it to me too.

"If I don't stay with them, then I should try and change my tickets and go home to see my dad."

He pushes off the wall and closes the distance between us. My heavy eyelids close as his hand caresses my cheek. His thumb whispers across my bottom lip.

"You don't want to stay with me? Or, you don't think you should?"

He still doesn't have a shirt on, and I swear I can feel the heat radiating off his skin calling to me like the warmth of the sun. I lean in, wrapping my arms around him. Time is slipping away too fast. I should tell him that five days won't matter. I should go home and spend time with my dad. I should let the heartbreak happen so the healing can begin. I should ... I should ... I should. It's history repeating itself. The first day Lautner asked me to the beach my mind scrolled through all the reasons why I should not have gone, and yet I ignored every single one.

"I'll pack my stuff."

———

I PACK while Lautner feeds Swarley. The note I leave for Elizabeth and Trevor is brief but at least they won't worry about me. However, my dear Aunt Elizabeth won't let it slide. I expect a call from her first thing tomorrow demanding I tell her everything.

Welcome home. Hope Trevor is feeling better. Staying with a friend until I leave for Paris. Text me when you get this so I know you made it home safe, and Swarley will be fed in the morning. Love, Sydney

"This everything?" Lautner gestures to my two large suitcases, small carry-on, computer bag, and purse all stacked by the front door.

"Yep."

"I'll carry them out while you make sure the doors are locked and everything is shut off."

I nod and turn toward the kitchen to find Swarley.

"Hey, buddy." I squat down and he falls like a tree on his side, kicking his legs in the air. Swarley shows no shame when he thinks a belly rub is coming. "I'm leaving but I'll be back to say goodbye again in a few days. Remember, sleeping on the bed never happened so don't get me in trouble by putting so much as a paw on the duvet. Understood? And you're back on dog food. I know it sucks but it's the price you pay for a few weeks of paradise." I release an emotion laden sigh. "I'm giving up something pretty great too, so you're not alone."

"Ready?"

I jump at the sound of Lautner's deep voice. He's waiting at the threshold to the kitchen. Standing, I clear my throat.

"Yeah, I'm ready." I take a deep breath and mentally say goodbye to yet another adventure in housesitting.

After we pull out of the drive, Lautner breaks the silence that we've kept since walking out of the house. "Hungry?"

I laugh, wondering if he's been hearing my angry stomach growling. "Starving. But I look and feel pretty nasty after all that cleaning. There's no way I'm going anywhere to eat."

He hands me his phone with a number already on the screen. "Chinese takeout?"

I take his phone and smile. "Sounds perfect."

We beat the delivery guy to Lautner's by thirty seconds at best. It's my first time being inside his apartment.

"Eat then shower?" He takes the containers out of the bag.

"Definitely." I turn in a slow circle. "Your place is ... surprising." I look around the large open space filled with a charcoal upholstered sofa accessorized with amber red, white, and black throw pillows. A rectangular, white-top coffee table with black steel legs sits on a large black and white Persian rug. The rest of the floor is wide, dark planked wood. The walls are a light gray with framed abstract paintings and photographs.

"Surprising? How so?" he asks, holding up a bottle of beer.

I nod and we both sit on the couch to eat. "It's all very Crate & Barrel."

"You don't like Crate & Barrel?" He takes a long pull of his beer.

"I love it. I guess I imagined more of a bachelor pad. You know, old leather sofa, team logo bean bag chairs, a weight bench in the corner, a TV about ten times the size of the one on your wall, framed football jerseys, pinup girls ..."

Lautner busts out laughing. "You're describing my dorm room freshman year of undergrad. I've matured a bit since then."

Swallowing a bite of my vegetable fried rice, I wipe my mouth with a paper napkin. "Everything is clean too. Are you a neat freak?"

He shakes his head. "No. I just haven't been here much to mess anything up. I eat two, sometimes all three, meals at the hospital. I don't remember the last time I sat on this couch. When I get home I either go straight to bed or work on my computer at the counter. You'll see that my bed hasn't been made and there may even be some socks on the floor in my closet."

"No roommate?"

"Caden and I used to rent a house together, but then his fiancèe decided to move in too, and that's when I started looking for a place of my own."

"Three's a crowd?"

"Something like that." He shrugs.

"No live-in girlfriends of your own?" I'm entering into a

subject I'm not sure I really want to discuss, but I can't help my curiosity.

"Live-in? No. I've had a few that have attempted to move in."

"Attempted?" I cock my head to the side with a curious smirk.

"An outfit here, a toothbrush there, then a makeup bag and an extra pair of shoes ... all very much on the sly."

"How many girls are we talking about?"

Dammit! The words are out and I can't take them back.

"Syd, you're leaving me in five days? Does it matter?" His eyes drop to his plate.

The laid-back feeling to our conversation has shifted. My impending permanent departure is the constant elephant in the room. The "leaving me" comment stings a bit too.

I set my half-empty takeout box on the coffee table and take a swig of my beer.

"It doesn't. I—I'm sorry. I don't know why I asked." I stand and look around. "Where's the bathroom? I think I'll take a quick shower if that's okay?"

"Syd—"

Shaking my head, I hold my hand up. "Don't. It's fine. Really. I'm just going to shower."

His furrowed brow and slumped posture makes me angry with myself. I've put him in an awkward position all for nothing. Me and my stupid questions. I grab my smaller suitcase by the door and take it with me.

"First door on the right. Clean towels are on the shelves under the sink," he calls out.

"Thanks." I close the door and lean back against it. "What the hell are you doing, Sydney? Jeez, five freakin' days until you're on a plane and *now* you decide to ask about his past relationships." I look up and see the crazy girl in the mirror talking to herself—hair a mess, no makeup, utterly lost. Scanning the bathroom, I can't help but smile. Everything is clean, yet he could not have known that I would end up here tonight.

"Not a neat freak my ass."

I turn on the shower and strip down. There's a knock at the door. I grab a towel and frantically wrap it around myself.

"Uh ... yes?"

The door opens. "Are we good?" His voice is cautious. I expect a white flag to be waved.

I nod feeling stupid for walking off.

Lautner grins and steps inside shutting the door behind him. "Thought we could conserve water." He tugs on my towel pulling it away from me. "What's this? Shy tonight?"

I roll my eyes. "Not everyone is as confident as the ringleader of the *Jock Club*."

"President, not ringleader," he says with a cocky smirk as he pulls his shirt over his head.

"How would your club have rated me?"

He steps out of his shorts and briefs. Then brushing my hair off my shoulders he purses his lips and crosses his arms over his chest. "Well, I'd say—"

"Wait! You have to imagine me without these." I point to my breasts. "I didn't have these back then. I also didn't have long hair *and* remember I ate bugs and shit like that."

His hands shift to his hips as he shakes his head. "No boobs, Peter Pan hair, and cricket legs stuck between your teeth? You would not have made the cut."

My mouth drops open. "Pig!" I scowl and get in the shower.

His naked body is pressed to the back of mine before the first drops of water make it to my feet.

"Pig? You think I'm a pig?"

I try to wriggle out of his iron hold but a case of the giggles robs me of all strength. "You only want me for my body. That really hurts."

A loud laugh escapes his chest and fills the room. He turns me toward him. Grabbing my wrists, he places them on his chest. "What do you want me for?" A single brow raise says *pot calling the kettle black.*

He's a visual orgasm, an erotic work of art. I want to photograph him, paint him, and sculpt him. He is my muse.

"If I could take a part of you with me it would be those fucking Medusa eyes."

"*Fucking Medusa eyes?*" He chuckles. "They're just eyes."

"Not to me." I slide my hands up his chest and around his neck pulling him down to me. The water cascades over us, enveloping our bodies in intimacy and sensuality.

His hands skim over my curves—breasts, hips, backside. I fist his erection with slow strokes. I love the moan he releases into my mouth as our tongues dance. I love that I do this to him. I love the way he worships my body with tender appreciation. I love everything about this man.

"Sydney—" His head falls back as I slide down his body to my knees and take him in my mouth. "Jesus—" His breath catches and his stomach muscles go rigid. I can't take all of him in my mouth, but it doesn't seem to matter. His mouth goes slack, and his hands press against the shower wall. My gaze is fixed on his face. When his heavy lids crack open, I smile and circle my tongue over the head several times.

"Stop ... Sydney—"

I take him as deep as I can then pull back and quickly repeat, sucking and teasing my tongue over every inch of him. Releasing him, I lick my lips.

"Are you sure you want me to stop?"

I know he's coming undone before me, and I've never felt so sexy. His hooded eyes sear into me. He fists my hair and I think he's going to bring my mouth back to his pulsing erection, but he gently tugs upward until I stand.

Lautner's control has been taken to the breaking point. I'm hiked up his body and barely able to get my legs locked around his waist before he's driving into me. I cry out his name as the intrusion completely fills and stretches me. I need a minute to adjust, but he's not in a patient mood right now. My back is pressed against the wall and he's thrusting into me. My arms encircle his neck and I just hold on. His pace quickens, shoulders tense, and a warmness pours into me as he stills deep within me.

"Sydney!" His forehead drops to my shoulder and I'm rocking my hips into him.

"Please ... don't stop!" I'm so close, but not quite there.

He continues with slow deep strokes, sucking my nipple into his mouth.

"Don't stop, right the—there." I cling to him in desperation as he pushes me over the edge.

"Ahh ... oh God!" I yell, digging my nails into his back. I'm seeing stars and the flood of sensation is dizzying. "That was ..."

"Amazing ..." He sighs, gently trailing kisses from my ear to my lips.

I'm boneless. My legs are sore from clutching his waist, and I'm not sure if I can stand. He inches me to my feet. I keep my arms around his neck for support.

"Okay?" he questions with a smile that captures his blue pools of infinity.

I nod, releasing his neck, but my body slumps into his anyway.

He chuckles, but doesn't say anything. Kind hands work soap over my body and shampoo in my hair. Occasionally, our eyes meet and we share smiles born of complete adoration. It's beautiful and painful, Heaven and Hell, love and sorrow.

Chapter Thirteen

June 28th, 2010

"**W**AKE UP, BEAUTIFUL."

I crack one eye open just enough to see that it's still dark. I must be dreaming. There's no reason for me to rise before the sun.

"Sexy goddess hair ..."

I hear the whisper of his voice again.

"Perfect skin ..."

Lips ghosting across my lower back.

"What time is it?" My sleepy voice is laced with a bit of early morning whininess.

"Five-thirty," he whispers over my goose bump covered flesh. "Time for breakfast."

"I'm not hungry," I mumble, hiding my face in my pillow.

"Come to breakfast with me. You can sleep all day while I'm gone."

He slides his hands under my body and cradles me in his

arms. "I'm feeling greedy. I want every minute. You're lucky I let you sleep at all." He plants me into a seated position at the foot of the bed, turns on the closet light, and rummages through my suitcase.

"As I recall, you didn't. I think I finally passed out. Are you on Viagra or something?"

Lautner kneels in front of me and slips on my panties and shorts. Then he lifts me to my feet and pulls them the rest of the way up. I reluctantly fasten them.

"You're my Viagra," he whispers in my ear, nibbling my earlobe.

I lift my arms and he pulls my shirt down over me.

"Don't I need a bra?" I raise my eyes in question.

He steps back and looks at my chest. His hands cup my breasts, thumbs running over my nipples bringing them to embarrassing peaks.

"There. Perfect." He grins all too happy with himself.

I roll my eyes. "Pervert." Stepping past him, I grab a hair tie out of my purse and pull my messy locks into a ponytail. He smacks my ass and walks out of the bedroom. "I wasn't until I met you."

I follow him down the hall. "Me?"

He grabs his bag and keys. Opening the door for me, he sucks in his bottom lip and nods. "Mmm hmm, the things I want to do to you."

I hurry down the stairs to the exit because between last night's sex marathon, his comment, and that predatory look, I'm feeling like the stalked prey. The physical intensity between us over the past twenty-four hours has been off the charts and out of this world. We can't get close enough to each other. Last night it felt like he was trying to physically consume me with his entire body.

Lautner, always the gentleman, hurries past me to the car door, opening it for me.

"Chivalrous ... so chivalrous." I wink and hop in.

He leans in and kisses me. It's soft, slow, patient, and filled with something I just won't acknowledge.

Releasing my lips, he looks at me, as in, *really* looks at me. Fucking blue irises striping me to my very core.

"I love you."

Ouch!

Why do those three words cut so deep?

I swallow the lump of emotion in my throat. No matter how loud the words scream in my head ... and heart, I can't say them. Blinking to hold in the teary sentiment of the moment, all I can do is nod.

The sad smile on his face magnifies the pain. His gaze falters as the smile fades. He closes my door and we drive in silence to the café. We order our standard cherry-almond galettes—still warm—coffee for him, tea for me. The beautiful sunrise graces us as we sit by the window.

"Still glad you chose pediatrics?" I break the uncomfortable silence.

He sips his hot coffee. "Absolutely. The attending physicians I'm working with are great. You hear about the nightmares of the first year of residency, but so far I feel like part of the team. It's a lot to take in, but I love it. It's not crying kids all day or anything like that. I could have ten difficult patients, but the one that I make a connection with, the one whose trust I gain, makes everything else disappear."

Of course I love Lautner. If he hadn't already stolen my heart, locked it up, and thrown away the key, then those words all on their own would have done it. I'm either immeasurably ambitious or monumentally stupid for walking away from him.

I smile. "I could listen to you talk like that all day."

He looks at his watch. "I'd love nothing more than to spend the day with you, but ..."

I finish the last bite of my pastry and grab my purse and tea. "But you need to take care of some kids who need you."

Standing, he pulls me into his side and we walk out to his 4-Runner.

After taking me back to his apartment and giving me a key, he leaves me with a kiss that I will be feeling on my lips for the rest of the day.

———

I CALL ELIZABETH. After receiving her text last night, I know they made it home and she's dying to talk. A little after one o'clock, she picks me up from Lautner's and takes me to lunch. She's older than my dad by ten years, but she's very hip and open-minded. On the way to the restaurant we do a quick run-through of how things went around the house and with Swarley while they were gone. But the moment we're seated and handed menus, Elizabeth has only one thing she wants to talk about.

"Spill it, young lady."

I smile and shrug nonchalantly while pretending to read my menu. "Spill what?"

She grabs my menu and pulls it away from my face. "This 'friend' you're staying with. A *he* I presume?"

"Yeah, the pool guy."

She tilts her head to the side and squints. I can't keep it in any longer. The story really is a great one, all except the ending which has yet to be written, but I know where it's going. I tell her everything, almost. By the time I'm done, she looks shocked.

"Sydney Ann Montgomery, please tell me you're going to marry this guy."

I fail to maintain eye contact. My nervous fingers twirl and knot in my hair. "I'm leaving for Paris in a few days."

"So. It's not like you're moving there."

"True. But I'm going to continue housesitting for the next year which will have me traveling every month or so, and then I'm starting grad school next fall. Lautner's just ..."

Elizabeth pushes her plate out of the way and rests her arms on the table leaning forward. "Just what?"

Shaking my head, I trace the pattern of the tablecloth with my fingernail. "The right guy at the wrong time."

"So, you're just going to leave. Walk away because the timing isn't perfect?"

My eyes snap to hers. "*Perfect?* It's not even in the same spectrum as perfect. I'm twenty-three and probably won't be done with school and offered my first real job until I'm nearly thirty. Lautner's going to be done with his residency in three years and ready for marriage, children ... a real life. Not some long-distance relationship with a college student. He's going to probably start his own practice, and when I'm done with school where does that leave me? Looking for a job around here? Do you know how hard it's going to be to find my dream job if I'm willing to go anywhere, let alone restricting myself to a fifty mile radius? It'll never work. Eventually one of us will resent the other. It's just not ... it just won't work."

"Is this job you're going back to school for really *your* dream." Elizabeth's voice is soft, hesitant, even sympathetic.

"I love art, and being a curator at a major museum or gallery would be an amazing opportunity ... a dream job."

"*Your* dream job?"

"Of course *my* dream job. Why else would I go through all this work to save money for school and then put myself through the grueling studies and long hours of grad school?"

She taps her finger on her chin. "I'm not sure. But you're my niece and I love you like a daughter so your happiness is important to me. Sometimes we find happiness where we least expect it. I'd just hate to see you pass it by. Jobs pay the bills and provide us with a sense of accomplishment in life. But they don't love you and comfort you. They don't take you to the beach and bring you flowers and pastries. They don't hold you at night and make you feel beautiful."

I don't know how to respond. Her words may hold some merit, but right now they're not comforting.

She leaves some cash on the table and stands. "But you're right, Sydney. You are young and making a life-changing decision after knowing a guy for one month is probably crazy."

I stand and grin. I know what she really means, but she's giving me an out. An excuse to leave and not feel like such a fool.

She drops me back off at Lautner's and hugs me tight. "I love you, sweetie. Whatever you decide to do will be the right decision. No regrets, okay?"

Secure in her arms, I let a few stray tears fall. There's a whole flood of them waiting, but they're reserved for the long flight to Paris in four days.

———

I SPEND the rest of the afternoon messing with photos on my computer. Then I respond to an email from a college friend requesting I be her photographer at her wedding in the fall. It happens to be a weekend I'm home between housesitting jobs so I agree. It's easy money and I need to save as much as I can.

By seven o'clock I'm hungry again but not sure whether to eat or wait for Lautner. I'm getting a taste of being with a doctor and it kind of sucks. Then again, he is a busy resident and I'm jobless right now. After scrounging through his kitchen cabinets, I find some granola bars and eat one to tide me over.

My boredom turns into curiosity and I find myself in his bedroom snooping around. I open his nightstand drawer and find a few books, mystery thrillers, some loose change, and a box of condoms. An opened box of condoms. I know none of them have been used with me so now I wonder how long he's had them and who he's used them with. Before my brain has a chance to think rationally, I'm counting the remaining condoms. There are four left and it was a ten pack. The expiration date is out a ways so they can't be that old.

"Snooping?"

A familiar female voice startles me.

"Claire."

She's in the doorway, staring at my lap. I look down and shove the condoms back in the box.

"How did you get in here?" I put the condoms back in the drawer with shaky hands.

She holds up a keychain with several keys dangling from it. Why the hell does Dr. Brown have a key?

"Does Lautner know you're snooping around?" Her lips

set in a tight, firm line and the smugness mixed with the hint of warning in her voice has me feeling like an errant child.

I stand and walk toward her. She retreats with each step I take until we're in the living room.

"What do you want?" I grab my phone and mess with it to look distracted and unaffected by her intrusiveness.

"Lautner said I could borrow a few books for research."

"Well I don't know where they're at maybe—"

She prances back toward the bedroom again. "They're on his bookshelf in here. I'm sure I know his bedroom better than you do."

I'm so unprepared for this conversation. She has a key and comes in without knocking. Now she's making subtle implications that there's more to them than I know.

Dr. Brown struts back out with several books in her arms. "Right where I remember them being."

I shake my head and scrunch my nose. "Am I missing something here?"

Claire laughs. "I'm sure you're missing a lot, so you'll have to be more specific."

"Cut the crap. You're dying to say whatever it is that has you so pissed off. Is this about Lautner being with me instead of you?"

She glares at me and I know I've hit a nerve, but she makes a quick recovery and a smirk plays across her face.

"Don't flatter yourself. You're not getting anything I haven't had. The difference is you're leaving and I'm staying."

What is she talking about? My stomach rolls and the ache in the back of my throat is compounded by the weighted feeling in my chest. I don't know how to respond. Am I upset with her for those biting words or Lautner for not sharing this piece of information? Do I even know what she's saying or am I jumping to the wrong conclusion?

God, I feel dizzy.

"What are you saying?" I press my lips together, avoiding eye contact.

"Oh dear. He didn't tell you, did he? Well, shame on me for letting the cat out of the bag."

I risk a glance. She's waving her hand dismissively in the air.

"I'd love to stay and share all the details, but I have more important things to do." Her head flips back as she reaches for the doorknob, giving me one last smirk. "Pleasure knowing you."

Staring at my phone, the urge to call Avery is overwhelming. Why do I feel like I just walked in on Lautner screwing some girl? Wrapping my brain around the idea of Lautner and Claire together is nauseating. He didn't cheat on me. This had to have happened before me, but it still cuts. Why did I feel like the intruder when she walked in here without knocking? With four days left, why does it matter?

I don't call Avery. This is something I can handle on my own. Technically, he never lied to me. There is no need to mention my visit with Dr. Brown. Lautner is twenty-seven, of course he has a history. I do too. Everything will be fine. There is no reason why I shouldn't be able to get through these next few days without mentioning today's incident.

Remembering the condoms in the bedroom, I put them back in the drawer. Six condoms, so what? Maybe they weren't with the same person. *Oh God!* No, I don't like to think of Lautner as the guy who sleeps around. It's better to think that he used them with the same girl. *Fuck!* No, that's no good either. That would seem like a relationship. Did he love her too? Maybe he loved her more.

"Sydney! Just let it go. Yeah, that's better. Talking to myself again like a freakin' crazy woman."

Stuck in Lautner's apartment by myself is not good. I notice a plastic storage container on the floor in the corner of the closet, so I tug it out and open the lid. It's filled with photos, trophies and his folded football jerseys both from high school and college. I slip on his Stanford jersey which swims on me. Pulling the front of it up to my nose, I smell it.

"Sweat, blood, and dirt."

I jump and my heart nearly stops. Lautner is standing in the doorway. I feel like a total snoop. He's caught me looking through his private things, overstepping all boundaries by miles.

"Shit, you scared me. I'm ... just ... God, I'm sorry. I was bored and curious and—"

He shakes his head and walks over to me. I'm fumbling to pull his jersey off. Taking it from me, he offers his other hand. I look at it for a second and take it. He pulls me to my feet.

"Take your clothes off," he demands.

I knit my brows. "Huh?"

"You heard me." His voice is deep but not angry.

The tangle of emotions running around in my head has arrested my ability to reason.

I remove my clothes leaving only my panties on. His head turns from side to side. "Keep going."

I sigh and roll my eyes, but remove my panties. He slips the jersey back on over me. It hangs nearly to my knees.

His tented shorts don't go unnoticed by me.

"Yes, I'm happy to see you." He grins and leans down

taking my mouth prisoner. I hum in satisfaction while his tongue explores familiar territory. His hands cup my face and he pulls away, leaving me dazed and breathless. "That jersey has scored a lot of points, but tonight it's going to see me break a few new records. Let's eat."

Another smack on my ass before he walks to the kitchen. I'm reeling with confusion, desire, excitement, and some residual embarrassment from getting caught. Jealousy, however, seems to be the emotion that is winning. I visualize Claire in this jersey sprawled out on his bed, quizzing him for a test, while his hands and mouth touch her the way he has touched me.

Closing my eyes, I try to shake the images from my head. The smell of pizza infiltrates my nose as I walk to the kitchen. Lautner grabs two beers from the refrigerator as I lift the lid to the pizza box.

"Oh my God. You. Are. The. Best! I love taco pizza."

He sets the beers down on the counter and pulls me into his chest. "And I love you in my jersey ... only my jersey." His cold hands from the beer slide up under his jersey and firmly grip my bare ass.

Sure buddy, was this your MO with Claire too?

"Dr. Sullivan, you are one kinky bastard."

His hands slide from my ass to just under my legs, and with an effortless tug, I'm lifted up. My bare sex rubs against the bulge in his shorts.

"You drive me crazy. I have to plead insanity around you." He bites my lower lip and drags it through his teeth with a low growl. Setting me back on my feet, he looks down and his lips curl into his signature sexy and oh-so-cocky grin.

My whole body flushes with embarrassment as I see what he's looking at. The wet spot on his shorts from *me*.

"I may never wash these shorts again."

My eyes shoot to his as I stand with my legs crossed, fingers fiddling with my hair. "You really know how to embarrass me."

He hands me the beers and grabs the pizza box, plates, and forks. "You shouldn't be embarrassed. You're sexy as hell, Syd and—"

There's a knock at the door. Lautner sets everything down on the coffee table by the sofa. I quickly sit down hoping the back of the couch will hide me from the front door. The jersey covers everything, but there's no question that I'm naked underneath it.

"Hey, Sully. Claire got called to the hospital. Just opened this bottle of Zinfandel, wanna hang out for a while?"

"Actually—"

"Mmm ... do I smell pizza?"

I turn toward the voice behind me. The wavy-haired blonde with large breasts, short shorts, and a tube top exposing her navel decorated with a rose tattoo stops behind the couch. I stand and face her large brown eyes inspecting every inch of me.

"Oh ... I didn't realize you had company."

Lautner is still standing by the door holding it open. "Yes, I have company." He sounds irritated but his polite smile doesn't show it.

She crosses her arms over her chest shoving her cleavage up closer to her chin. "Well, aren't you going to introduce us?"

I pin Lautner to the door with my narrow-eyed stare. He glances upward and blows out an exasperated breath that rattles his lips. "Rose, Sydney, Sydney, Rose."

"Oh, so *you're* Sydney?" She openly stares at me. "Interesting." Her mouth twists to the side.

I can see how she and *Dr. Brown* are friends. Has she been with Lautner too?

"So you're Rose? I've heard so much about you," I say with a fake smile and extra flutter to my eye lashes.

"You have?" she asks with a high-pitched enthusiasm to her voice—chin up, shoulders back, chest out.

"Yes, Lautner just said he hoped Claire and Rose would keep to themselves tonight while he fucked me on the couch, kitchen counter, the hallway wall and, of course, tied to his bed."

Rose audibly gasps, hand covering her mouth, wide eyes darting back and forth between me and Lautner. The muscles in his jaw tick, lips quivering to hold back his grin. She turns and clicks her heels out the door.

"Rose wait—" Lautner calls, but she holds up her hand behind her and huffs off to the stairs.

Lautner closes the door and leans back against it with his arms folded over his chest. I tip my beer up and turn my back to him.

"You do realize after you're gone I'm going to have to deal with two very pissed off neighbors upstairs."

I shrug. "I'm sure you'll find a way to *smooth* things over with them."

He sits down beside me and runs his finger along my bare leg.

"You'd better also realize I'm a man of my word. So if I said I am going to 'fuck you on the couch, kitchen counter, hallway wall, and my favorite ... tied to my bed...'" he looks at his watch "...then I'd better get started."

The patience and self-control I fought for after Claire

left was teetering on the edge when Lautner came home. Now it's been blown to oblivion. The one-two Claire-Rose punch knocked me down, but I'm back up and angry as hell.

"Not happening. I'm going for a run." I stand and walk to the bedroom.

"Wait ..." He's right behind me. "Are you upset?"

Tossing clothes everywhere, I find a pair of shorts and a sports bra. "I'm just going for a run." Tossing his jersey aside, I slip into my clothes without one peek in his direction.

"Now? You're going for a run ... now?"

Finding matching socks, I shove my feet into my shoes and tighten the laces. "No, I'm going in the morning. I just thought I'd sleep in this. Yes! I'm going for a run NOW! Jeez, Dr. Sullivan, thought you were smarter than that."

He's blocking the door, but I try to squeeze around him. Before I can get past he shoves me to the wall, gripping my arms.

"What the fuck is wrong with you? You're blindsiding me with this attitude and I have no idea what the hell I did?"

I shove at his chest, but he doesn't budge. "Blindsiding? Wow, that's rich." I fight again to wriggle out of his grasp, but my attempts are futile.

"What are you talking about?" The creases in his forehead continue to deepen.

My eyes widen as my head juts forward. "Dr. Bitch and now Rose the hussy roommate?"

He shakes his head and releases me. "God, Syd, I'm too damn tired to play this stupid game of Charades with you, just tell me what you're so pissed about." With a deep sigh, he runs his hands through his hair and leans back against the opposite hallway wall.

I cross my arms over my chest. "Why didn't you tell me you and Claire were together?"

He bites his upper lip and rolls his eyes to the ceiling. "We weren't *together*, it was one fucking night a year ago after we went out with some friends. We both drank too much and ... it was just a stupid mistake. That's all."

He looks at me. "How do you even know about it?"

I tilt my head to the side and smirk. "Claire told me when she came in here earlier. With. Her. Key!"

Lautner lets his head drop back against the wall, eyes closed, hands lace behind his neck. "This is just ... stupid. Why are we—"

I stomp toward the door. "You're right. This is stupid. Me being here is stupid."

"Syd, wait!"

Slamming the door, I sprint out of the building. With no idea where I'm going, I just run. Not a jog, I'm running fast and hard, fueled by toxic emotions. If I can keep going, maybe I can leave it all behind—the hurt, anger, jealousy. I don't want any of it. My lungs are burning, legs fatigued, as I come to an abandoned park on my right. Slowing to a walk, I clasp my hands on top of my head fighting to catch my breath. The salty taste on my lips is a mix of sweat and tears.

There's a bench ahead facing a small pond filled with ducks, geese, and a few other migrating birds. Collapsing on the bench, I rest my elbows on my legs and drop my head. The dam breaks. Sobs wrack my body in uncontrolled waves. I'm so lost. My sister is five hours away, my dad even farther, and my mom is gone. My feelings are so irrational and raw. The more I try to ignore them, the louder they scream at me. The agony is crippling. How can I want to leave and stay at the same time?

"Hey ..." Lautner's soft voice calls to me.

Lifting my head, I'm greeted with blue irises. Sad. Blue. Irises.

He's hunched down in front of me, and I throw my arms and legs around him. Falling back onto his butt, he hugs me to his chest with strong arms. I bury my face in the crook of his neck and cry. He rests his cheek on my head and gently rocks me. The last time I felt this safe, comforted, and loved was in my mother's embrace.

"I'm sorry, baby. I'd rather die than hurt you."

Sniffling, I shake my head. "No, I'm just—just s-s—so messed up. It's not y-you." I take a deep breath, hold it, then let it out with a slow release. "Your personal life is none of my business and—"

"Stop!" He pulls back and cradles my face in his hands, wiping my tear-stained cheeks with his thumbs. "What are you talking about? This. Us. Nothing has ever felt more *personal*. I'd bare my soul to you if you'd let me. Do you get that? Do you have any idea how I really feel about you?" His face is tense, etched with pain.

Biting down on my lips while my eyes rapidly blink away more impending tears, I nod.

He presses his lips to mine, closing his eyes.

Life. Is. So. Cruel.

Releasing me, he skims his fingers along my jaw, eyes bright and adoring. "I'll tell you anything you want to know. Even if it's not what you want to hear. Okay?"

"Okay," I whisper with a weak smile.

"You're killing me, Sydney Ann Montgomery." He shakes his head. "I'm not a greedy guy, so this ... *feeling* is hard to handle."

"Feeling?"

252

He nods. "Wanting something more than anything else in the world, but knowing you can't have it ... knowing *I* can't have *you*."

———

I'M DRUNK ON LAUTNER. He's my drug of choice. When I'm high on him, the rest of the world fades away. Naked, sated, and wrapped in his arms, I am at peace.

"Are your arms sore?" His voice chimes through the silent darkness of his bedroom.

Tracing the muscles in his arms circled around my waist, I smile. "Hmm, the only thing I'm feeling right now is bliss."

That smile, the one that sends chills through my body, is pressed against my shoulder. I wonder if he knows the smile I *feel* on my skin is my all-time favorite. My eyes see what they want to see, my ears hear what they want to hear, but that touch, that tactile emotion is real and undeniable.

"Claire has a key because Rose likes to *entertain* so I let her use my apartment to study or do research when I'm not here."

My body stiffens at the mention of her name alone and he squeezes me tighter.

"And Rose ... have you—"

"No." He laughs. "Jeez, I'm not that guy."

"That guy?"

"The one who puts notches in his bedpost."

Six condoms. Why does that bother me? I should ask him, but I'd hate myself for being *that girl*.

"I know." I say the words to reassure myself more than him.

June 29th, 2010

THE REPEATED ringtone of my phone brings me out of my sleep. The sun is up and I'm alone in bed. I don't even try to make it to my phone, which is out on the coffee table. I'm not that quick in the morning. Stealing the sheet from the bed, I wrap it around my naked body and go retrieve my phone. I don't remember hearing it ring more than once, but there are two missed calls, one from Avery and one from Elizabeth.

Something catches my attention as I yawn. I do a double take and notice a large—no, a gigantic—bouquet of flowers on the kitchen counter. They are a rainbow of vibrant colors and must have cost a fortune. Lautner has to be related to a florist because there are simply no flower shops open when he leaves before sunrise. What brings an enormous smile to my face are the two ACE bandages tied in bows around the stems. The same ACE bandages Dr. Kinky Bastard used to tie my arms to his bed last night. And holy fuck … did he do things to me that I will never be able to share with even my oftentimes crude sister. How he puts on his scrubs and tends to sick children, like the male version of Mother Teresa, after last night is beyond me.

I dial up Avery but it goes to her voice mail so I leave a message. Next I try Elizabeth.

"Sydney, Avery tried calling you but you didn't answer —" Elizabeth's voice is rushed.

"I know. I just tried her but it went straight to her voicemail."

"She's probably in the air already."

"What? Where's she going?"

"Sydney, your dad was taken to the hospital early this morning. They think it's his heart."

The bottom to my world just came out and I'm free falling into my own hell. "Wh-What? Is he—"

"He's fine right now. They're going to run some tests, but they won't know more until later. I've booked us a flight out at noon. It was the earliest I could get."

I hear her words but they're not registering. My dad is fit and healthy. This can't be.

"Uh ... okay, yeah I'll be ready." The clumsy words stumble from my mouth.

"I'll pick you up in two hours."

"Okay ... um, bye."

The tears fall faster than I can wipe them away. I can't lose my dad too. This just isn't right. My eyes flicker to the flowers again and I think of Lautner. I'm leaving in two hours. Then the enormity of the whole situation hits me. My dad is in the hospital and I can't get to him fast enough. I'm supposed to be leaving for Paris in three days, and I won't get to see Lautner again ... ever.

He deserves to know, so I send him off a quick text before packing up my stuff.

> My dad's in the hospital. I fly out at noon. Sorry I have to leave like this. Call you tonight from Illinois. ~Syd

I head to the bedroom, toss my phone on the bed, and start throwing things into my suitcase. "In Your Eyes" plays from my phone.

"Don't go ... just wait!" Lautner's panicked voice sounds in my ear.

"I'm sorry. I have to go. I didn't want to end things like this but—"

"Just WAIT!" he yells and the line goes dead.

My heart is being ripped apart in two directions. I have to be with my dad. This wasn't how I wanted to say goodbye to Lautner, but I no longer have a choice. After my suitcases are packed and set by the door, I do a final check around in the kitchen and bathroom. Elizabeth won't be here for another half hour so I text my sister to let her know I got the message and I'm on my way.

My breath stops when the front door crashes open almost being torn from its hinges. Lautner stands before me in his green scrubs, chest heaving. In a heartbeat, I'm in his arms and a lifetime of emotions pour from me—worry, heartache, sadness, fear, and ... love.

"Shh ... I'm here." He soothes me with his voice.

I feel and hear his heart pounding against his chest like it's beating only for me in this moment.

"What happen to your dad?"

I lean back enough to see him, finding comfort in blue irises. He cradles my face and wipes my tears.

"Heart ... som-something with his ... heart." I sniffle between broken sobs.

"Is he in surgery?"

I shake my head. "I don't thin-think so. They're doing some tests." I pull in a deep breath and hold it for a moment before letting it out slowly to calm myself down.

His large hand cups the back of my head and I rest against his chest. He presses his lips to the top of my head and leaves them there. We hold each other without words. I don't know how he was able to leave the hospital but it doesn't matter. He's here and I need him. I need this goodbye so I can move on. I need closure.

"Your dad will be fine. I'm sure he's in good hands. They'll run the tests, figure out what's wrong and fix it. Okay?"

I pull back. "God, I hope so."

He leans down and kisses me. Then he pauses. I feel it. The building emotion, the reality of the moment. "Come back." He brushes his lips against mine.

I take a step back and shake my head. "I can't. You know that."

"Why not?" he asks with wavering words.

"Because I have to work and then go back to school. I'm twenty-three. I can't throw away my future, my dreams on some guy."

His head jerks back. "*Some guy?* Is that what I am to you? Just some guy?"

"No!' I turn and rake my fingers through my hair, stepping away to distance us even more. "God! You're not just some guy to me, Lautner. You're probably *the* guy, but it doesn't change anything."

"It fucking changes everything!" He steps inside and slams the door shut so hard a framed picture falls from the wall, shattering glass everywhere.

The roar of his voice and the glass hitting the floor sends frigid chills through my body. I've never seen this side of him.

I turn and look at him and then the mess on the floor that he isn't acknowledging. His eyes are searing into me.

"Jesus, Lautner! We knew this day was coming. I never once promised you anything more. You're living your dream.

Would you give it all up for me?" My voice is an all-out yell, and I resent him for making me lose control.

"Yes." Just one word, but he speaks with complete certainty and without hesitation.

It's a punch in the gut, knocking the wind out of me. How can he say that? Even more, how can he mean it?

"Bullshit," I say with a defiant edge to my voice. "You would give up your dreams for me?"

"Yes." His eyes are filled with tears that haven't been breached, but mine are all down my face. I've lost control over my emotions. I've lost control over my life.

I sweep them away with the back of my hands. "Well there's the difference. I would never ask you to." I can't hide the defeat in my voice. "You'd resent me."

"No." He shakes his head. "I would never resent you."

"That's just it. Once again, it doesn't matter. I'd resent myself for everything you'd give up to be with me. I'd resent you for making me feel so awful about myself." I shake my head and suck in my upper lip to fight my emotions. "It would eventually tear us apart."

"I love you," he whispers.

"Don't," I say with anger in my voice.

"I will always love you." He takes a step toward me.

"Shut up." I clench my teeth, looking anywhere but at him.

"Damit! Look at me!" He cups my face and drives the knife completely through with those fucking blue irises. "I. Love. You. Period. It's a goddamn soul-shattering love that will never, *ever* be matched. My love for you is unapologetic and forever."

There's a knock at the door but Lautner ignores it. I know it's Elizabeth.

"I have to go," I whisper and walk to the door.

"GODDAMMIT!" his thunderous voice echoes.

I whip around to see him hurl an empty beer bottle at the wall, followed by another. I cry for him. I cry for me. He's like a bomb with a lit fuse—clenched jaw, furrowed brows, piercing eyes, fisted hands, heaving chest.

The door opens.

"Sydney?" Elizabeth's uneasy voice calls out.

I'm sure she's heard the commotion and is concerned about me. I turn and look at her.

"I'm coming." I try to force a sad smile, but there's no hiding the emotional disaster she's walked in on.

"Uh ... okay, I'll take one of your suitcases down."

I nod. All my emotions are colliding and it's tearing me up inside. I don't want to love him ... I don't want to hate him. But the truth is I hate him because he made me love him. He made me pause just long enough to doubt myself. He cracked open the door to my heart and whispered *what if.*

Lautner is standing in the kitchen with his back to me, hands on the edge of the counter, head down.

The words are stronger than my control over them. I feel regret before they ever leave my mouth. "You have four condoms left in your box. I'm sure you'll survive without *me.*"

Jealousy feels like the tongue of Satan. The words feel venomous. Would he love me less if I hurt him? Would I love him less if he hurt me?

I sling my bags over my shoulder and bend down to get my carry-on and other suitcase.

I turn and tug my stuff into the hallway.

The piercing pain in my arm makes me grimace as I'm being whipped around.

"The fucking condoms! Is that what you've been carrying around in your head since yesterday?"

The tightness around his cold eyes, the seething words, and his bruising grip frightens me. I haven't seen this side of him. My bag falls off my shoulder as he pulls me back into his apartment and straight to his bedroom. Ripping the drawer from his nightstand he pulls out the box of condoms.

"How many condoms?" He's holding the box in front of my face.

I swallow but can't speak.

"HOW MANY?"

My body shakes and tears run out of control down my face. "Ten," I choke.

He dumps the remaining condoms on the bed.

"Count them!" I don't recognize the voice in my ears. He's so angry.

"Four," I whisper.

He pulls his wallet out and tosses two more on the bed.

"Now how many?"

I release a sob. "Six."

He jerks my arm again pulling me to his closet. Digging out a pair of shorts from his hamper, the ones he wore the first night we had sex without condoms, he retrieves two more foil packets and tosses them on the bed.

"How many?" he demands between clenched teeth.

My sobs strangle me. "Stop ... please," I plead.

"Count the fucking condoms, Sydney!"

"Eight ... eight ..." I cry.

I don't know what hurts more, my arm or my heart. Yes, I do ... my heart. He's shattering it.

He drags me out of his apartment and past a shocked Elizabeth, who is getting the rest of my bags. Lautner doesn't acknowledge her as he pulls me down the stairs behind him.

"You're hurting me ... stop!" I beg.

"Sydney!" Elizabeth's voice calls from behind us.

Lautner opens the passenger door to his 4Runner then opens the glove compartment and pulls out ... two ... more ... condoms.

"Say it," he says with a menacing voice.

I shake my head, nose running, eyes swollen, tears bleeding in a river down my face.

"Goddammit, SAY IT!" His roaring words sever something deep inside.

Elizabeth's concerned voice sounds like an echo miles away, even though she's standing only a few feet away. Everything is in slow motion like I'm watching the past month with Lautner in slow motion—visions people aren't supposed to have until they're dying. Is that what's happening? Am I dying?

"Ten." The painful word cuts past my raw throat.

He tosses them on the seat and stares at me. Jaw clenched and ... *oh God* ... tears. His eyes are filled with tears.

"The day..." he swallows "...the day in the rain. I felt terrible. You looked so rejected and ... God, I wanted to be with you too."

One. Blink.

Blue irises releasing tears. Nothing, *ever,* has felt so heartbreaking.

"You ..." He bites his upper lip so hard I think he breaks the skin. Sucking in a shaky breath he moves his head from side to side. "... They were for you, only you ... always you."

I start to move my hand to his face, but he flinches and steps back shutting the door.

The rejection and pain I feel right now is indescribable.

He walks around to the driver's side.

"Lautner—" His name rips from my throat.

A resurgence of tears fill my eyes.

He stops, holding the driver's door partially open with his back to me.

My arms are hugging my nauseous stomach, nails digging into my skin.

Through my teary, blurred vision I don't see him approach. His lips violently collide with mine. The physical pain momentarily blinds the emotional. This is what a last kiss feels like.

Infinite emotion. Beautiful pain. All consuming. Utterly shattering.

"I hope you find your dreams, Sydney ... my ... beautiful ... Sydney," he whispers in my ear with a cracked, broken voice.

One last look. One last moment. One last chance.

Pleading blue irises call to me, begging for three words. The three words he deserves to hear. The three words that would let him know he owns me. The three words that would ruin my future.

I say nothing.

Closing my eyes—One. Last. Nod.

Car door slams. Engine roars. Tires screech.

I open my eyes to see my *what if* driving off into the distance.

"I love you." I let go of the words; holding them inside would kill me.

Chapter Fourteen

ELIZABETH KNOWS WHAT I NEED. I don't have to ask. Words are too painful. When we arrive at the airport, she digs my sunglasses out of my purse and shoves a wad of tissues into my hand. As we wait in line, she rubs gentle circles on my back. It's her way of being there for me and I love her for it. No "I told you so," just unconditional love like a mother's love.

The trip to Illinois is torturously long. Then again, every breath feels like a lifetime. Time … the funny thing about time is it flies by like a freight train when I'm falling in love, but it creeps by one agonizing second at a time when it's mending my broken heart. I need to see my dad and know he's going to be okay. Part of me died today and I can't lose him too.

By the time we get to the hospital, I'm a complete wreck. We find my dad's room and he's sitting up in bed with Avery by his side. I know he notices my swollen eyes despite the cold water bottles Elizabeth had me press against them in the cab.

"Daddy!" I hug him and the tears come again. I feel like a little girl in his arms, his little girl who got her heart broken today.

"Oh, hey, baby girl. What's this all about? I'm going to be fine. You girls didn't need to rush back home."

I release him and sit on the edge of his bed.

Avery rolls her eyes. "Jeez, Dad. You have an eighty-percent blocked artery and the doctor said you need a stent. Don't make it sound so benign."

"So you're having surgery?" I ask with a sniffle.

"*Minor* surgery. I'll probably be out of the hospital within twenty-four hours."

"When are they doing it?"

"Tomorrow," Avery says.

"I'm going to cancel my trip to—"

"No way," my dad cuts me off. "You're going to Paris. You've been waiting to see Paris since you were a little girl. If I die you can stay, but anything short of that you're getting on that plane. Do you understand?"

"Don't say that, Dad." I wrinkle my nose because him even saying the word death makes me nauseous.

"It's going to be fine," Elizabeth says. "Besides, my little brother has the Big Man on his side."

Dad laughs. "I'm not afraid of dying. God can have me whenever He needs me. Besides, the love of my life is waiting for me."

Ugh! Could I feel anymore punched in the gut today?

"Mom has eternity now. She can wait for you." Avery leans down and kisses his cheek.

The nurse comes in and tells us she needs to go over some stuff with my dad before his surgery tomorrow. Elizabeth stays with him while Avery and I go down to the cafeteria for some food.

"You not hungry?" Avery asks, looking at my lonely bottle of grape juice.

"Not really." I fight to find a smile.

"Everything is going to be okay," she says, wrapping her hand over mine and giving it a tight squeeze.

"I know. It's a pretty common surgery."

"I'm not talking about Dad." Her voice is soft and heartbreakingly sympathetic.

The stupid tears return, but I refuse to blink and let them win. I take a deep swallow and nod, focusing on the label of the glass juice bottle.

"I'm moving," she announces.

God, I love her for knowing when to change the subject.

"Moving home?"

Avery snorts. "Hell no! Just closer to the beach. One of the massage therapists I work with is looking for a new roommate. One that doesn't play the bagpipes."

We both laugh.

"Well she'll love you then. You're never home anyway."

Avery eats her chicken sandwich, and I manage to finish my juice before we go back up to see Dad. It's getting late and his surgery is early in the morning so we decide to head home and let him get some rest.

June 30th, 2010

WE ARRIVE at the hospital by 7:00 a.m. to see Dad one more time before his surgery. Avery and Elizabeth make a coffee run while I stay in the waiting room. I didn't sleep worth shit last night. My head was throbbing and Advil didn't touch it, probably because I couldn't stop bawling. Avery crawled in my bed a little after midnight and held me the rest of the night. I know that's why she's extra desperate for coffee this morning. Operation Broken Sydney is exhausting. Nothing sounded more appealing than drowning my sorrows in a six pack of beer or a bottle of Jack, but I couldn't with Dad having surgery this morning.

I don't remember falling asleep. But when Avery nudges me to let me know that Dad's out of surgery, I have to wipe a string of drool off my cheek.

"Nice, Sam. Real attractive." Avery laughs as Elizabeth loops her arm around mine and walks me to Dad's room.

The surgery went well and they plan on releasing him the next morning if all his tests look good. We stay in his room most of the day talking about Avery's move, Elizabeth and Trevor's trip, and my bucket list for Paris. Dad dozes in and out of sleep until finally kicking us out of his room after he eats his delectable plate of hospital food.

"You three hens head home to finish all your clucking," he says jokingly. But we know he's quite serious.

"We'll be back in the morning to get you," Avery gives him a kiss.

"If we're not up too late *clucking*." Elizabeth gives him a big hug.

"I'll be right there," I say as they leave the room.

I start to sit in the chair by the bed, but he pats a small area beside him. Taking his hand, I sit next to him.

"I leave at six in the morning, so I won't see you until I get back from Paris."

He smiles. "Live it up, sweetheart. Be smart ... but live it up. I'm so proud of you. Your mom would be too. You worked so hard in school and you continue to work hard to see this through. I can't wait to see you, my baby girl, as a museum curator someday. Probably at The Louvre." He winks.

I laugh. "No doubt. I'm sure they'll probably offer me a job while I'm there. An apprenticeship of sorts."

"The sky's the limit. In spite of everything, God has truly blessed us."

I wipe a stray tear and hug him. "Yes, he has. I love you, Daddy. I'll call you when I get to Paris."

"I love you too, sweetheart. Be safe."

"I will."

———

ON THE WAY HOME, we stop by the printshop. I e-mailed a few photos yesterday to have prints made. I tell Avery and Elizabeth they're photos I took for a friend and they don't question me. When we get home I go to the basement and dig out some frames I'd bought years back on clearance. I frame the photos and write inscriptions on the back. After wrapping them in brown paper, I leave them with some cash and an address for Avery and Elizabeth to take to the shipping store tomorrow.

"Palo Alto?" Avery questions.

"Just do this for me."

She nods without further questions and hugs me.

"So which one of you two *hens* is getting up not so bright but early and taking me to the airport in the morning?"

Avery raises her hand. "I drew the short straw."

Elizabeth grins. "I'm too old to get up that early."

"Baloney, I slept in your bed. Ever heard of room darkening shades?"

She waves her hand in the air. "Ah, the sun doesn't wake me up."

"Well if not the sun then your dog sure does."

"You mean Trevor's dog. I don't get up with Swarley unless Trevor is out of town. A girl needs her beauty sleep, don't you know."

I giggle. "I knew it was Trevor and his regimented OCD."

Avery's busy messing with her phone but even she laughs at that truth.

"He doesn't have OCD."

I cock my head to the side. "Really? You're going with that answer?"

"He's just ... clean and orderly."

"Your spices are alphabetized."

"A lot of people do that."

"So are your refrigerated condiments. Barbecue sauce, ketchup, mayonnaise, mustard, pickle relish, ranch dressing, steak sauce, Thousand Island dressing, and Worcestershire sauce. In. That. Order."

"Yeah, that's just not right." Avery laughs.

"He does get a little weird when I put the pickle relish after the ranch."

"Mmm hmm." Avery and I nod with tight-lipped smiles.

"It's neither here nor there. I'm off to bed, young things. Give me a hug."

I squeeze her tight.

"Have a safe trip, Sydney. Love you."

"You too, Elizabeth."

Avery winks at me. "Goodnight," we reply as Elizabeth goes upstairs.

We plop down on the couch and stare at the wrapped pictures leaning against the chair. Lautner haunts me. I've gone longer than twenty-four hours before without seeing or hearing from him, but it was different. I knew I would see him again. That's no longer the case.

Avery knows where my mind is. "Please tell me you're going to get piss-ass drunk on the plane tomorrow and forget about Dr. What's His Name."

I smile, still staring at the wrapped frames. "Can't. I'm flying alone. I'm going to wait until the family I'm housesitting for leaves, and *then* I'm going to get piss-ass drunk and forget about Dr. What's His Name."

"You'd better screw a few hot Frenchmen for good measure as well."

I weave my fingers through my long hair. "Of course. What's the point of getting piss-ass drunk if not to wake up in a stranger's bed."

"That a girl," Avery leans into me and rests her head on my shoulder. "I'm exhausted. Some bawl baby kept me up all night."

I lean my head down on hers. "She sounds truly pathetic."

"Totally."

Chapter Fifteen

June 22nd, 2013
THE WEDDING

"**READY, SWEETHEART?**" The deep voice on the other side of the door soothes me.

"Yeah. Come in, Dad." I two-fist my white ballerina length tulle skirt and turn.

My dad has aged well. His thick black hair has some distinguished grey highlights, but his fit physique takes a good ten years off of his real age. I know he never imagined the circumstances that have led to this day or that it would have happened so soon for me. When I shared my news with him, the disappointment in his eyes couldn't be masked, even behind all the love he's given me.

Here we are and time has changed him too. He's ready to walk me down the aisle *and* officiate over the ceremony. My father, the preacher, has accepted "God's hand" in the events that have taken place over the past several years. And now he, too, gives thanks for the blessings that have been so unexpectedly bestowed upon us.

"Stunning." He shakes his head and I fight back the tears.

My mouth curls into a tight lipped smile as I swallow a sea of emotions that stem back to the ten-year-old girl who lost her mom too early. "Thanks, Dad."

"Your groom's a little nervous."

I cock my head to the side. "Really?"

"He never thought he'd see this day. You two have been through so much. He told me it still feels like a dream."

I shrug. "Fate."

He laughs. "This coming from my daughter who doesn't believe in fate."

"Yeah, well sometimes it's the only explanation."

"Here." He reaches into his coat pocket and pulls out a small box.

I open it. "Oh, Dad ..." I'm at a loss for words.

"They were your mother's—"

"I know," I whisper, staring at the white gold and blue topaz teardrop earrings. "My birthstone. Mom told me you gave them to her the day I was born."

He nods. I sense the emotions lodged in his throat.

"My something borrowed and something blue." I smile, removing them from the box.

"Just something blue, sweetheart. They belong to you now."

The corners of my eyes sting with tears as I put on the earrings.

"I'll be right outside. Take your time."

I think my dad needs his own private moment to gather his composure. Grabbing my bag, I dig through it until I find the folded up piece of paper that is nearly disintegrating after being handled, folded, and unfolded so many times. With a deep breath I read the words that have been etched in my head for years ... for the last time.

Sydney,

I've held off writing this letter until the last possible minute. Today my hands are shaky and my body is weak. You and Avery just left with your dad to go home for the night. Since I've been at hospice the past week, every hug feels like the last. Every kiss feels like the last. Every goodbye feels like the last.

I know what I believe happens after death, and I hope the stories are true. I need you to always picture me in a wonderful place, healthy, happy, and watching you grow up into the beautiful woman I know you'll be. It's so unfair to ask this of you, but I want you to take care of Avery. She's going to need you, the way she's needed me. Love her unconditionally and lead by example.

You're too young to understand this now, but someday you'll read this again and know exactly what I mean. Don't be afraid to fall. Sometimes the perspective we need most is from the ground. Don't be afraid to succeed. Sometimes we don't shoot for the sky because we don't look high enough. Hence, the view from the ground. Follow your dreams with steadfast determination. Never settle. Open your heart to endless possibilities, and risk it all for a moment, when the moment is right.

Life may not always seem fair, but that's how you'll know you're living it. I'll always be watching you, and I want you to take me with you for as long as you need me. Then someday ... maybe five years from now, maybe twenty, you'll be ready to let me go. When that day comes ... do it! Set me free and you'll feel the weight of your past lift. Spread your wings and soar, my sweet baby girl. Make a difference in the world—make your mark.

Sydney Ann Montgomery, you will ALWAYS be loved by me.

I'll see you in the stars. ~Mom

I fold the fragile letter for the last time and lay it to rest in the trash.

"I've found my wings, Mom. I've even made my mark on the world already." I laugh. "I've read your letter hundreds of times and it's been both a blessing and a curse. I wanted you to be proud of me. I wanted to live the life that was stolen from you. I wanted redemption ... for the both of us. But then I risked it all when the moment was right. I opened my heart to endless possibilities and I found the unexpected ... I found myself." I dab away the moisture from the corners of my eyes with the pads of my fingers.

There's a knock at the door. I look high in the sky out the window. "Goodbye, Mom."

"Hey, talking to yourself again?" Avery asks, peeking inside the room.

"Just a conversation between me and my two best friends."

Avery raises a single eye brow in confusion.

I smile. "Me, myself, and I."

She shakes her head. "Let's go, princess. Everyone's waiting on you."

"How's my groom?"

"Nervous, handsome, fidgety, but completely sexy and dying to see his beautiful bride."

"Well then, let's not keep the good doctor waiting any longer."

"Where's my flower girl?" I ask my dad as he leads me down the hall toward the sanctuary doors.

"Your sister took her to the bathroom one last time. She was dancing a jig."

"Mommy!" I hear my favorite voice in the whole world call to me as I turn around and watch bouncing brunette curls atop a white tulle dress with daisy inlays come barreling at me.

I bend down and open my arms to catch her. "Hey, baby girl." Her smile is infectious and her cheeks are rosy from running around all morning. I kiss her forehead to mother-test for a fever. She's been running a high fever off and on over the past twenty-four hours. I've considered postponing the wedding but Dr. Know It All insists it's just a viral infection and she'll be fine. She still feels warm, but I chalk it up to all the running around. I sigh, looking past her long eyelashes into breathtaking blue irises that sparkle with life.

Daddy's eyes.

"Where's your ring bearer?" I ask.

"Avy ... doggie."

"Here he is." Avery's voice calls from the side door.

Swarley, AKA the ring bearer, trots over to us. He's dressed in a dog tux and has a special collar with a box, that presumably, has the rings in it.

"Little Miss Ocean Ann, take your doggie's leash and follow Aunt Avy down the aisle just like we practiced last night."

"Mommy." She smiles and kisses my cheek, I melt.

"Ready?" My dad confirms as we wait the final few seconds before the piano starts to play Elvis Costello's "She."

Nodding, I take a deep breath as I round the corner and watch everyone stand and turn to look at me. A quick glance at Avery and Ocean then my eyes go straight to my awaiting groom. He's the epitome of handsome. I don't take my eyes off his until my dad gives me away and takes his spot at the altar.

I'm a little nervous but his large hands steady mine and calm my nerves. My mind is everywhere. I try to focus on the words my dad is saying. He's worked hard on his sermon and choosing the appropriate scriptures, but his voice is white noise to me. This day is so significant. The weaving of events that has led to this moment is surreal.

Focus, Sydney!

"Dane, do you take Sydney to be your lawfully wedded wife, to ..."

Chapter Sixteen

July 17th, 2010

PARIS IS NOT what I imagined it would be. It's more. A plethora of famous buildings, chic fashion, and a perfect mix of old European and contemporary culture. Then there is the art. There are no words. Books, photos, and even YouTube videos don't do it justice. Of course Musée du Louvre consumed my first week here. The Tuileries Gardens behind the Louvre are formally French landscaped gardens with contemporary sculptures. I ate lunch all three days at a café there. In a few weeks the Fair of the Tuileries, the second largest Parisian fair, begins. I've been told there will be slides, trampolines, bumper cars, and a big wheel merry-go-round. It's said to be more reminiscent of fairs in old films.

My attempt to drown my sorrows in a tall bottle of wine backfired on me, more than once. I'm not sure if I caught something on the plane or what, but I've struggled with a persistent stomach bug. I've been passed out on the couch feeling miserable almost as much as I've been checking things off my Paris bucket list. Today doesn't look too promising for venturing out. The hidden blessing is there is no pet requiring attention. However, I would be lying if I said I didn't miss Swarley to some degree. The crazy pooch grew on me, or it's possible he let me feel a little less insane. With him around it didn't feel like I was talking to myself all the time.

"Oh, God—" I race to the bathroom, heaving the remainder of my stomach contents, which isn't much.

Kneeling on the floor, I glance up and suck in some much needed air. Something catches my eye.

"No. Fucking. Way."

The box of tampons sitting on the toilet topper is a flashing neon sign. It doesn't take much thought; I know exactly when I started my last period. After all, I posted a sign on the door.

"Oh my God. I'm late ... really late."

A quick trip to the pharmacy on the corner with the signature green cross above it and I'm back with six sticks.

Pee. + "No!"

Pee. + "Shit!"

Pee. + "Shit shit shit!"

A large glass of water and fifteen minutes later.

Pee. + "Damit!"

Pee. + "Fuck ... no!"

Pee. + *Tears...*

———

NUMB. Nauseous but numb. I recall this feeling, or lack thereof. Our parents sat me and Avery down in the living room and explained that "mommy is sick." It was the moment I realized everything I thought I knew was no longer true. The trip to Disney postponed ... then cancelled. Every parent in the bleachers watching their child swim in the State Meet except mine. Birthday cakes in a box from the store—no more frosting covered beaters to fight over or spoons to lick.

Right now, everything I thought I knew is a lie. I'm not going to grad school. My father will no longer be proud of me. Redeeming the future that my mom lost is now just a tarnished memory. I'm a fucking failure a half a world away from my heart I left behind in Palo Alto.

"Jesus, Lautner." Tears stream down my face as I sit in a chair with my knees hugged to my chest.

He's pursuing his dreams. Three demanding years of pediatric residency. I'm sure he'll be ecstatic to see me on his doorstep until the moment I tell him I'm jobless, knocked up, and his new responsibility. It's too overwhelming. All I want to do is wakeup from this nightmare, but I can't. Tears aren't this wet in dreams and when the pain is this intense, the dream ends.

I have to call Avery. It's too much to take on by myself. We've always been there for each other to share the emotional burdens of life. This though ... this will blow her mind.

"You do realize it's still early here right?" She answers her phone with her characteristic smart ass commentary.

"Ave—" I release a sob.

"Sydney, what's wrong?" Her tone changes.

I hear her concern through the phone, see her wrinkled face, feel her arms around me.

"I'm—I'm—pregnant." My voice breaks.

The words hang heavy in the air. The silence on the line says it all. She's shocked too, and there are no words of comfort. Avery knows me too well. She understands that this is the worst possible thing that could happen to me and not just because I'm twenty-three, unmarried, and not finished with school. It's our mom. As many times as I have denied it to her, Elizabeth, my father, and myself, I wanted to achieve what our mom never did.

"Sydney ... are you sure?"

"Yes, God, yes. I pissed on six fucking sticks. They're all positive." I wipe my nose with the back of my hand and sniffle.

"What are you going to do? I mean are you going to ke—"

"Jesus, yes, I'm going to keep it! Dad just had surgery on his heart, this is going to disappoint him beyond words but ... an abortion would put him in the grave."

"He wouldn't have to know," Avery says with slow caution.

"Mom would ... and so would I."

"Are you going to tell Lautner?"

I pause as if to think about my answer, but there's nothing to think about.

"Yes."

"When?"

"When I come home. I'll change my tickets and fly to Palo Alto instead of going back to Illinois. Lautner needs to know before Dad. But I don't want to tell him over the phone. This has to be said in person."

"Sydney ... it will ..." Avery doesn't finish.

It's our unspoken no bullshit rule. She can't tell me it's

going to be okay and I can't tell her I'll be fine. So we share the only thing we know for certain.

"I'm here for you, Sydney, and ... I love you."

"Love you too, Ave."

———

July 25th, 2010

My Paris bucket list is a joke. Three weeks and I can't remember the feeling I had when I took the sunset cruise on the Seine watching the monuments come to life with slow illumination. The cold tile under my knees, the echo of my heaving stomach, the ghostly reflection in the mirror, and those damn plus signs are all that are seared into my mind. Sure, I have memory sticks filled with photos but they might as well have been taken by someone else because I don't remember being in those places.

The twelve hour journey back to the West Coast is exhausting, especially in a crowded plane with a barf bag in hand in case the toilets are occupied. Other than needing to escape the herd-like claustrophobia, I'm in no hurry to get ... *anywhere*. For the first time that I can remember, I have no direction. Where will I be living in a week ... a month ... a year? What job will I find with a bachelors degree in Art History and a baby? How will my dad react? How will Lautner react?

Lautner. There's a hollowness inside me from missing him so much. Time didn't ease the pain, it multiplied it. There is a slideshow on my computer with his pictures and Peter Gabriel's voice reminding me how complete I felt in his eyes. I've played it at least a hundred times. My head tells me to forget, but my heart won't allow it. It's been nearly a month since I've seen his face, heard his voice, felt his touch. No calls or texts asking about my Dad or Paris or *me*. The day I left, there was the moment when I felt like something severed inside me, like something died. It was my heart. Not the shattering that I felt when he yelled at me, not the heavy shame of not trusting him, it was Lautner letting go of me. The connection between us being ripped apart ... severed.

———

THE VIOLENT POUNDING of my heart intensifies my already nauseous state. I step out of the cab and spot a black 4Runner. He's here. It's a little after nine o'clock at night, and there's a mugginess in the air. Lugging my suit cases into the entry, I leave them and take the stairs to Lautner's apartment one shaky step at a time. My pulse is a rhythmic bass in my ears. Drawing in a calming breath, I push back the unsettling churning in my stomach.

"Here goes everything." I knock on the door.

No answer.

With more force I knock again. Wringing my hands together, I chew on the inside of my cheek. Just as I start to turn away, the door opens.

Lautner's making love to me for the first time, lazy afternoons by the pool and at the beach. Flowers, tea, and pastry bags waiting at the door. Blue irises. Lips pressed against my skin. Condoms. Tears. Taillights in the distance.

"Claire." Her name releases from my lungs like my last breath.

Her cold eyes and hard smile slice through me, but it's her wet hair and naked body wrapped in a bath towel that sucks every ounce of life out of me.

"You're too late ... Samantha? Right?" She adjusts her towel, tucking it in tighter above her breasts.

If I could move, I'd physically remove that smug grin off her face. The conniving bitch knows my name, but I can't tell her that. I can't speak at all. The graham crackers I ate at the airport are on their way back up. Turning, I sprint down the stairs, fly out the door, and hurl in the bushes.

"Oh God!" I cry as my stomach continues to contract until I'm dry heaving.

The unforgiving concrete digs into my knees as I fall to the sidewalk—gasping, sobbing, broken.

"Why ... why ... why?" I weep, folded over hugging my stomach.

I can't breathe; my lungs feel like their spasming out of control.

Coughing. Choking. Heaving.

"Are you okay, Miss?"

I lift my heavy head to the sympathy laden stare looking down on me. A young woman, maybe my age, is resting her hand on my shoulder.

"Yes," I croak with a barely audible voice, stumbling to my feet. "Just ... sick."

"You sure?"

I swallow back my burning stomach acid. "Yep." I nod.

"Okay ..." She hesitates, but I give her a weak smile and she continues into the building, glancing back once more before the door shuts.

Fumbling through my purse, I find my phone and call Elizabeth.

"Bonjour!" She answers with high pitched enthusiasm.

"Elizabeth ..." My voice is raw.

"Sydney? What's wrong. Where are you?"

"Can you come get me?" The words feel like sandpaper.

"What? I'm mean yes ... sweetie, where are you?"

"Lautner's." I squeeze my eyes and release a strangled sob.

"I'll be right there."

After pulling my bags to the curb, I sit and wait. It has to be eighty degrees, but chilling shivers wrack my body.

"Sydney." Elizabeth's soft voice calls.

She's standing before me, but I didn't hear her pull up. All my senses are dulled, shock has set in, and I'm stuck in a teeth-chattering daze.

Wrapping her arms around me, she helps me up and puts me in the car. I have a vague awareness of her loading my luggage and getting in next to me. Head pressed to the window, I watch the road blur by like my life—fast winding curves and unexpected bumps.

The minute we walk through the door, I bolt to the bathroom. My abs are sore, knees bruised, hair matted with sweat.

"How far along are you?" Elizabeth pulls my hair back away from my face with one hand and rubs my back with her other.

"Avery?" I have to assume Avery told her.

I sit back on my butt and lean against the wall opposite the toilet.

Elizabeth tucks her dark shoulder-length hair behind her ear, leans back against the vanity, and smiles. "Nope, just a hunch."

Stretching my legs out on either side of the toilet, I sigh. "I don't know yet. Maybe a month."

"And Lautner? Are you ready to talk about—"

Holding my breath and biting my lips together, I shake my head and blink back the tears.

"Okay, when you're ready, I'm here."

"Thank you," I whisper.

Chapter Seventeen

August 1st, 2010

H<small>OPE</small>. God, I need something ... just a flicker of light to bring me from my darkness.

Elizabeth and Trevor have been making my meals, forcing me out back for fresh air and sunshine, and insisting I shower and brush my teeth every day. What they haven't done is ask any more questions. I called my dad and told him I'm hanging out with Avery a few weeks before I head home. What he doesn't know is Avery is on her way to be with me. Missing him, because I haven't seen him since his surgery, is the easy part. Telling him I'm pregnant is going to be unimaginably difficult.

Avery knows no more than Elizabeth at this point. I'm sticking to my ten-year-old mentality that if I don't say the words, if I don't tell them what I encountered at Lautner's, then maybe it's not true. Denying that the man I love, the father of my unborn child, has moved on with a woman I despise won't last forever.

"Avery called last night and said she'd try and meet us there unless she hits heavy traffic or road construction." Elizabeth gives me a quick glance.

Keeping my eyes focused out my window, I return a reflexive bob of my head. We're heading to my OBGYN appointment Elizabeth scheduled for me the day after I returned from Paris. This isn't how I imagined my first prenatal visit going. Not to sound old-fashioned, but I pictured being in my thirties, married, holding my husband's hand, and ... happy.

Arriving fifteen minutes early, I fill out my paperwork. I'm still under my dad's insurance and I have no idea if it has maternity coverage. The moment they file this claim the clock starts. It will only be a matter of weeks until my dad receives notification in the mail regarding this claim. I think it might be best if he finds out from me first. Then again, maybe by messenger while I'm still halfway across the county would be a better idea, at least for me.

"Sydney Montgomery," the nurse calls.

Elizabeth follows me back. We stop in the hall and the nurse gets my height, weight, blood pressure, and temperature. Avery hasn't arrived, but I hope she does soon. I feel like I'm being prepped for execution instead of examined for a new life growing inside of me. The nurse escorts us to the room and asks me a few more questions that were not on the form I filled out. Then she instructs me to strip from the waist down, sit on the table, and cover with the blue disposable paper blanket. Just as she's leaving, Avery walks in.

"Sydney." She hugs me tightly to her.

Having played the role of mother and protector to her for years, it's a humbling experience to have our roles reversed.

"I'm so glad you made it," I whisper through a thick throat.

She sits next to Elizabeth while I get undressed and situated on the table.

"So, are you nervous?" Avery questions.

"About?" I tilt my head, eyes wide.

"The ultrasound." She rolls her eyes.

"I'm nervous about telling Dad, finding work, dealing with this nasty morning sickness, and giving birth. The ultrasound is nothing."

"Lautner?" Avery stares at me with a tight painful smile.

Elizabeth nudges her and gives her a barely detectable head shake.

There's two quick knocks at the door.

"Good afternoon, I'm Dr. Wiggins." The petite doctor with brunette hair pulled into a tight bun offers her hand.

"Sydney." I gesture to the side. "My aunt Elizabeth, and my sister Avery."

Dr. Wiggins shares a kind smile and nods as she sits on an adjustable rolling stool. She repeats all the same questions the nurse already asked me. I'm tempted to give her completely different answers just to see if she's really listening or simply going through a routine spiel. The nurse recorded all my answers already; this seems unnecessarily redundant. It's no wonder doctors are always running late.

"Well let's take a look."

Securing my feet in the stirrups, I take a deep breath and try to relax while she inserts a wand into me. There is a little pressure but it doesn't hurt.

"There's your baby." She points to the screen. "Heart rate is perfect and..." making a slight adjustment, she continues to look at the screen "...measuring about six weeks."

There it is ... the rapid rhythmic beating of *hope*. Avery grabs my hand and squeezes it. I turn toward her and we share a few tears.

The nurse knocks and slips in the room. She types a few things into the computer before Dr. Wiggins removes the wand.

"I'll get you a prescription for prenatal vitamins and Eileen will print out your ultrasound pictures and get you some information about taking care of yourself and your baby since this is your first pregnancy. Do you have any more questions for me?"

I wipe my eyes and shake my head. There has to be a million questions to ask, but I can't think of anything right now except the life inside me—a perfectly woven combination of me and Lautner.

———

THE RIDE HOME is just as silent as the ride there. I can't stop staring at the blob on the photos. Through the corner of my eye, I see Elizabeth sneak an occasional glance at me. My mother would have tied me to a chair and interrogated me by now, but Elizabeth has had saintly patience with me.

Trevor has left with Swarley to run some errands while Avery and Elizabeth make dinner. I haven't said a thing to either one of them since we returned home. Elizabeth sets a bowl of trail mix on the table for me to munch on while dinner is being made. My computer is in front of me, but my eyes stay glued to the two blob photos next to it.

"He's moved on." My monotone announcement silences the kitchen.

Avery and Elizabeth stand frozen in place—one holding a knife, the other with a potato and peeler. It's as if it's the first time I've ever spoken. I can tell by their wide eyes and parted lips that they are afraid to say anything or even move a muscle. My gaze shifts from them to the pool out back. Visions of Lautner, sans shirt, running the skimmer through the pool play in my mind. I blink and all I see is Claire wrapped in a towel looking at me with condescending eyes and a you-should-have-stayed-away smirk.

"I knocked on his door and Claire, *Dr. Brown,* answered—wet and wrapped in only a towel."

The chuckle that escapes me is sheer disbelief. "Not even a month and he moves on ... with *her.*"

At the end of a deep sigh, I force a smile and look at the frozen statues by the kitchen island. "So I'm having this baby by myself and we're going to be fine." I exert as much conviction into those words as I can. Once again, if I say it then it's true.

Avery sets her knife down on the chopping board and twists her lips, but her eyes remain down. "Don't you think he has a right to know? That maybe he should assume some responsibility for what has happened. After all, he's a freakin' doctor. Hasn't he heard of a condom?"

Condoms? Yeah, he has a whole box of condoms. Ten to be exact. The knife in my gut digs in a little deeper.

I fiddle with my hair and divert my eyes back out the window. "We did use them at first, but then I sort of told him ... we didn't need them because I had been taking my birth control pills."

"Had you?" Elizabeth breaks her silence.

"Yes!" I respond with a defensive edge to my voice. "I mean ... I hadn't been taking them regularly but then the first time we almost..." I look at them and roll my eyes toward the ceiling "...*you know*, I started taking them every day. But it's not like we had sex right away. I had my period for five days before I even saw Lautner again."

Closing my eyes, I run my hands through my hair and shake my head. "What does it matter anyway? I'm pregnant. How, when, or why doesn't change what *is*."

"I still think you should tel—"

"Ugh! Ave, I'm not going to tell him. I thought I knew him. But the guy that made me believe I broke his heart when I left last month was not in that apartment the other day. *That* was someone else. There is no way in hell I'm going to tell him now."

"Because you're afraid he'll choose her?" Elizabeth questions.

"No, because I'm afraid he'll choose me."

They both share the same blank expression.

"Lautner's too much of a boy scout. He'll choose me because I'm carrying his child. But I don't want to be chosen because I'm some charity case ... and even if he never said that, I would always think it." I rub the back of my neck. "I won't marry someone who would rather be with someone else, and I certainly won't bring a child into that type of relationship."

Avery resumes her slicing, shaking her head. "If he ever finds out, he's going to hate you for not telling him."

Picking up my computer and photos from the table, I shrug. "Yeah, well, I hate him right now."

August 3rd, 2010

Avery went back to L.A. yesterday. She has a job, bills to pay, and for now, there's nothing she can do for me. I'm nauseous half the time and fighting a severe case of anxiety. My intention was to go back to Illinois to tell my dad, but flying in my miserable condition is not an option right now.

"Can we talk?" Elizabeth hands me a glass of ginger-lime iced tea.

I'm soaking up some sun and fresh air by the pool and for the first time today my stomach feels settled.

"Sure, what's up?"

"I don't know what your intentions are for your ... future. But if you decide not to go back to Illinois to have the baby and stay with your dad, then I have a proposition for you."

I push my sunglasses down on my nose and look at her over the rims. "A proposition?"

She sips her tea. "Trevor and I purchased a condo in San Diego, we're moving next month—"

I sit up in my chair. "Oh jeez, you need me to leave. I can be out—"

"Sydney!" She shakes her head and smiles. "Let me finish. As I was saying ... we haven't put this house on the market yet, and Trevor won't accept anything short of what he wants out of it, so it could sit here for a while. In the meantime, we'd like you to stay if you want, under one condition."

"Which is?"

She grimaces. "Swarley stays too."

I look over at Swarley stretched out on the chair beside me. He lifts his head, ears perked up.

"The condo association won't allow large pets. We're

looking for a new home for him, but if you stay here it will buy us more time to find the right person. We'll pay for the utilities and everything, you'll just have to find a job to pay for your food, transportation, and other personal expenses. When it sells we promise to give you at least a month to find a place of your own."

I pinch and tug at my lower lip. The past thirty days have been a train wreck for me. My life has taken it's own course without informing my brain.

"You don't have to decide right—"

"I'll do it."

I really have to stop being so agreeable. Looking back, it's quite possible that's how I ended up in this *situation*.

I flip my sunglasses up on my head. "I mean, it's a generous offer and I'd be crazy not to take you up on it. The morning or *all day sickness* prevents me from going back to Illinois right now, and the thought of moving back in with my dad to have my out-of-wedlock baby is terrifying. So ... I'll do it. I'm sure I can find a job around here and it will give me some time to figure out what I am going to do or where I want to be when the baby comes."

Elizabeth reaches out and grabs my hand. "It might not be a bad idea to stay in this *area* for a while."

Standing, I adjust my top and walk to the edge of the pool. "It doesn't matter if Lautner is five or five hundred miles away. We're over," I declare, diving into the pool.

Chapter Eighteen

September 1st, 2010

NORMALCY. Eleven weeks into my pregnancy and I *finally* feel normal again. The misery of feeling sick all day has faded. My tummy has expanded only enough for me to notice, and it's only when I try to button my shorts or jeans. Skirts, sundresses, and yoga pants are my outfits of choice. I've had to buy larger bras, but I'm not complaining about that. In fact, I think I'll breastfeed this child until they're ten if I get to keep the perky boobs. Sadly, I've read that's not the case. One mom blogger said her kids sucked the life out of her breasts. They went from grapefruits to silly putty.

Fabulous!

Elizabeth and Trevor left for San Diego yesterday. Lucky for me their condo is smaller so they left a fair amount of furnishings here. Trevor thought it would help the house show better.

My dad is leaving tomorrow to drive my car with the rest

of my belongings out here. One of the worst moments of my life was making the call to my dad to tell him I'm pregnant. He's been doing great since his surgery and I didn't want to send him into cardiac arrest with my revelation. The agonizing silence on the line after I told him lasted for an eternity. Then one of the best moments of my life followed. He said, "I love you and I'm here for you." That's *all* he said. At the moment it was my heart that was in danger. He offered me unconditional love and I cried harder and longer than if he would have yelled at me and expressed his utter disappointment in me. Sometimes I think my mom's soul bonded to his when she died because he speaks in his voice with her heart.

I'm not sure where I will go when this house sells, but I'm leaning toward moving down to L.A. to be closer to Avery. It would also put me closer to Elizabeth and Trevor. Swarley's been on my mind lately too. They haven't found the right home for him yet and my pregnancy hormone controlled brain thinks I should keep him. I've talked to him more in the past three months than anyone else. What can I say ... he gets me.

Over the past month I've also managed to find some work as a freelance photographer thanks to Elizabeth's connections. I've taken engagement pictures, baby pictures, family pictures, and I even was the photographer at a birthday party for a dog. Yes, some people have that much money.

———

SINCE ELIZABETH AND TREVOR LEFT, I don't have transportation until my dad arrives in a couple days with my car. Swarley is the recipient of my newfound energy, and with no wheels our ventures have to stay within walking distance. We both finished dinner an hour ago and now we're on our way to the park before it gets too dark.

"I'll let you off your leash, but you have to show some manners. No humping, no pissing on anything man made, and keep the crotch greetings exclusive to your four-legged fury friends. Got it?"

Swarley nods because I've made him part human over the past few months and I'm pretty sure I saw him roll his eyes at me too. Guess I'd better start getting used to sassiness and eye rolling ... read that on a parenting blog too.

Note to self. Find more positive bloggers that paint the picture of parenthood with rainbows, fairies, and pixie dust.

"Sydney?"

I turn. "Hey, Dane!"

He bends down to let his dogs off their leashes. "Gosh, I didn't think you'd be back. How was Paris?"

Which part? The view of the ceiling from the couch or the drain from the top of the toilet?

"Great!" Extremely sugarcoated ... maybe teetering on an outright lie.

"So how long are you staying?" He rests his hands on his hips.

Dane is adorable. I'm sure grown men don't like to be called adorable; hell, I didn't like it when Lautner said it to me, but Dane is just that. Tall, dark, and admittedly handsome with a boyish grin that makes me want to take him home, bake him cookies, and pour him a tall glass of milk.

"I'm not sure. Trevor and Elizabeth just moved to San Diego and I'm staying at their house until it sells or until I find something else."

He cocks his head to the side. "Yet, they left Swarley?"

Turning my gaze to look for the wild pooch, I shake my head. "Their condo association doesn't allow large pets. They've been looking for a new home for him, but for now I have him."

"You two have come a long way since the first day you showed up at my office."

Clasping my hands behind my back, I look down and kick at the dirt. "Yeah, you're right. As of lately, I've considered taking him myself. But until I know where I'm going to end up, offering it would be a little premature if not irresponsible."

"Grad school with a dog. You'd have to find some place to live that allows pets."

My faces wrinkles as I peek up at him. "I'm not going to grad school, at least not for a while. Something's kind of come up."

"Oh?" Dane's hands shift from his hips to crossing over his chest as he widens his stance.

I blow out a long breath, scrubbing my hands over my face. My fingers trace my eyebrows as I meet his eyes again. "I'm ... pregnant."

Dane's eye are going to pop out of his head and the dogs will be chasing them if he opens them any wider. "I'm sorr— or congrat—or—"

I smile because his adorableness doubles when he gets all nervous and starts stuttering.

"It's congratulations now ... 'I'm sorry' was last month."

He nods in slow motion. "So you came back for Lautner?"

"No ... well, yes, but that backfired on me. He's ... *moved on.*"

"Moved on? Are you serious? From ... you?"

I shrug, bobbing my head up and down.

"Well ... he's a fuc—a freaking idiot."

As much pain as this conversation brings me, I still manage to let a giggle escape with an accompanying smile.

"You're right. He is a fucafreaking idiot."

Dane grins.

"Especially because he's with Claire."

His eyes go wide again. "Dr. Brown?"

I nod. "Dr. Fucafreaking Brown."

Dane mouths *WOW!*

"Exactly."

"So what did he say about the baby? Are you staying in Palo Alto so you don't have to shuffle a child back and forth long distance?"

Jerking my head back, I squint my eyes. "What? No ... I mean he doesn't ..."

Telling Lautner and considering the possibility that we would raise our child in a shared custody situation never crossed my mind. Now that Dane has mentioned it, I don't like the idea one bit.

"I didn't tell him."

His mouth falls open. "You didn't tell him? He doesn't even know you're pregnant?"

Digging my teeth into my lip, I shake my head.

"Sydney..." he scratches the top of his head "...it's none of my business, but he deserves to know."

I hate that he's right. This fear I have is paralyzing me and making it impossible to think rationally.

"Dane, I know what he'll do. He'll say he wants to be with me, but I'll never know if it's really about me or the baby. Two months ago I would never have questioned it. I felt like he loved me more than anything or anyone. But when I saw Claire and it had only been a month ... everything changed. I can't trust his feelings for me anymore."

Dane shrugs. "Then don't tell him you're pregnant ... at least not right away. See if he chooses you, just you. If he does, then you'll know it's not about the baby."

"And if he doesn't?" The words cut through my chest.

He sighs. "If he doesn't, then you won't marry the wrong guy for the right reasons."

———

September 3rd, 2010

I'VE SPENT the past two days thinking about what Dane said. The night I showed up at Lautner's and Claire answered the door I hit rock bottom. I felt rejected by him without even seeing him. The idea of being rejected face to face is something so far beyond imaginable I can't begin to conceive of it. However, I have to do it. Everyone I love and count on for support has given me the critical eye for my decision to not tell Lautner. Telling him, no matter the outcome, will take away the constant guilt I feel around everyone.

My dad called when he was an hour away and that was about an hour ago. I sit on the porch, knee rapidly bouncing up and down, eyes glued to the drive. A familiar grey Jeep Cherokee turns in the driveway and I leap to my feet.

"Dad!" I yell, flying down the stairs as he gets out.

"Hey, baby girl." He hugs me and I sense the emotion in his weak voice as I fight back the tears.

"I'm so glad you're here," I whisper in his ear.

"Me too." Releasing me, we both smile. "Let's get your stuff unpacked ... or I'll do it. You probably shouldn't be lifting anything too heavy." His eyes drift to my belly that is still flat.

I roll my eyes. "Maybe in another three or four months, but for now I'm fine. Besides, you're the one who just had surgery on his heart. I feel guilty that I asked you to load up my stuff by yourself and drive it out here to me."

He waves a dismissive hand in the air. "Nah ... I'm fine. Good as new." He opens the back and we both grab a load to haul in.

By the time we get everything inside and unpacked it's late.

"I think I'm going to head to bed. We'll talk more in the morning," he suggests.

I hug him. "Sure, I'm tired too. Love, you."

"You too, sweetie."

———

September 4th, 2010

WE BOTH TAKE Swarley for a walk. My dad is supposed to get some form of low-impact exercise everyday. After breakfast we sit out on the deck and, having exhausted all small talk earlier this morning, the looming topic is breached.

"So this *guy* ..."

"Lautner," I correct him.

Dad nods. "Lautner ... has he stepped up and taken responsibility yet?"

My hand rubs my nonexistent belly. "I haven't told him—"

"You what—" My dad's voice elevates.

I hold up my hand. "Let me finish."

He relaxes back into his chair, lips in a firm line.

"I haven't told him, because I needed to figure out what to do and say that would make it so he doesn't take me back as his pity project. Just because my dreams have been shattered like mom's were, doesn't mean I should settle for someone who doesn't love me."

Dad's eyebrows squish together, lips tuned into a frown, and he's moving his head from side to side. "Whoa! Wait a minute. Why would you say that?"

"Say what?"

"That your mom's dreams were shattered. Where did you ever get that impression?"

I swallow, feeling a growing lump in my throat. "I heard her ..."

My dad leans forward resting his elbows on his knees. "You heard her what?"

It's been over a decade and I was young, but I still hear her voice, her anger, her anguish.

"You and mom were fighting. It was late and Avery was asleep, but I wasn't. I sat at the top of the stairs; you were both in the kitchen."

My dad's shoulders slump, head bowed like he knows what I'm going to say, like he remembers.

"You were arguing about money. She said you should have chosen a different profession if you expected her to stay home barefoot and pregnant. You told her she spent too much money on herself ... me ... and Avery." My voice breaks as a few tears come.

"Sydney, don't—" The tight look of anguish on his face is nearly as painful as the memories.

I draw in a breath and look out at the pool. "Honeymoon baby." I laugh, wiping away the tears and shaking my head. "I suppose in your line of work it was better to say that I was a honeymoon baby than an out-of-wedlock baby."

"Please, Sydney don't—"

I hold up my hand. "I was too young to fully understand. It took me years to put it all together. She said you knocked her up and stole her future, that you made her dependent on you." More tears come fast and furious. "You said—" I choke on the words, bottom lip quivering. "You said she was acting like a whore before you saved her from damnation." A sob escapes. "Then I heard something shatter and I ran back to my room."

His hand reaches for me, but I shake my head and pull away. "Do you have any idea how I felt as the significance of that fight came to light ... one word at a time?"

My dad's eyes are red and filled with tears and regret.

"It was a goddamn punch in the gut when I learned what 'knocked up' meant, and 'whore,' and 'damnation!'"

His jaw tenses. I know I've offended him with my language, but I don't care.

"Sydney, I'm so sorry—" he cries.

Running my hands through my hair, I sigh with a shaky breath then wipe my face. "Don't, I'm not mad anymore. I never wanted you to know I knew, but now things are different. I'm so sick of everyone not understanding me and why I've been so driven to make something of myself. It wasn't just the cancer, it was everything. I hated Mom for blaming you, and I hated you for blaming her. Then later I realized I was most upset with both of you for settling for something less than amazing." I find my dad's gaze again. "I never wanted to be dependent on anyone. I never wanted to sacrifice my self-worth and dreams. I never wanted to *settle*."

He reaches for my hand again; this time I let him take it. "What you heard that night was a culmination of emotions that had been building for years. When things don't go the way we think they should, it's easier to find a scapegoat than it is to look in the mirror. I wish I would have known that you've been dealing with this all these years. You've been trying to put together a puzzle that you don't have all the pieces to."

"What do you mean?" I tilt my head to the side.

"It's hard to explain and there are just some things—"

"Tell me! Jeez, I'm an adult, I can handle it ... the truth please."

He sighs. "Both your mom and I had some personal issues we were dealing with when we met. Maybe that was part of the initial attraction. I was crazy about her and she was a *temptation* for me." He diverts his eyes as if he's embarrassed to admit he was physically attracted to my mom. "You were conceived because I felt like taking *precautions* was somehow more sinful since it was planned." His face contorts into a grimace. "Then when we found out your mom was pregnant, I wanted to get married right away so it could appear that you were a honeymoon baby. Your mom wanted to ..."

Head down, his eyes look up to mine and the pain in them is palpable. He's not speaking, yet I hear his plea begging me to understand so he doesn't have to say the words. The realization gives me chills and my heart sinks.

Knocked up. Saved from damnation.

"She wanted an abortion."

He squeezes my hand tighter and answers with a single nod.

"Was I her first?"

He shakes his head.

Whore.

My hands splay over my stomach. Could I abort my baby?

"Time changes people, Sydney." His dark eyes capture mine. "We all say things we don't mean. We all do things that we regret. I know what you heard, but the reason we fought with such intensity was because we were in love. That, I know in my heart for sure. We loved each other and we loved you girls. Calling your mom a whore is something I will always regret, and knowing you heard me say it ... well, it guts me. What you don't understand is she was my first, but I wasn't hers. When she was seventeen she got pregnant and had an abortion. I hated that she wasn't the 'pure' virgin I imagined finding, but our hearts don't always agree with our minds."

He smiles and looks down.

"I wish you would have been eavesdropping on the conversation we had after she received her cancer diagnosis. The one where she broke down and cried in my arms for hours, eaten alive with guilt. She wanted more time with us —more movies, more bike rides, more camping in the back yard and roasting marshmallows on the grill. The list of regrets was so long and painful to hear, but she *never* said she regretted having you and your sister, *and* she never regretted being a mom instead of an architect."

I'm a flood of emotions. The searing honesty I see as his eyes find mine, lifts the weight of guilt I've been suffering under for years.

His hand moves to my face and I lean into it as he wipes my tears. "That, my sweet girl, is the conversation you should have taken to heart and set your goals and dreams on."

We embrace and I feel two sets of arms around me, his and *hers*. I will read the letter my mom left me with a new set of eyes, and starting today, I will reclaim *my* future, not hers.

Chapter Nineteen

September 6th, 2010

I DROP my dad off at the airport and drive straight to Lautner's. It's Sunday so there's a chance he might be home. Preparing to see him with Claire when I knock on the door has been difficult, but I have to do this. It's the only way I can move forward. I owe it to our baby and I owe it to him.

I don't see his 4Runner, but the lot is large and unusually crowded, so it's possible it's here somewhere.

Once again I feel nauseous climbing the stairs to his apartment, but this time it's all nerves. With a deep breath, I knock on the door.

No answer.

I knock again.

No answer.

"Can I help you?"

I turn and my eyes home in on the rose tattoo I've seen before. "Uh ... I'm just here to see Lautner."

Rose stops on the bottom step so she's looking down on me. "He's at the hospital."

I nod. "I'll go there then."

"They won't let you in unless you're family."

I squint my eyes. "What are you talking about?"

"His mom, duh."

My wrinkled face of confusion remains.

Rose rolls her eyes. "His mom is having surgery today. The cancer came back, but now it's spread. Chemo, radiation ... all that good stuff. Anyway, he's been a wreck. I rarely see him. Claire said between his residency and his mom he's barely hanging on. She's been with him night and day. Doing his laundry, grocery shopping, and checking in on his mom when she gets a chance. I don't know what he'd do without her right now."

My face has relaxed. I have no expression, and the only thing I feel is shock. It's the numbing balance between feeling his pain and my own.

"Do you want me to tell him you stopped by?"

I look at her, back at his door, then down at my hand resting on my stomach. "No ... no need."

My body is on autopilot since my mind is mush. That's the only explanation for how it is I'm back home and on the couch. I don't remember leaving his apartment building or driving home. There no longer is an obvious solution to any of this. How do I mosey back into his life right now? If he's hanging by a thread, one that is being held together by Claire, how can I break that? What will it do to him?

I'm hurt, angry, and confused. I need some advice because I can't trust my instincts if I don't have any.

Chapter Twenty

March 10th, 2011

"**P**USH! SAM, YOU CAN DO THIS." Avery squeezes my hand and encourages me.

The pain is insane and opting out of the epidural was an astronomically huge mistake. Too late now.

"I can see the head. You're doing great, Sydney." Dr. Wiggins' voice, while calm, is irritating as hell.

She's been "seeing the head" for the past forty minutes. I'm drenched with sweat and exhausted. Maybe I'll just stay pregnant forever. This baby obviously doesn't want to come out.

"I'm too tired..." I breathe "...it's not working. There's not enough room."

Dr. Wiggins laughs. "Your baby is fine and you're fine. This is a marathon, Sydney, not a sprint."

Fucking marathon. Does she have any idea how much I hate running?

"No, no, no!" I yell, feeling my belly tighten and the pain

sinking its ugly claws into me as another contraction builds with unrelenting force.

"Now! Push with everything you have, Sydney," Dr. Wiggins instructs.

The burning fire is so intense. It feels like I'm being ripped apart.

At the end of the contraction, I thrash my head from side to side and moan.

"Give me your hand, Sydney." Dr. Wiggins guides my hand between my legs. "Feel that?"

I nod and swallow. It's warm and slick, but it's not me.

"That's your baby. Push it out, Sydney. It's time to meet your baby."

Another contraction begins. With my fingers still on my baby's head, I push with everything I have.

"Aaahhh!" I cry in agony as Dr. Wiggins tells me to stop pushing.

"Oh, Sam!" Avery has tears running down her cheeks. "The head is out. It's your baby. Oh my God."

"Okay, Sydney, one more push, you've made it past the hard part."

Finding strength from some unknown place, I push once more and the room erupts into cheers, laughter, and tears.

"You did it!" Avery is ecstatic.

The nurses congratulate me as Dr. Wiggins hands me my baby. "Meet your daughter, Sydney."

I take her in my arms and she cries for the first time. It's the most beautiful sound in the world. Nine months of emotion pours from my eyes. I can't stop the tears. I'm in love, and yet the moment is bittersweet. Avery has been my rock, but she's not the person I imagined holding my hand and cutting the cord.

"Do you have a name picked out?" the nurse asks.

With gentle strokes, I brush my fingers over her dark hair and she opens her eyes.

Blue irises.

I read that most babies are born with blue or grey irises, but somewhere inside I just know she has her daddy's eyes.

"Ocean ... Ocean Ann." I whisper looking at the most amazing sight I have ever seen.

I look up at Avery and I think of my mom and her letter to me.

I just made my mark in this world, Mom.

———

March 12th, 2011

SIX MONTHS ago I made the difficult and anguishing decision to not tell Lautner. Two days after I left his apartment with the new knowledge about his mom, I ended up in the hospital after passing out. Luckily, Dane and I were supposed to meet at the dog park and he came looking for me when I didn't show up. The doctor said it was a combination of stress and dehydration.

My priorities shifted. I couldn't risk adding Lautner's stress to mine. The only thing that mattered was our baby. Now I know she's the only thing that will ever matter. My hands were made to hold her and my heart beats to love her.

Trevor and Elizabeth sold their house in November. I contemplated finding a place to rent in L.A., but I'd already booked freelancing jobs in both Palo Alto and San Francisco into the middle of February. Enter Dane. He owns several rental properties and one became available in December. He offered to let me rent it month-to-month—an offer I could not refuse. It's a quaint little two-bedroom, all-brick home with a fenced-in backyard perfect for my adopted son—Swarley. I stand by the simple truth ... he gets me, and now I've got him.

"Shh ... quiet, Swarley!" Avery chastises his loud greeting as she sets the baby carrier down by the sofa.

"He's just welcoming her." I laugh, taking a still sleeping Ocean out of her carrier. "She's been hearing his 'voice' for months. I'm sure it won't phase her."

"What can we get you for lunch?" Elizabeth asks, following my dad through the front door.

Sitting on the couch with the whole world swaddled in my arms, I smile. "Whatever. There's not much here."

"Dane is at the store as we speak, but for now we'll go pick something up." My dad bends down and presses a gentle kiss to Ocean's head. The adoring sparkle in his eyes is stirring.

"Dane has done way too much already. He shouldn't be buying my groceries." I roll my eyes.

Avery sits next to me as Elizabeth and my dad leave to get lunch. "Yeah, you try and tell him that. He would sacrifice his left nut before he'd let you want or need for anything."

I shake my head. "I know. He's such a good friend. I don't know how I would have survived these past few months without him."

"Pfft ... *friend?* Whatever. Dane has complete Sydney tunnel vision. He could be in a room full of naked models and still choose to rub hemorrhoid cream on your ass."

"Shut up." I giggle. "I don't have hemorrhoids, and Dane and I are just friends."

Chapter Twenty-One

June 3rd, 2011

OCEAN IS ALMOST three months and I've never adored anything so much. Her beautiful blue eyes are both haunting and mesmerizing. Avery keeps sending me listings for rentals in L.A. She thinks we should get a place together so she can help with Ocean. It's tempting, but I don't want her life to revolve around mine. For now, I'm content with my life in Palo Alto. Avery thinks it's the close proximity to Lautner, but it's not. At least, I hope I'm not that pathetic.

I continue to book more jobs, keeping them to evenings and weekends per Dane's suggestion. When I tried to place an ad for a part-time nanny, he came completely undone. He insisted I work my schedule so he can stay with Ocean, even going so far as to roping his assistant, Kimberly, into being his backup in case he gets called away for an emergency.

Lautner has taken up permanent residency in my thoughts. I'm not sure I'll ever be able to look at Ocean and not think of him. Recently, I've thought about telling him.

He has no idea he's missing out on part of his own life, a perfect and beautiful essence of us. What's been most surprising is Dane, who played Lautner's advocate for months after he found out I was pregnant, is now the one who's making me doubt my decision to tell him. He thinks Ocean will not remember this time in her life, so risking a custody battle is unnecessary right now. I can't fathom the idea of Lautner and Dr. Brown driving off with my baby for a weekend, a week, or longer. The protectiveness I feel toward her is fierce.

"There are two bottles in the fridge and frozen milk in the freezer. Extra diapers are in—"

"Go, Sydney." Dane laughs while playing with a cooing Ocean on the floor. "I know where everything is. The quicker you leave, the sooner you'll return so just ... go."

Kneeling on the floor, I nuzzle her neck then playfully pinch Dane's cheek. "You're too good to me."

He winks.

I grab my purse and camera bag. "Call if you—"

"Go!" he yells with a huge grin.

———

THE REHEARSAL DINNER photos take about two hours. It's the seven plus hours I'll be gone tomorrow photographing the wedding and reception that will cause major Ocean withdrawal.

It's nearly ten o'clock by the time I pull into the dark drive. Easing the front door open, I'm greeted with another irresistible photo opportunity. Dane is reclined on the sofa with Ocean hugging his chest like a koala bear as they both sleep. I snap several quick photos and before I get my camera put back in my bag, Dane wakes.

"Hey," he whispers, easing to a sitting positing.

I smile as we make the gentle baby exchange. After laying her down in the bedroom, I pad back out to the living room. Dane is by the door slipping on his shoes.

"She give you any trouble?"

He tucks a strand of hair behind my ear, leaving his hand lingering against my skin. "She was perfect, just like her mom."

I'm paralyzed with something ... fear? Bending down, his lips hover over mine. He moves the last inch and I turn just enough to offer my cheek instead.

"I can't ... I'm sorry. It's just—"

He shakes his head. "It's fine. I don't want to push you. I just ... *like* you ... a lot."

I force a smile. Calling Dane an amazing guy sounds generic. He's more than that, but I don't have the right words yet, so I say nothing.

"Goodnight. I'll be here by noon tomorrow."

I nod. "Thank you."

He turns to leave but before he gets out the door, I grab his wrist. "I mean it. What you've done for me ... what you're *doing* for me is just—"

He shrugs. "It's fine. I wouldn't do it if I didn't want to."

Another forced smile tugs at my lips, but my eyes don't quite reach his before he pulls away and walks to his car.

Chapter Twenty-Two

November 16th, 2012

WHERE HAS THE TIME GONE? Ocean is getting ready to celebrate her second Thanksgiving. Dark brown wavy hair and *ocean* blue eyes rule me. She's the alpha and omega of my life. This girl of mine has had more photos taken of her than any celebrity ever.

Dane has become a part of our lives as much as Swarley. Not that I'm comparing him to a dog. Okay, maybe I am. The truth is ... he is like family—I just have yet to define his role. We're definitely friends, and the line between that and *more* is blurry. Holding hands in the park and eating dinner together almost every night is the *more* part. There has been the occasional kiss too, but it doesn't lead to anything else. Dane is waiting on me, I can feel it. I think he would wait forever.

The lingering thoughts of telling Lautner about Ocean have nearly vanished—*nearly*. There's no doubt in my mind that it's the fraction of doubt, the damn *what if* that's holding me back from completely moving on. Dane knows it too. I see him trying to fill the father role with Ocean, but I won't completely allow it. Do I want Ocean to know her father someday? Will she hate me like I know Lautner would? These questions are agonizing and the answers aren't so simple.

Dane has been out of town for the past week at a conference. He gets home tonight and it's pathetic how eager I am for some adult conversation. In the meantime, Ocean and I are on our way to the park, specifically the park Lautner took me to watch Brayden fly his remote control plane. Ocean loves watching the kids, and since it's unseasonably warm today, I can't resist getting some fresh air with her.

"Do you want to see some air planes?" I ask her while unfastening her from her carseat.

Her bright-eyed enthusiasm matches mine as she bolts from the car running toward the grassy hill. Those little feet of hers can barely keep up with the energy of her eager legs.

"Ocean, wait for Mommy!" I grab her jacket and chase after her.

Nabbing her before she makes it to the top of the hill, I maneuver her squirmy body into her pink fleece jacket.

"Look!" I point to the sky where a low flying remote control plane buzzes over us.

She squeals with delight as her mouth tries to form the correct word. "Pane!" Her attention is quickly stolen by the little soccer ball I toss down by her feet. "Ball." Ocean picks it up and starts running with it, obviously partial to her dad's type of football, not mine.

The park is crowded today; we weren't the only ones who decided to get out and enjoy the warm weather. I keep a close distance behind my wandering daughter as I take in the diverse crowd. Families, couples, groups of guys with more expensive hobby planes, and even a few single people with their K-9 companions are spread out over the large open area. Guess I'd better not tell Swarley there were other dogs here.

Something catches my eye, or *someone* catches my eye. It's been two and a half years and there's probably fifty yards between us, but I'd recognize that figure anywhere.

Lautner.

He's wearing faded jeans and a black hoodie and his back is to me. I don't see anyone else with him. His head tilts back as he follows a plane overhead. My heart pounds in my chest. This is it. I'm not sure why, but this feels like the moment.

"Ocean?" I call out and she runs to me.

I scoop her up in my arms. "Want to meet your daddy?" I whisper more to myself than to her.

I take a tentative step forward then stop. "Oh my God!" I breathe. My lungs fight for air as the life is sucked out of them.

As if out of nowhere, a woman with long black hair appears and wraps her arms around him and he's ... kissing her. He's holding her in his arms and lifting her petite frame off the ground. The kiss is intimate. I know because he once kissed me like that. Visions of thunderstorms and Lautner hiding the keys flash in my head. Our wet bodies moving with eagerness and desperation. Caressing hands. Hungry lips. Blue irises.

Fight or flight takes over. I'm running toward the car with Ocean in my arms gasping for each and every breath.

"Ball," she cries.

The ball is back beyond the hill, but I can't go back.

"Ball!" Her voice escalates as I fumble with the latch to her carseat.

"I know, sweetie. Mommy will get you a new one. I promise."

Tears form in her eyes and she's fighting against my efforts to get her fastened in, legs kicking, arms flailing.

After I finally get her in, we make the emotional drive home. Ocean cries for her ball. I cry because I just got the closure I needed but not the closure I wanted. I had a moment's glimpse, when I first saw him, of us as a family. An indulgent and unrealistic part of me thought he'd turn around and see us and fall in love with Ocean for the first time. I thought he would fall in love with me all over again. I was wrong.

Ocean has cried herself to sleep. I carry her limp body inside and put her in bed. I'm tempted to crawl in next to her and go to sleep too. Maybe I'd wake up and realize this was all a nightmare. All this time I've imagined Lautner with Dr. Brown. I should feel relieved that it wasn't her in his arms, but I'm not. Seeing him with anyone else is an excruciatingly painful feeling—one I may never forget.

The bottle of Merlot in the kitchen calls to me. I pour myself a glass, stick my phone in the dock, and play some music. "In Your Eyes" plays. Out of over a thousand songs, the shuffle mode picks this one. Life is cruel.

By the time I finish my second glass, I decide to quit. Ocean is my world now, my first priority, and I need to be a responsible and sober mom to her.

"Hey ..." Dane calls from the back door.

"In here." My voice lacks the enthusiasm it should have. After all, I've been missing him all week.

He sits down beside me, pulls me into his arms, and

kisses the side of my head. "Where's the little bundle of energy?"

"Swarley's out back. Didn't you see him?"

Dane laughs and squeezes me tighter. "You know who I'm talking about."

I slide my hand along his chest, returning his embrace. "She's out. Running around the park exhausted her. Then we lost her ball and she had a complete meltdown in the car."

"Hmm, bummer. I missed her and couldn't wait to get home to see her."

I tilt my chin up to look at him. My body feels a slight warm buzz. "Just her, huh?"

He swallows. "No—"

Grabbing the back of his head, I find myself making a bold move I never imagined making. I kiss him. He starts to pull away so I climb up on him, straddling him, and show him I don't want him to stop. Today, I lost a part of myself and the void is raw. I need this. I need to move on. I need … Dane.

Chapter Twenty-Three

June 22nd, 2013
THE WEDDING

"**D**o you, Sydney, take Dane to be your lawfully wedded husband to—"

"Ocean!" Avery's shrill voice sends chills through my body.

"Ocean!" I yell. "Somebody, get help!"

My baby girl, my heart, my whole entire world is passed out on the ground. Her body is rigid with convulsing waves shaking her and her eyes are rolled back into her head but not closed.

"Oh God! Somebody, please help!" My voice cracks.

Her little lips are tuning blue.

"No! No!" My pleas seem to be falling on deaf ears. Why isn't anyone helping?

"Sydney, calm down. She's going to be fine." Dane's voice is calm but it feels like sandpaper on my nerves.

"She's not fine! Her lips are blue. She's not breathing!"

"She's had a seizure. Look, honey, she's breathing. It's going to be okay."

All the voices around me turn to echoes. I pray for God to save her, to take me instead. My baby ... my sweet little Ocean ...

The ride in the ambulance is a blur. I'm being asked so many questions and my mouth is moving, but I'm not sure what I'm saying. Ocean's eyes find mine. *Blue irises.* She's coherent and breathing. Color has returned to her lips but she's crying. My baby is scared. The bottom part of her dress is soiled, and a section of my tulle skirt is ripped from climbing into the back of the ambulance in frantic desperation.

They ask me if I have a hospital preference but I can't answer. We're in L.A. and nothing is familiar. Dane suggested we have the wedding here since Avery lives here and his family is here. They've been wonderful help planning everything, but right now, I wish we were in Palo Alto. Dr. Erickson, Ocean's pediatrician, would set my mind at ease. She's been more than a doctor to Ocean; she's been a friend to me and helped me though all my concerns and apprehension of being a new mom.

"Mommy!" Ocean cries.

"I'm right here, baby." I lean over and hug her, trying to calm her nerves. The lights and strangers looking down on her has to be scary.

We arrive at the emergency entrance and Ocean's cries become louder as they wheel her inside. Dane, Avery, and my dad are right behind us. The nurse shoves a clipboard at me and all I want to do is smack her in the face with it. Lucky for her, Dane takes it and starts filling out the forms.

My stupid dress catches on everything and the ripped pieces at the bottom keep getting caught on my heels.

"Miss or Mrs. ..." the nurse questions.

"Miss, I mean Mrs., wait no we didn't ... Sydney, my name is Sydney." My jumbled brain can't piece anything together. I should be Mrs. Abbott, but I don't think we officially made it that far. I'm sure the big white dress has her confused.

"Sydney, we're going to run a few tests then the doctor will speak with you."

I nod. My heart is broken. The sound of her cries has crushed me. She was calling my name, but there was nothing I could do. Now they've taken her for these tests and I know she's scared and she needs me.

Time is irrelevant. I haven't looked at a clock. Maybe it's been an hour, maybe it's been ten. To me, it feels like eternity.

"We're done with the tests. I'll take you to her room," the nurse says.

"Baby!" I can't hold back the tears as I embrace her frail little body. Her red eyes are glazed and her eyelids are heavy. I kiss her tear-stained cheek, brushing her dark hair away from her face.

"She was dehydrated so we're giving her IV fluids and, as you know, we gave her a mild sedative for the tests we did. It should wear off in an hour or so. The on-call pediatrician will be in shortly to discuss the test results."

"Thank you," Dane responds while rubbing gentle circles on my back.

Ocean's eyes close, I kiss her forehead, and pull up a chair right next to her bed.

My dad hands me a bottle of water. I shake my head. "Drink it. I don't need two of my girls dehydrated."

Reluctantly, I grab it and take a few sips. "We should have postponed the wedding. I knew she wasn't feeling well. God, I feel like such a terrible mo—"

"Shh ... stop." Dane massages my bare shoulders. "I know how scary it looked, but it was most likely a febrile seizure caused by fever and a viral infection. She's going to be fine."

I fold my arms and rest them on the edge of her bed with my head down. Dane's trying so hard to be reassuring, but it's not helping. This place is driving me crazy. I just want to be back home with my little girl. To hell with the wedding, to hell with everything. Yesterday, when she first started feeling sick, my instincts were to postpone, but everyone tried to talk me out of it, saying I was overreacting. Well, who's overreacting now?

"Hi there I'm—"

My head jerks up so fast I'm certain I've given myself whiplash. No. Fucking. Way!

The room is silent with the exception of Ocean's monitors.

"Oh shit." I hear Avery whisper.

He clears his throat. *Lautner* clears his throat. "Dr. Sullivan, I'm Dr. Sullivan."

Blue irises.

He quickly diverts his eyes from mine to the peanut gallery behind me.

"We'll just ... wait outside while the good *doctor* does ... uh ... his thing," Avery suggests to everyone.

Our families trail out of the room in a single-file line. I glance back at Dane, but he doesn't budge.

"Can you give us a minute," I whisper.

His frown shows his obvious displeasure. He leans down and kisses my neck then exits the room without acknowledging Lautner.

I wish I could say after three years he didn't affect me, but I can't.

"Hi," I whisper, nervous hands fiddling with my tulle skirt.

His eyes fall from mine back to the chart in his hands, his lips in a firm line. He swallows hard. "Ocean Ann Montgomery ... you had a baby."

It's not a question. In fact, I'm not sure if he's even aware that he's saying the words aloud.

I'm chewing a crater on the inside of my cheek. He looks at me and I give him a slow nod. The tension is thick and suffocating.

His eyes travel over me. "Nice dress." He frowns.

I stare at my hands. After all this time the words should be here but they're not. My last nerve has been frayed today and my brain is ready to explode.

"The ER doctor ordered blood and urine tests, CAT scan, and an EEG. She had a febrile seizure, most likely from a fever caused by a viral infection. Nothing of any concern showed up on the tests. This is not an uncommon occurrence in young children and she should be just fine. However, since she was dehydrated we're going to keep her overnight, but she should be able to go home in the morning. Do you have any questions?"

I hear his voice but I can't make out all the words. The frigidness of his tone and the lack of emotion has rendered me speechless.

"*Mrs. Abbott*, do you have any questions?"

The jab is obvious and intentional and what I need to snap out of my shock. My back is up and I'm ready to strike back.

"Mommy." A soft voice sounds.

"Hey, baby." With gentle hands, I brush back her hair and kiss her forehead.

"Hi, Ocean. I'm Dr. Sully." His voice has magically transformed into a soothing harmony. "Do you want to listen to my heart?" He holds out his stethoscope.

Her eyes are barely open, but she grabs for it anyway. Gently adjusting it in her ears, he holds the opposite end to his chest. Her kissable little cherry lips curl into a soft smile. He grabs for something in his coat pocket.

"Can I look at your eyes?"

She nods, still struggling to open her eyes.

I hold my breath as he uses one hand to hold the instrument with a light on it up to his eye and his other hand to pull up her eye lid. My whole world starts to collapse around me.

"Your eyes are ... beautiful." His voice cracks, then he clears his throat and takes the stethoscope from her. "Can I listen to *your* heart now?"

She nods.

Lautner doesn't look at me, not one glance even acknowledging I'm still in the room.

He drapes the stethoscope around his neck and squeezes her hand. He might as well be squeezing my heart. "You're perfect, but since it's getting late, I think you should stay here and go home in the morning. Would that be okay?"

She looks at me and I squeeze her other hand and smile. "I'll be right here all night. I'm not going anywhere."

She nods.

"I'll make sure you get something to eat, then I'll be back in the morning. Okay?" He's still holding her hand.

She smiles at him and I can barely breathe. All my blue irises—it's too much.

I stand, waiting for him to look at me, but he doesn't. He turns and leaves the room.

What the hell?

"Dane, Aunt Avery, and Grandpa are outside. Do you want to see them?"

Ocean smiles. "Yes."

I poke my head out the door and they're all standing there. There's no hiding the questions they have etched on their faces, ready to jump off their tongues, but I can't answer them now.

"She wants to see you."

Everyone rushes in except for Dane.

"Go on in. I'll be right back."

He doesn't respond. His eyes fall to the floor and he walks past me into the room.

Lautner is standing at the nurses' station, typing something into the computer. I lean up against the counter in front of him. He ignores me.

"Can we talk?"

He still ignores me. The nurse next to him looks back and forth between us.

"Lautner?"

He looks at me with cold steel eyes then turns and strides down the hall.

"Lautner?" I yell after him.

He ignores me as he slams open the door leading to the stairwell.

He's down the first set of stairs by the time I make it through the door.

"Lautner, stop!" I call after him as the door shuts with a loud bang behind me.

He stops, hands on his hips, back to me. "She's mine." Again, it's not a question.

I chased him down the corridor and yet words fail me again.

He turns, chest heaving, eyes piercing.

Fear slams into me and my protective mommy shield comes up. I shake my head.

"I saw her date of birth. Don't lie to me!"

Tears sting my eyes as I continue to shake my head.

"SHE HAS MY FUCKING EYES! DON'T. LIE. TO. ME!"

A sob rips its way out of my chest. "I—I—wanted to tell —you."

"You what?" He looks toward the ceiling and shakes his head while laughing. "Un ... believable. You wanted to tell me. How is that even possible? I've lived in the same apartment until three weeks ago. My cell phone number hasn't changed. Yet ..." he glares at me "...you expect me to believe you wanted to tell me?"

I wipe my eyes and can see from the black smudges on my fingers that I've just smeared my mascara across my face. "I went to your apartment."

His forehead wrinkles in confusion.

I cross my arms over my chest. "*Dr. Brown* answered the door ... In. A. Bath. Towel."

Lautner shakes his head. "I don't even know what the hell you're talking about."

"Now who's lying? I'm not going to stand here and let you make me feel guilty. I tried to tell you." I turn, open the door, and stomp back down the hall.

"Wait just a goddam minute!" His voice is a growl again as he clenches his fingers around my arm and spins me toward him. "You're not getting off that easy. Make up all the excuses and lies you want, but it's been three fucking years and I'm not buying any of it."

"I suggest you take your hand off her *now!*" Dane's deep voice sounds behind me.

Lautner's gaze shoots past me as he releases my arm. "Well played, Dane." He shakes his head with a sadistic smirk on his face. "You could have said something ... but you didn't. Well, you can have *her.*" His eyes fall to me for a brief second then focus back on Dane. "But you're sure as hell are never going to have *my* daughter." He turns and heads back toward the stairwell.

I collapse into Dane's arms—scared and confused.

———

June 23rd, 2013

DANE and I didn't speak anymore of Lautner last night. Ocean was our focus and with our families hovering it wouldn't have been the opportune time anyway. Everyone is waiting for my instruction. Will the wedding go on? If so, when? Should out-of-town guests stay or go home? Then there's all the food from the reception, cake, and gifts waiting to be shuffled to a new location.

Dane has gone to get us breakfast and caffeine while I

wait with my bright-eyed baby for her to be discharged. Ocean seems to be feeling much better this morning. She has color back in her cheeks and her signature sparkle in her blue eyes.

She's sitting on my lap, dressed and ready to go. Dr. Sullivan is taking his sweet time this morning, no doubt planning his next venomous attack on my already fragile psyche.

"Good morning! How's my favorite patient?" The irony in his comment brings an immediate frown to my face.

He can't see it though, because once again, he's looking only at Ocean. Holding out his hands, she willingly goes to him and it feels like my heart is being ripped from my chest. He sets her on the bed and starts baby talking to her while he checks her over.

"My girl is perfect!"

My? The hell!

"Let's go, Ocean." Swooping her up in my arms, I head toward the door just as Dane walks in.

"She's fine. Let's go." I try to push him back out of the room, my eyes pleading in desperation for him to just go with it.

"Sydney?" Lautner's cool voice calls.

I sigh and roll my eyes, handing Ocean to Dane. "Go. I'll meet you out front."

He nods and takes her. I turn but stay in the door way.

Lautner sits on the edge of the bed, resting his hands on either side. "I don't want to fight with you, but I'm not going to let you just walk out of here with her as if nothing has changed."

I hate the rebel tears that fill my eyes. "I can't lose her," I whisper, shaking my head and biting my lips together.

He stands and walks to the door. I flinch as his hand

nears my face. Pausing for a moment, he looks at me with a tense, pained expression. Then he moves his thumb to my cheek and wipes away a stray tear. I fight the urge to lean into his touch.

"I don't want to take her away from you, Sydney." His voice is soft and kind. It's the first bit of compassion I've felt from him in three years. "I promise. I just want to see her. I want to be her dad."

I sniffle and clear my throat. "We live in Palo Alto, not here in L.A."

He shrugs. "So what? I'll come visit or maybe she could stay here with me and Emma for a few days each month."

"Whoa, what? Who's Emma?" I take a step back. The scene from the park comes to mind. I think I know who Emma is.

He chews on the corner of his lip. "She's my fiancée."

I'm still wearing my wedding gown, so I'm not sure why that last word cut so deep ... but it did.

I shake my head. "No way. You're not taking my two-year-old child and using her to play house with your fiancée. She's doesn't know you *or* Emma, and she's not old enough to understand." I turn and walk toward the elevator.

"Sydney?" Lautner calls.

The doors open but before they close he manages to squeeze through them.

"Don't do this. Please don't turn this into a stupid battle," he pleads, but I hear a slight edge of warning in his voice.

I sigh and stare at the red numbers counting down the floors. "You can come visit and when my schedule allows I'll drive her down here, but she stays with me. I go where she goes."

The elevator chimes and the doors open. I step off and

turn back toward Lautner. He's slumped against the back of the elevator, arms crossed over his chest.

"Take it or leave it," I say with a firm voice.

"I'll take it. Next weekend I'm coming up. Clear your schedule." There's no humor in his voice as the doors slide shut.

Chapter Twenty-Four

June 24th, 2013

IT FEELS so good to be home, even if my wedding turned into an epic catastrophe. Dane's parents and my family tried to delay the events until Ocean got out of the hospital yesterday, but I couldn't. Putting one foot in front of the other to walk to the car was difficult. Speaking was even more challenging, so continuing a marriage ceremony was out of the question. I can't think about the money, or confused relatives, or my fiancé and his shattered ego.

Ocean and Lautner. That's it, that's all I can think about. There is no way to explain this to a two-year-old. What will I say about Lautner's new presence in her life? The poor child will think she's sick all the time with Dr. Sully around. I need to find some books on this matter or seek professional help. It seems like there are probably windows of opportunity to introduce a new parent into a child's life. The first one of course would have been when she was an infant. In my completely unprofessional opinion, the next opportunity shouldn't be until she's older and able to understand what happened, like maybe in ten years. I'm sure Lautner will go for that. *"Hey, big guy, sorry I kept this from you for three years, but if it's all the same to you, I think we should wait another ten. I'll call ya."*

Yesterday's trip home and settling in is a blur. I'm not sure if Dane and I said more than two words to each other. Now this morning he's gone for a run. Ocean is still sleeping and I'm trying to figure out where to put all of our stuff. Last month Dane found a renter for the house we'd been living in. We're now moved into his house, our house.

"Hey," Dane says though labored breaths as the front door opens.

Standing in the middle of the living room surrounded by boxes, I feel quite overwhelmed.

"Hey." I smile.

"Are you thinking of unpacking or taking off?"

His question is a sucker punch.

"Dane ... I'm not ... just because I did't go through with everything doesn't mean I'm leaving."

He hangs his head and shifts his weight side to side. "It's just that ... I saw the way you looked at him and—"

"Wait! How did I look at him? Like I was scared out of my mind that he was going to know? Like my whole damn world was falling apart around me? Like my baby girl was going to be taken away from me? Because that's it. Whatever else you think you saw is in your head not mine."

The grimace on Dane's face sends waves of regret through me. I sigh. "I'm sorry. I don't want to take this out on you. My head is ready to explode and the last thing I need is to have to worry about you feeling insecure." I move to him and take his hands in mine. "We *will* get married. Okay?"

He nods then walks to the stairs.

"Dane?"

He turns.

"What did Lautner mean by 'you could have said something?'"

He runs his hands through his sweaty hair and shakes his head. "I saw him at a coffee shop a month before you had Ocean. But it wasn't my place to tell him."

"Why didn't you tell me?"

He shrugs. "For the same reason you didn't tell him. You didn't need the stress. Ocean was your number one priority and, well … both of you were mine."

———

June 25th, 2013

DANE and I were supposed to be honeymooning in Mexico, but there has to be an official marriage to make the honeymoon legit. Since he's had this week marked off on his schedule anyway, he's decided to do some needed maintenance around his clinic. Ocean and I have been unpacking and reorganizing. One of the spare bedrooms is filled with wedding gifts, gifts I refuse to open or even acknowledge until I'm officially Mrs. Abbott.

Ocean is in her booster seat eating peanut butter and jelly. "In Your Eyes" plays from my phone sending the most unnerving chills down my spine.

"Hello?"

"Hi, Syd." The sound of his voice saying my name sends shivers through me.

There's an awkward pause.

"I rearranged my schedule so I have Friday off. We'll drive up to my dad's Thursday night. Can we go to the beach or something Friday? Then I thought Saturday we could go to the zoo or a childrens' museum or—"

"Lautner?"

"Yeah?"

"Just ... stop. She's two and still takes a nap. An hour at the park wears her out, so don't over plan anything." I sigh. "Besides, you can't go dictating our schedule on a whim just because you've rearranged your schedule."

"Oh, excuse me for not wanting to wait another minute to get to know my daughter after going three years without even knowing that we'd conceived a child and—"

"Stop! I get it. Okay? Call me Friday morning."

I press *End* before he responds.

"Silly girl." I grab the abandoned crust off of Ocean's plate and pop it in my mouth. "You're leaving behind the best part."

She grins and takes a swig of water from her sippy cup.

This isn't the life I imagined for myself at all. It's a waste of time even thinking it, but I can't help but wonder where I would be today if I would have told Lautner.

Chapter Twenty-Five

June 28th, 2013

LAST NIGHT WAS A JOKE. I'm not sure why I even crawled into bed. My mind raced all night while my body tossed and turned. Dane looked equally exhausted when he took Swarley for a run this morning. I'm surprised he didn't kick my ass out of bed, but then again, that's not Dane. He loves me, without question, I know he would lay down his life for mine or Ocean's in a heartbeat. A restless night probably doesn't phase him.

It's sunny and a pleasant eighty-three degrees. Dane's not back and I haven't heard from Lautner, but I'm anticipating a beach day. From the *we* comment Lautner made on the phone, I'm assuming Emma will be joining us today. Good thing there's nothing awkward about this situation.

"No word?" Dane asks as he and Swarley drag their tired asses through the door.

I shake my head while helping Ocean piece together her wooden dog puzzle on the floor.

"Well, I got a call from Mrs. Fitzgerald. Her schnauzer has a thorn or something lodged in his paw. I'll have to catch up with everyone later."

"Are you serious?" I whine. The thought of being with Lautner and Emma without my own backup is not something that's settling too well with me.

He bends down and kisses Ocean then me. "Sorry, honey. Maybe we can all grill out later or something."

"Grill out? Now you're inviting them to dinner at our house?"

He starts up the stairs. "We're going to be in each others lives, might as well make friends now."

Ugh! I hate that Dane's a better person than I am. I know his insecurities are still there, but he hides them so well. Must be a guy thing.

Peter Gabriel sings and I answer before the lyrics paralyze me.

"Hey."

"Good morning, is everyone up for the beach today?"

I'm having trouble feeling the excitement that Lautner exudes in his chipper voice.

"Sure. I've already packed our lunch. Where do you want to meet?"

"I was thinking the beach we used to go to—"

"No!" I reply while walking into the kitchen so Ocean doesn't hear me.

"What? Why not?" He sounds so dumbfounded.

"I'm not taking my daugh—"

"*Our* daughter ..." he interrupts.

I roll my eyes and release an exasperated breath. "I'm not taking *our* daughter to meet you and your fiancée at the same beach where we ..." I can't say it.

"Made love," he whispers.

Why did he say it? Why did he say it like that?

"Just pick a different beach."

"You and Dane choose then. I don't care."

"Dane's not going. He's ... been called into work." I don't mention the grill out because at this point I'm going to feel pretty lucky if I manage to survive a few hours at the beach.

"Then we'll pick you both up in a half hour."

"I'll drive. Ocean's carseat is in—"

"Syd, I bought a carseat."

Whoa! Why does that admission bother me? It's not that I thought he'd see her a few times then decide he no longer wanted to be her father. But for some reason, in spite of what he said, it feels like I'm losing her one piece at a time.

"Uh ... okay, then we'll see you ... in a little bit."

"Sydney?"

"Huh?" I answer with a shaky voice.

"I need your new address."

"Oh, um, I'll text you it."

"Okay, see you soon."

―――――

"Stay hydrated and wear sunblock." Dane hugs and kisses both of us before leaving.

Ocean and I sit on the porch swing and wait for Lautner and Emma. All she knows is that we're going to the beach. Since we can't have the who's your daddy conversation yet, I've decided to not say anything and wait for her to form her own questions.

"Here they are."

Lautner still drives the same black 4Runner. He has two

surfboards strapped to the top just like our first date at the beach.

We stand as they get out.

"Hi, Ocean." Lautner's voice is soft and his fucking Medusa eyes cast their spell on my little girl.

Another little piece of my heart rips away when I see the recognition in her eyes and she willingly goes to him. He scoops her up and gives her a gentle hug.

"Remember me?"

She just grins.

"I took care of you when you were sick. Remember, I'm Dr. Sully but you can call me ..." he hesitates and looks at me then Emma.

I'm holding my breath. If he says Dad, Daddy, Father, or anything like that I'm going to lose it.

"Sully, just call me Sully."

All Ocean can do is grin.

"Ocean, this is Emma."

Emma smiles. "Hi, Ocean. I love your name and your beautiful blue eyes."

Seriously? She has to mention the eyes. Talk about fingernails on a chalk board.

"Emma, this is Sydney."

I dig so deep it's painful, but I manage a polite smile as I offer her my hand.

"Nice to meet you." Her voice is soft and sweet; it matches her smile.

I recognize the long black hair from the park. She's about my height with a few more pronounced curves, but still very toned and ... beautiful. She can't be older than me. If anything, she's younger with perfect olive skin, which makes me hope that she's not older and looking that good.

"Nice to meet you too. Shall we?" I gesture to the car.

Lautner secures Ocean in her seat while Emma gets in front and I put our bags in back.

"Shoot, I forgot our cooler and water bottles. I'll be right back." I jog to the house and into the kitchen.

Our water bottles are in the refrigerator. Grabbing them, I turn to close the door and my breath catches. Lautner is right here, inches from me. I almost bump into him. Looking up, I meet blue irises and they're melting me. My heart struggles to keep up. He's stripping with his eyes, but not physically—it's an emotional branding that will never go away. Three years later and I still feel it, I still feel him. He doesn't speak, his face is stone, void of all emotion. I close my eyes and break the trance.

"I'll get the cooler," he whispers so close to my face I smell the mint from his toothpaste.

I nod and swallow back a surging river of emotions.

———

"Hey, baby girl." I lean over and give Ocean a quick kiss before fastening my seat belt.

Emma turns and smiles. Then I see blue irises in the rearview mirror as we back out of the drive.

Fucking Medusa eyes.

Just kill me already. The man who took everything from me then gave it back one hundred fold nine months later is torturing me with unspoken words while the life we made together sits beside me and his fiancée next to him. I'd better take on some extra work because the therapy I'm going to need will be pricey.

"So, Emma, are you from L.A.?" I'm forcing the small talk like I do with new clients.

"Hawaii. My mother still lives there and my father and his new wife live here in Palo Alto. He's Chief of Staff at the hospital, that's how Lautner and I met."

Lovely.

"Are you a doctor or in med school?"

She laughs and gives Lautner a sideways glance. He winks at her.

"No, I own a website design business. I did a year long technology internship in China. In fact, my dad sent Lautner to the airport to pick me up when I came home last year." She reaches over and rests her hand on his leg. "He was holding up a silly cardboard sign, per my dad's suggestion, and what can I say ... it was love at first sight."

Screw therapy. I'm going straight to the looney bin.

"Wata," Ocean says.

I give her a sip of water.

"Lautner told me you just got married ... to a vet. Are you a stay-at-home mom or do you work outside the house?"

We make brief eye contact in the rearview mirror, then I smile at Emma. "Actually, we're not officially married yet. Ocean had her seizure during the ceremony so we postponed it."

I see Lautner's brows knit together but his gaze stays fixed to the road.

"As for me, I'm a photographer but I work mainly evenings and weekends so I don't have to find daycare for Ocean. It's the best of both worlds really."

"A photographer, huh? What do you photograph?"

I shrug and look out my window. "Everything."

"My dad pulled some strings and got Damon Michaels

to agree to do our wedding photos? Can you believe it? Have you seen his work ... I mean surely you have. He's done a ton of celebrity weddings. Isn't he just ... amazing?" Emma sounds like a seventeen-year-old girl who just found the perfect prom dress.

"I've seen his work, it's ... predictable."

Her head jerks back. "Predictable? You can't be serious? The only thing that I've seen that beats his work is the artist whose work Lautner has on his walls. Some unknown photographer took these incredible shots of him for an art project. They're black and whites of his body ... hands, calves, each defined muscle of his abdomen and back, and Oh. My. Gosh. His eyes. I wanted *her* to do our wedding but my forgetful fiancé can't remember her name and has no way of contacting her. You should see them sometime ... talk about insane talent, just ... wow!"

I can't hide the smile that pulls at the corners of my lips. Lautner won't look at me in the rearview mirror and he's squirming in his seat.

"She sounds *amazing*!" I look back out my window and grin.

"An understatement ... but, yes, amazing." She leans her head back against the headrest and sighs.

IT'S NOT OUR BEACH, but it's not too crowded, and my sweet beach baby is all smiles with her little fingers and toes digging into the cool, wet sand.

"Here, let's put on your hat." I fasten the straps to her pink and white floral sun hat under her chin and sit next to her and all her shovels and buckets.

Emma is sprawled out on a towel in her string bikini a few feet behind me and Ocean. Lautner's been catching some waves but now he's walking our way ... wet, tan, and mouthwateringly sexy. I flip my sunglasses down over my eyes so my blatant staring isn't so obvious.

"Eee!" Ocean squeals as he drops to his knees beside her and shakes his wet head like a dog, splattering us both with cool water.

"Whatcha making?" he asks her.

"Sand," she replies.

"You're up Em," Lautner says. "Unless you want to go?" He smirks at me.

"I'm good, thanks." I don't give him the satisfaction of acting like I see the humor in his question.

"Watch and learn, hot stuff." Emma struts past us with her board, swaying her perfectly sculpted booty the whole way.

She's from Hawaii, of course she's a fucking surf queen.

Lautner jabs at the sand with one of Ocean's plastic shovels. "So you're not married?"

"Not yet."

He doesn't look at me as he fills a bucket and pats it firm with his palm.

"So when?"

I shrug. "I don't know. When's your wedding?"

"August second, and I'd love for Ocean to be our flower girl."

Talking about Lautner and Emma's wedding is crushing. A part of me still belongs to this man and now that he's back in my life, I fear my feelings for him will never dissolve. I can't be near him without wanting him. My body craves his touch, and my heart aches for his love.

"I don't know, Lautner. It's so soon. You just met her last week."

"I love her." He looks at me, eyes firm, jaw clenched.

I shake my head. "You don't even know her."

He looks out at the water. Emma is showing off, but I don't think he's paying much attention to her. "When did you love her?"

"What?" I ask.

"Our daughter, when did you first love her?"

I blink back the tears, grateful that my eyes are hidden behind my glasses. "She's my everything. My head remembers not knowing her, but my heart can't remember not loving her."

"Then you know how I feel."

I nod, biting my lips together, praying my emotions stay in check. "So the airport ... love at first sight, huh? Sounds like *fate*."

He sucks in a breath. "Syd, it wasn't—"

"Never mind, I've changed my mind. I don't want know." I stand and brush the sand off my legs.

Lautner jumps to his feet and lifts Ocean up. "Let's go dip these cute little piggies in the water."

He carries her to the water's edge, and holding her under her arms, he swings her little body like a pendulum. Every time her feet drag through the water she squeals with delight. I grab my camera and start clicking. In a perfect world I wouldn't see Emma walking up the shoreline, or feel the need to check in with Dane. I let my mind wander, just for a moment, to what might have been if I would have come back here after my dad's surgery instead of going to Paris.

The dreamy illusion vanishes as quickly as it came. Emma sets down her board and takes Ocean from Lautner.

She twirls her around in circles and the excitement in Ocean's face is Breaking. My. Heart. I stop taking pictures. The happy family I see through my lens triggers jealousy and fear—a lethal combination. Turning away, I put my camera back in it's bag and grab my phone.

"Hey, honey. How's it going?" Dane answers.

I draw in a shaky breath. "Fine. How's the schnauzer?"

"Rodney is fine. It was a nasty thorn, but I got it out. Are we still on for grilling out?"

I glance back and see the three of them sitting in the sand. Closing my eyes, I breathe in a fresh breath of air. *This is for Ocean ... This is for Ocean ...*

"Probably, but I haven't checked yet. I'll text you in a bit."

"That's fine ... Sydney?"

"Yeah?"

"How are you holding up?"

I may never love Dane the way he loves me, but right now he ranks pretty high.

"I'm dying."

"I'm sorry, wish I were there."

"Me too."

"You can do this. You're the strongest woman I have ever known."

"Thanks."

"Talk to you soon." He disconnects our call.

"Mommy!" Ocean calls, running at me, her little legs working hard to escape the gripping hold of the sand. "Flower ... me ... flower."

"Hope you don't mind, Lautner said he talked to you about Ocean being our flower girl," Emma says with an apprehensive wrinkle to her nose. "I'll need to get her measured for a dress, like, yesterday. Maybe we can do it tomorrow morning."

Lautner squints and mouths "I'm sorry." He knows damn well I didn't say yes to this.

"Yeah, sure, whatever." I turn and grab some hand wipes and grapes for Ocean. "Uh ... Dane wanted me to invite you over for dinner tonight. He's grilling out."

"Oh that sounds like fun. He's not serving red meat or pork is he?" Emma asks as she adjusts her top.

"I don't know, probably fish or something." I'm glad my sunglasses hide my exaggerated eye rolling.

"We'd love to, thanks," Lautner says, digging through their cooler.

"So is this a big wedding you're having?"

Lautner sits on his towel and Emma plunks herself down between his legs. "Only about five hundred," she says.

Luckily, the grape I just popped in my mouth hasn't made it past my teeth or else I'd be choking on it. *Only five hundred?*

"Then we're off to Bali for ten days of..." she giggles and leans back, kissing his neck "...you know."

"Yeah ... well, we should be getting back. Dane might need my help." I shove our stuff in our bags and brush the sand off Ocean. The visual dagger Emma just threw at me has my eyes watering and my heart bleeding.

Through the corner of my eye, I see Lautner standing. He's looking at me, but I refuse to look at him.

"Let's get your toys, sweetie." I hold her hand and pull her toward the pile of sand toys.

Lautner squats down beside me and helps empty out the sand and put them in the mesh bag. "I'm sorry," he whispers.

I can't talk. If I try to talk, I'm going to cry. And I'm sure as hell not going to cry in front of Lautner and Emma.

"Sydney ..." His voice is soft.

I shake my head and grit my teeth. Standing, I lift Ocean. Lautner takes the bags from my shoulder and I let him because I feel like collapsing. It's taking everything I have to hug Ocean to my body and carry her to the car.

"In you go, baby." I fasten her in and brush the sand off my feet before getting in.

Lautner loads everything up as Emma situates her towel over the front seat.

"Hope we have time for a shower before dinner." Emma laughs as she picks at the sand under her perfectly mani-cured nails.

We've been on the road for five minutes and Ocean is out. Emma is messing with her phone and I'm slumped down with my head resting against the window. The tears fall to my cheeks, one at a time, and I wipe them away before they trail below my sunglasses. God, why does this hurt so bad?

Lautner clears his throat. He's glancing at me in the mirror. Then I notice his left hand reaching back between his seat and the door. It's holding a tissue. I swallow hard and reach for it. My fingers graze his palm as I take it and he closes his hand around them. I rest my head on the back of his seat, still holding his hand, my fingers curling around his. I've missed his touch so much. Emma continues to mess with her phone, completely oblivious to everything and everyone else.

"Babe, my dad wants us to come to brunch on Sunday before we leave. What do you think?"

I sit back, taking the tissue from Lautner. He moves his hand back to the steering wheel. "We're in town to spend time with Ocean, it's not that I don't want to see your dad ..."

"Maybe we could take Ocean with us. I'm sure my dad would love to meet her." Emma looks back at me. "Would that be okay with you?"

I sense Lautner's eyes on me. "Um ... I don't know. Can we see how tomorrow goes?"

"Sure." She faces forward again. "I'll tell him we're a maybe."

The rest of the ride is fairly quiet. Lautner pulls into the drive and I unfasten before he comes to a complete stop. I shove the wadded tissue in my purse and unlatch Ocean's harness.

Lautner opens my door. "Let me carry her. You grab your bags."

I turn and hesitate for a moment then nod and get out. Emma stays in the 4Runner while Lautner carries a still sleeping Ocean in the house. She looks so tiny in his strong arms. I remember feeling small in those same protective arms.

"Hey," Dane whispers holding open the door.

Lautner nods and I give a sad smile. Dane's forehead wrinkles. He knows me too well. Lautner follows me up the stairs and into Ocean's room. He lays her on her bed and presses his lips to her forehead. I take a deep breath. There's nothing I need more than a hot bath and a glass of wine.

Lautner turns and moves closer to me. "Thank you ... for today. She's just ... more than I could have ever dreamed of."

I nod and he eases my sunglass from my face. My eyes feel puffy; I'm sure they're red too.

"Why?" he whispers, brushing the back of his hand over my cheek.

I shrug and look away, biting my quivering bottom lip and swallowing.

"I just ... it's ... nothing." I look at him with a tight-lipped smile. "It's just been a long week, a lot has happened. I'm a little overwhelmed, that's all."

"Emma shouldn't have—"

"Everything okay?" Dane's quiet voice sounds at the door.

I take a step away from Lautner and turn. "Fine. I'm going to take a bath." I look back at him. "See you in a couple hours?"

He nods and shares my pathetically weak smile.

———

OCEAN WAKES while I'm in the bathtub. "Mommy," she calls with a groggy voice.

"In here, sweetie."

Rubbing her eyes, she grins. It's a familiar grin, the one that says she wants in the tub with me.

"Come here." I reach out and help her undress. "Go potty, then you can get in with me."

"Bath ... ducky." She giggles.

We go through this routine several times a week. I ask Dane to keep her occupied while I take a relaxing bath. He gets distracted and she sneaks upstairs and gives me the grin I can't refuse. Then I have to drain half the water and add cold because I like *hot* baths. Within a few minutes I'm freezing and crowded out of the tub by all her toys. On a good day I make it out without slipping on a toy and falling back into the tub, sending a tidal wave of water onto the floor, and sparing Mr. Ducky's head from being lodged into my ass by mere inches.

Ocean plays until all the soapy bubbles are gone and the sand at the bottom of the tub is visible. I help her get dressed and dry her hair before sending her down with Dane. Looking in the mirror, I admire the nice color the sun added to my cheeks today. My eyes, however, are still a little red. After squirting some drops in them, I apply some eyeliner, mascara, and lip-gloss.

"Sydney, they're here," Dane calls.

I hustle to dry my hair then slip on some dark jeans and a white sleeveless button-down top. Taking one last glance in the mirror, I release a big breath. "Round two of torture Sydney. Ding. Ding. Ding."

"Hi." I greet Lautner and Emma as I open the back door.

They're sitting on the deck drinking beer and wine while watching Ocean chase the three dogs.

"Small world, honey. Emma's dad, or her dad's cats are patients of mine." Dane grins and flips the burgers on the grill. Lucky for Emma they're turkey burgers.

"Yeah, I had no idea your husband, or soon to be husband, is the infamous Dr. Abbott, or cat whisperer, as my dad calls him." Emma is sitting on Lautner's lap teasing her fingernails along the nape of his neck.

"Dane's gifted all right," I mumble and grin.

"Mommy!" Ocean's blood-curdling cry sends my body into action.

I run out to her. She has fallen in the rocks and scraped her knee.

"Shh ... it's okay, sweetie." I cradle her in my arms and carry her to the house.

"Let me put these on a plate and I'll get you the first-aid kit," Dane says.

"It's fine. I'll get it," I tell him as Lautner holds the door open for me.

Ocean sobs into my chest as I carry her upstairs with Lautner right behind us.

"Shh ... it's just a scrape, baby girl." I reassure her, setting her on the bathroom vanity.

"Can I see?" Lautner asks.

She nods between strangled sobs.

I grab the small first-aid kit. Lautner cleans the scrape and puts some ointment on it. I hand him a Band-Aid. He looks at it.

"I'll be right back," he says.

Hugging Ocean to me, we wait.

"Here we go. Look what I found in my car?" He holds up a Winnie the Pooh Band-Aid.

"Pooh." Ocean giggles and the tears are magically gone.

"There, much better." He bends down and places a kiss over the Band-Aid.

Up until this moment he was a doctor, but that kiss was all Daddy.

He lifts her down and she bolts out of the room and down the stairs like nothing happened.

I throw the wrappers in the trash and lean back against the vanity with my hands on either side. "I'm sorry about earlier. I'm not sure why I was so emotional."

He shoves his hands in his jean pockets. "Emma shouldn't have said what she did about ... Bali. I know she didn't say it to upset you, but she still shouldn't have said it."

I laugh and roll my eyes. "Jeez, Lautner, she's going to be your wife. I'm not under any illusion that you're not going to have ... or do ... *that* on your honeymoon."

Holy crap! I can't believe we're having this conversation, and I can't believe that I said *that* instead of sex. What am I? Twelve?

He shrugs. "I'm just saying that if you were upset by her words ... I'd understand."

"Understand what?"

Running his hands through his hair, he shakes his head. "Nothing." He turns and steps toward the door.

"No, not *nothing*. What were you going to say?" I cross my arms over my chest.

Lautner turns and shuts the door behind him. Before I can blink, he's hovering over me with his hands pressed to the counter on each side of me. "I was going to say I understand if the idea of me being with someone else bothers you." His voice is deep and demanding.

I lean back more to keep our faces from touching.

"Because even though it shouldn't, it drives me fucking crazy to think of Dane's hands on you!"

He's breathless, but I'm not because I'm holding mine. There's no more room for me to lean back, but he continues to inch closer. I feel his arousal against my stomach. His eyes are on my lips and his mouth is almost touching mine.

"Coming, Sydney? Dinner's ready." Dane's loud voice carries up the stairs.

Lautner stands up, but I don't move. We stare at each other for a moment, then I stand up straight and walk out the door.

"What were you doing?" Dane asks, handing me a beer and a plate of food.

Lautner is only a few seconds behind me.

"Uh ... Lautner was just giving me a few first-aid tips for future injuries. Butterfly bandages, properly cleaning wounds ... you know, that kind of stuff."

Sucking the air from my lungs. Hardening my nipples. Drenching my panties.

"Well, Miss Ocean is pretty smitten with her Winnie the Pooh Band-Aid," Emma says, standing on her tiptoes to give Lautner a quick smooch.

I sit next to Ocean and Lautner sits on the other side of her. As I cut up her food, I risk a glance at him. His eyes are hot, blue hot, like a blow torch searing into me.

"What's on the agenda for tomorrow?" Dane asks, sitting opposite of me.

"We're taking Ocean to get fitted for her dress. Did Sydney tell you she's going to be the flower girl in our wedding next month?" Emma's enthusiasm is probably contagious to most people, but it makes me want to vomit.

Dane looks at me. I smile around my mouthful of food.

"I guess we'd better get that date on the calendar then. We'd hate to pick the same day for our wedding. That would be a real conflict," Dane says.

I'm not sure if it's sarcasm in Dane's voice or a polite reminder to me that we're not married yet but should be. Although we never finished it, we've had our *wedding*; I'm not feeling up for a redo. Too much money has already been wasted, including my dress and Ocean's. At this point, a justice of the peace feels appropriate.

Wiping my mouth with a napkin, I swallow and clear my throat. "I'm sure we can work around their weekend."

"So where is your wedding taking place?" Dane asks.

"San Francisco at Bently Reserve. Of course, due to

limited space for the ceremony, only three hundred and fifty of the five hundred guests will be invited to both the ceremony and reception," Emma says.

"Five hundred?" Dane chokes.

I grin and kick him under the table.

"My dad's new wife comes from a large affluent family, then of course there are all my dad's friends and colleagues. With all the doctors it's going to be like a medical convention." Emma laughs and Lautner shakes his head with a hesitant smile.

"Done," Ocean says.

"Do you want some more strawberries?" I ask.

She shakes her head.

"Okay." I wipe her off and help her out of her booster seat.

"Swing!" she yells, running to the toddler swing Dane hung from the large oak tree.

I roll my eyes. "Why don't you play for a bit while we finish eating?" I call after her.

Lautner scoots back in his chair, wiping his mouth. "I've got this"

I give him a weak smile and a single nod.

"So where are you going on your honeymoon?" Dane asks Emma.

That's my cue to leave. I grab some fetch toys from the rubber bin on the far side of the deck and whistle to the dogs. All three come running. I toss them out as quickly as they retrieve them. Every time I look over at Lautner and Ocean he's smiling at her, but his eyes quickly find mine, like he senses my gaze. We're a good fifteen yards apart, but when his blue irises are on me I feel him as close as we were in the bathroom.

The bathroom. God, what happened there? How is it that less than a week ago I was in the middle of my wedding vows to Dane—and Lautner is getting married in a month—but when I'm near him the three years we've spent apart seem to vanish? This is such a mess.

Chapter Twenty-Six

June 29th, 2013

MONDAY CANNOT COME QUICK ENOUGH. I need some serious psychiatric help.

Lautner and Emma left shortly after dinner and Ocean was asleep by nine. Dane, however, was feeling frisky—like a cat. Part of me questioned if he'd been bit by one and caught some feline virus like Peter Parker and the spider bite. He kept rubbing up against me while I was doing dishes, and he nuzzled into my neck and licked me. His tongue felt dry ... like a cat's. No joke. When he hummed in satisfaction, it sounded like a purr. Then I just about passed out from shock when I looked over and saw him licking the top of his hand. I thought "Holy shit! He's cleaning himself." But then I realized he had some frosting on his hand from cleaning up the rest of Ocean's cupcake.

I'm losing it. Lautner is back in my life in the worst way imaginable. I can't get him out of my head. After Dane snapped out of his freakish feline phase, he turned into a dog in bed. More licking, but not sexy licking. It was the kind of licking that makes one feel the need to wash it off. A Dr. Brown and Swarley situation was what it felt like. Dane must have hydrated before bed because his dry cat tongue became a slick, slobbery lubricating wand. His hands were sandpaper on my skin which was crawling from his every touch. The moderate but not Lautner-sized erection in his briefs was rubbing my skin raw on my thigh as he humped my leg and fondled my breasts. Even my nipples were scared as they inverted like turtles hiding. I lay there silent and limp like a corpse until Dane asked if something was wrong. The response I swore I'd never use in bed came out automatically as a desperate plea. "I have a headache."

Sipping my tea while waiting for Dane to return from his run and Ocean to wake up, I'm seeing things differently. Dane used the same moves on me last night as he has since the first time we had sex. Lautner has fucked with my head. I even tried to imagine Lautner having sex with Emma, hoping it would stir some anger and make me want Dane more, like the time I saw them in the park. Nothing worked.

"Good morning, sunshine. How's your head?" Dane asks in a cheery voice, taking Swarley's harness off.

"Much better, thanks." I smile.

"When's the dress fitting, measurement taking, whatever thing happening?"

I shrug. "Not sure. I haven't received that call yet."

"Is this a girl thing or are we all going?"

"Don't know that either." I sip my tea. "Emma wants to take Ocean, just Ocean, with her and Lautner to her dad's for brunch tomorrow. What do you think?"

Dane finishes guzzling down his water then wipes his mouth with the back of his hand. "I know Dr. Kane. He's a great guy. It's up to you, but I wouldn't be too concerned, unless you don't trust Lautner."

"It's not a trust issue. Ocean's just young and I don't want her to be scared."

"She is a real mama's girl, but I think she'll do fine. Maybe it's a good idea to let her go for a few hours before they decide they want her to spend the weekend in L.A. with them."

My head snaps up. "Why do you say that? Did they say something?"

Dane tosses his plastic bottle in the recycling bin. "While you were playing with the dogs and Lautner was swinging Ocean, Emma mentioned the possibility of Ocean staying with them next weekend. She thinks they should spend as much time together as possible before the wedding so when they get back from their honeymoon it's not like starting over with her."

My head is screaming "over my dead body," but I don't let on to Dane. "One day at a time. I can't make any promises yet."

———

I GET the call from Lautner shortly before ten o'clock. Dane finds a lame excuse not to come with us, something about a leak with the backyard spigot. So to not come across as anti-social, he suggests dinner again tonight at an Italian restaurant near campus.

The drive to the bridal store in San Francisco is uneventful. Emma dominates the conversation, talking about her new design accounts and lots of wedding talk.

"Mags!" Emma chimes as we enter the lavish store.

A tall thin lady, probably in her forties, with chin-length blonde hair hugs Emma. "Darling." She greets in an I'm-just-that-stuck-up voice.

"I want you to meet Ocean." Emma takes her hand and I reluctantly let her go. "Lautner's daughter."

Mags looks her over and smiles as much as her Botox infused face will allow. "Well, aren't you just a real button." She taps Ocean's nose with the tip of her acrylic nail. "Come on back, let's get you measured and pick out the perfect dress for you."

I start to follow them and Emma turns around. "She'll be fine, if you want to wait out here."

No fucking way!

Ocean is grinning, eyes sparkling. She's all girl, unlike her mom was, and the lace, satin, and tulle dresses surrounding us transform her into princess mode. Truthfully, I don't care to help with Lautner and Emma's wedding, but being cut off from my daughter pisses me off.

"There's a coffee shop across the street. Take your time and meet us over there when you're done." Lautner attempts to make peace before my wrath is unleashed.

I look once more at Ocean and bend down to give her a kiss. "I love you. I'll be right across the street. Okay."

She nods and follows Emma to the back of the store.

I turn and look at Lautner, not able to hide the frown on my face.

He opens the door and gestures for me to go out.

"She'll be fine," he mumbles as we cross the street.

I turn as soon as we reach the opposite sidewalk. "Don't! Don't say that to me. You've known her for two goddamn seconds. I know you can't understand it yet, but the farther I get from her the harder it is to breathe. So don't you dare try and make me feel like my concern for her is somehow an overreaction. Understand?"

He holds up his hands. "Understood."

I move past him and he catches up to open the door to the coffee shop. "And whose fault is it that I've known my daughter for *two goddam seconds*?" he says in my ear with a low gravelly voice as I walk inside.

"Ask Claire, or did you have to officially sever all ties with her when you decided to be monogamous with Emma?" I grit though my teeth while forming a fake smile for the barista at the counter.

"What can I get for you?" She smiles back.

"Small green tea, please." I set a ten dollar bill on the counter. "And whatever he wants." I don't wait for Lautner to order or my change before walking off and finding a seat near the window.

He brings our drinks and tosses my ten back at me. I roll my eyes.

"What is your issue with Claire?" he asks with an edge of disgust to his voice as he removes the lid to his coffee.

I laugh. "You mean aside from the fact that you didn't wait a month after I left before you started screwing her again?"

He squints his eyes. "What the hell are you talking about?"

"I told you. Claire ... at your door..." I raise my eyebrows, waiting for my words to spark some recognition in his brain "...in a towel."

He shakes his head and I can't believe he's acting like he doesn't remember.

"July 23rd, 2011, nine o'clock at night. I'd just gotten off the plane after a twelve hour flight from Paris—pregnant and so fucking nauseous. The cab took me straight to your apartment."

He's still looking confused.

I sigh and continue. "Your 4Runner was there ... so *you* were there. It took everything I had to knock on your door, then ... *she* answered, her naked wet body wrapped in one of your bath towels. She said I was too late." I look out the window to the passing cars. I can still feel the pain from that day.

"Jesus, Sydney ... I ... I didn't sleep with her."

I hate that after all this time he can't just be honest with me.

"I wasn't there—"

My head whips around. "Your car was there!"

"But *I* wasn't!" His voice escalates and we both look around to see if people are staring at us. "Claire had some plumbing issues in her apartment and they couldn't get out until the next day to fix it. So I told her she could shower at my place *while I went for a jog!*" His voice isn't as loud, but his tone is still firm.

I shake my head. It doesn't make sense or maybe it does. Did she want me to think that something was going on? Or did I jump to that conclusion on my own?

"What did she say after that?" he asks.

"After what?" I whisper, my mind still reeling.

"After 'you're too late?'"

I can't stop shaking my head. "I ... I don't know. I was so sick and I ran out of the building and vomited over and over. Then I ... God, I collapsed on the ground and cried. Couldn't stop—couldn't stop crying. It felt like I was ... dying."

Lautner's elbows rest on the table, his forehead pressed against his palms, voice shaking. "I'm so sorry, I didn't know you ..." He lifts his head. Tear-filled blue irises hit me hard. "... You came back?"

I think it's a question, but he says it with such disbelief I'm not sure.

"I came back," I whisper.

"Mommy!" Ocean calls as the coffee shop door chimes upon opening.

She hops up on my lap and hugs me tight. Lautner clears his throat and wipes his eyes.

"Babe, you look like you've been crying." Emma outs him.

He clears his throat again. "Coffee went down the wrong pipe."

She hugs his arm and leans up to kiss him. "Poor baby."

He pulls away first. "So where to now?"

"Zoo!" Ocean yells loud enough for everyone to hear.

We all laugh.

"Someone's been putting ideas in your head," I tell her while nuzzling her soft neck.

Emma holds her palms up. "Guilty."

"The zoo it is." Lautner declares, standing up.

———

"I MIGHT RENT A STROLLER," I announce as we get out of the vehicle. "If I would have known we were going to end up here I would have brought hers."

"Nonsense." Lautner swings Ocean up and plops her on his broad shoulders.

She releases her signature happy squeal. I can't hide the smile that plays across my face. Seeing them together is, at least part of, a dream come true. Following them to the entrance, reality smacks me in the face again. Emma wraps her arm behind Lautner and slides her hand in his back pocket. There are four of us so there shouldn't be a fifth wheel, but that's what I feel like.

"What do you want to see first?" Lautner asks Ocean as we make it through the gates.

"Zoo!" she cheers, grabbing onto his ears like handles.

"Alright, I'll choose." Lautner laughs, holding her feet.

Two hours later we've seen all the major exhibits. There hasn't been much adult conversation. It's been all about Ocean. Fine by me. We buy some snacks and head to the playground area.

Lautner surprises me when he pulls a packet of wipes out of his pocket and proceeds to wipe Ocean's hands before she eats her soft pretzel.

He glances up at my dazed stare. "What?"

"Nothing." I smile and look away.

Ocean takes three quick bites before she's running off to go play with the other kids.

"Dane feels bad," I lie, "about missing the outing today. He suggested dinner at some Italian place near campus tonight."

Lautner looks at Emma. She shrugs and nods her head.

"Sounds great." He smiles back at me.

"Have you thought about brunch tomorrow?" Emma asks.

I keep my eyes on Ocean; she's on her third trip down the slide. "If she's fine with going, then I'm fine with it too."

"Great! I'll let my dad know." Emma grabs her phone from her purse.

Lautner's foot taps mine under the table. I turn.

"Thank you," he whispers.

I nod but can't quite find a smile. He has no idea how hard it's going to be for me to watch the three of them pull out of our driveway tomorrow.

———

"I USED to come here all the time," Lautner announces as we're seated at the Italian restaurant Dane picked out. "They have the best grilled Tuscan chicken."

"Pata." Ocean claps her hands as Dane lifts her into her seat.

"Yes, pasta for you, sweetie." I hand her some crayons and a coloring page.

The waitress brings us our drinks and takes our order. Lautner traces Ocean's hands on the paper and she giggles like he's tickling her. Small talk about our day at the zoo fills the awkward space of time until our food arrives.

"Pata!" Ocean cheers.

"Shh ... yes, pasta." I laugh while cutting up her spaghetti.

"You like pasta?" Lautner smiles at her.

She nods with enthusiasm. "I eat pata." She spoons some up and shoves it in her mouth. Several pieces are stuck to her chin.

"Missed some." Lautner leans over and press his lips to her chin, sucking in the missed pieces.

She giggles and I feel myself falling in love with Lautner all over again, but this time it's with Daddy Lautner. It's only been a week, but I see the adoration in his eyes ... and hers too.

"Are you heading back to L.A. after brunch tomorrow?" Dane asks.

"Yes, I have some charts to go through before Monday," Lautner answers between bites.

"Did you want to talk to them about next weekend?" Emma looks over at Lautner with her eyebrows raised.

He pats his mouth with the napkin and swallows. Before he can say anything, Emma continues.

"Since everything seems to be going so well and ... well, we just adore Ocean, so we wondered if she could come stay with us next weekend. You know, keep the bonding going. I mean, if you're not comfortable with it until our attorneys get everything in writing we completely under—"

"Whoa ..." I shake my head. "What are you talking about?" My heart is in my throat, blood surging through my veins.

"Nothing ... it's not what you—" Lautner starts to talk.

Shoving my chair back to stand, it falls over from my abrupt movement. "No ... No ..." I shake my head in defiance. "You promised..." I glare at Lautner and toss my napkin on the table before storming out of the restaurant.

My world is unraveling. He played me, made me trust him. Now I'm going to have to fight to keep Ocean out of a custody battle. God, I can't breathe. Emerging from the restaurant, I fight for air. One labored breath at a time, I stumble down the sidewalk and turn into an alley. Falling back against the side of the building, I slide down and tug at my hair. "No ..." I cry. Something's wrong. I can't breathe. This must be what a panic attack feels like.

"Syd ..." Lautner's voice startles me. He's hunched down in front of me.

"No ..." I scream, lunging at him, punching and smacking him. "You promised ..." I cry. "I hate you!"

He grabs my arms and holds them to my chest, pressing

me back against the wall. "She—she—she's mine!" I try to suck in air but it feels like I can't, like there's no air to take in.

"Shh ... calm down, Syd." His voice is soft and steady, but I don't buy it. I know he's playing me to get what he wants.

"I—can't—brea—breathe—"

"Slow it down. Take in a slow breath, Sydney. Feel your body. Start with your toes. Can you move your toes?"

"Go—away!" I try to push him back. "She's—mi-mine."

"Slow it down, baby. I'm not taking her from you."

"Don't—call—me—th-that—"

His mouth is on mine. It's hard and demanding. I fight him. I fight for air. Then I feel them—my toes, my legs, my fingers, my arms. Finally, I suck in air through my nose and my lungs accept it. Our tongues reunite; it's been way too long. He's breathing life back into me and I don't ever want him to stop. As his hands relax around my arms, I slide my palms up to his cheeks.

I hate him.

I love him.

I need him.

I want him.

Then he slows his movements and releases me.

I see the instant regret in his tense eyes and I realize ... I can't have him. He's not mine anymore.

"I'm not taking Ocean away from you. Okay?" he whispers, brushing his thumbs over my tear-stained cheeks.

"Why did Emma say—"

He shakes his head and closes his eyes briefly. "I was upset. That night I left the hospital after finding out, I vented and said things I shouldn't have. Emma thought I should get an attorney given the circumstances, and that night I did too." He swallows and I see the pained wrinkling of his forehead. "But things are different now. I see the way she looks at you and *needs* you. No attorneys. We'll work it out, okay?"

"Why did you kiss me?" I whisper.

He steps back and drops his head while slipping his hands in his front pockets. "To calm you down. I—I'm sorry. I shouldn't have."

Rejection. It's a sick, nauseating, awful ache. I suck in a controlled breath and release it. There's nothing else I can do but add this incident to the "101 Reasons Why Sydney is Fucked Up" list that I'll be taking to therapy as soon as I get it scheduled. I start to walk back toward the restaurant, but Lautner grabs my arm.

"What about tomorrow? Can Ocean still—"

I yank my arm away. "Yes, you can pick her up in the morning." My hurt is disguised as anger in my voice. Lautner has a slumped defeated posture, but I don't care. I can't care. I'll only get hurt worse if I do.

Chapter Twenty-Seven

June 30th, 2013

TICKTOCK. Lautner and Emma should be here any minute. Ocean seems excited which eases my anxiety over her being scared, but there's still the irrational part of my brain that thinks they're going to kidnap my baby. It's only 9:30 a.m. and Dane thinks I'm going with him and the dogs to the park after Ocean leaves. Wrong! I'm prying the cork out of the bottle of Riesling in the refrigerator and numbing my nerves.

"Here they are," Dane says, looking out the window.

I stand and mess with Ocean's hair. "Do you need to go potty once more before you go?"

"No."

"Okay, are you sure you want to go?"

"Yes." She smiles and breaks my heart ... a little.

We take her out front.

"Good morning, my beautiful girl!" Lautner picks her up and hugs her.

We haven't explained the father situation to her, but

every time Lautner sees her, he tells her with his body language that she's someone special in his life.

I follow them to the car.

"Hi, Sydney," Emma says from the front seat.

"Hi," I reply with a hesitant voice. I can only imagine what she thinks of me after last night's little display at the restaurant.

Lautner gets Ocean secured in her seat and steps back. I lean in and kiss her, resenting the tears that are stinging my eyes.

"Love you, sweet baby. See you a little later, okay?"

"Okay." She kisses me again. I close the door and turn toward the house before my stupid tears break free. Lautner grabs my wrist and turns me back around.

Burying his nose in my hair, he whispers in my ear, "Please don't cry. I'm bringing her back, okay?"

I nod once and continue walking back to the house. Dane sees the tears escaping and embraces me.

"Don't say anything," I plead.

"I won't." He rests his hand on the back of my head.

———

DANE FROWNS when he sees me on the couch with a large glass of wine. He kisses my cheek and leaves with the dogs. Kudos to him for biting his tongue so hard. It's not about being away from Ocean for a few hours. I've done that many times before. That's why Dane doesn't understand me. I can't tell him that my fear over losing Ocean mixed with my messed up feelings about Lautner has me spinning out of control.

I'll never forget how broken Lautner looked the day I left

him to go back to Illinois. There's this sick feeling I have that Lautner's looking for revenge. I'm a moth to his flame and he's drawing me in. It's only a matter of time before I get burned. Is that what he needs? Revenge? Does he need to bring me to my knees so I can feel what he felt? He loves big, so I know that he loves Emma. Would he rather die than hurt her? Is his love for her a *soul-shattering love that will never be matched?*

"In Your Eyes" plays and I jump and grab my phone. It's not a call, just a text.

You're KILLING me, one sad tear at a time.

Great, this has to be code for "get a grip, you pathetic loser." I'm sure he and Emma laugh at what a bawl baby I am. She's probably in on his revenge plan.

"Sydney, Karma, Karma, Sydney. Oh jeez, that's probably their master plan. Drive Sydney insane and then snatch her baby after she's been committed. Gotta hand it to ya..." I hold up my glass "...I'm halfway there. I don't even have the dogs here, so it's official ... I'm talking to myself." I shake my head and gulp down the rest of my wine. "You're a crazy bitch, Sydney." My eyes close.

"Sydney ... Sydney!"

"What?" I'm startled out of my sleep.

"They're back." Dane gestures with his head to the front window.

I jump up and grab my head. "Ugh!"

"Too early for wine?" Dane smirks, holding the door open for me.

"Shut up." I roll my eyes but can't hide my embarrassed grin as I walk out front.

Lautner is carrying Ocean toward the house. She's asleep in his arms.

"Does she ever stay awake in the car?" he asks.

I shake my head. "Rarely."

"I'll take her." I hold out my arms.

"I've got her." He continues into the house and right up the stairs.

Dane stays outside chatting with Emma.

Standing against the wall in the upstairs hall, I wait for him to lay her down. He slips out, pulling the door partially shut.

"She did great. Emma's dad fell in love with her."

I shrug. "Of course he did. She's amazing."

"She's you," he whispers.

"Stop."

He squints his eyes, cocking his head to the side. "Stop what?"

"Everything." I brush past him and hurry down the stairs.

Grabbing my wine glass from the sofa table, I take it to the kitchen.

"Can you elaborate on *everything*?

I set my glass in the sink and turn to him.

"Touching me, kissing me, being so good with Ocean, handing me tissues when I'm crying, telling me how much it bothers you to think of Dane's hands on me, texting me bullshit about 'killing' you with my tears … just EVERYTHING!" I run my hands through my hair. "I get it. You're pissed that I left you and this is your chance for revenge. Time to make Sydney pay. Well, mission accomplished. Job well done. I'm miserable, hurt, and a fucking jealous, raving lunatic. So stop trying to make me love you again just to run off with someone else."

He jerks his head back. "Love me *again*? Again?" He turns and shakes his head. "You have to love someone *once* to love them *again*."

"What's that supposed to mean?" I follow after him as he walks to the front door.

He grabs the knob but doesn't look back at me. "Why would I think you ever loved me?"

"Why wouldn't you?" I wrinkle my face in confusion.

"Because you never said it." He opens the door and walks out, pulling it shut behind him.

Chapter Twenty-Eight

July 1st, 2013

I WAKE up with a miserable headache from finishing the rest of the Riesling after putting Ocean to bed last night.

Serves me right. It's time to Get. It. Together. I dug my way out of this miserable pit when I was pregnant with Ocean, I can do it again. I'm going to focus on my family, starting with setting a date to make my marriage to Dane official. Then I'm going to see an attorney. Lautner and Emma are right; there has to be some boundaries set. It's the only way to have any sense of organization and respect for each other's time.

Grabbing my phone off the dresser, I sneak past Ocean's room and down the stairs for some much needed tea with a boost of caffeine. When I turn on my phone, I see a missed text from Lautner.

> Thank you for the time with Ocean. Sorry if
> I led you on. Wasn't my intention. Are you
> by any chance visiting Avery over the
> holiday weekend? I'd love to see our
> daughter again, but I'm on call so I can't
> leave town.

Heating the water, I decide to wait to respond. I need to be sure I'm in my new frame of mind. The fourth of July has creeped up on me, and to my knowledge we don't have any plans. Avery, on the other hand, most likely has something planned. I call her first, before Dane.

"My client will be here soon, what's up, Sis?"

"Hi to you too."

"Just kidding." She laughs.

"What are your plans this weekend?"

"Vegas. What are yours?"

"Seriously? You're going to Vegas?"

"Uh ... yeah. Girls' weekend, sorry we didn't invite you, figured you were doing the family thing."

"Whatever, I'm not calling for an invite. Just thought of coming for a visit and bringing your favorite niece."

"Ocean's my only niece, but yes, favorite. I'll come visit the following weekend if I can reschedule my clients. How's the 'who's your daddy' thing going?"

"Crazy, confusing, but mostly good for Ocean. She likes him a lot and he's smitten with her. We need to figure out visiting times and all that. Oh ... and she's going to be the flower girl in his wedding."

"Wow! Nothing weird about that. So will you be at the wedding too?"

Good question. I hadn't thought about that. Can I watch Lautner marry Emma? Doubtful.

"I hope not."

"So when's your wedding?"

"Soon. But it's not going to be a redo wedding. I'm thinking justice of the peace."

"Dr. Dane okay with it?"

"I haven't brought it up, but—"

"But you've had his balls wrapped around your fingers for years, so of course he'll be okay with it."

"Nice, Ave." I roll my eyes.

"Gotta go. Give Ocean a big hug for me. I'll call you after my wild weekend."

"Be careful."

"Yes, Mom."

For my own sanity I need to get things with Ocean and Lautner figured out. This weekend would be a perfect opportunity to discuss what we each expect so we know how to proceed when we meet with our attorneys. However, I'm not sure Dane is going to be too excited about spending another weekend with Lautner and Emma. I sure as hell am not looking forward to it.

I call Dane.

"Hey, honey."

"Hi, are you with a patient?"

"Not at the moment. Why?"

"Just seeing what you'd think about going to L.A. this weekend?"

"I can't go. We're walking rescue dogs in the parade Saturday morning."

"Crap, that's right. I forgot."

"But if you don't mind going without me, then I think you should go. Avery's probably dying to see Ocean."

"Uh ... yeah, I'm sure."

"Go for it then."

I chew on the inside of my cheek, feeling like shit for not being honest with him. I'm not sure how he would feel about me taking Ocean to L.A. just to see Lautner. Dane said I shouldn't go out of my way, that if Lautner wants to see Ocean, then he can drive his ass up to Palo Alto. Lying to Dane makes me feel like Lautner is my dirty little secret. But maybe after I get things set straight this weekend, I won't feel so guilty.

"I think I will go. Thanks, Dane."

"Bye, honey."

I text Lautner.

> We'll drive down Friday morning. We need to talk. Send me your address.

Chapter Twenty-Nine

July 4th, 2013

> Just stopped for gas. We'll be there in 10.

OCEAN WAKES up from her car nap and needs to go pee, like ... now! So I gas up the car while we're here. We can't check into our hotel until after three-thirty, so we're going to Lautner's first. I'm carrying a nice load of guilt with me on this trip. Avery's not in L.A. but doesn't know that I am. Dane thinks I'm visiting Avery, but I'm not. Lautner thinks I'm staying at Avery's, but we're actually staying at a hotel several miles from Lautner's house. Oh, the web I'm weaving.

We wind our way into the hills until we reach his house. Wow! It's a gray two-story home set in a secluded urban oasis with a deck that appears to wrap around the entire house. I pull up into the steep drive, making sure to set my emergency brake.

"We're here, sweetie."

Lautner comes out the double French entry door with a million dollar smile. Ugh! He's already making this hard on me. I can't help staring at him in his cargo shorts and a snug grey T-shirt. He opens the back door.

"Hey, there's my girl!" He unfastens her and she clings to him with an eager smile.

We walk toward the house.

"Where's Dane?"

"He couldn't come. His clinic volunteered to walk some shelter dogs in the parade."

We step inside to an open living room with a fireplace, stone floors, and walls of windows.

"This is amazing!" I follow the windows around to the back and I'm greeted with the most spectacular panoramic view of Hollywood, including the sign off in the distance. "Must be rough waking up to this view every day."

He laughs, setting Ocean down. "It's not too bad."

Ocean runs straight to the windows, smacking her hands on them.

"Oh, sweetie, don't put your hands on the clean glass." I pull her back.

Lautner squats down behind her and grabbing her hands, puts them back on the windows. "You can put your little hands here..." he moves them to a new spot "...or here..." he moves them again "...or anywhere you want. I'll see your adorable hand prints and never want to wash them off." He kisses her on her neck and she squirms with a giggle.

"Your fiancée may not agree, and besides, you're teaching her bad habits. By the way, where is Emma?"

"Her mom had surgery on her foot so she's in Hawaii with her for the weekend."

This is not good ... not good at all.

"Why didn't you go with her?" I ask still mesmerized by the view.

"On call, remember?"

I nod.

"Want to check out the back?" He gestures with his head.

"Sure."

I was right. The deck wraps around the entire house with built-in bench seating.

Stone stairs lead to a large square section of paving brick with a rustic outdoor chair and table set. Another set of stone stairs leads farther down to a gravel path.

"Wow ... I mean just ... wow!" I shake my head.

Lautner smiles. "Glad you like it."

"Where does the path lead?"

"It winds down the hill a ways then works its way back up to the side of the house. Come on, I'll show you."

He scoops up Ocean and carries her down the second set of steps which are fairly steep.

"There you go." He sets her down and she squats to pick up a rock. A few steps later she finds a stick.

"This is her routine. When we take walks she spends the whole time in search of the next best rock and stick."

"What else does she like?"

I know he's trying to know her better, but I feel a pang of guilt that he's missed out on the first two years of her life and I have to tell him about his own daughter.

"She loves fruit, any kind of fruit, and yellow ponies. When I put her to bed at night we read *Guess How Much I Love You?*, and when she wakes in the morning she wants to cuddle on my lap for a good twenty minutes before break-fast. She hates spiders but is intrigued by snakes. I've bought her numerous soccer balls, but she insists on running with them like that other 'football' sport."

Lautner laughs, tilting his head back and resting his hand on his stomach. "I love it! She's her daddy's girl."

I shake my head with a goofy grin plastered on my face. Then I playfully shove him. "She's her mommy's girl. You should see her swim."

He nudges me with his elbow, giving me a sideways glance. "Always so competitive."

I roll my eyes. "You do realize how laughable that is coming from you?"

"Stick." Ocean turns around and stops, pointing her stick out, but not giving Lautner enough time to stop.

"Ahh!" He stops with a slight grimace on his face, rubbing his hand over his ... *area*.

My eyes double in size. "Oh my gosh, are you okay?"

He nods as a smile pulls at his lips. "She just nicked my sac is all."

I giggle. "Told ya she's a mommy's girl."

"No, she's a daddy's girl!" He scoops her up and sets her on his shoulders. "Should we race your mommy?"

"Ra mommy!" Ocean squeals.

Lautner takes off with her, and I try and catch up but I'm in flip-flops and he's in tennis shoes, so it's hardly a fair race. They're already seated on the bench, looking all cool and casual by the time I make it to the top of the hill.

"What took you so long?" He smirks.

"Mommy!" Ocean cheers.

"Cheaters," I mumble, squinting my eyes at him.

"What? I had an extra twenty pounds on my shoulders."

I shake my head and continue inside. "Water, I need water."

Lautner gets us water and sets out some cut up strawberries. Ocean's eyes widen with delight.

"Traberrries." She grabs for one.

I tap the side of my glass. "You called her d.a.d.d.y'.s girl, and yes you are her d.a.d.d.y, but do you think it's confusing for her to hear you refer to yourself as that?"

He sighs and clenches his jaw then relaxes. "Does she call or think of someone else as her d.a.d.d.y?"

I know who he means by *someone* and I see the possibility irritates him.

"Dane and I haven't been together very long ... at least not in *that* way, so she calls him Dane."

"How long?" he's looking at me, but I stay focused on Ocean and her strawberry-stained mouth.

"Last November. I saw ..." I stop myself.

"What?"

"Nothing."

"Not nothing, what did you see?" His strained voice has a hint of exasperation to it.

I meet his eyes. "You," I whisper.

"Me?" He pulls his head back.

I swallow and try to tell him like I'm talking about someone else ... like I'm telling someone else's story. A story that didn't crush me.

"I took Ocean to the park. The one where they fly the planes. She was carrying around her pink soccer ball..." I smile "...like a football."

He grins too.

"Then I saw you. You were a ways away and your back was to me, but I knew it was you. It was the first time I used the word daddy in front of Ocean. I asked her if she wanted to meet her daddy. Something about the moment, the timing, felt like fate. Which says a lot, since I'm not a big believer in fate. We started to walk toward you then—"

"You saw Emma," he says.

I nod. "I couldn't get out of there fast enough. We even left her ball behind and she cried all the way home."

I did too, but he doesn't need to know that.

"I don't know. It's weird. I never wanted us to be together just because I got pregnant, but for the longest time there was this part of me that was ... holding out for you."

I shrug, focusing my gaze on the Hollywood sign in the distance. "Anyway, it was that night I moved on. After two and a half years, I stopped holding out and moved on ... with Dane"

Lautner's body is rigid, completely still. He's looking at something on the floor beside him, or maybe he's looking at nothing. I can't tell if he's confused, upset, or just thinking.

"I think it's someone's nap time."

Ocean yawns.

Lautner still doesn't move.

"So ... mind if I take her upstairs and lay her down for a nap?"

He nods ... at least I think he does. It's too slight to tell. I'm not sure what I said that has him in such a daze, but I decide to let him be.

———

THERE ARE TWO BEDROOMS UPSTAIRS. I choose the smaller one, assuming the larger with the king-sized bed is his or *theirs*. I have her go potty then we lie down and cuddle. Lautner's odd reaction to my story frustrates me. What did I say that was so shocking?

It's been ten or so minutes and Ocean is out. I could go downstairs but I think Lautner needs time or space or something. Just as I decide to close my eyes, I feel the bed shift. Lautner is lying on the other side of Ocean, facing me. We stare at each other for a while. I wish I knew what he's thinking.

The pain in his eyes mixed with the silence that's screaming something is too much. I ease off the bed and go downstairs to sit on the deck. There's a light breeze and I close my eyes and focus on the air in my lungs and the sound of the leaves rustling on the trees. I hear the door open then shut with a soft click, but I don't open my eyes.

"I proposed to Emma that night."

Now I'm the one who cannot move or speak.

"That's how I know what you saw. We had a picnic in the park that afternoon, then I proposed to her that night after I took her to the symphony."

"Why are you telling me this?" I open my eyes, biting together my quivering lips.

"Don't you wonder what if—"

"No!" I stand and rest my hands on the railing. "I don't. There's been a lot of what ifs that have eaten at me over the past three years, but that day is not one of them. If I would have introduced you to Ocean before Emma ran into your arms, you still would have proposed to her. You're a good man, Lautner. You would never buy an engagement ring for someone you didn't love. We were over and looking back the 'fate' part of the day was me finally realizing it." I laugh, shaking my head. "It must be a photographer thing ... 'a picture's worth a thousand words.' It wasn't like seeing some girl in a towel at your door. That day at the park was different. I saw you ... in love."

He stands next to me and slides his hand over on mine. "I'm sorry."

Drawing in a shaky breath, I pull my hand away and wipe a few stray tears. "Don't be sorry for finding someone and falling in love. I left you. I returned at the wrong time. I assumed you were with Claire. Hell, I was the one who got pregnant in the first place ... probably missed a fucking pill or something." I wipe a few more tears. "But I don't regret Ocean, not for one moment. The crazy part is ... of all the stupid choices I've made, she's the one thing I did right."

"Sydney ..."

I sniffle and wipe my eyes. "I know ... you're sick of my tears. I'm so pathetic."

I head in the house and hurry up the stairs to check on Ocean. She's still sleeping. Remembering I forgot to call Dane when we arrived, I start back down the stairs to get my phone from my purse.

"Hey." My breath catches rounding the landing, avoiding a near collision with Lautner coming up the stairs.

His jaw is set, lips in a firm line, and eyes fixed on mine. "Don't speak."

"Wha—"

He palms the back of my head and smashes our lips together. His demanding tongue thrusts into my mouth. I moan into him while his other hand feathers down my neck and over my breast.

"Lautner—" I protest, turning my head to the side.

"Don't. Speak!" He devours my neck with his desperate lips.

I close my eyes and try to form a coherent thought as my nipples awaken under his touch. My knees go weak. He reaches out a hand behind me and lowers us to the stairs. I can't resist him ... he's my drug. As his lips reclaim mine, my hands find his hair—clenching and tugging. His hands slide up my bare legs taking my sundress with them. I relax my legs, allowing his body to cradle into mine. We should stop and I know it, but his hands feel like they were made to touch me, his lips to kiss me. How can something so beautiful and perfect be wrong?

"Mommy," Ocean calls from the bedroom.

Her voice, although the sweetest sound in the world, is a bucket of cold water poured over us. Lautner sits back on his knees. I hurry to pull my dress down and adjust the straps. We're both breathless, lips swollen, speechless, and ... fucking stupid.

"Coming," I yell and run up the stairs. "Hi, sweetie. Did you have a good nap?"

She nods, rubbing her eyes. Sitting on the bed, I lift her on my lap, hugging her to me. "Mmm ... who loves you?"

"You wuv me." She clings to my neck.

Lautner may be my addiction, but Ocean is my cure for everything. When she's in my arms everything magically makes sense again.

"Daee."

I hold her back to see her face. "What did you say?"

She smiles. "Daee."

"Daee what?" I wrinkle my brow, not understanding where this is coming from.

"Daee." She points to the door.

Turning, I see Lautner leaning against the door frame with an I-just-won-the-lottery grin. I'm sure in his mind he just did.

It's official and bittersweet, she's no longer solely mine.

"Yes, sweetie. That's your daddy." I exhale and let the reality of the moment sink in.

Lautner saunters in like he's all that and opens the California blinds. "Took her less than two weeks to say my name. How long did it take her to say yours?"

I roll my eyes and set her down. He picks her up and throws her in the air eliciting a high pitch shriek followed by a run of giggles. "You just stole my heart." He hugs her and kisses her cheek.

They both stole mine a long time ago.

"I'll be downstairs. I have to make a quick call."

He tosses her on the bed and tickles her. "We'll be bonding."

The moment is bittersweet.

———

Dane doesn't answer, so I leave a message.

"Hey, sorry I didn't call earlier. We made it here safely and I'll try you later."

A dazzling flood of blue irises comes down the stairs as I drop my phone back in my purse.

"Look!" Ocean holds up a football that's about the size of her entire torso.

"Sweetie, that's not going to roll very well when you kick it."

"Ha ha! Your mom thinks she's funny." Lautner sets her down and she runs to the couch and flops on it while still hugging the ball.

"Toudown!" She giggles.

I raise my eyes at Lautner. "Someone's expanding her vocabulary with a bunch of useless words."

"She's going to need to know that when I take her to her first Stanford game this fall." He flips on the TV and turns it to Dora.

"Dora!" Ocean cheers, scooting back on the couch.

"What should we do for dinner before fireworks?" He calls from the kitchen.

I join him and sit at the table. "We need to check into our hote—I mean ..."

"What?" He shuts the refrigerator door. "Hotel? I thought you were staying with Avery."

I fiddle with my hair. "She's in Vegas."

"You came to L.A. just for me?"

"No ... I mean, sort of. I thought we should talk."

"Well, you're not staying at a hotel. No way. You'll stay here."

He turns and opens the refrigerator again. I walk up behind him with my hands on my hips. "I don't think that's a good idea." Pulling out a glass dish, he sets it on the counter and faces me. "Why not?"

"Well for starters, because of what happened earlier."

A devious smirk pulls at his lips while he grabs a pot from the wood and wrought iron hanging pot and pan rack. "I don't know what you're talking about." He dumps what looks like soup from the glass container into the pot.

"Lautner, you know damn well what I'm talking about. The stupid smirk on your face says so."

Lighting the gas stove, he shrugs. "I'm just happy because the most beautiful girl in the world, no offense..." he glances over with a wink "...called me her daddy today."

"You're impossible!" I throw my hands up in the air. "Fine, we'll stay but I'm sleeping with Ocean."

"Me too," he adds.

"No ... not you too."

"Will Ocean eat chicken tortilla soup or should I make her something else?"

"She'll eat it if it's not too spicy and if you have avocado to go on it. AND you're changing the subject."

He smiles holding up an avocado. "Sorry, what was the subject? Because all I heard was Charlie Brown *wah wah wah*."

"You're getting married." I throw at him, hoping he'll take me seriously.

"So are you." He throws back.

The frustrating irony of this is he's beating me at my own game. He's acting like not acknowledging what happened somehow makes it less true. That's my MO.

"Whatever." I leave to check on Ocean and cancel our hotel reservations.

Lautner walks out of the kitchen while I'm on the phone and takes Ocean and the football out front. I watch out the window as she runs with the ball while he chases her. For this small moment, I allow myself to imagine the man in the front yard, the man that I love, is mine. I imagine how amazing it would feel to not carry the pain and the guilt in my heart.

Lautner looks at the window and motions for me to come outside. I wave and nod.

"Think fast," he says, sending the football through the air in my direction.

I catch it and kick off my flip flops.

"Get Mommy!" he tells Ocean and she toddles toward me.

I jog in the opposite direction but she quickly loses interest when she sees all the butterflies in the front bushes.

Lautner grins and squints his eyes as he hunches down ready to chase me.

"Don't embarrass yourself, you'll never catch me."

His grin turns into a full smile and he races toward me. I take off running, but he hooks his arm around my waist and pulls me to the ground on top of him. The ball falls out of my arms. Our faces are inches apart and we breathe into each other. The moment is too familiar. I shouldn't feel at home in his arms.

"Who's embarrassed now?" he says with a labored breath.

I lunge for the ball, but his long arm reaches it first. Holding it with one hand, he runs in the opposite direction. I scramble to my feet and chase after him. Ocean sees us and joins in. He lets her catch him and dramatically falls to the ground. She giggles with delight and climbs on his large chest stealing the ball back and running off again. I shake my head and hold out my hand. He grabs it, letting me pretend I have the strength to help him up.

"Thank you," he says.

I roll my eyes. "Whatever, you got up on your own."

"No." His voice is serious as he nods his head toward Ocean. "For her."

I shrug. "I'm sure you'll have more kids someday." Staring at my toes, I curl them into the cool grass.

"I hope so."

His eyes are fixed on me as I look up. I give him a weak smile then look over at Ocean rolling in the grass.

"When did you know she was the one?"

"Who?" he asks.

"Emma."

He walks over and sits on the porch step, resting his arms

on his knees. "I'm not sure. So much had happened in my life, then one day I just realized that I no longer felt alone and she was the reason. She gave me hope when I needed it. For me it wasn't love at first, but it was definitely a special friendship. My heart felt something again. I was drowning and she pulled me to the surface." He laughs. "She was relentless. It didn't matter how many hours I worked at the hospital, she went out of her way to be with me. I don't know how many times she drove forty minutes to spend five with me. I tried to push her away, feeling guilty for not having time for her, but she wouldn't let me. Surfing, football games, camping ... she loves it all. My dad thinks she's the female version of me."

His eyes find mine. I cross my arms over my chest. "Was she upset when you told her about Ocean?"

He shakes his head. "Upset, no. It happened before we knew each other. Disappointed, maybe. She imagined giving me my first child."

"What about you?" I swallow hard.

"Do I regret Ocean?" he asks with a grimace.

"Not Ocean, I don't mean that. I mean is it bittersweet to have a child that's yours but not hers?"

Ocean grabs my legs and looks up at me. I smile and pick her up.

"Let's eat." Lautner smiles and stands leaving my question unanswered.

———

"Eeee ... look!" Ocean yells in delight at the fireworks. We have the most breathtaking view of them from Lautner's deck.

She crawls back and forth from my lap to Lautner's, until finally settling on the bench by the railing. I stand behind her, making soft strokes with my fingers through her hair.

My body tenses with Lautner's touch. He slides his hand around to my abdomen and pulls me back against his hard body. His other hand sweeps my hair to one side and then his lips press to my neck.

"Lautner ..." I whisper.

"Shh ..." He breathes in my ear.

Ocean is enthralled with the magical light display, but I'm still nervous she's going to turn and see Lautner touching me in a way that may confuse her. The problem is, I want him to touch me, I need him to touch me.

His hand on my abdomen inches down between my legs and the thin material of my dress and panties doesn't do much to dull the sensation of his middle finger stimulating my clit with slow firm circles.

Dear God ... this is *so* wrong, but it feels so good. My eye lids are heavy and when I blink, I see my own fireworks display, building one glorious starburst at a time. He's working me up to my own finale.

"Bedtime." My voice squeaks the word between heavy breaths.

Lautner releases me.

"No!" Ocean protests.

Thankfully the finale starts and she goes crazy jumping up and down and clapping her hands. She turns to give us a quick look and her eyes are huge with excitement. It's complete sensory overload for her. I can relate, thanks to Mr. Magic Hands.

When all that's left are the city lights in the distance blurred by a residual smoky haze, I take her inside while

Lautner brings our bags in from the car. It's way past her normal bedtime but she insists on a book. Lucky for her I packed several.

"I'll read to her," he offers.

I hesitate at first. "Uh ... okay, I'll go shower. Goodnight, sweetie."

"Night, mommy." She hugs and kisses me.

In the shower, I replay the day's events in my head. I'm in a bubble that's no doubt going to burst in a few days. Today, I got a glimpse of what it would feel like to be a family with Lautner and Ocean. When I'm with him and he's looking at me the way he used to, touching me the way he used to, I can push away the guilt. However, Dane is home waiting for me and Emma will be back in a few days. Then what? I'm not a cheater, I never have been, yet here I am allowing intimate moments with a man who is engaged to someone else. And I should be married to Dane. What are we doing?

After slipping into some Victoria's Secret lace bottom lounge shorts and a fitted tank, I peek around the corner to check on Ocean. The nightstand light is still on and she's tucked under Lautner's arm resting her little hand on his broad chest. He has one leg hanging off the edge of the bed, and they're both sleeping. I tiptoe through the hall and down the stairs to grab my camera. I return, pleased that neither have moved. Click after click, I take numerous shots then take my camera back downstairs.

Kicking myself once again for forgetting, I call Dane.

"Hi, got your message," he answers.

"Good, hope I'm not waking you."

"Nope, just watching a movie with three dogs sprawled out on the couch with me."

"Hmm, what are you watching?" I ask while walking into a room opposite of the living room. I flip on the light and my breath is taken away.

"Sydney?" Dane says.

"Uh ... yeah?"

"Did you hear me?"

"No ... uh what?"

"I said we're watching *Marley and Me*."

"Uh huh."

"Sydney?"

"What?"

"You sound distracted."

I turn and Lautner is standing at the door wearing a pair of navy boxer shorts and nothing else. My eyes reacquaint themselves with every curve and ripple of his body.

"I'm just tired. Long day of driving."

"Are you sure?"

"Mmm hmm."

"Okay, honey. Goodnight, I love you."

"Yeah ... uh ... you too."

I press *End*.

"Like my photos?" Lautner asks with a smirk.

Peeling my eyes off of his delicious flesh, I survey the walls of his office again. They're covered with the photos I took of him, except they're not the originals that I sent him. They've been enlarged and reframed. To an outsider it would look like he's full of himself with all these black and white prints of various parts of his body, but not to me. I see his obsession with the photographer, not the muse.

"They're okay. I mean, they're no Damon Michaels, but there's some potential there."

He chuckles. "No, they're definitely no Damon Michaels masterpieces, but I'll give the artist an E for effort."

I turn and walk over to him. "I'm sure she did the best she could given the lame bodied model she had to work with."

"Shut up."

"Hey, don't tell me to—"

He does it again. Lips, tongue, hands … he seizes my body and my mind. God, I love the way he shuts me up. My hands are tingling they're so anxious to feel his naked skin. I run them down his chest, one muscle at a time, and then up his back the same way. Guilt and conscience are playing their loud drums in the back of my head and chanting *adultery … cheating … affair.*

Why can't my body and mind agree? Everything is out of sync.

"Lautner …" I whisper.

"Shut up," he mumbles, biting, licking, and sucking every inch of my neck. "I hate that it makes me some sort of prick, but it's not bittersweet to have a child with you." He sucks at my neck, brushing his lips down to my shoulder. "It's a goddamn dream come true."

Grasping the back of my legs, he lifts me up, walking forward until we're at the desk. He sets me down and shoves everything off the desk except the lamp in the opposite corner.

Holy crap!

I've only seen this done in the movies. Lautner is too organized for this type of behavior. It may take him hours to reorganize everything he just swiped to the floor. I wonder if his mind is already regretting such rash behavior. Maybe I should suggest we stop and I can help him get everything tidied up.

"Lautner ..." My needy voice tries to gain strength.

"Don't speak!" He slides my tank up my torso and over my head.

He pauses, taking in my exposed breasts. His chest heaves and his hooded eyes are more of a smoky blue in this light. It's agonizing how slow he moves his hand to one breast —lifting, kneading, caressing my nipple.

My head falls back, eyes close. His other hand follows suit.

"Ahh!" I moan.

"Shh ..."

How does he do this to me? Every nerve in my body has a hair trigger to his touch. Moving his right hand to my sternum, he gestures for me to lie back. Then, with both hands, he slides my shorts and panties off. Blue irises never leave mine. Resting my feet on the edge of the desk, I watch him push down his boxers. Just the sight of his large cock springing free sends me to near convulsion.

Oh God ... we're really doing this. The waves of guilt continue to build and I feel them spread over my face as I grimace. Why, why, why is this wrong? The magnetic force drawing us together has herculean strength. We have a child together ... we should be together. So why is my mind poisoning this moment?

"Lautner ..." I sit up.

He pulls me to his body, turns, and slams my back against the wall. With one hand, he pins both of my wrists above my head.

"Just. Stop. Talking!" He growls, thrusting up into me.

I cry out, feeling him completely fill me with brute force.

His mouth covers mine, absorbing my loud pleas. Lautner has never been this animalistic with me—demanding, dominating.

I feel his anger, desperation, and … pain. My body feels like it's on the verge of breaking every time he slams into me, but I don't want him to stop—ever.

His mouth moves to my breast, sucking in my nipple so hard my teeth dig into my bottom lip drawing blood. I want to die in this man's arms. Even if it's in Hell, I don't care. I just want to be with him. The pain that this is a stolen moment, an unforgivable, epic mistake draws tears from my eyes. With one last thrust, he stills and growls dragging my nipple through his teeth causing me to climax around him.

Releasing my wrists, he rests his head on my shoulder. I ease my fingers through his hair with the same tenderness that I do with Ocean. He just went alpha male on me, yet all I feel from him now is a childlike vulnerability.

What. Are. We. Doing?

He lifts his head.

Blue irises. They're bleeding with pain. He looks at my lips and runs his tongue along my bloodied lower lip, then gently sucks it into his mouth. I close my eyes and melt into his tender touch. His soft lips brush over my tears as I run my tongue over my lip.

With slow ease, he slides out of me and my feet find the ground. His eyes drag along my body then he slips on his boxers and leaves. No explanation. No apology. No words.

One more lonely tear. That's all I allow myself. After a quick trip to the bathroom, I slip into bed next to Ocean. Hugging her to my body, I close my eyes and wait for my world to make sense again.

Chapter Thirty

July 5th, 2013

BLUE IRISES.

"Good morning," he whispers.

Ocean is no longer nestled next to me. She's navigated to the other side of the bed and is snuggled into Lautner's bare chest, still sleeping. I don't remember him coming in last night. After our encounter in his office, my body was exhausted so it's not surprising I didn't hear him.

"Morning," I return with a cautious smile. "I think she likes you."

"I'm in Heaven right now." He kisses her head.

Me too, but mine is an illusion.

"Nature calls." I ease out of bed.

As tempting as it is to slip back into the bed of blue irises, I exit the bathroom and go downstairs. It's a beautiful morning and I can't get enough of the view. I feel like a god, surrounded by beautiful flowers and a quiet tranquility, looking down on the rest of the world. From here, the large city looks so small. Maybe that's what this weekend is—a taste of paradise, a slice of Heaven. Can I make love to Lautner and still marry Dane? Is that even what we were doing? Was that making love or just a release of emotions—a slow goodbye?

"Tea?"

Turning to my left, Lautner is holding out a mug.

"Thanks. Ocean still sleeping?"

"Yeah, she's out." He sips his coffee. "What should we do today? Pacific Park? Universal Studios? The Aquarium?"

So this is how it's going to be? Like last night never happened. The same way the close encounter on the stairs never happened. Is this how it's going to be when his fiancée comes home? Will he take her upstairs and make love to her like he didn't just fuck me against the wall in his office?

"We should talk."

He sighs and walks over to the railing with his back to me. "You're right, we should. I'll go first."

Uh ... okay ...

"Were you ever going to tell me I had a daughter?"

Whoa! I see we're back to this. He didn't think to ask me this before now?

"I think so."

He turns, leaning back against the railing. "You *think* so? What's that supposed to mean?"

"It means I don't know. It means since I struck out all three times I went to tell you, I thought it might be best to wait until she was older."

"Wait ... three times? You tried to tell me twice." He frowns, squinting his eyes.

I stare down into my mug, shaking my head. "Three times. Shortly after my first doctors appointment I went to your apartment." I laugh. "Honestly, I wasn't exactly going to tell you right away that I was pregnant. At the time I assumed you were with Claire. The last thing I wanted was you leaving her to be with me because I was pregnant. But I knew if you did, you'd never admit that was the real reason." I take a calming sip of my tea. "I didn't want to settle. I thought that's what my mom had done and I didn't want that to be me."

"You felt being with me was *settling*?"

"Yes ... er ... no. I wanted to be with you, but I wanted you to want to be with me too—just me, for me, not because I was having your baby. I knew I wanted you, I just didn't know if you still wanted me."

He rakes his fingers through his hair. "So it was okay for you to decide you wanted to be with me *after* you found out you were pregnant with my baby, but I had to choose you *before* knowing it?"

Oh, shit! He has a point. I never thought of it that way. Stupid pregnancy brain.

He laughs, the laugh that keeps someone from tipping over the edge of insanity. "Jesus, Sydney! I chose you. I chose you before you ever left in the first place. I chose you before either one of us knew you were pregnant. *YOU* however, did *not* choose me."

"I would have," I whisper.

He bends forward slightly, placing his cupped hand behind his ear. "Excuse me, what did you say?" He can't seem to shake the sarcastic tone from his voice.

My eyes find his. "I said I would have if I'd known that everything I thought was true about my parents was just a lie. My mom slept around, got pregnant, had an abortion. I wasn't a honeymoon baby, I was a child conceived out of wedlock and my mom was going to abort me. All I've thought about for years was making something of myself so I felt a sense of accomplishment and would never have to rely on a man like my mom did. I knew she loved us, but I've always thought she lived in regret. But now I know she didn't. Having me and Avery changed her life, but in a good way. We gave her life purpose, with us she made her mark in this world more than any job or any amount of success ever would have." I close my eyes, take a deep breath, then open them. "I know it doesn't matter now, but my heart chose you, my brain just didn't listen."

His mouth opens then closes again as the sweet sound of Ocean chimes through the open kitchen window.

I jump up and head inside. "Good morning, sweetie."

She grins, holding her arms up. I pick her up and shower her with kisses and hugs.

"Waffles with fresh fruit?" Lautner asks, looking solely at Ocean.

Her happy sparkling eyes and irresistible smile is the only answer he needs.

———

Pacific Park here we come.

"Will this be her first time at an amusement park?" Lautner asks as we pull out of his driveway.

"Yes. Mine too."

"What? You can't be serious!" Lautner's eyes bug out and his jaw is resting on his lap.

"My mom never thought the rides went through proper inspection, and my dad assumed all the people working there were drug addicts or child molesters. But I got to ride the carpet slide at the state fair once."

"I—I'm speechless. Drug addicts and child molesters? Doesn't he follow the Ten Commandments … thou shalt not judge?"

I laugh. "That's not one of the Ten Commandments."

"Well it's in the Bible some where."

"Luke 6:37."

"Preacher's daughter showoff."

I roll my eyes.

"Well, I'm honored to be the one who takes both of you to your very first amusement park."

"Don't be. The carpet ride made me vomit."

"Well I've dealt with your vomit before. I can do it again."

Keeping my gaze out the window, I can't help but smile. I think that's when I knew Lautner loved me. There has to be some pretty strong feelings to clean up someone's vomit and stick around to tell them about it.

We find our parking spot and sure enough, Ocean is asleep.

"Do you mind if we let her sleep for a little bit? She'll stay in a better mood if we let her have a small nap."

Lautner cracks the windows and shuts off the vehicle. "Fine by me. The two of you are my plans for the weekend, so I'll do whatever you want."

I slip off my Keens and rest my feet on the dash. Lautner's phone vibrates on the console.

"Hi," he answers in a voice that says he knows who it is.

"Miss you too. How's your mom?"

My heart speeds as my body stiffens. It's Emma … and he

misses her too. Was he missing her last night when his dick was buried in me?

"Yeah, we're at Pacific Park, but Ocean fell asleep on the way so we're waiting for her to wake before we go in."

I feel like I'm eavesdropping, but I can't help it. Should I get out and give them some privacy? Maybe he should get out.

"Okay, then I'll see you at the airport ... love you too, bye."

Reality check! Punch in the gut. Slit my wrists. Bullet to the heart.

Is it all men or just the ones I fall for? How could he be so insensitive? I feel like someone stabbed me with a syringe and injected liquid anger into my veins. My blood is past boiling, it's in massive volcanic eruption mode.

"Emma says 'hi.'"

What ... the ... fuck?

My body acts on its own accord as my brain has a waiting line today for all thoughts that need rational consideration.

Smack!

I hit him so hard I expect Ocean to wake up just from the sound alone. Then there's the grunt type growl that escapes him as his hand covers his check.

"What the hell?" he whispers at the highest possible decibel to still be considered a whisper.

"Emma says 'hi.' Really? You fucked me so hard last night I thought there was going to be a permanent mold of my ass in your drywall and less than twenty-four hours later you're *missing her* and *loving her too* right in front of me. And then you have the nerve to say 'Emma says hi' like we're all BFFs!"

We both look back. Ocean adjusts in her seat but settles in again without waking.

"I'm sorry." He runs his fingers through his hair.

"Sorry for what? Fucking me or loving her?"

He leans his head back against his headrest and closes his eyes. "Both ... neither ... I don't know."

"Well don't get your knickers in a knot. I didn't come down here this weekend to steal you from your bride. You were right to begin with. We should talk to our attorneys about a legal custody agreement. If we put things in writing so we both know what to expect, it will be easier on everyone."

Tilting his head upright again, he turns toward me. "That's why you're down here ... to discuss custody?"

Slipping my feet back into my sandals, I chuckle. "Well, I sure as hell didn't come down here to have my heart ripped from my fucking chest ... again. That appears to just be a bonus. Lucky me."

I open the door and hop out, deciding Ocean has slept long enough. She really hasn't, but even with the windows cracked, the air in the car is too thick to breathe.

―――――

THE RIDE back to Lautner's is just as uncomfortable as the three hours at Pacific Park. Ocean is the focus for both of us. We talk to her but not to each other. She's loved every minute of the day. I've taken so many photos today it's going to take hours to sort through all of them. I'm contemplating leaving to go home tonight, but it doesn't seem fair to Ocean. She loves being with Lautner, even if I can't stand to be near him. If we stay it will be for her and I'll add it to my list of motherly sacrifices.

"You didn't finish telling me about the other time you came to my apartment." Lautner breaks the silence as we drive through the hills nearing his house.

"It doesn't matter." I shrug, staring out my window.

"It does to me."

"Why?"

He sighs. "Because I'm trying to wrap my head around how we got here, to this messed up situation."

"Bad timing ... I guess." I shake my head. "It was a little while after my first OB appointment. You weren't home, but Rose came down the stairs and said you had been going through a tough time because your mom's cancer came back. She said you were hanging by a thread and that Claire was basically holding you together. I didn't want to be the one to break that thread so I decided to wait. Shortly after that I ended up in the hospital. I was dehydrated and stressed out. It was a wakeup call. I knew right then that I needed to put my baby first, so I decided not to try and contact you again until after she was born."

I remember Lautner saying he and Emma stayed at his 'dad's' last weekend. Giving him a quick sideways glance, I contemplate asking the question.

He nods but doesn't look at me or say anything.

"Did your mom ..." I can't finish.

His head snaps to mine. "You don't know?" He asks with tense confusion in his face.

I shake my head. "No, how would I know?"

Lautner pulls into the drive, shuts off the car, and hops out. "Unbelievable. I should have known." He gets Ocean out of her seat and carries her to the house.

"What are you talking about? I chase after him.

He sets Ocean down and goes into the kitchen. I lay her new coloring book and crayons on the coffee table and she's all smiles, dumping the crayons out of the box.

Lautner is chugging a sports drink by the refrigerator as I come into the kitchen.

"What is *unbelievable?*"

He finishes it and tosses the empty bottle on the counter. "My mom died two days before Christmas that year."

"I'm so sorry," I whisper.

"Me too." He plants his hands on his hips and looks out back. "Dane knew, so I assumed you did too."

Now he's talking gibberish. How would Dane know?

"Dane didn't know."

"YES, he did. I saw him the following spring at the hardware store. Ocean would have been close to two months."

My mind stirs with jumbled thoughts. This still doesn't make sense.

"When I asked Dane what you meant at the hospital, he said he saw you at a coffee shop a month *before* Ocean was born. He said it wasn't his place to tell you I was pregnant and he didn't tell me because he was looking out for me and Ocean."

Lautner whips around. "Are you serious? Nice guy you've got, Syd. He's a fucking liar."

I raise my eyes and gesture with my head toward the young ears in the other room. He sighs with regret then goes out back. I follow him.

"Dane wouldn't lie to me." I cross my arms over my chest.

"Then ask him about our conversation at the hardware store *after* Ocean was born. See if he tells you that I told him

I was a complete wreck after losing the two most important women in my life within six months of each other. I told him it had been almost a year and I couldn't even look at another woman yet because you marked me so deep. Then I asked him if he'd heard from you or if Elizabeth or Trevor had said anything about how you were doing." His voice has worked its way up. Each word is filled with pain, but the emotion behind it is pure anger.

I collapse on the bench, shoulders slumped, head down. "Why would he lie?" It's a question to myself.

"Because he wanted what should have been mine!" Lautner yells.

Scrubbing my hands over my face, I shake my head. "No, it doesn't make any sense. He was the one who originally convinced me to tell you. He's the reason I showed up that day when Rose was there. It doesn't make any sense that he would be on your side then lie about this."

Lautner laughs. "Maybe once he got in your pants, his conscience became clouded."

"Fuck you!" I squint my eyes at him. "Dane's the one that found me passed out and took me to the hospital. He's done nothing but look out for me and Ocean, even when I spent years hung up on you, thinking by some miracle we'd end up together. He's always made sure we've had a house to live in and food on the table. When I needed to go back to work, he spent all his free time babysitting or walking my dog. So don't you dare make it sound like Dane's only goal has been to *get in my pants*!"

"Then why didn't he tell me? Why didn't he tell you? 'Hey, Sydney, I ran into Ocean's dad and he just lost his mom and misses you so much he can barely focus on his next breath!'"

Lautner's face is red, his chest heaving, every muscle in his neck and arms is strained. It's me this time, or maybe it's just us because when we're together it's all or nothing. I close the distance between us so fast I can't remember what it felt like to not be in his arms two seconds ago. My lips demand him this time and he doesn't deny me. The feelings I have for Lautner are second only to Ocean, and since I've had her and seen his eyes in hers every single day for the past two years, my feelings have only intensified.

Breaking our kiss, I press my face into his neck and hug him so tight my muscles start to ache. "Why did this happen? It's just not fair."

"I know," he whispers into my hair, holding me tight.

————

THE ANGUISH and pain around us the rest of the evening is unbearable. We say very little, sharing the occasional sad smile over dinner and during the movie we rented for Ocean. It should be simple. Tell Dane and Emma that we can't live without each other and let the healing begin and start our lives together as a family. But it isn't that simple. My feelings for Dane are complicated. Then there's Lautner's feelings for Emma. I've seen them together and when he looks at her there is love in his beautiful blue eyes. I would never ask him to choose me, because I'm no longer sure he would. He no longer has to be with me to have his daughter and he knows that. Emma's not a fling; I know what they have is real.

"I'll carry her upstairs," Lautner whispers, picking up our sleeping baby from the couch as the movie credits roll up the screen.

I flip through the channels trying to find something to take my mind off the ache in my heart.

"Come with me." Lautner holds out his hand.

I look at it then blue irises. Clicking off the TV, I take his hand. He leads me upstairs. I can see straight ahead into his bedroom. Ocean is in the middle of his bed. Turning left, he pulls me into the guest room where we slept last night. He shrugs his shirt off and sits on the edge of the bed, pulling me to stand between his legs.

I press my palms to his cheeks, brushing my thumbs under his eyes. "Don't want Emma to find out I was in her bed?" My voice is soft and sad. I bite my lips together and blink back the tears. My own jealous emotions are ripping me apart.

His gentle fingers cover my left hand and he presses his lips to the inside of my wrist. "It's not for her. It's for you ... always you, Sydney."

I suck in a shaky breath and hold it, then release it with my tears.

He brushes his thumbs over my cheeks, catching my watery emotions one at a time. I close my eyes as his lips touch mine with tenderness. Last night he took, tonight he's giving.

Keeping his lips slow dancing with mine, his patient fingers work the buttons of my shirt before pushing it over my shoulders, releasing it to the ground. I unclasp my bra and let it join my shirt. My arms wrap around his neck and his around my waist as we fall onto the bed. Our tongues slide together—tasting, teasing. His hands skim up my back and tangle in my hair.

"You're a fucking goddess." His lips move down my neck as he flips me on my back.

The carnal appreciation in his voice drives me crazy. Arching my back, I moan as his mouth covers my breast. My fingers curl into his hair, my pelvis rocking into him. He continues to move down my body, stopping to unfasten my shorts, then standing to pull them off with my panties. I love, love, love the way he looks at my naked body. It's a slow perusing of his eyes over every inch. He wets his lips, like a hungry predator ready to attack. How does he do that? I can physically feel his eyes on me. This will never go away. What we have is longer than time and deeper than eternity. Even if we live out our lives in the arms of another, I have to believe we will be together again ... somewhere, someday.

I start to squirm, but he doesn't move. Is he having second thoughts? God, I hope not. I'm half way there. He has to touch me ... soon! Maybe he's waiting for me to beg. Am I that desperate?

Yes.

Sliding my hands under my hair, I fan it out over my head.

That's right ... come get your goddess. Touch me, dammit!

I move my hands to my breasts, rolling my nipples between my fingers.

Holy shit! That feels good. I've never touched myself like this. I'm good!

His mouth opens and his breaths are coming closer together. My eyes are on his, but his are on my hands. He's getting close.

This nipple stimulation is playing havoc with a certain area a little lower.

"Lautner ..." I say in a needy whimper.

His eyes flash to mine and he smiles. Cocky shit thinks

this is a game. I've gone from tears to touching myself in a matter of minutes. That's the effect he has on me.

Screw it! I've come this far.

I slip two fingers into my mouth and with slow control circle them with my tongue, eyes on him the whole time. Then I drag them down my neck, between my breasts and lower … all the way. Sliding them between my legs I rub them over my clit. His smile is gone, eyes hooded, hands working the button and zipper on his shorts.

Good Lord, I'm really good.

Who knew? All these years I didn't touch myself because my parents told me masturbation caused blindness. I've always looked judgmentally at blind people wondering if they felt shameful.

If he doesn't hurry up, I'm not going to need him. "Oh God," I moan, closing my eyes.

I open them as I feel him crawling up between my legs. He grabs my hand and stops my motions. With his eyes on mine, dark and hungry, he sucks my two fingers into his mouth.

"Sydney Ann Montgomery, you're quite the little temptress." He grins, kissing his way up my stomach, stopping to give my breasts equal attention.

"Lautner … I can't wait."

He traces his tongue up my neck and sucks in my ear lobe. "I know, baby," he whispers, sinking into me.

"Oh God …" I moan, pulling my knees back letting him plunge deep into me.

He pauses then inches out before easing back in at an equally slow pace. I'm no longer in a hurry. At this moment, I'm praying we stay frozen in time. I never want to forget this feeling. He completes me physically and emotionally.

"Don't stop ..." And just like that my emotions flip and the moment brings back the tears. "... Don't. Ever. Stop."

"Sydney ... say it." He breathes, looking into my eyes with something ... *Desperation?*

"Don't you feel it?" He kisses me, letting his tongue dip into my mouth with the same rhythm as his pelvis.

Closing my eyes, I try to control the building sensation that's on the verge of exploding. His pace picks up and his breathing is erratic.

"Say it ... please, baby, say it."

Say what?

I can't think. What does he want me to say? The stars are coming and it's an incredible slow release. Thrashing my head from side to side I cry out, "Please don't stop ... that feels ... so ... good ..."

One, two, three more thrusts and he stills emptying into me then collapsing on me.

I can barely breathe beneath the weight of his strong body, but I don't say anything. I'm used to the crushing feeling in my chest and around my heart when we're together.

My fingers trace the muscles of his back and I turn my head and kiss the side of his. He turns and looks at me for a moment before kissing me. It's patient, soft, and ... perfect.

He rolls over, pulling out of me, and I repress the painful gasp from feeling the empty space he leaves inside me. Pulling me into his chest, I rest my ear against his sternum and fall asleep to the soothing beat of his heart, a heart I used to think beat for me and only me.

"I love you ... always you." His words are so quiet—barely a whisper. I'm not sure if he meant for me to hear them.

Chapter Thirty-One

July 6th, 2013

A FEW RAYS of morning light sneak through the tiny gaps in the blinds. There is a warm body pressed against mine—not the one I fell asleep against; this is a tiny body and her messy hair is in my face. I inhale her scent. We're alone. Lautner is not here. I'm still naked under the sheets. Not really wanting to play twenty questions with my two-year-old as to why I'm not wearing my jammies, I slip out of bed and put on a T-shirt and shorts.

I hear some noise in the kitchen as I tiptoe downstairs. Rounding the corner I freeze.

Oh shit!

"Good morning. Hope I didn't wake you running the coffee grinder." Emma scrunches her nose.

I'm trying my best to hide my deer in the head light look, but I'm shocked and unsure of what to say. It's now quite clear why he put Ocean back in bed with me. When did she get home? Where is he?

"Coffee?" she asks, reaching in the cabinet for another mug.

"Uh ... no, I'm fine thanks." I smooth back my hair, knowing I must look like a hag this morning.

"Not a coffee person, huh? It's my survival, especially after my long flight. I was supposed to fly home tomorrow but they canceled the flight, so my choices were a late flight last night or not until Tuesday. Luckily, Lautner got the message I left him before boarding the plane. I chastised him for not answering his phone when I called, especially since he's on call this weekend. He said Ocean was playing with it and it took him a while to find it after she fell asleep."

Oh he did, did he?

I'm letting her do all the talking because she knows the story, not me. A heads up from Lautner would have been nice.

"Where is he?" I ask, thinking it's a safe question.

"On the way back from the airport early this morning he got called in to work, so he dropped me off and headed straight to the hospital. He texted me a few minutes ago and said he'll be home soon." She takes a sip of her coffee. "Bummer about your sister's place."

Hmm, she's going to have to elaborate. Wish I would have gotten a text with a script for today. Instead, I'm stuck doing improv.

"Um ... yeah ..." I nod my head.

"Bedbugs can be a nightmare. She should do a better job of checking the hotel mattresses when she travels."

"Mmm, yes, she should."

Bedbugs? What the fuck, Lautner?

"So, how's your mom?" I find a subject that doesn't require me to walk through a minefield.

"She's doing pretty well. My brother showed up early to stay with her; that's why I was able to take the earlier flight. She'll be fine by herself in a few more days."

"That's good." I smile and walk to the windows. "Your view is spectacular."

"It is. I'm going to miss it when we move."

I turn to her. "You're moving?"

"Soon as we find the right place. Still in L.A. of course, just something more child-friendly. We want to start our own family right away and now the surprise of Ocean has made us even more determined to find something as soon as we can. Maybe when our kids are grown we'll trade in the big backyard and swing set for a view like this again."

This is all so awesome. I haven't felt this nauseous since I was pregnant. Thinking of Lautner and Emma starting a family and growing old together is just ... *fabulous!*

"Oh, by the way, did Lautner mention the dress fitting next weekend?"

With a tight-lipped smile I shake my head.

"Ocean's dress will be ready. She just needs to try it on so they can make any last-minute adjustments if needed." Emma puts her empty cup in the dishwasher.

"Sure ... um, I have a wedding I'm photographing next Saturday, but I'm sure you and Lautner can take her."

"Oh ... you landed a wedding gig, good for you. Did you see the photos in his office I was talking about?"

Yes, I stared at them while your fiancé was fucking me against the opposite wall.

"I did. You were right, that photographer has some real talent."

"I know, right?" She looks at the clock. "Lautner should

be back any minute. I'm going to run up and take a quick shower if you don't mind."

"Go right ahead," I offer my prizewinning fake smile.

As soon as I hear the water going upstairs, I fly up to the bedroom and start packing our bags while Ocean continues to sleep. We have to get the hell out of here ASAP!

Setting aside a clean outfit for Ocean, I take our bags out to my Jeep just as Lautner pulls in.

I'm not going to cry ... I'm not going to cry.

"Need some help?" he calls, walking toward the back of my Jeep.

"Nope, I'm just fine on my own." Attempting to stay pleasant and unaffected fails me.

I toss the bags in as he sits on the back bumper.

"I'm sorry."

Looking at him is not an option in Sydney survival mode. "Don't be." I start walking back to the house.

"Sydney?" he calls after me, but I don't stop.

Kneeling by the coffee table, I shove Ocean's books and toys into her bag.

"We need to talk."

I shake my head while keeping my hands busy and my gaze away from fucking Medusa eyes. "There's nothing to say."

"There's everything to say!" he says with a low, firm voice.

I stop what I'm doing and look at him. "Are you going to tell Emma what happened this weekend?"

He wrinkles his forehead. "I-I-are you going to tell Dane?"

"Yes," I deadpan.

"You are?" His eyes are big.

"Yes."

"So you're not getting married?" he cocks his head to the side.

I laugh. "Are you?"

Lautner's mouth falls open but no words escape.

"Look who just woke up," Emma says, coming down the stairs in a bathrobe, holding Ocean's hand.

Standing, I hold out my arms and she runs right into them. "Good morning, baby girl." I hug her. "Let's get you dressed, we're going home soon."

"I'll get her some breakfast." Lautner heads to the kitchen.

"Don't bother. I'll pick her up something on the way."

He turns with a frown, but I don't acknowledge it. Instead, I take her upstairs and get her ready to go. If only I had a magic wand, we would be back in Palo Alto right now instead of trying to make our escape from here. I don't know if I'm going to tell Dane about my infidelity; it was more of a test. I needed to see the look on Lautner's face. My answer came fast and clear. He's scared shitless to tell Emma, which means he doesn't want to lose her. That's all the answer I need.

"Okay, let's go." I walk Ocean down the stairs, but pause for a moment.

"God, I missed you," Emma says. Then I hear her moan. I think they're kissing. "After they leave we need to get reacquainted."

"Mmm ..." he hums.

A crashing ball just hit my chest. It's the feeling I had in the restaurant. I can't breathe. Tears swell in my eyes and I. Can't. Breathe.

"G-go down—I'll b-be right—there." I struggle to get the words out to Ocean.

She doesn't notice my state. Instead, she continues down the stairs. I run into the bathroom, unintentionally slamming the door behind me. Sitting on the toilet seat, I fight to slow my breathing. I did this. I allowed this to happen. Now I'm paying the painful price for a weekend of pleasure. The door cracks open, but before I can push it shut or say anything Lautner comes in and closes it behind him.

"Breathe, baby ... breathe. Slow it down." He squats down in front of me, resting his hands on mine.

I hold my breath then try to control the release, searching for my toes, feet, and fingers, focusing on one breath at a time and connecting it to the rest of my body. As I begin to calm down, he wipes away my tears.

"I should not have—"

"Don't! Don't you dare say it. If you say you regret what happened this weekend, I'll hate you forever, so just ... don't." My voice is still shaky.

He puts his hands on my face and kisses me. I put mine on his and kiss him back between broken sobs and a flood of tears.

I rest my forehead on his. "You love her." It's not a question.

"I love you," he whispers.

"You love her too."

He doesn't say anything, but I feel his head nod against mine. I'm going to leave and he's going to make love to her. He's going to marry her, and I'm going to have to watch the two of them live happily ever after because we share a child.

"Go put Ocean in the car."

"Sydney."

"Just go!"

He stands while I wad some toilet paper and wipe my eyes and nose. Grabbing my purse from the floor, I dig through it and find my sunglasses.

"Go!"

He leaves and I finish cleaning my face before donning my sunglasses. I look into the mirror. "Epic, Syd. If you're going to dive down to rock bottom, might as well do it in a fucking fireball of flames."

Emma is still in her robe standing by Lautner, who is talking to Ocean through the open backdoor of the Jeep. I hop in and buckle up.

"We'll check with you about next weekend, I've got to go dry my hair," Emma calls back with a wave, heading to the front door.

"Bye, my little princess." Lautner gives Ocean one last kiss then shuts her door. I start my Jeep and try to shove it in gear, but I'm not quick enough. Lautner opens my door.

"Sydney."

"Shut the door."

"Say it, why won't you say it?"

What is he talking about?

"Say what? I don't know what you mean so shut the door. I think Emma's inside waiting to get *reacquainted*."

He shakes his head, clenching his jaw then shuts the door.

———

It's an agonizing drive back to Palo Alto. What did Lautner want me to say? Leave Emma, choose me? Don't go inside and make love to her? I'm sorry? What? It's sending me over the edge of insanity that I'm always teetering on with him.

"We're home, baby girl." I lift a groggy Ocean out of her seat.

I'm surprised Dane isn't rushing out to greet us. The garage door is up and his Lexus is here. Ocean walks to the house while I get our bags.

"Hey!" I smile at Dane, who is sitting on the couch with a frown on his face that he manages to disguise with a small smile just for Ocean.

"Hi, doll." He gives her a big hug, then she runs out back to see her doggies.

I set our bags by the stairs then sit next to him on the couch. "What's wrong?"

He rests his elbows on his knees and runs his fingers through his hair. "How's Avery doing?" The cold tone of his voice tells me he knows.

"Dane ..."

"Did you sleep with him?" This is a new side to Dane. I've never seen him look so angry. His fists are clenched and his jaw muscles are twitching.

"We should talk—"

"Did. You. Sleep. With. Him?"

Biting my quivering lips together, I nod and blink back my tears. He stands and takes the stairs two at a time.

"Dane!" I chase after him.

He's changing into his biking gear.

"Aren't we going to talk about this?"

Pulling his shirt over his head, he laughs. "Talk about what? You lying to me. You cheating on me? There's nothing to talk about." He brushes past me and my tears cannot be held back.

"Dane, wait!"

Before I get to the top of the stairs, I hear the front door slam shut.

"Mommy?" Ocean calls.

Wiping my tear streaked face, I suck in a deep breath and hold it for a moment before releasing it. Ocean doesn't need to be in the middle of this mess. I have to get it together for her. She's all that matters.

"Coming, sweetie."

After getting her a snack, I greet the dogs. It would be easy to regret what happened with Lautner, especially if I lose Dane and Lautner marries Emma. However, I don't regret it, not one moment. Nothing so wrong has ever felt so right. Hurting Dane, though, I do regret. I don't expect him to forgive me, and even if he did, things would never be the same between us because he would never forget and neither would I.

After two hours, I start to worry. The sun is setting and Dane's not back yet. I try his phone but it goes to voice mail. Ocean wants a bath so I take her upstairs and watch her in the tub. My phone rings but I don't recognize the number.

"Hello?"

"Sydney Montgomery?"

"Yes."

"My name is Jillian, I'm a nurse at Standford Hospital. You were listed as an emergency contact for Dane Abbott on his running shoe ID tag."

Oh God, oh God, oh God!

"What happened? Is he okay—"

"He's been injured in an accident. A motorist hit him on his bike—"

I drop the phone and my breath is stolen again. Ocean plays in the tub, oblivious to my alarmed state.

Breathe slow ... slow it down ...

Karma, this is Karma. I did this.

"Come here, baby." I pull Ocean from the tub and dry her off.

My instincts kick in and I get us out of the house and to the hospital.

"Can I help you? The nurse at the desk asks.

"Dane Abbott, a nurse called and said he—"

"Yes, room 238."

I pick Ocean up and carry her so she doesn't have to run to keep up with my fast pace.

My stomach is knotted and my heart beats with a dull pain in my chest as we enter the room. Dane is sleeping with a sling around his left arm and shoulder and his leg is elevated with a cast from his knee to toes.

"Dane," Ocean whispers.

"Shh ... sweetie, Dane got hurt on his bike. He needs to sleep."

The relief that washes over me is indescribable. I imagined all sorts of things since I dropped my phone before the nurse finished talking. Massive head injury, spinal cord injury, I even feared ... the worst.

"Are you Sydney?" a soft voice behind me asks.

I turn. "Yes."

"I'm Jillian. I called you—"

"Oh God, yes ... I'm sorry I panicked. My daughter was in the tub and—"

"It's fine. I should have started with 'he's fine,' so that's my fault. Are you his wife?"

I start to hold up my left hand but notice my ring isn't

there. It's the first time I've realized I haven't worn it since the wedding. We never made it to the exchanging of rings. I'm honestly not sure where our rings are.

"Fiancée. What happened?" I turn back and move closer to the bed, setting Ocean in the chair then holding his free hand.

"Witnesses said he was crossing an intersection when a motorist turned right on red. He has a concussion, dislocated shoulder, and a fractured tibia. We're keeping him over night to monitor his concussion, but he should be able to go home tomorrow."

"Thank you."

She leaves and I fight so hard to hold back my tears. I don't want Ocean to think I'm worried about Dane. Although that's part of it, it's not the main reason for my emotions. Guilt is tearing me up inside.

Dane's hand twitches as his eyes fight to open.

"Hey ..." I hate myself for not knowing what to say beyond "hey."

"Hey," he murmurs back.

"Dane," Ocean calls.

I lift her up and he forces a smile for her. "Hi, doll."

"Owie?" she asks.

"Yes, owie. I fell off my bike."

She squirms down and climbs back on the chair digging through my purse, probably for a snack.

Tears fill my eyes and his too. Something tells me the emotional pain he's experiencing is far worse than the physical.

"I'm sorry," I whisper, wiping away a tear.

He shakes his head moving his eyes to Ocean. "Not now."

I nod. "Do you want me to call your parents?"

"I'll call them tomorrow when I get home."

"Do you want me to see if Heather next door can take Ocean for the night so I can stay with you?"

He closes his eyes and shakes his head. "Just go."

A few more tears spill, and I wipe them away and sniffle. He's angry and hurt. I can't blame him or expect him to feel any other way. The rejection I feel from him is painful as well, but I deserve it and then some.

I squeeze his hand. "Okay, I'll be back in the morning to get you."

He nods once.

"Tell Dane goodnight, sweetie. He has to stay here tonight just like when you stayed at the hospital. But he'll be home tomorrow."

He cracks open his eyes for her. "Night, doll."

I lean her down and she gives him a kiss. "Night."

Chapter Thirty-Two

July 7th, 2013

Dane didn't want me to call his parents last night, but I did anyway. It's the mother part of me. I can't imagine ever not worrying about Ocean or wanting to know if something happened to her, whether she's two or thirty-two. They left early this morning to get here in time to be with Ocean while I pick up Dane from the hospital.

"Are you sure you don't want us to go get him?" his mother, Shirley, asks.

"No, since he didn't want me calling you, I don't think you showing up at the hospital to pick him up is such a good idea. I can tell him in the car on the way home." I grab my purse and open the door. "I'll be back soon, hopefully."

"Okay, dear. Drive safe."

"I will."

I get to the hospital and Dane is awake and watching TV.

"Good morning."

He looks at me. The corners of his mouth try to curl into a smile, but I can tell it's a struggle.

"Brought you some clothes." I hold up a bag.

"Thanks."

He doesn't want my help getting dressed, but it doesn't take long for him to realize he *needs* it. After he's discharged, I pull my Jeep up as he waits at the entrance in a wheelchair with the nurse. His left arm and leg are out of commission so he has to use one crutch under his right arm. The nurse helps me get him in and we head home.

"Don't be pissed but—"

"God, Sydney, what now?" he grumbles.

"I called your parents last night. They drove up early this morning. That's who's staying with Ocean right now."

"Great ... whatever." He turns his head and looks out the window.

"I called Kimberly too. She's cancelled your appointments for the next week."

He laughs. "For the next *week?* Look at me, Sydney! It's going to be a helluva lot longer than a week before I'll be able to do my job again."

I fight back the emotions because I deserve his wrath. He went from finding out I cheated on him to getting hit by a car, and now he can't do his job. To top it off, he's going to be stuck at home with me, relying on me, needing me when I'm sure he'd like nothing more than to tell me to take a hike.

The words *I'm sorry, I didn't mean to hurt you, will you ever forgive me,* are dying to escape, but I know how generic and pathetic they'll sound. Lautner tried to apologize to me and it pissed me off more that he was trying to say them than had he not said them at all.

Dane's dad, Phil, helps me get him inside. Shirley over

mothers him, propping pillows behind his back and under his leg, fixing him food, lining up the TV remotes near him. Ocean crawls up next to him and he wraps his good arm around her. He thinks of her as a daughter and I know she loves him too. As time ticks on, I continue to feel worse about ... everything.

After lunch, I take Ocean upstairs for a nap. As soon as she's asleep, I go to my room—Dane's room—and call Avery.

"Hey, Sam."

"Hey, you busy?"

"Nope, I don't have anymore clients until tonight. What's up with you and Dane. Did you guys get your signals mixed this past weekend? He left a message on my phone and said you weren't answering yours. I called him back and told him I was in Vegas. He apologized and said it was just a miscommunication."

"I took Ocean to see Lautner."

"This past weekend?"

"Yes."

"That was nice of you. Dane didn't go?"

"No, he couldn't, but he thought I was visiting you so ..."

"Oh, shit! Sorry, Sam. I didn't mean to out you. Why didn't you tell me?"

"I don't know. Things are such a mess right now." I sigh.

"What happened?"

"The short version is I went to L.A. so Ocean and Lautner could spend time together and so we could talk about some sort of visitation or custody arrangements. Emma was in Hawaii with her mom and we ended up staying at his place but I didn't tell Dane."

"Well he can't be too upset, it's not like you ... Jesus, Sam, please tell me you didn't ..."

"Yes, we had sex."

"Oh my God! What does this mean? Does his fiancée know?"

"No."

"But Dane does?"

"Yes. He asked me and I couldn't lie to him."

"What are you going to do?" Her voice is soft and sympathetic.

"That's just it. The story gets *better*. After I admitted to him what had happened, he took off on his bike. A few hours later I got a call from the hospital that he'd been hit by a car."

"Oh my God! Is he—"

"He's okay. It could have been so much worse. He has a dislocated shoulder and a fractured tibia. They kept him overnight last night because he had a concussion too."

"Sam ... I don't know what to say. Do you want me to come up?"

"His parents are here. I don't know how long they're going to stay. He can't work and I don't know how long it's going to be before he can. I ... I've messed up so bad and for what?"

"Love. You messed up for love."

I shake my head and lean back on my pillow. "It doesn't matter. Lautner loves Emma. He's going to marry her. The reality of it makes this past weekend seem so selfish and now seeing what happened to Dane ..."

"You and Ocean should come stay with me."

"I can't! That's just it. Dane's parents aren't going to stay here forever. They don't know what's happened between us. Dane needs my help, as much as I'm sure he doesn't want it, he needs it. I can't leave him ... I owe him."

"Have you told Dad?"

"What? No way!" Avery doesn't know about the personal and very revealing conversation I had with our dad. The last thing I want to do is tell him I've turned into my mother ... a *whore*. "And I'd appreciate it if you wouldn't say anything right now either."

"Hey, your secret's safe with me. Promise me, though, that you'll call me if you need anything."

"I promise. Thanks, Ave."

"Love you, Sis."

"Love you too."

———

I STAY UPSTAIRS WAITING for Ocean to finish her nap. If I go downstairs without Ocean there for a distraction, Shirley and Phil will easily pick up on the tension between me and their son. My phone vibrates, it's Lautner. I don't want to answer it, but I can't avoid him forever.

"Yes," I answer in a somber voice.

"Hey, you okay?"

Yes, I'm great. Why wouldn't I be?

"What do you want?"

"We should talk." His words are slow.

"About?"

"Us."

A sarcastic laugh escapes me. "Us? Really? What us? The us that you couldn't wait to forget about while fucking Emma after I left? The us that Dane found out about before I ever got home? Or the us that landed Dane in the hospital after he took off on his bike, hurt and angry? Which us are you referring to?"

"Jeez, Syd, is he okay?"

"Okay? Yeah, he's definitely okay. He's out of the hospital but pretty banged up. We're not sure how long it's going to be before he can work again. Oh ... and let's not forget. I'm pretty sure he hates me, but he needs my help so we're stuck with each other until his leg heals and he can physically kick my ass to the curb. So how are the wedding plans going?" There's a natural progression from anger to sarcasm and sometimes it goes even further to complete insanity ... that's me right now.

"Sydney ..."

"Sydney what? Did you call to tell me that you told Emma? Did she leave you?"

He doesn't say anything.

"That's what I thought. So I'm sure the dress fitting is still on. No problem, whatever. You know where we'll be."

I press *End* and toss my phone on the bed.

Chapter Thirty-Three

July 12th, 2013

Dᴀɴᴇ'ꜱ ᴘᴀʀᴇɴᴛꜱ decide to stay the week. I take his lead on everything. He's decided to play the happy couple and I go along. The truth needs to come out on his terms when he's ready. The anger in his eyes has faded a bit, but the pain is still there. Ocean has been a nice buffer, and I've found plenty of time to escape since the role of dog-walker has fallen on me. I'm not complaining.

A big part of Shirley and Phil's decision to stay is the wedding I have scheduled to photograph this afternoon. Lautner and Emma should be picking up Ocean any minute, but Dane still needs help. I keep a close eye on the drive. The last thing we need is Lautner coming to the door. A face-to-face encounter might be the final straw for Dane.

His black 4Runner appears in the driveway. I pick up Ocean and head outside.

"Hi, Ocean. I missed you." He takes her from me and gives her a gentle hug and kiss on the cheek.

The passenger's seat is empty.

"Where's Emma?" I ask as he fastens in Ocean.

"Uh ... she wasn't quite ready so I decided to come get Ocean then stop back by and pick her up." He closes the door.

Crossing my arms over my chest, I smirk. "You're afraid I'm going to tell her, aren't you?"

He shrugs. "Nope. If you want her to know, then tell her." He holds up his phone. "Do you want me to dial her up?"

Ugh! What's his angle here? Why would he say that?

"It's not my place to tell her. You should tell her."

He cocks his head to the side. "Do you want me to tell her?"

Fucking mind games!

"I said you *should* tell her."

"I asked if you *want* me to tell her."

I turn and walk off. "Tell her, don't tell her. It's none of my business."

———

THERE's nothing quite like photographing a wedding to take my mind off my own wedding that will not be taking place or Lautner's wedding that will. By the end of the reception, I've filled all my memory sticks so there has to be some great pictures, but today I didn't feel inspired; my artistic side was not feeling it.

As I leave the reception, my phone vibrates. It's a text from Lautner with an address and message saying Ocean is still with them and I can pick her up at his dad's when I'm finished. I'm exhausted by the time I reach his dad's house. It's been a long day.

"Hey." Lautner smiles, opening the door. "Come in."

I'm not in the mood to visit, but since he has my daughter held hostage I don't have a choice.

"You remember my dad, James?" he says as we enter the great room.

James is in a recliner and Ocean is sleeping on his chest. He smiles. "Nice to see you again." He kisses Ocean's head. "Thank you for giving me such a beautiful granddaughter. She has Rebecca's eyes."

I nod with a small smile, tired but not completely unaffected by his words.

"Hey, Sydney." Emma walks into the room. "Here." She hands me a bag. "We went shopping after the fitting. Just some girly clothes I couldn't refuse and a new baby doll."

I take the bag feeling Lautner's eyes on me, but I don't look at him. "Thank you. Well, it's late and I'm tired so ..."

"You get her stuff, I'll carry her out," Lautner says, taking Ocean from James.

I wave at James and Emma while holding the front door open for Lautner. "Goodnight."

He fastens her in without waking her up and shuts the door. I open up the back and put her bags in, jumping at the feel of his hands snaking around my waist. I look around worried that someone is watching, but I'm parked in the driveway on the side of the house away from all windows and tall shrubs line the other side of the drive.

Turning in his arms, I place my hands flat on his chest and sigh. "Why are you doing this?"

He bends down and kisses my neck. "Say it," he whispers.

I close my eyes, curling my fingers into his shirt. "Say what?" My voice is weak.

His lips work their way up to mine. His tongue thrusts into my mouth. I moan. Where the hell is my self respect? I am such a junkie; I keep coming back for more thinking eventually I won't want it ... I won't need it. What if Emma or his dad come out? Doesn't he care?

I cling to him, wanting him to be mine so bad. "I want you." I breathe against his lips.

"I want you too," he whispers back, tangling his hands in my hair. He kisses me again.

I wrap my arms around his neck and kiss him back with everything I have. Can't he feel this?

Tugging on my hair, he pulls our mouths apart and rests his forehead on mine. "I love you," he whispers.

Tears sting my eyes. This is torture. "Then don't marry her," I plead.

There. Is that what he wanted me to say? Fine, I said it. My voice is desperate, what more can I do?

He grabs my hands, removing them from his neck. Squeezing them tight he bends down to my eye level. "Why?"

"Why shouldn't you marry her?" My face is contorted in confusion.

He nods.

"Because you love me! That's why!" I yell, louder than I should.

Standing straight, he drops my hands and walks away. There's nothing more I can do or say. I asked him not to marry her. I asked him to choose me. There's nothing left.

Dane is asleep on the sofa. He hasn't slept upstairs since his accident. His parents think it's because of how long it takes him to get up the stairs. I know he's not wanting to share a bed with me.

After getting my half-sleeping baby into bed, I grab a snack from the kitchen. I haven't eaten since noon.

"How was the wedding?" Dane's groggy voice mumbles.

I take my plate and sit on the edge of the coffee table next to the end of the couch where his head is at. "Long." I crunch on a chip. "How are you feeling?"

"Restless."

I give him a sad smile. "Are your parents still planning on leaving tomorrow?"

"Just my dad." He tries to readjust himself so he's sitting up a little more. The grimace shows the pain that's still there every time he moves.

"Why just your dad?" I take a bite of my sandwich.

His eyes fail to meet mine. "She knows you're moving out."

I stop mid-chew. His gaze meets mine. With a slow nod, I continue chewing.

"He's still marrying Emma."

Dane shakes his head. "Doesn't matter."

"I care about you." I rest my hand on his.

"Do you love me?"

My head jerks back. "Why would you ask me that?"

"Because you've never said it."

"What do you mean? Of course I've said it."

"No, I've said it and you've said 'you too.'"

"Same thing."

"Is it?" He raises a brow.

I look away. "Does it matter?"

"It does to me. If you can look me in the eye and tell me

you love me, not like a friend or a brother, but as a husband ... as your lover, then maybe we stand a chance."

I look him in the eye, but not to say those words. "Why did you lie to me?"

He looks away.

"You didn't see Lautner before Ocean was born. You saw him after. He told you his mom died. He told you he wasn't with anyone because he still loved me. Lautner was broken and you could have said something ... if not to him, then to me. Why, Dane?"

His jaw muscles twitch as he continues to look away.

"I wanted you, then I saw Ocean and this protective side of me took over. But I did it because I loved you." His eyes meet mine. "I may have lied to you, but I didn't screw anyone."

"You screwed me!" My voice elevates and I pause a moment to make sure I'm not waking anyone. "You screwed me, Dane. You stole Ocean's chance at having a real family, not some split situation where she's being shuffled between two homes, but a real family with her mother and father together. The life you got to have. You took that away from her and now it's too late. So, you can be pissed at me because I made a last ditch effort to get that back for her and myself, but we wouldn't be having this conversation if you would have told *me* the truth."

He's hurt. My words were meant to hurt him. I'm willing to take responsibly for my actions, but I won't let him put it all on me. Dane has given me so much, but he's also taken so much away.

Chapter Thirty-Four

July 27th, 2013

Two weeks ago I packed up my belongings, my daughter, and my dog and said an emotional goodbye to Dane. We shared some tears and by the time I pulled out of the driveway, things felt better between us. The fact that Dane was willing to even consider taking me back was a real testament to his love for me. A love I never was able to return. My feelings for him may not have been as strong, but I care for him too much to take away his chance at happiness. He deserves a love like the one I had with Lautner. I know saying goodbye to Ocean was just as hard. She has asked about him more than once, and I know over time the memory of him will fade from her mind, but she will forever be in his heart.

As for my sister ... she has taken us in temporarily. Her roommate agreed to stay with her boyfriend until we found our own place. In return, I have taken over paying for her part of the rent. Swarley has been the challenge. Avery's not allowed to have pets so we've been sneaking him in and out of the building.

Lautner and Emma's wedding is next weekend. I've only communicated with him through texts and those have been about Ocean. He hasn't seen her either in two weeks and I know it's killing him, especially since he won't get to see her while he's in Bali doing *stuff* with Emma.

Somehow I failed him. I saw it in his eyes that night at his dad's. I'm not sure if he was looking for an apology, a promise to never lie to him again, or what, but my words weren't good enough. I've come to the conclusion that since he's going through with the wedding, then he's meant to be with her. I won't show up and barge through the doors in Hollywood fashion drama and beg him to not marry her just before the minister makes everyone hold their peace forever.

"So since Dane's out, who are you taking to the wedding?" Avery asks as we eat our breakfast.

"Actually, I'm not going."

"What do you mean you're not going?" She gives me a disapproving glance over her coffee mug.

I shrug and hand Ocean part of my toast. "I wasn't invited."

"What? Of course you're invited. Ocean is the flower girl."

"Which means Ocean is invited. Lautner texted me and I'm supposed to drop her off at his dad's house late Friday afternoon. She's going to the rehearsal, then rehearsal dinner, and then she's staying overnight with them at his dad's so she can go with the girls to the salon in the morning."

"And you're okay with her spending the night with them?"

I reach over and brush Ocean's hair out of her eyes. "No,

but I don't have much of a choice. After all, she's going to be doing it in the near future anyway."

"So what are you going to do while all this is going on?"

I laugh. "That's the fun part. Apparently, Emma's rich family is putting me up in a nice hotel and even throwing in some fancy spa treatments for me and a *friend* of my choosing. So what do you say *friend*?"

"Uh ... heck yeah, I'll go live it up on someone else's tab." Avery's grin is enormous. "You think room service is included?"

I grin. "Well, I'm not giving them my credit card number so I'd say yes. Food, champagne ... whatever we want."

"Watch out world, the Montgomery sisters are going to get hammered!"

I shake my head.

Chapter Thirty-Five

August 2nd, 2013

WE'RE a few block's from Lautner's dad's house. I'd like to say that my anxiety over Lautner and Emma stealing Ocean has subsided, but it hasn't. The overnight part is what has me worried. She could wet the bed, have a bad dream and be crying for me. What if she gets sick like she did at my wedding?

"Knock it off," Avery says with a smirk on her face.

"What?" I reply with a quick sideways glance.

"Stop obsessing."

"What—I-I don't know what you're talking about." My voice jumps an octave.

"I can hear the cogs turning in your head. You're worried about leaving her and who's going to cut up her food tonight, and what if she doesn't get a bedtime story. Tomorrow she could get sick or scared or stolen by her father and his new bride."

"Pfft ... you think you know me but ... that ... no ... not even close."

"Lying like a rug, Sam ... lying like a rug." She laughs as we pull into the drive. "Want me to come with you?"

I roll my eyes as I open my door. "Thanks for your concern, but I'm a big girl. I can do this."

After getting Ocean out of her seat, I sling her two bags over my shoulder and walk her up to the door. It's like I'm leaving her off at camp.

Don't cry ... don't cry.

"Ocean!" James answers the door with such excitement to see his granddaughter. "Sydney, nice to see you too."

I smile. "Where's Lautner?" I try to sound casual, like it doesn't matter and I'm not sure why it does.

"He and the groomsmen are still out golfing, but they should be back soon. I offered to stay back to be here for Ocean. He wanted to but I told him it would be wrong for the groom to miss his own golf outing with the guys."

"Oh, okay .... um ..."

James pats me on the shoulder. "She'll be fine. I'll guard her with my life."

I blink back the tears and swallow hard with a hesitant nod. "Come here, baby girl. Give me a hug and kiss."

Ocean hugs me and a little too willingly walks into the house.

"So, you'll call me after the reception and I'll pick her up here?"

"You bet. We'll see you tomorrow." He goes to shut the door.

"And you have my cell phone number?"

"Got it."

The door closes and I know I'm going to receive a ration

of crap from Avery for my pathetic watery eyes, but she can just kiss my ass.

———

"Holy Crap! *This* is where we're staying?" Avery gasps as we pull up to the valet parking.

"Close your mouth. You're embarrassing me." I laugh, getting out of my Jeep.

The valet greets me as if I just pulled up in a Bentley. Nice!

Check-in is simple because everything has been handled ahead of time. I wonder if it's a distraction. Keep the deranged Sydney preoccupied so she doesn't show up at the wedding and ruin everything. Looking around at the posh surroundings, I inwardly smile. For the first time in my life, my craziness pays off.

"Would you look at this?" Avery runs over to the windows as we enter the room.

I dig in my purse to tip the bellboy, but he holds up his hand. "It's all been taken care of, ma'am."

"Thank you." I smile.

It's not a room, it's a luxury suite larger than the house I rented from Dane.

"Get over here, now!" Avery calls.

French doors open to a massive private balcony overlooking the bay and part of the city. "Not bad."

"Not bad? Okay, Miss I've-traveled-the-world, but for those of us who haven't, let me tell you this is unbelievable."

I grin and nudge her. "I'm kidding. I have seen a lot of the world, but this is still amazing."

She turns and skips inside to check out the rest of our palace for the night. I check my watch.

"We need to get going. We have spa treatments in half an hour," I call to her.

She waltzes out of one of the bedrooms, jabbering in her ridiculous British voice. "Ah, yes, we should most certainly participate in a little pampering."

I roll my eyes and open the door. "Shall we?"

We arrive early and fill out our necessary forms while being offered any beverage imaginable. Avery jumps at a glass of champagne, while I opt for iced tea deciding to wait to drown my sorrows in alcohol until after my treatments.

"So no regrets, right?" she says while we sip our drinks waiting to be taken back.

"Regrets?" I tilt my head.

"This weekend. The love of your life is marrying someone else, I'm just saying ... no regrets?"

"I laid it on the line, told him not to marry her, yet, here we are. I don't know what else he wanted me to say."

Avery nods and sips her champagne.

A young couple exits the spa and stops to look at some of the products on the shelves next to us. He wraps his arm around her and kisses her. "I love you," he says.

"I love you," she returns.

I smile and try not to stare. How sweet, I think to myself.

TOMORROW WE ARE SCHEDULED for massages; tonight we're having manicures and pedicures. Avery goes for wild hot pink polish with glitter. I do sex red on my toenails and a French manicure.

"Did you bring a cocktail dress for the fancy restaurant here?" Avery asks as our nails are under the heated dryers.

"Yeah, but it's probably not fancy enough."

"Your eyebrows could use a little touch up. Want me to see if they can fit us in for a quick wax."

I shake my head. "My eyebrows are fine. You thin yours out too much. Must be an L.A. thing."

"Well I'll be up in a little bit then, I'm not passing up *free* treatments."

I wave my hand at her as I exit. "Enjoy, don't be too long or I'm going to dinner without you."

As I leave the lobby of the spa, I think back to the couple we saw earlier and my short conversation with Avery.

Regrets ...

Entering our suite, I set my purse down and dig out my phone.

Regrets ... "Say it ..." The couple downstairs ...

I tap the letters on the screen. "What the hell are you doing, Sydney?" I ask still crazy, still taking to myself.

With one hand I hold my phone, and with the other I mess with my hair.

"Screw it!" My thumb grazes over the *send* button and off it goes.

I toss my phone on the couch, grab my dress and makeup bag, then head in the bathroom. After applying my makeup, I slip into my silver sequined cocktail dress and look in the mirror again.

"Oh shit! What did I do?" The reality of my impulsive text hits me. I hear the door to the suite shut.

"Ave ... you're not going to believe what—" I open the bathroom door.

Oh ... dear ... God!

442

Flowers. Dim lights. Soft music. *Lautner*.

He's about ten feet away wearing a black suit and a titanium tie. I've never seen him dressed up like this. He's ... perfect. Holding up his phone, he shakes his head. "Got your message ... finally."

My newly applied makeup is in serious danger. There's a lump in my throat the size of Saturn and it's making my eyes water ... a lot!

He takes a step closer. "So here's how this is going to go ... I'm going to drain you of all your tears because that's what I do best, then you're going to say these three words to me..." he holds up his phone again "...then I'm going to get down on one knee and ask you a very important question. Then you're going to say yes. After that, I'm going to remove your clothes and make you scream until the Golden Gate Bridge collapses, *then* we're going to make slow ... passionate ... love ... for the rest of our lives. Okay?"

The most painful sob escapes as my tears come so fast I can barely see him, but I manage to nod.

He takes another step. "Here's the problem. I don't know how to live if I'm not loving you. It's like asking my lungs to expand without air, my heart to beat without blood, my eyes to see without light. It's just not possible. And yet, you're so stupid ..."

I laugh and sob at the same time, eyes swollen, nose sniffling.

"How could you ever think I would love someone the way I love you?" He takes a step closer, reaching into the inside of his jacket, pulls out a hankie and blots my face one gentle pat at a time. "You obviously didn't hear me the first time so I'll say it again."

He smiles. "Are you ready?"

I nod and sniffle.

"I. Love. You. Period. It's a goddamn soul-shattering love that will never *ever* be matched. My love for you is unapologetic and forever." He puts his hankie back in his pocket and cradles my face.

Blue irises.

"I love you ... only you ... always you ... forever you." He reaches in his pocket and pulls out his phone showing my text on his screen. "Are you done crying?" He smirks.

Sniffling, I nod and smile.

"Good, your turn." He wiggles his phone a few times before sliding it back in his pocket.

"Laut—"

"Uh, uh ..." He shakes his head and puts his finger to my lips. "Three words, Syd, that's all I want to hear." He slides his finger off my lips and presses a chaste kiss to them.

In this moment I've discovered a truth that I never thought I would believe. Fate is a real, undeniable force and not all fairytales are fictional.

"I love you." I've never put so much emotion into three simple words.

A lifetime of happiness shines from his smile and beautiful blue irises. I can't believe it took me so long to say those words.

He drops to one knee, reaches into his other jacket pocket and pulls out a ring. "My mom gave me her diamond ring before she died." He releases his own rebel tears with a deep swallow. "She told me to give it to the girl who captured my soul." He closes his eyes while I brush my thumbs over the tears running down his cheeks. "I didn't give this ring to Emma."

Our eyes meet and he doesn't have to say anymore. There's nothing left to say. He just said it all.

"Sydney Ann Montgomery, love of my life, keeper of my soul, mother of the most angelic baby girl ever to grace this Earth ... will you marry me?"

"Where is my baby gir—"

"Sydney! One word, baby. I told you how this was going to go."

I giggle and hold out my left hand. "Yes!"

He slides the ring on my finger then kisses it.

"Where's my sister? Where's Ocean? Why aren't you—"

He silences me in the only way he knows how. As I relax and surrender to his silencing demand, he releases my lips. Looking down at my bare feet he bites his bottom lip. "What do your shoes look like that you brought to wear with this?" He skims his hands down my hips.

"Silver stilettos, why?" I sniffle.

"Put them on."

"Why? Are we—"

"Put. Them. On." He interrupts with a firm voice but a sly grin tugs at his lips.

I roll my eyes, dig the shoes out of my suitcase, and slip them on. They have a four inch heel and look like something a pole dancer would wear. I only wear them when I go out with Avery.

He's standing by the glass balcony doors. My eyes meet his sexy, heated gaze. Are we going to sit out on the balcony? Why do I have to wear these for that? He crooks his finger at me. I follow his silent request. Standing in front of him, he explores my body with his eyes as he shrugs off his suit jacket.

"Are we staying in? I ask as he loosens his tie.

He nods.

I continue to watch him remove his shirt while I wet my lips.

"Are you taking off *all* your clothes?" My words are breathy.

He nods.

I chew the inside of my cheek and fiddle with my hair while thinking about my stilettos. "We're going to do something kinky, aren't we?"

He grins as he removes his boxer briefs. I gasp as he stands before me naked and very aroused. Taking a glance out the window first, I look back at him with wide eyes.

"No one can see us." He smirks, turning me around and unzipping my dress. My strapless little number falls to the floor and I'm left with just my black thong and silver stilettos.

"Step out."

I step out of my dress. He grabs my hands and places them flat on the window.

"Spread your legs."

"When did you become so kinky?" I look back at him.

He brushes my hair to one side, exposing my neck and running his tongue along it, then continues down my back with open-mouth kisses. "Says the girl who pleasured herself in front of me," he mumbles over my skin.

There it is ... the smile. I feel him smile against my skin and it makes me tingle all over.

"It was awkward." I sigh as his hands slide around to my breasts.

"It's was fucking sexy." He cups my breasts then pinches my nipples.

"Ahh ..." I arch my back, pushing my breasts farther into his hands and my butt toward him.

"Baby, you're so damn sexy." His cock slides between my legs, rubbing against my thong. "And you're mine ... all mine."

Inching his right hand down my stomach, he slips his fingers under the front lacy part of my panties. I tilt my head back next to his as he circles my clit.

"Lautner ..."

"What is it, baby?"

"Oh ... God!" I cry.

"I can't hear you, Syd." He pinches my nipple harder.

"Ahh! Lautner!" I yell as he works my nipple and my clitoris.

He fists the delicate fabric and with one quick jerk my thong disintegrates into a small lace scrap of nothing. Rocking his pelvis, he thrusts into me. My nails scrape against the glass as my knees give a little.

I look up and watch our reflection in the glass, surprised by how much it turns me on. His hands at my breasts and then moving lower, between my legs. I see him watching us too. Our eyes meet in the glass.

"Not kinky baby—just—sexy." His voice is strained and labored with each thrust he makes into me. "My God ... I love ... every inch ... of you."

"Lautner!" I yell again, tipping my head back and his expert fingers work me.

"I'm close ... Oh God ... so ... close!" I cry as he hits every bundle of sexual nerves I have.

He slams into me harder, more erratic, and I push back against him, tightening around him.

"Yes! Yes! Yes!" I scream like I'm trying to wake up the

city. I convulse around him in wave after wave of glorious sensation. My forehead drops against the window.

He slams into me one more time. "Sydney! God, that's so good!" He growls, pouring himself into me while wrapping his arms around me.

My legs are gone. I'm thankful he has a strong hold on me. He turns me around, picks me up in his loving arms, and carries me to the bed. Pulling down the covers, he lays me on the bed and eases off my shoes, massaging my feet.

I grin and shake my head. "Sexy my ass ... say what you want, that was kinky."

He kisses each one of my newly pedicured toes. "Yes, your ass is sexy, and since I'm officially keeping you forever, then we should throw in a little kink every now and then to keep things ... unexpected."

I hold out my left hand and gaze at my ring. "It's beautiful. How will your dad feel about me wearing your mother's ring?"

He crawls up the bed toward me planting kisses the whole way. "He's thrilled."

I lift my head. "He knows?"

"Of course."

"Hmm ... interesting."

He kisses me on the lips. It's slow, almost lazy, like we have all the time in the world. I smile inwardly because it's just now sinking in that we do. Please don't let this be a dream and if it is, I never want to wake up.

I tug his hair and he releases my lips. "I love you."

His lottery winner grin reappears. If he smiles that big every time I say it to him, then he's going to hear it at least a hundred times a day.

"I love you too." He rolls me so I'm sprawled on his chest, his face in my hair, his heart at my ear.

"So ..."

"Here we go, twenty questions." He chuckles knowingly.

"Okay, smarty-pants..." I dig my nails into his chest eliciting a slight jump from him "...if you're so smart, then don't make me ask, just tell me."

"Where to start. Let's see ... Ocean is at my dad's tonight with ... let's just say family and you'll find out more tomorrow."

I start to lift my head but he puts his hand on it, pressing it back to his chest. "Just listen. The wedding was cancelled two weeks ago right after I last saw you..." He keeps my head pressed firmly to his chest knowing I'm dying to look at him and ask for more details. "...but I think I knew I wasn't going to marry Emma the moment I found out you hadn't married Dane. So to answer your next question ... I plead temporary insanity for not breaking it off sooner, and I'm quite certain I'd better hang onto my current job because I know a certain chief of staff who will no longer be giving me a glowing recommendation. However, Emma doesn't hate me. She said she envies what we have and knows she'll find a guy that looks at her the way I look at you."

I relax, although my next question is not one I should want to know and no good can come from asking it but ...

He releases his hold on my head and I look up at him with mixed emotions.

"No," he says.

I furrow my brow. "I haven't even asked you anything yet."

"You want to know if I had sex with Emma after you and Ocean left my house."

I look away and nod.

He tugs my chin, forcing me to look at him. "Let's just say I've had some unusually bad headaches and long hours at work." He winks.

Biting my lips together, I fight to hide my pleased smile. "I love you."

"I know you do. I've always known it."

"Then why the drama? Why make me say it?"

He tucks my hair behind my ears. "I needed you to know it ... admit it to yourself. I didn't want your love for me to be a hidden emotion or a guilty pleasure. I wanted you to say it, feel it, show it. Surrender to it, to me, to us."

I kiss him. "I surrender."

"Mmm ... it's about time," he mumbles.

I smile against his lips.

"You planned this without knowing I was going to text you. What were you going to do if I didn't say it first?"

"Let's just say you'd still be in your heels and plastered up against the window."

My mouth falls open. "You were going to pound a confession out of me?"

"Something like that."

Squeezing my ass, he rocks his hips into me.

"Mmm ... what was next on the list?" I wet my lips and wiggle my hips over his erection.

He flips me on my back, settling between my legs and sinking into me. "Making slow ... passionate ... love ... for the rest of our lives."

Chapter Thirty-Six

August 3rd, 2013

"**I** LOVE YOU." *Kiss.* "I love you." *Kiss.* "I love you." *Kiss.*

"Baby ... what are you doing to me?" Lautner's groggy but sexy voice vibrates.

He hasn't opened his eyes yet, but his mouth is twisted into a grin as I kiss the back of his legs, along the firm muscles of his ass, and the bumpy terrain of his sculpted back.

"Sorry, I couldn't sleep. Had to make sure you were still mine," I whisper in his ear.

"Well, don't stop. I'm yours, baby, all yours."

I straddle his butt and massage his back. "So, I probably should have mentioned this last night, so you knew what you were getting into, but I'm sort of homeless right now with a child and a dog. Is that going to be a problem?"

He chuckles. "I got it covered. Found a new place for us to live after we get married."

"Oh." I bite my tongue, no need to press my luck. However, I need a place to live, like *now*. It's only a matter of time before Avery gets in trouble for having a dog at her place.

"Breakfast then sex or sex then breakfast or sex for breakfast?" he asks.

I pinch his sides and he rolls over bucking me off his back then pinning me to the mattress. "What's it going to be?" He interlaces our fingers above my head.

"Hmm ... how about sex for breakfast therefore breakfast, then, well ... more sex, and by that time we might actually need some food."

He grins. "Sex in bed, the tub, or shower?"

"Yes, yes, and yes!" I smile.

"God, I love you, Syd."

———

As promised the day before, I get a massage and even my hair done at the salon. Although, I feel much more guilty knowing that Lautner is the one paying for this elaborate overnight stay and spa services. I'm itching to get back to Ocean, but Lautner wants to keep me to himself for a few more hours after we check out of the hotel.

We drive down the coast and enjoy the view and each other's company. He holds my hand, occasionally playing with the diamond ring on my finger.

"You do realize my dad is going to kill you when he finds out you proposed without asking him first."

He laughs. "Now I *know* 'Thou shalt not kill' is one of the Ten Commandments. What religion did you say your dad is?"

I grin. "He's going to freak. When I told him it was over

with Dane, he suggested I try it on my own for a while and not rush into a new relationship."

"He'll just have to deal with it."

"Someday, that's what Ocean's boyfriend is going to say about you."

Lautner frowns. "Yeah, well we'll discuss that when she's thirty."

"Marriage?"

"Dating," he says with a serious tone.

We pull up to a familiar empty dirt parking lot. *Our beach.*

"My suit is at the bottom of my bag in back."

He leans over and kisses my lips then slides his hand up under my sundress, massaging my thigh. "I'm pretty sure we're not going to need our suits for what I have in mind." His deep seductive voice has me squirming in my seat.

He hops out and comes around to open my door.

"Why, Dr. Sullivan, I didn't know you were into public fornication." I step out and he smacks me on the butt.

"Remember, a little kink is a good thing, baby."

"Oh, I remember. The muscles in my legs are still burning. Next time you wear the stilettos."

A roar of laughter escapes his chest as he grabs my hand and leads me to the path around the grassy knoll. Our private beach comes into sight and I stop. He squeezes my hand and looks at me with adoration and love. I look back at the beach.

His dad. My dad. Avery. Ocean. And ... Swarley.

Our dad's are dressed in nice shorts and button down shirts. Avery and Ocean are wearing sundresses and holding flower bouquets.

"Mommy!" Ocean runs to me, I pick her up and hug her tight. "Fowers." She hands me a small bouquet.

Of course, I'm crying.

Lautner kisses Ocean and then me. "We'll make it legal later, but marry me ... today ... right here."

Ocean squirms so I set her down and she runs back to the beach.

I have no words.

Lautner pulls me into him and wipes my tears. "Marry me, Sydney," he whispers.

I nod. "Yes!"

He kisses me and it's all consuming.

"Ah hem!" I hear my dad walking toward us. "I haven't given you permission to kiss the bride yet."

Lautner releases me and shakes my dad's hand. "Tom."

Then my dad pulls me into his arms.

"How ... when ... you're here," I stutter.

"I got a call ten days ago. Some guy claiming to be Ocean's dad wanted to know if I'd marry him and this girl he's crazy about ... on a beach."

Lautner walks toward the beach but turns and gives me a smile and sexy wink. I shake my head, wiping my tears.

My dad kisses my forehead. "Happy, baby girl?"

I nod. "All my dreams have just come true."

"Shall we?" He offers his arm and I take it.

Numerous hearts have been carved in the sand, and there is a trail of rose petals leading to where Avery, Ocean, James, Swarley, and Lautner are waiting.

My dad gives me away with a kiss on the cheek and Lautner takes my hands ... and my whole heart.

My dad keeps it short and sweet, then Lautner says his vows to me.

"Sydney Ann Montgomery, I promise you a long life of flowers, chai tea lattes, and cherry-almond galettes. I promise to teach you how to surf and play real football ..."

Everyone laughs.

"... I promise to listen to your every word, even though most of the time you're talking to yourself."

I squint my eyes and shake my head.

He clears his throat and lowers his gaze to our hands for a moment then looks back at me with teary blue irises. "I've wanted many things in my life until I met you. Then I wanted nothing ... except you. My existence is for you..." he looks at Ocean "...every part of you. Never doubt my love for you. If I'm breathing, I'm loving you. Only you ... always you ... forever you."

I reach up and brush my thumb along his wet cheek, and he leans into my hand. The love I feel for him cannot be expressed in words, yet it's my turn to form something that I know will fall so short of my true emotions.

"*What if* you wouldn't have taken a wrong turn for the right reason? *What if* the moment would have slipped away? *What if* for the rest of our lives we would have to live with the excruciating agony born from the soul-snatching *what if*?" I shake my head and smile. "BEST pick up line ever."

Lautner grins and in this moment it doesn't matter that nobody else understands our vows. It's just us and the rest of the world has always ceased to exist when we're together.

"Blue irises ... you were right. I see my reflection in your eyes. My Whole. Entire. World. Is in your eyes. My past, my present, my future ... it's all there. When I'm lost, I find myself in your eyes. I see my heart beating in your eyes. I see everything beautiful about life in your eyes. I see an ocean of infinity in your eyes."

I look at Ocean. "I see *our Ocean* in your eyes. Lautner Asher Sullivan, if I'm given a million lives to live, it will never be enough time to show you how much I love you, but I do. I. Love. You."

I look at my dad and he has tears in his eyes. Clearing his throat, he continues, "Lautner, do you take Sydney to be your wedded wife, to love and cherish so long as you both shall live?"

"I do." He grins and squeezes my hands.

"Sydney, do you take Lautner to be your wedded husband, to love and cherish so long as you both shall live?"

"I do." My giddy smile rivals his.

"I now pronounce you husband and wife. You may kiss my daughter."

Lautner looks at my dad and laughs. "Thanks, I think I will."

We kiss and our small gathering cheers as Ocean squeezes between us. Lautner lifts her up and we both hug her between us.

"Congratulations!" Avery pulls me from Lautner and into her arms.

"You! Are a real sneak." I hug her and shake my head. "How long did you know?"

Releasing me, she grins. "Not that long, maybe a week. But I've been dying watching you sulk around, knowing your Prince Charming was getting ready to sweep you off your feet."

I brush my finger over her eyebrows. "Did you really get them waxed?"

"Heck yeah, free treatments!"

I roll my eyes.

James touches my back. I turn and he grabs my left hand and smiles. "Perfect. Rebecca would be elated."

I blink back a few tears. "Thank you." We embrace until I'm once again being pulled away, literally. Lautner scoops me up in his arms and carries me toward the water.

"Lautner!" I squeal as he carries us into the crashing waves until we're completely drenched. He kisses me, taking his time to explore every inch of my mouth. As he releases my lips, I wrap my arms around him and he leaves my face cradled in his loving hands. "So, *Mrs. Sullivan*, I hear you have a housing issue ..."

Epilogue

September 3rd, 2013

MY SEXY, doctor, ex-wide receiver husband is charitable enough to take in his homeless bride, our angelic love child, and rambunctious Weimaraner. We have a huge backyard framed in large trees, a swing set, and a pool. I have to mention that my pool guy is off-the-charts hot ... somedays even a little naughty.

My wedding present from him is a bonus room above the garage that has been converted into a photography studio. I feel a little guilty that I haven't found the perfect gift for him yet, but I'm sure I'll know it when I see it.

Lautner's birthday is tomorrow so Avery picked up the kids, Ocean and Swarley, and is keeping them overnight. He should be home any minute and I have dinner on the table, candles lit, and Ed Sherran plays through the speakers. My red dress is tight, short, and paired with black heels that could lead to some kink. Originally I had my hair up but

Lautner loves the long-haired goddess look so it's down again.

My stomach is unsettled, it has been all day. We've been intimate in every way possible so I don't know why my nerves are knotting my stomach so much.

He's here!

I dim the lights and hop on the kitchen island with my bare legs crossed and my hair flowing over my ample cleavage. He opens the back door and freezes.

"Happy birthday, Dr. Sullivan," I say in a low sexy tone.

Hungry blue irises peruse my body as he wets his lips. Tossing his keys on the counter, he grins in appreciation, sauntering toward me like a jungle cat.

"Mrs. Sullivan ..." He uncrosses my legs and settles between them, hiking my dress up farther. His hands skim down my bare legs. "... Nice shoes. Hope they're comfy because I think you're going to be in them for awhile." Full, greedy lips take mine. I tug his tie, holding him close, and moan as our tongues dance—a welcome greeting after a long day apart.

"Dinner—" I try to say over his lips.

"It can wait." His hands slide back up my legs and under my dress.

"I don't want it to get—"

Oh God!

I shove him away, hop down, and sprint to the bathroom, somehow managing to avoid turning an ankle on the way. Loving hands pull back my hair as I heave into the toilet.

Lautner sits on the floor straddling his legs around me, pulls me back into his chest, and hands me a wet wash cloth. "How's my baby?"

"Ugh! I'm not feeling so good."

He laughs. "I can see that, but I meant how's my *baby*?" I feel his hand rubbing circles on my tummy.

"What are you talking about? I'm not pregnant." I lean my head back against his shoulder.

He kisses my neck. "We've had sex every night since I proposed to you. I haven't seen any 'stay away' signs on the door or tampons in the trash, and your breasts are ... well, let's just say I'm not complaining."

Holy shit! He's right.

"For heavens sake! Why are you always trying to get me pregnant?"

"Me?" He chuckles. "You're the one who takes her pill 'most of the time.'"

I stand and give him a scowl then brush my teeth. He leans against the door frame looking cocky as hell.

Spitting, I toss my toothbrush aside and turn. "For a doctor you're terribly irresponsible when it comes to birth control." I squint my eyes and poke my finger into his chest. "If you've known I can't be trusted to take my pills, then why haven't you worn a condom?"

Grabbing my hand, he kisses my accusatory finger. "Because you seem to be hell-bent on having my babies, and you know I can't deny you."

"You wanted me to get pregnant? Both times?" My voice escalates with each word.

He shrugs with an I'm-the-ultimate-stud smirk.

I brush past him. "You have a twisted mind, Dr. Sullivan."

Grabbing my arm, he spins me around and into his chest.

The playfulness is gone, but his eyes sparkle with love and adoration. "I love you, Sydney." He kneels in front of me and removes my shoes. My toes scream in delight. Wrapping

460

his arms around me, he kisses my belly, blue irises peering up at me. "We're having another baby."

I grin and run my fingers through his hair. "We're having another baby."

He just got his wedding present.

———

April 3rd, 2014
PAGING DR. SULLIVAN

ALMOST FOUR YEARS AGO, I met my wife. She didn't know it, but I did. Sydney landed in Palo Alto for one reason ... to be with me. When did I know she was the woman for me? Easy. The day she crawled onto the beach after trying to catch a few easy waves. Sharks? Hell, there were no sharks in a two mile radius. Even they swam away, embarrassed for her, after watching her capsize into the water so many times. On all fours, she crawled out of the water, stopping at my feet—her sexy goddess hair a matted tangled mess and an enormous sand turd sagging from her bikini bottoms. Two thoughts went through my mind. One: "Man! This girl is one, sexy, awkward, stubborn disaster." Two: "Yep, I'm probably going to marry her."

Being with her is my survival; loving her is effortless. She is the shining center of my universe and her love is the moon that pulls the tide of my heart. The best part of my day is coming home to the squeal of "Daddy" from our brown-haired, blue-eyed baby girl followed by the tug of my tie as Sydney pulls my lips to hers and seductively whispers, "How was your day, Dr. Sullivan?"

Perfect. That's my day ... everyday.

"Oh God! It hurts!" Sydney yells clenching my hand.

"I know it does, baby, but you're doing great."

"The hell you do! How many babies have you pushed out of your vagina?"

Dr. Mackey, our OBGYN, perched on her stool between Sydney's spread legs, glances at me, and I know she's smirking behind her mask as is the nurse next to her.

"Well, none but—"

"Then. Just. Don't. Talk." She clenches her teeth as another contraction seizes her.

"That's it, Sydney. One more hard push and the head will be out."

Hmm ... why does Dr. Mackey get to talk?

"Ouch!" Sydney yells one last time.

"You're up, Dr. Sully," Dr. Mackey declares as I pry my hand from Sydney's to finish delivering our baby. Sydney's not stopping in spite of Dr. Mackey's instructions to stop pushing. It's out. *He's* out. I catch him with ease—the best catch I've ever made ... and I've made a lot. I suction his mouth eliciting an immediate cry and hand him to his mom.

"Oh my gosh!" She looks at him and then at me with tears freely flowing from her irresistible hazel eyes.

I'm gone. Grown man or not, I can't hide my emotions. The most beautiful woman in the world has given me another child, a son.

She reaches her free hand up to wipe my face. "You can speak now." She grins.

"Amazing. You, my love, are amazing." I kiss her and then our son.

"I love you, sweetie."

"I know you do, baby. I love you too."

Sydney tells me all the time how much she loves me.

They're just three simple words, but they're food to my soul. I waited so long to hear them, and I'll never tire of the way they sound coming from her or the way she holds my gaze until I smile in acknowledgment.

I cut the cord and hold our son, Asher, for the first time. I lay him under the heat lights and look him over. Ten fingers, ten toes, and a strong set of lungs.

Perfect. That's my day ... everyday.

———

August 17th, 2014
REAL FOOTBALL

"Ocean, turn your shinguards around, it's obvious your dad dressed you for your first practice."

"I heard that, and she dressed herself," Lautner says behind us, carrying the mesh bag of soccer balls to the practice field.

I remove Asher from his Ergo carrier and try to hand him off to Lautner. He holds up his hands.

"Nope, sorry, I have to run practice, baby."

"I'm the coach, you're the assistant coach," I say between gritted teeth.

He picks up a soccer ball and dribbles it on his knees just to prove he's all that.

"Well, the moms at the team meeting said they'd like to watch *me* run practice."

I roll my eyes. "Oh, I'm sure they'd love to *watch* you do anything. As I recall, I had to hand out tissues at that meeting so they could wipe the drool off their faces."

He kicks the ball to Ocean as more cars start pulling into the parking lot.

"You're not jealous are you, baby?" he whispers in my ear before kissing Asher on the cheek. "Because after the way you touched yourself for me last night, you have no reason to be—"

"Lautner!" I glare at him with raised brows as I look to see if anyone can hear.

He chuckles at my red face. "Now if you'll excuse me, the moms, I mean ... the *kids* are waiting."

I shake my head, but my smile contradicts the mock annoyance I'm trying to show.

Lautner has given me nothing I thought I wanted and everything I can't live without. In the past year he's mastered the art of making cherry-almond galettes and concocted a "top-secret" chai tea latte recipe, which led to him learning firsthand why I drink them down with the satisfaction of an orgasm. When he's not donning his scrubs as Dr. Sully, he's fulfilling his role as father of the year by teaching Ocean about American football, preserving our waters to make Grandpa Sullivan proud, and balancing on a surfboard in our swimming pool.

Asher, Lautner's mini-me, isn't as demanding of his time yet since mommy's still the food source. However, they bonded in the delivery room. I, *apparently,* did the easy part by pushing him out; Lautner caught him, cut the cord, and checked him over, eliciting his first scream. For once, I wasn't the only one in the room with tears trailing down my cheeks. Blue irises were watering hard that day.

"Mommy! Mommy!" Ocean yells. "I did it! Goal!" She's already an athlete at the tender age of three.

"Awesome! Good for you, baby girl." I stroke her hair as she hugs my legs.

"Pizza!" She grins at me.

"Ah, did Daddy promise you pizza?"

She nods as my *assistant* coach walks our way having given the kids an hour of fun and the moms a visual to use with their vibrators.

"So how'd I do, coach?" He smirks, taking Ocean's hand as we walk to the car.

"There was too much tackling."

"They weren't tackling. Sometimes they just get tangled in each other's feet." He shrugs.

"Tackling," I murmur.

We fasten them in their carseats and before pulling out of the parking lot, we both look back at them and then at each other.

"They're amazing, just like their mommy." Lautner leans over and presses a slow kiss to my lips.

Blue irises.

Lost in the eternity of his eyes, his love, his heart—I smile. "They're you ... undeniably you."

The End

Also By
Jewel E. Ann

Standalone Novels

Idle Bloom

Undeniably You

Naked Love

Only Trick

Perfectly Adequate

Look The Part

When Life Happened

A Place Without You

Jersey Six

Scarlet Stone

Not What I Expected

For Lucy

What Lovers Do

Before Us

If This Is Love

Right Guy, Wrong Word

I Thought of You

Acknowledgments

To my family, your support is my lifeline—my existence.

To my readers, thank you for justifying my addiction. I LOVE YOU!

To the amazing blogging community, you are THE BEST! You read, review, share, spotlight, recommend, and, in general, promote the hell out of books! Indie authors like myself would not see our dreams come to fruition without you.

About The Author

Jewel E. Ann is a *Wall Street Journal* and *USA Today* bestselling author. She's written over thirty novels, including LOOK THE PART, a contemporary romance, the JACK & JILL TRILOGY, a romantic suspense series; and BEFORE US, an emotional women's fiction story. With 10 years of flossing lectures under her belt, she took early retirement from her dental hygiene career to write mind-bending love stories. She's living her best life in Iowa with her husband, three boys, and a Goldendoodle.

Receive a FREE book and stay informed of new releases, sales, and exclusive stories:
www.jeweleann.com

Made in the USA
Monee, IL
07 August 2025

22805742R00266